# TINY
# TIN
# HOUSE

# tiny tin HOUSE

by

L MARISTATTER

ISBN: 979-8-9866311-0-3

Library of Congress control number has been applied for.

This novel is a work of fiction; any names, characters, incidents, or places are products of the author's imagination and are not to be construed as real. Any resemblance to actual events, locales, organizations, or persons, living or dead, is entirely coincidental. "His Eye is On The Sparrow," written by lyricist Civilla D. Martin and composer Charles H. Gabriel, is in the public domain.

*Content advisory: Some mild profanity and violence.*

FIRST PRINTING EDITION 2022.

*Cover images used under license from Shutterstock.com.*
*Book cover and interior designed by Lisa Hewitt.*

Printed by NiffyCat Press, in the United States of America.

NiffyCat Press
PO Box 915
Sheboygan, WI 53082

www.niffycatpress.com
info@niffycatpress.com

*For Mom, who never stopped believing in me,*
*holding fast to the dream when I couldn't, and loving me.*
*I can never repay you—*

*and I love you more.*

*Because the Sovereign Lord helps me, I will not be disgraced.*

*Therefore I have set my face like flint,*

*And I know I will not be put to shame. ~ Isaiah 50:7*

# I. GOΠE

The Guardian Angel told me Mom was dead in the same tone of voice he'd use to tell kids on the sub to stop climbing over the seats and sit down.

And I sat—rational thought impossible, legs turned to jelly, I collapsed on the worn chintz sofa, hard.

The news drove the breath out of me. I experienced a split second of terror—that, to my shame, drove thoughts of Mom straight out of my head—wondering if I would ever breathe again. Still, I found it poetically appropriate that Mom and I would go out almost at the same time, close as we were. Stars swam in my vision and gray encroached, and I'd almost yielded to the idea of dying when air flowed into my lungs.

The breath came as though my will had nothing to say about it, and I suppose that's true. I gasped a bit in protest, but yes, it was a breath, and the stars cleared and the gray retreated. My fingers curled into my palms, nails cutting skin. The breath meant I would live, and I wasn't sure I wanted to. I wanted to scream until the men went away. Scream until my vocal cords shattered the walls of our shabby little apartment and everyone left me alone with Mom.

The following exhale came with a quiet little noise—an almost dog-like whine—and the Guard looked at me sharply. At his expression, I slammed my mouth shut, the knife edge of my fear severing the sound. Grief didn't mean I could break the law.

Standing in the dining room with the other Guard, my stepfather whirled to face the sunflower-patterned wall, his head down.

The wallpaper had been Mom's idea. "It'll bring the outside in," she'd said, standing on a stepladder in the dining room, her red hair tied up in a kerchief, smiling as she smoothed the paper into place. "And aren't sunflowers cheerful? Won't it be fun to wake up and see their happy faces every morning at breakfast?"

The Guard put his hand on Ray's shoulder in a gesture of condolence.

*Condolence.* Livid bile rose in my throat. I tried to swallow, but my mouth felt like a patch of sand.

The Guard standing in front of me did not try to touch me and I was glad. "Miss Esselin," he said. "I will need your statement. Come with me."

"Flint." It came out a bare whisper.

"What?"

I cleared my throat. "Flint." Better. "My name is Flint, not Esselin."

To my surprise, he didn't react—just motioned toward the door. "Let's step outside."

Seizing my jacket, I followed him out of the apartment and down the walkway with its chipped black metal railing, rust pooling under each spindle. He kept moving until we were out of earshot of those inside the apartment. Not that it mattered: gossip was rife in our community, and even though not a soul was in sight, I knew someone would overhear what we said and bring it back to Ray. A frigid wind from off the bay swept around the buildings and scissored through me, but I didn't feel it. I was frozen inside.

Guardian Angels—the Reformation Directorate's guardians and law enforcers—wore white to symbolize the purity of their mission. When I was a little girl, I used to wonder who washed their uniforms and how much bleach they used. When I asked Mom, she laughed.

He turned to me. "May I?"

It seemed an odd courtesy—a Guardian Angel could read my chip without my knowledge or consent—but I nodded and held out my right arm. As his implant accessed my data, he blinked rapidly, like a woman swooning. I wasn't even tempted to laugh.

A Guard's brain implant was mandatory because it couldn't be hacked, altered, or removed. I thought it was a major downside of the job. Not that I could ever be a Guard, anyway, since I was a girl. Another drawback was that most people—at least, people I knew—feared and hated the Guards. Only Governance and Exalted Castes called them Guardian Angels, or Angels. To the rest of us, they were just Guards.

It always bugged me that any Guard could know who I was and where I lived or worked just by looking at me on the sub. I told myself that if I was careful to follow the law, I had no reason to be afraid.

At this moment, however, I was grateful for the invasive technology; I wouldn't have to endure more questions when all I wanted to do was scream.

*No screaming, Meryn.* I bit my tongue, hard.

"Worker Caste. Flint, Maryan Athena," he murmured, reading aloud.

"It's pronounced MARE-in, sir." My correction was polite, automatic.

He went on without acknowledging. "Age: eighteen. Height: five feet, nine inches. Weight: 130. Hair: brown, curly. Eyes: gray. Skin tone: 3.5." His eyebrows went up. "You work at On the Mark?"

I nodded.

"How long have you been employed there?" He knew that, too. I figured he was testing my honesty. *Why would I lie? Do people actually lie to the Guards?*

"About seven months. They hired me April fourth."

"That's at the mall, right?" His eyes quivered slightly, unfocused. That meant he was still accessing data from the Guard network.

"We have several locations, but yeah, my store is across from the Silvermine Mall." I swallowed.

Now his eyes met mine. "Okay. What happened here?"

"Um . . ." I looked at the pavement, wondering what would happen if I told the Guard I couldn't remember. *What if I get a detail wrong?*

An hour earlier, I'd been getting ready for work: the closing shift, noon to eight. Mom and Ray were celebrating their anniversary, and Ray had sprung for pork chops—real pork chops!—for their dinner, to be followed by a romantic afternoon together.

I'd eaten a fried eggplant sandwich, Mom whispering that she would save part of her pork chop for me. She was generous that way, even though I knew Ray would finish it off before it ever got to the fridge.

While Mom cooked dinner in the kitchen, I sat on my bed, her sewing kit open next to me, trying to reattach a button on my work uniform. She came down the hall just as I cursed under my breath.

"Oh, honey, there's a trick to this type of button. Let me show you." She settled next to me, taking the repair out of my hands.

As Mom worked, I'd studied her face. Unlike many women who looked worn and sad at thirty-six, she was still youthful, beautiful. Her parents, my Gamma and Gampa Flint, had been well off, so Mom was GM—a Genetically Modified baby. Gamma had requested Mom's curly red hair, porcelain skin, and eyes as green as the sea on a summer morning. Mom also had a slender frame—the unkind would call her "frail." Her natural grace still drew admiring glances from men on the bus.

Most people who could afford tinkering engineered a boy, although the mid-level castes—Management, especially—tried to craft girls who would appeal to high-caste families as potential mates. The rest of us were known as NMOs—Non-Modified Organisms. It wasn't unheard of for an NMO girl to marry up, but it was rare.

Mom never told me her birth caste. "We're with Ray. Nothing else matters now," she always said, her lips compressed in a firm line that told me the subject was closed. I'd never had the courage to ask her about my dad's caste.

I looked at her, bent over that button, a thoughtful *hmmm* coming from her throat as she checked the position of button and buttonhole. *I could ask . . . No. She's busy.* I bit my lip.

Me, I was NMO. Mom called me "homegrown," with her musical laugh. Engaged at seventeen and suffering the kind of overwhelming love that shuts off a girl's brain, she had yielded to her fiancé's demands and slept with him before the wedding. I came along nine months later. I'd never known my dad—didn't even know his name. He broke their engagement when he discovered she was pregnant, just before she went into hiding in her mother's parents' basement. No unmarried woman in our society dared go out visibly pregnant; the Guards were always watching, always hoping to make their quota. She told me my father died soon after I was born. I didn't know if that was true.

"You'll want to make the loops larger." Mom's voice was soft, her head still bent over her work. "If they're too tight, the button seats itself in the fabric and it won't go through the hole. So you leave a little slack." Her eyes darted a glance at me, smiled. "Kind of like life."

When I'd reached sixteen, I reached her height. Standing next to her, I looked like her sister—same curly hair, but brown. Same heart-shaped face, but light brown skin, not white. And my frame is tougher and hippy, not birdlike and slim. "You'll be better off," she'd told me when I remarked on the differences. "Your babies will come easier." Mom had almost died delivering me, despite the GM tinkering; somehow Gamma Flint got the bleeding stopped. The hospital could have been a death sentence for her. Sometimes good intentions backfire.

Mom rose and held up the blouse with a muted cry of triumph. "There! Let's try it."

I shrugged into the lace-trimmed orange top and buttoned it. The repair worked perfectly, and I hugged Mom, blowing out a sigh. "It was driving me nuts."

Mom smiled in her gentle way. "There's just a trick to it."

"Rose!" Ray's bellow echoed down the hall. "Why aren't you at the stove?"

Her face changed—the sea before a storm—and her breath sucked in. "The pork chops." Her arms dropped and she bolted to the kitchen.

I wasn't worried. Mom was known throughout our apartment complex for her mouthwatering cooking, and she hadn't been away from the stove for more than a minute or two. Slipping my blue Caste Ring on my left index finger, I waited a beat for it to shrink to the correct size, then picked up the eyeshadow palette.

Ray's voice came again. "Why the heck weren't you paying attention?" His words slurred—he'd started celebrating early with his favorite bootleg beer.

Mom's response wasn't audible. She always tried to defuse his anger by "speaking softly," as the Bible put it.

"No, they're not! I work my butt off to bring you real pork chops, and you can't even stay in the kitchen?" A loud *clang*—Ray must have thrown something. A gasp. Angry whispers, then footsteps. Mom and Ray often went into their bedroom to argue, as if by closing the door they could keep me from knowing about it.

I held my breath and turned away from my open bedroom door. Lately their arguments had become more frequent. I knew better than to get involved.

The bedroom door slammed, muffling the words, but Ray's voice grew louder. A moment later, Mom cried out. I whirled away from the mirror, eyes wide; before I could take a step, a terrible, hollow *THUD* rocked the apartment. Then silence—an odd silence that balled in the pit of my stomach and made it hard to breathe.

The bedroom door opened. Uneven steps, meandering down the hall to the living room. The *psssht* of a bottle opening.

"Mom?" Wary, I poked my head into the hallway. Silence. I slipped down the hall and peeked into Mom and Ray's room. "Mom!"

She lay on the floor, her face obscured by a curtain of red curls. At my voice, she tried to rise, but her body flopped, a broken marionette.

I darted into the room and lifted her onto the sagging bed, cushioning her head with the pillow. Her eyelids fluttered, her eyes struggling to focus.

"Mom?" Fear knotted my midsection. "Mama?" I hadn't called her that since I was six. I smoothed curls away from her face, and my breath sucked in—a reddish, dusky bruise marched across her left temple, and blood seeped from a cut on her scalp. "Ray!" I shrieked, running down the hall. "Call emergency—Mom's badly hurt!"

"Huh?" Ray looked up from his easy chair. "Nah, Meryn, she's fine. Stupid witch." He belched, turning back to the football game on the house screen. "She burned the pork chops."

I grabbed his cell phone from the table and shoved it in his face, too panicked to be tactful. "You call the medAngels *now*, you worthless drunk!" I hissed. I couldn't do it myself; I was low caste and female. They'd just hang up.

Ray's face distorted with fury. I had never spoken to my stepfather that way. Not waiting for his reprimand, I dashed back to the bedroom.

"Mom?" As I eased down next to her, I heard Ray on the phone in the living room. He was indeed calling the medAngels, but I didn't relax. Who knew when they would come—the Governance and Exalted Castes had their own first responders, but the rest of us shared just a few stations. And Worker Caste neighborhoods were low on the priority list.

"Meryn." Mom's voice was distant. "'s okay, sweetie. I'm okay." A long trail of cooking oil marred the front of her dress, and her right forearm displayed a vivid streak of burn. Her eyes opened and immediately screwed shut, as if seeing was more than she could handle. The white of her left eye was occluded by a fierce red that took my breath away.

"Of course you are," I said, struggling against panic. "The medAngels are coming, Mom. Just rest. They'll be here in a minute, okay?" Tears pricked my eyes, and I held one of her hands in both of mine. The bones felt tiny, like the bones of a sparrow. When had my mother become so fragile? How had I not noticed?

Mom put her other hand on my arm. "Mer-child. Listen." She winced, blinked. "Bright." A tear—pink with blood—crept from her left eye, trailed across her temple and melted into her hair.

"I'm here, Mom. I'm listening," I whispered. The tightening knot in my gut was turning to ice.

The sound of water running in the kitchen—Ray was rinsing out his beer bottles. I knew he'd hide them before the medAngels arrived.

Mom whispered, too, her words slurred. "You were . . . right." Her hand lifted, flopped. "Ray . . . not safe. Promise if . . . you'll go."

I frowned fiercely, forehead cramping with the effort to hold back the tears. "Mom, no! You'll be fine! You—"

She interrupted. "Go. If—" She blinked, eyes unfocused, and squeezed my arm, hard. "Promise!"

My tears were collecting in a little pool at her collarbone. "I promise, Mom," I whispered, my mouth twisting. *Whatever she wants. Just—oh God, please—*

A spot of blood gathered below her nostril, and I wiped it away, gentle. She released my arm, reaching up to touch my face. "Mer-child, don't cry. I love you so. I'll be fine—'course I will. You'll, too." She frowned, puzzled. "D'you hear . . ."

I shook my head. "Hear what, *Mama?*"

"Music," she said, her face dreamy, distant. "Beautiful. Better than DNN . . ." And she hummed a little melody, but it was nothing I could identify—certainly none of the hymns broadcast hourly on the Divine News Network.

She coughed, wincing, then her eyes opened, her expression so lucid I was startled. "Meryn," she whispered, her voice firm. "Top drawer . . . Christmassss . . . ahh . . ." She blinked, disoriented. "Christmasssoo . . . go . . . Mer . . ." The rest of my name vanished, unaspirated. Her eyes closed, her breathing morphing into a series of gasps.

I didn't try to understand. I held her close, unable to stop the tears, my whispers desperate, half-articulated prayers.

Commotion at the front door, then down the hall. A medAngel entered the room and came straight to the bed. Ray lurked in the hallway, his hands clenching and unclenching on a kitchen towel, his face finally registering concern.

"Help her!" I pleaded, unable to stop the sobs even though I risked arrest. "Please, help her!"

"Let them work." A man's voice, behind me. I knew it was a Guard, but I couldn't see him—I couldn't take my eyes from Mom, the medAngel kneeling at her side, opening his kit, taking out a stethoscope, then a syringe . . . The man took my arm, not unkindly, and led me to the living room.

# 2. CLİFF

On the balcony, I pulled up my jacket collar against the cold and an odd guilt. I hadn't told the Guard about my intimate, whispered exchanges with Mom.

"Did she have any last words?" the Guard asked.

And I, who had been trained from childhood not to lie and threatened with dire warnings of hellfire for doing so, looked him full in the eyes and said, "No, sir."

My biometrics mustn't have so much as blipped, because he shrugged. "That's all I need, Miss Flint. Thank you for your cooperation. God comfort you in your bereavement." It came out wooden and impersonal, as if he were giving directions to Pentz Concert Hall. I nodded, oddly disappointed, and annoyed at myself for expecting anything different. *I wanted compassion? From a Guard?*

We entered the apartment, Ray and the other Guard murmuring low in the dining room. At that moment, the medAngels came down the hall, pushing the antigrav gurney that bore Mom's body. A gasp escaped me. *They're taking her?* My hand came up and my eyes veered to Ray, but his head was turned away. The medAngels brushed past, and my hand dropped. My stomach contracted into a quivering mess.

"So . . . am I going to jail?" Ray's voice. Nervous.

"Unlikely," the Guard replied. "Typical domestic dispute. We have to file it, but it's doubtful they'll prosecute your case." His shoulder twitched. "Too many others just like it. And you have a dependent. No worries, Mr. Esselin. You can always remarry."

Ray blew out a lungful of air, smiling.

*Remarry.* My right hand curled into an impotent fist. Somewhere deep inside me, a scream was building.

The Guards turned toward the door. They were going to leave me alone in the apartment with the man who had just killed my mother.

*No!* Pulse pounding, I pushed past the men, fleeing to the safety of my bedroom. Makeup tubes and palettes still lay in a random scatter on the dresser, but I ignored them, my eyes lifting to the cracked mirror. The face behind the tearstained ruin of my mascara wore an expression I didn't recognize: haunted, shattered—*old*. The change frightened me, and I stepped back.

*What now?* The woman in the mirror shook her head, her eyes wide with panic. As a little girl, I'd fancied that my reflection was an alternate me—a girl smarter and richer, living a much nicer life, despite the identical Worker Caste bedroom. But the woman peering at me from the other side of the glass looked like she'd just lost her best friend. Did her mother tell her to run? "Are you going to?" I whispered.

"Going, too?" she whispered back.

I heard the echo of Mom's voice: *You're not safe. Promise you'll go.* I sank to the bed. *I have to. But where can I possibly go? I don't have a brother or male cousin for protection. God help me! And what about my Duty?*

Mom's request was no small matter. She was asking me to go against Sanctioned Church doctrine. She was asking me to go against *God.*

Family Duty meant that as a young woman I had an obligation to remain chaste until my stepfather gave me in marriage to my future husband. My behavior must never violate—or even appear to violate—that Duty.

When I was thirteen, Sarah, a neighbor girl two grades ahead of me, ran off with a boy. They were gone three whole days before the Guards caught up with her. She became a pariah—a branded woman, destined for hell, forced to stay at home under the protection of her father for the rest of her life. It wasn't long; within a week, she slit her wrists. No one found her until it was too late. Her father, talking with Ray in the courtyard, said the shame had driven her to it, but I thought he didn't seem all that upset about it—almost as if she were an embarrassment he was glad to be rid of. I don't know what became of the boy; Sarah's father just said the whole incident was her fault for not having the sense to say no. Standing appropriately silent with Ray and Mom, I'd looked up at Ray, wondering if he would cry if the same thing happened to me.

I closed my eyes at the memory, avoiding my reflection, and warm tears oozed down my cheeks.

But a moment later, the chaos in my mind quieted, and I had an answer. An idea. *You're not running off with a boy. Go to work. Pack only food, clothes . . . and memories. Take what she would want you to have. Do it now.*

It was a start. The face that greeted me when I opened my eyes was still lined with grief, but resolute. I nodded, and so did she. *It's what Mom wanted.* Taking a deep breath, I rose and wiped away tears and the ruin of my makeup.

As I slipped into Mom's bedroom, low voices murmured in the living room—the Guards hadn't left yet. Deliberately turning away from the empty bed with its bloody pillow and scattered medical paraphernalia, I faced the battered dresser and opened Mom's jewelry box.

She didn't have much. Ray wasn't rich, and I had no interest in the cheap baubles he'd given her. But a few pieces were hers by right, gifts from her parents. She would want me to have them. If I were to leave today, I had to take them now.

At once I found what I had come for: Mom's cloisonné mermaid pin. It looked just like her, with green eyes, porcelain skin, and long, curly red hair coyly covering the bosom.

Mom was a romantic. She'd always believed in magical creatures—as much, I sometimes thought, as she believed in God—so I grew up hearing stories about fairies and mermaids, witches and trolls, elves and wizards. Far from eroding my faith, such stories helped me believe that anything was possible, and that God's magic gilded life with purpose and joy. The pin in my hand reminded me to believe.

The other item was Mom's coral necklace, a gift from her parents for her high school graduation. The necklace's tiny, polished beads reflected Mom's love for the sea and echoed the wild freedom of her spirit. When I turned thirteen, she let me borrow it for special occasions, and wearing it always made me feel grown up, like her. As I retrieved it now, tears leaked down my cheeks, leaving wet splashes on the scratched dresser top.

"What the hell do you think you're doing?" Ray's angry voice stopped my tears.

My hand was closed over the mermaid pin. As I turned, lifting the necklace, I slipped the pin out of sight in my pants pocket. "Ray, could I wear this to work today?" I didn't have to fake the grief.

Ray's expression changed from anger to something warmer. "Sure, of course." His voice was gruff. He moved forward, arms up as if to embrace me. My stomach churned, and I took a quick step back. I hadn't let Ray touch me for more than three years.

His face shifted to confused regret. His arms dropped. "You—uh, you sure you want to work, Peanut? Call in. They'll understand."

I shook my head. "I can't, Ray. I . . . have to do something." *I have to get out of here.* From the corner of my eye, I could see the bloody pillow. And the syringe.

"You could, uh . . ." Ray ran his hand through his hair. "You could come with me. We'll get something to drink."

"At the bar. I'm eighteen, my mother just died, and you're inviting me to an illegal bar." My face froze, and I shook my head. "I'll pass."

Ray stepped back, eyes lowering, and retreated to the living room. As I looped the necklace over my head, his voice echoed down the hall. "Constance? It's me." A chuckle. "Are you going to The Watering Hole some—you are? Got the password? Good. See you in ten."

Astonishment, and white hot rage burst through the numbness of my grief. *How DARE he!*

I bolted down the hall . . . just as the front door closed behind him. I stood rooted to the floor in open-mouthed shock, tears of naked fury streaming down my face, wishing I had the courage to open the door and scream his crime for the world to hear.

Instead I sank to the worn blue carpet, sobbing into my hands, my heart breaking all over again. *Oh, Mom! How long has he . . .* Through my despair, I wondered if Mom knew. *She must have. She knew everything about me, so I'm sure she could sense Ray's . . . And yet she got up every day and fixed breakfast, and smiled at both of us as if—*

*Meryn.* A tiny voice in my mind interrupted my thoughts. *You don't have time for this. Get up now. Get up!*

Surprise felt distant. *God? Mom?* I resented the intrusion, but I wiped my face, pushed myself to my feet and lurched back to my room. At the threshold, I hovered, indecisive. *Suitcase? No. Too obvious.* I dug my biggest tote out of the closet, then chewed my lip, fiercely scrubbing away tears that wouldn't stop. *Okay. The house is on fire. You have five minutes. What do you take?*

The first thing I grabbed was the hologram of me and Mom at the beach. Ray had taken it two years earlier when we'd spent a blissful afternoon at Silvermine's only swim-safe stretch of sand. Mom's smile beamed at me as I tucked it into my Bible next to my Gamma Maya's cross-stitch bookmark, then I dropped the book in the bag. Atop it went *Mystical Tales*, the enchanting children's stories I'd grown up on. Before she gave it to me, the book had been Mom's; it was now banned. My childhood rag doll, Magicia, fitted neatly beside the books.

I tossed in makeup, folded my second uniform and laid it on top. A utilitarian skirt and T-shirt, socks, underwear. My high-heeled sandals I wrapped in a limp plastic shopping bag before stuffing them down next to the clothes. I didn't wear heels much, but they were too expensive to leave behind. The cheap athletic shoes on my feet would serve for daily wear.

I looked around the room, seeing Mom everywhere: the wall hangings she'd crafted, the unicorn painting we'd worked on together when I was eight, the bedspread Mom had quilted in my favorite colors of lavender and light green, my fish tank with its tiny denizens darting and playing. I'd have to leave it all behind. I turned away, scrubbing my face with my sleeve.

As I zipped the tote, my chip tingled in my wrist, and I grabbed my phone. The message was from my manager, Mary-Sarah.

*Meryn, are you aware you were scheduled to come in at noon? We're extremely busy and I could use you.*

I gasped—I was an hour late. Quickly I dictated a reply. "I'm so sorry, Mary-Sarah. My mother just went home to Jesus, and the Guardian Angels needed my statement. I'm on my way."

Using the phone almost made me burst into tears again. Mom had given it to me for my eighteenth birthday, and the extra speed and chip sync made it worth its weight in gold. We couldn't afford the brain implant that would give me the phone's full functionality, but I didn't want it, anyway. Too many people went crazy from implants. I sent the message and pressed *mute*. I didn't have time for questions or condolences. Hefting my tote, I headed for the kitchen.

A startling sight greeted me. A frying pan lay upside down on the floor, two pork chops and a fork lying next to it in a pool of oil. One pork chop looked raw, the other browned. Frowning, I looked closer. *Wait! That pork chop isn't burned!* Picking up the fork, I flipped over the ruined slab of meat, and fury shot through me again. *What was that lying blackheart—*

*Meryn.*

The fork clattered to the floor. "Mom?"

In my mind's eye I saw a replay of Mom's last moments, including her words about a top-drawer Christmas. I bit my cheek, my nose reddening. Mom loved Christmas, and she worked hard to make the season special, even when we had nothing. *No. I can't think about that now.*

The burner was still aflame, so I shut it off. Then I hopscotched the oily spots on the floor and rifled through the pantry, taking packets of cold cereal, dried tofu, nori, crackers, peanut butter—anything that might keep me going that didn't need cooking.

Pausing at the small whiteboard on the wall next to the fridge, I scrawled a quick note to Ray.

*I'm not coming back. Please don't call the Guards—I'll be fine. I just can't live here anymore. I hope you understand. Take care.*

Ray would reprogram the door lock to reject my chip. I took a last look around, hefted the tote to my shoulder and headed for the door.

*Meryn. No!*

I stopped, uncertain. "Mom! What am I supposed to do?" I waited, hearing nothing but the clock ticking, and sighed. *Meryn, you're silly—*

An interruption in my mind, another echo of Mom's last words. "Top drawer . . . Christmassss . . ."

*Wait. Was Mom trying to tell me something? Top drawer. The top drawer of her dresser? Or nightstand?*

Dropping the tote, I sprinted to the bedroom and yanked open her drawer, where an organized array of undies, bras, and rundled stockings marched in neat rows.

"Socks!" I whispered. "Mom's Christmas socks!" She wore them every year: a whimsical touch that helped make Christmas special. Frantic, I pawed through the clothes until I found the wreath socks at the back, covered by a scarf. Two neat rolls, side by side.

*Two rolls? Mom doesn't have two pairs of Christmas socks!* The sock unrolled in my hand, heavy and round, and when I withdrew the contents, I gasped: a fat roll of Reformation Directorate scrip, secured with a rubber band.

The implant chip had rendered paper scrip almost entirely obsolete. Husbands liked it that way—they could easily track their wives' spending. But Mom loved giving parties and little surprises. She'd talked Ray into giving her a small weekly allowance for the purpose, calling it her "mad money."

Obviously, she'd been squirreling part of it away for some time. The top note was 20GP— "God's Provision" dollars. *If the rest of it is twenties . . .*

I didn't waste time counting. I carried the socks to the living room and stuffed them in my tote. Then my shoulders dropped, and my lungs released a breath I wasn't even aware I'd been holding. "Thank you," I whispered.

I heard nothing.

Looping the tote over my shoulder, I opened the front door . . . and stopped, paralyzed. Pausing before the walkway, I felt as if I were standing at the edge of a cliff, about to jump. The only sound was the metronomic ticking of Great-Gampa Flint's clock from its spot on the living room table. *Where am I going after work?* Fresh anxiety knotted my stomach. *Will a hotel even rent to me?* A single woman, unescorted by a male—the odds weren't good. In my mad preparations, I hadn't even considered it, but it was my only option. Gamma and Gampa Flint were gone, killed in a hovercar wreck when I was three. And Ray's parents had died before he even met Mom. He had no siblings that I knew of. *Should I stay with Ray? No. Not possible. Even if Mom hadn't told me to go. What do I do?* Cold oozed in. I wondered what the woman in the mirror was doing.

I glanced over at Gampa's clock. Centuries old and notoriously unreliable, the thing gained ten minutes every month and required weekly winding with a special key. I never understood why Mom kept it.

But now, its quiet tempo calmed me. The clock had marked every minute of Mom's life, every minute Gamma and Gampa Flint had lived, and their parents before them, and on and on, going back at least to the American Reformation. *The clock survived, and I will, too. Somehow.*

Echoes of a hymn drifted from the courtyard below—someone watching DNN's afternoon programming. I jerked with recognition.

*Why should I feel discouraged?*
*Why should the shadows come?*
*Why should my heart feel lonely*
*And long for heaven and home?*

*When Jesus is my portion*
*A constant Friend is He*
*His eye is on the sparrow*
*And I know He watches me.*

The hymn was Mom's favorite. She had often sung it in her lovely, light soprano while fixing dinner. I sometimes sang harmony with her, us smiling at each other across a stir-fry or soup pot. Memories overwhelming, I stood in the doorway, eyes closed, my toes on the sweep, letting the music wash over me as tears leaked down my cheeks. *God, why? WHY?*

*I sing because I'm happy*
*I sing because I'm free . . .*

To my surprise, a tendril of peace wrapped my aching heart, easing my grief, muting the anguished wailing of my soul, giving not answers, but comfort. In a quiet corner of my mind, I heard a familiar verse: *I will never leave you nor forsake you.*

My mouth twisted bitterness, and I stifled an angry thought as the song faded. A brief silence, and a prinister launched into a sermon. I couldn't make out the words and I was glad.

*Time to go.*

Did God speak? Or my own thoughts? I didn't know.

I stepped off the cliff, shut the apartment door and headed for the bus stop.

# 3. ADRIFT

As I boarded the bus the scanner beeped, registering my chip and deducting the fare from my RD Bank account. The vehicle smelled of body odor and urine and was noisy, crowded with afternoon-shift workers. I passed the first section of red seats reserved for Governance Caste passengers (always empty), then the next two rows of Management Caste green seats (almost always empty).

The bus lurched forward as I reached the blue Worker Caste section, and I grabbed an overhead bar to keep from falling into the lap of the balding, heavyset man in the second seat. His grin was kind, but I couldn't smile back. Embarrassed to have met his gaze, I looked away. *A lady never looks at a man directly.* The blue section was full, so I headed to the Indigent section in the back. There I somehow found an empty brown seat and settled in with a sigh, balancing my tote on my lap. I couldn't sit in a section reserved for a higher caste, but while going down caste might earn me a few frowns, it wouldn't get me arrested.

Later I would realize I was in shock. At the time, I couldn't understand why everyone was behaving normally. Anger curled around the edges of my devastation. Didn't they understand that the world had just lost a brilliant, loving human being? My anchor, my support? How could they act as if nothing had happened? That twentysomething man in the blue section, laughing at the program on his phone—*how dare he?* I wanted him to feel pain like I was feeling pain. I wanted to scratch his eyes out.

I wanted the sun to fall out of the sky.

My nose reddened; my hands clenched the tote handle so hard that the stiff plastic bent double. *Jesus, please help me with this. Help me not to hit anyone until I get to work. Well, not even then because I will lose my job, and I need my job. Thank You.*

With a double handful of other riders, I disembarked at the Reagan Avenue stop and followed the queue to the subway entrance. A dozen elderly women sat on the freezing concrete apron outside, holding battered plastic cups and handmade signs that read *Please Help*. Known as "tin widows," they were there every day, regular as clockwork, hoping to beg a packet of crackers or a bit of scrip to stave off starvation. Each woman wore a brown MT—the standardized, full-length dress the RD required married women to wear in public—under her coat or blanket, the garment's dun color denoting their Indigent Caste status. Behind them, a filthy, glazed bank of snow towered higher than our heads, bits of trash embedded firm in the ice, and sometimes it seemed to me that the women were frozen into the snowbank, too, not to move until the spring thaw.

The crowd flowed past the women, ignoring their outstretched hands, and down the steps to the sub. "Worthless hashers," a man muttered. My jaw tightened at the slur, but I didn't dare look up; he wore a green Management Caste Ring, and today of all days I didn't need a Caste Insult charge levied against me. A woman in her thirties wearing a blue MT paused, her eyes frightened, then covered her face with her scarf and hurried past.

I used to get angry at people who didn't help the widows, until Mom told me not to. "It isn't for us to judge," she would say gently. "Many people simply can't afford to give a dime."

Today, I got angry. I couldn't help it. I knew it would've upset Mom, and guilt seasoned my rage.

I stopped next to the woman wearing a red hat—Charity, her name was.

"Good afternoon, Meryn." Her wide smile revealed a complete lack of teeth. "You're a bit late today, aren't you, dear?"

"Hello, Charity." My throat closed and tears threatened. "Bad day." I managed to get it out, my voice a squeak. "Very bad day." I pulled 5GP from my pocket for her.

She accepted it with a cold-reddened hand, her smile fading. "Oh, my dear, I will pray for you." Her brown eyes were frank, concerned.

Something crashed into my shoulder, almost knocking me onto Charity. I whipped around, my face reddening, and the man stopped, shoving his fist in my face to display his green ring. "Submit, Martha," he snarled, and I immediately focused on the concrete at my feet, anger draining into fear.

The words were from the Women's Code: behavior guidelines drafted by the Reformation Directorate. The biblical Martha was known as a hardworking, submissive housewife, and the phrase was meant to remind a woman to exhibit appropriate behavior.

The RD frowned on social interaction between the castes, and this man was calling me out on my conversation with Charity. While this stricture was not always honored—enforcing it without exception would make it impossible for society to function—it was often used by the higher castes to harass those below them.

Now he spoke, his tone conversational, but his eyes roved across my body like hands, and I squirmed, discomfited. "Do you know why I'm Management Caste and you aren't, little Worker Bee?"

I kept my eyes on the sidewalk. He paused, forcing me to answer, my voice barely above a whisper. "No, right honorable, distinguished sir."

"Because I'm not afraid. Not afraid of the upper castes, not afraid to try, not even afraid to fail." He eased closer, too close, and I could smell the coffee on his breath, real coffee, but I didn't dare move. "And someday, I will trade in this green ring for a red one, but you"—he reached out and took my hand with its Caste Ring, a horrible violation of the law, but I wasn't about to call him on it—"you will always wear this blue ring. Unless someday you trade yours for a brown. Because you are afraid of everything. Everything, little bee. And you always will be."

The cold ate through my shoes and numbed my toes as I stood, hoping he was finished—hoping he was wrong. Finally, the man took a casual step back. He dropped my hand to gesture toward Charity. "Stop hanging out with this trash." Turning toward the entrance, he tossed over his shoulder, "And for God's sake, put on some makeup. You could be pretty." He vanished into the station.

After a long moment, I lifted my head. Humiliation scorched my cheeks, but relief was stronger; my exhale came out in a cloud of steam.

Charity was shaking her head, her face etched with sorrow. "Someday God will enlighten them," she said. "We must pray."

"I guess I deserved that," I said ruefully, rubbing my shoulder.

"Pray." A woman sitting some feet away snorted and waved a derisive hand, swollen and black from frostbite. "Why would anyone pray for that management scum."

I didn't show my shock at her irreverent attitude. I gave her my second fiver, and handed another to the woman sitting at Charity's right. "Here, Mother, get yourself some warm soup tonight."

The old woman bowed her head and folded her rag-swaddled hands in front of her as befit her caste, refusing to meet my eyes. "God's blessings rain upon you," she said, her voice shaking. It was the standard, acceptable reply to one of a higher caste. Although I'd tried to draw her out, to show her she had nothing to fear from me, I'd met with no success. I didn't even know her name. Charity—who clearly used to belong to a higher caste—shot me a regretful look, which took the edge off my frustration at a poor, nameless old woman who'd done nothing but thank me. Shame warmed my cheeks. More than once I'd wondered how Charity ended up on the street, but it would be rude to ask.

I forced a smile and dashed down the concrete steps, averting my eyes from the other women I couldn't help and trying to ignore the guilt. My eyes veered to the Reformation Directorate Message Board as I blew past; no, no new regulations to memorize.

The turnstile beeped, registering my chip, and I pelted for the sub, brushing past an ancient janitor scrubbing away fresh graffiti: "LIBERTÉ!" defiled the otherwise pristine subway tile. My stomach tightened with memory, my eyes sliding away from the red paint as if it were toxic. A Guard patrolling the walkway turned toward me, and guilt pulsed my veins. *I didn't look! I didn't!*

My body slid through the car's doors just before they hissed shut. As the train started, I braced against its motion, working my way back until I found a blue seat against the bank of windows. The other passengers chatted or looked at their phones. No one on the subs had a brain implant, of course. Folks who could afford an implant—usually Governance Caste—could also afford a hover-car. You saw brown and blue and sometimes green MTs in their coordinating sections on the sub. But red or pink MTs were rare as clear skies over Silvermine, and purple MTs nonexistent.

I closed my eyes, grief pulling me into fatigue. *So this is why Ray told me to call in and cancel. Too late now.*

Three stops later, I exited into the cold wind, following the other afternoon workers toward the Silvermine Mall. Coughing, I covered my mouth and nose with my scarf against air thick with exhaust. A stream of hovercars flew thirty feet above us, leaving shimmering trails of gravity displacement, outpacing the old-fashioned gas-engine vehicles in the street lanes below. The mall's bulk grew as we approached, its ancient, mold-streaked marble walls looking like worn battlements, or the prow of a mighty ship in the afternoon gloom.

The mall was a survivor, a relic from before the Reformation that had been reborn under the Humboldt administration's pro-business policies. It attracted masses of chain stores but few local shops, as permits were too expensive for a fledgling business. Local shops tended to shutter within a year, anyway. Some people bought online, but too many purchases ended up lost between buyer and seller. The wealthy could afford drone delivery; the rest of us shopped in person.

My friend Bree gave me beta on the ins and outs of retail when I started looking for a position. So I focused on the larger chains. I wanted my job to have a fighting chance at lasting more than six months.

On the Mark wasn't in the mall itself, but on the access drive. After a few minutes following a woman wearing a blue MT, I turned to the right, leaving the crowd behind, and picked my way across the fractured concrete parking lot to the big double doors.

Inside, a horrific mishmash of the store's orange and navy logo colors emblazoned displays and shelves stocked with cheap polyester clothing and plastic household items most of us could easily do without. Life-sized cutouts of our mascot, Marky—a tall, handsome man wearing a navy uniform—pointed an orange bow and arrow to the most prominent sale racks.

Mary-Sarah wasn't kidding: the place was packed. I forced my way through surging crowds of women clad in their brown and blue MTs, most of them carrying a baby or pushing a stroller as they argued over sale clothing or dug through clearance bins. Runny-nosed children pelted between the displays, their mothers screaming various versions of *stop that* and *come back here right now*. A toddler squatted in the middle of the main aisle, wailing, brown liquid oozing across the linoleum from his neglected diaper. *Not my mess*, I thought, making a mental note to tell Mary-Sarah before crowds tracked the ick all over the store.

The stockroom's swinging doors closed behind me, shutting out the worst of the noise. I leaned forward, my eyes closed, forehead against the time clock.

"Are you sure you want to work today?" At the gravelly voice, my head jerked up. Mary-Sarah, round and efficient, stood in the doorway, several garments folded over one arm. Her normally sharp eyes were sympathetic.

I nodded, not trusting myself to speak.

"Okay, Meryn. Where would you prefer to serve?"

She *never* asked that.

"The floor," I said at once, even though I was scheduled to unpack stock. The floor was always a madhouse; unpacking would have left me alone in the stockroom with my thoughts. She nodded her assent, and I stowed my tote and fled into the busy, laughing, hostile, needy crowd.

~

The closest hotel was a frigid, five-minute walk from the downtown sub station. Feigning confidence, I pushed through the door and stood for a moment, absorbing the quiet, relieved to be out of the wind. The warm lobby invited lingering, with a deep gray faux leather sofa and elegant tables, and I unwound my scarf.

Depending on what was in Mom's stash, I could afford maybe two or three nights. I chewed my lip. *No one can do this for you, Meryn. And it's just for tonight. Tomorrow you'll . . . figure out what to do.* I doubted the hotel would rent to me, but it was the only chance I had.

A thin man with greasy black hair stood behind the marble counter, typing staccato on a tab.

He looked up and raised his scanner at my approach, his eyebrows lifting at the chip readout. "We don't take Sweet Peas here." His back ramrod straight, he busied himself behind the counter. "Take your services elsewhere."

My mouth dropped open, my shield of confidence dissolving. *I'm not a prostitute!* "I'm not—that's not why I'm here! I have a reservation."

His eyes glittered. "You're unmarried and without your father. You know I can't rent you a room."

I bit my lip. "But . . . I . . . ." An idea formed. "My dad's out of town on a business trip, and our heat's not working. If I stay home, I'll freeze." *Forgive me, Lord.*

I hated lying. It always brought the worst in prinisters during confession. But the truth wouldn't get me a room.

"Then have your father call us." He turned back to his console.

"He's not available." I forced irritation into my tone. "He's traveling in New Korea and he's behind the firewall. You know how long it takes to get communications approved by that government. I don't expect to hear from him for at least three days."

"New Korea." The man folded his arms on the countertop and looked me in the eyes. "Your father works for the City of Silvermine, Miss Flint. You want to try again?"

He'd picked that up from my chip. My heart pounded, but I refused to look away. "Like I don't know where my father works? Look, I have a job." I held out my bundle of scrip. "I can pay you for three nights, right now. By then he should be in touch again. He can verify my story."

The man looked at the roll of cash. "Where is your mother?"

"My mother is . . . deceased." Despite an effort at control, my voice trembled.

For a long, anxious moment he hesitated, his eyes dark, and I realized he'd seen that in my file, too. Slowly he shook his head. "I'm gonna get fired for this," he muttered, but he picked up the scanner and checked me in.

To my surprise, he accepted the scrip without argument. My gut relaxed.

"The door will read your chip for the next three nights." He leaned forward and his voice dropped. "If anyone challenges you, don't change your story, Miss Flint. I have it on file. Understand?"

*Why would I change my story?* I didn't understand, but I nodded and quit the office, struggling against the cold wind to Room 145. Sighing, I waved my wrist over the panel and stepped inside.

My mouth dropped open.

I wasn't expecting anything palatial, but the room I'd entered looked nothing like the splashy photos on the website. The double bed sagged like an old porch, its wrinkled scarlet bedspread covered with odd brown stains. Next to the door sat a small table with two chairs, their faux red leather cracked and torn. Across from the bed, a chipped dresser leaned to one side, precariously supporting an ancient media screen. A door at the room's other end opened into a small bathroom. My nose wrinkled at the reek: a combination of dirty feet, urine and strong citrus disinfectant. *Well, I don't have to stay longer than tonight. At least I'm off the street.*

As I shut the door, my wrist buzzed. *Ray? Already?* Stomach knotting, I dropped my tote on the bed and dug out my phone.

But the text was from Bree, and I relaxed. We'd met in school and even though she was three years my senior, we hit it off at once—I think because unlike most of our classmates, neither of us was interested in finding a husband. At twenty-one, the age when most women were facing impending spinsterhood, she'd only just gotten engaged. Not that she hadn't had other offers; she simply hadn't accepted any (to my utter astonishment). Bree worked at Mrs@18, an upscale clothing store in the mall, and we often met after our shifts to catch up.

*You off yet? Kilte just told me the most hilarious story.*

Kilte was Bree's fiancé. I sighed, looking at the bed, and debated whether to remove my shoes. Finally deciding that Mom wouldn't want me to further soil the bedspread, I pulled them off and tucked my feet under me, careful not to touch the floor.

She picked up at once.

"You are not going to believe this!" She was laughing. "He had the most—"

"Bree," I interrupted.

"No, Mer, I'm sure your shift was horrible, as usual, but I promise this will cheer—"

*"Bree."*

At my tone, she stopped. "Mer? What's wrong?"

I wanted to answer—I was prepared to answer—but when I opened my mouth, nothing came out.

"Mer?" Pause. Her voice, now thick with concern. "Mer, are you okay? Should I call the medAngels?"

That broke my stasis. "No!" I gasped and started crying.

# 4. FLAILING

I don't know why I didn't tell her I was staying at a hotel. Maybe I didn't want to be rescued. Maybe I didn't think she'd have any better ideas. And it wasn't like she could take me home with her—if she were caught sheltering a runaway, she could go to jail. She was understanding, worried; I told her I was fine, I was coping, and then I just couldn't talk anymore and got off the call as quickly as possible without being rude.

In the quiet, my pulse pounded its surf in my ears. I dove for the remote, turned on the room screen with the volume up loud, and headed for the shower. I stood under the spray, letting my mind drift, toxic thoughts draining out with the water, memories blurring . . .

*Ding.* The room's AI came through the speaker. "Room . . . 145. Water is rationed. You have ninety seconds of water remaining. Water allowance resets at midnight." It went on in a loop.

Hurriedly I shut off the water and wrapped myself in a towel. And then it hit me: *I have no pajamas. I have no robe. And it's freezing in here.* It seemed the temperature in the room had dropped since I entered, but how was that even possible? *Okay. I'll get under the covers and warm up.*

That's when I discovered the bedspread was thin, and the bed had no blanket. I had just picked up the bedside phone when a tap came at the door, followed by a male voice. "Management."

*Well, thank God.* I didn't bother to edit the cynicism in my thought. Leaving the chain lock fastened, I cracked the door. The dark-haired man stood outside, and I felt a wash of relief. "Yes?"

"I uh . . . I just wanted to make sure everything was okay, and the room met your expectations." His expression was polite.

*Are you kidding?* I forced a smile, dropping my eyes to the pavement. "Actually, sir, I was wondering how to turn up the heat. It's pretty cold—"

"Temperature in the rooms is controlled by the front office," he interrupted. "All rooms are the same."

I blinked, shivering in the icy air from outside. "Oh. Well, could I possibly get a blanket? I'm not sure the bedspread is thick enough."

He smiled. "Of course. I'll be back in a minute." He turned away as I closed the door.

I quickly pulled on undies and looked around for my tote, but before I could dress, he was back. I rewrapped myself in the damp towel. Sure enough, he held a thick blanket.

"Thank you." I opened the door wider and reached out with my free hand, but he pulled the blanket away. "Miss Flint, there's a—umm—surcharge." He wasn't quite smiling.

"A surcharge?" I forced myself not to meet his eyes.

"Yes, miss. Anything additional not in the room—"

*This is unbelievable.* "Fine," I interrupted, reaching for the blanket, "I'll pay for it in the morning."

He pulled back. "It isn't *that* kind of a surcharge, Miss Flint."

I'm sure my confusion showed on my face. "Excuse me?"

His mouth curled, and he looked at the sidewalk, then at me. "My break's coming up, and I thought I'd spend it here. With you."

*WHAT?* A shock of adrenaline turned me colder.

He chuckled. "I promise, the charge will be . . . minimal."

I flushed, pulling the towel tighter across my breasts. "You're asking me to . . ." I couldn't finish.

"It's your option, of course. It does tend to get cold overnight, though. The occasional warm-up is generally"—he looked my towel-clad body up and down, his eyes anticipatory—"welcomed. And you may need other items. Room service."

"Other items." *Is he serious? But Prinister Severs told us—*"You—you're a man! You're supposed to protect women, not—"

He laughed, harsh and casual, like it was the biggest joke he'd ever heard. "You ain't my wife, darlin'."

My heart pounded in my ears. "I'm a virgin!" I didn't know a person could talk while inhaling, but that's how the last word came out.

His expression went reassuring. "Oh, I won't ask for *that*." He licked his lips. "Just—you know—pretend I'm a lollipop."

This time, no words came. My gorge rose, and I closed my mouth and swallowed hard. It was all I could do not to slam the door in his face.

"Well, all right." He shrugged, smiled. "When you change your mind, just pick up the phone."

Rage burst through my composure. My eyes pinning his, the words came fast now, the worst insult I could think of. "I'll change my mind when you're ice skating in hell!"

His expression didn't change, but he sidled closer to the open door, his tone conversational. "You know, Miss Flint, I bent some rules to check you in. I can check you out. Or"—he examined his fingernails in the spitting light of the walkway—"I could call the Guardian Angels. Or your daddy. Verify your story."

For a long moment I stared at him, frightened, furious; then I slammed the door and locked it. *He wouldn't! Would he? No. I can't worry about it. I've already paid him. He can't. And the Guards—what will they say if I tell them what happened here? Will they believe me?* I hovered by the door, a shaking hand over my mouth, listening as his footsteps faded.

The penetrating cold forced me to focus on the immediate problem.

Returning to the bed, I pulled off the bedspread, folded it, and placed it over the side I planned to sleep on. I frowned against the cold, tucking the towel more tightly around my shivering body. *Not enough.* My eyes fell on my tote, and I upended it, unpacking every item, and spread clothes across the bed. Then I threw my coat on top. *Okay. What else?* I strode to the bathroom, returned to the bed with dry towels from the rack, and laid them over the clothes.

It would have to do.

Shivering, I climbed under the covers with the screen remote. A brief, fleeting thought beckoned me to read my Bible. But I pushed it away, clicked on the broadcast, found a vid and let the story carry me—some ancient film about how God rescued a pregnant woman, desperately trying to escape the DRUSA's Secret Police before they forced her to abort.

Slowly, the bed warmed. Exhaustion crept along my bones, but my eyes were wide open. How could I sleep? My life was a thousand knife-edged pieces, hovering just beyond the vid's end. Long after the movie had finished, sometime around midnight, I dug through my tote and took a dose of allergy medicine.

*It's not going to work. Not this time. Of course it will work. It always works. God, please help it work. I need to sleep. It's not going to work. I'm wide awake. Please . . .*

Twenty minutes later I drifted off, the screen flickering light shadows across the smudged walls of the hotel room.

~

My wrist tingled.

*No.* I fell back into sleep.

Another tingle. *What?* I was incredibly comfortable, warm, cozy. *My phone. Late for work?* Eyes blinked open, shut. *No.*

Odd odor. *What?* Eyes blinked open. *Where . . .*

I sat up, my coat falling to one side. The screen's test pattern dimly illuminated the stinking hotel room. Sounds coming through the wall from an adjoining room brought a flush of heat to my face.

And Mom. *Oh, God. Mom is dead.*

It felt as if someone had punched me in the stomach. I coughed, and tears glassed my eyes. My wrist tingled again, insistent. Blinking away moisture, I clicked on the light.

The holo displayed a message from Ray, and the image of Ray in full fury. *Where the Sam Hill are you? Are you nuts? You get your fanny home THIS INSTANT, YOUNG LADY!*

The display showed an early morning hour, and my mouth tightened. *I should ask where you've been all this time, you whoring blackheart!*

Instead, I typed, *I'm fine. I'm staying with a friend for a few days so I can sort things out. Please don't worry—I'm quite safe.* I hit *send.*

Tingle.

*Are you at Steffan's?*

"What?" Surprise was so strong, I said it aloud. Steffan was an old boyfriend. A dark memory chased away the remnants of sleep. Ray knew better—or should.

*Are you kidding? Why would I restart that fiasco? And risk the fornication charge? I'm at a friend's. A female friend.*

Tingle.

*You stupid, reckless witch, you're just like your mother. You don't think!*

White-hot fury bloomed. I bit my lip, counted to ten, and typed, *Why, thank you. I am going back to sleep now. Might I recommend you do the same.* I thought, *So you can sober up,* but I didn't type that. Instead I shut off my phone, disconnecting it from my chip. Pulling the covers up to my chin, I tried to relax. But roiling anger forestalled any hint of sleep.

I sighed, my eyes unblinking on the ceiling, studying the contours of a large brown water stain.

*He was out with her. Drinking with Constance.* My mental tone slurred the name into a curse. *Constantly Ready Constance. I wonder if she opened her arms and her legs?* I shocked myself a bit with the raw thought. *And he has the nerve to yell at me?*

*But you don't know for sure he met her.*

*And I don't know for sure he didn't.* Angry, I rolled over, avoiding God, avoiding everything, and pulled the covers over my head.

~

"Excuse me, Miss?"

From the rack where I was replacing inventory, I paused, sighing inside. Worry had clawed at my mind the whole morning, and my work persona was on autopilot. Forcing a smile, I turned. "Yes, sir, how can I help—" The words died on my tongue and my smile stiffened.

"Hey, girl." Leaning against a display of men's jackets, Steffan Hagen chuckled. In his late twenties, he was still the same impeccably dressed, flaxen-haired specimen of Nordic masculinity my stepfather had brought home some eighteen months earlier during his campaign to find me an appropriate husband. Per church rules regarding Family Duty, Ray chaperoned us on our first three dates, after which Steff was permitted to see me without supervision.

Well-heeled and Governance Caste, Steffan wooed me like a pro—until the novelty wore off, I suppose. About six months into the relationship, we'd had a nasty fight. I remembered the scene vividly—Steffan's incandescent anger, my confusion, his sudden violence. It took three weeks for the bruise to fade. The only thing worse than the side-long and pitying looks from friends and neighbors was the fact that not one person asked me how it happened. Mom just sighed and gave me an icepack. It was as if every woman in my orbit knew exactly the story that lay behind that vivid purple mark—as if it were a story each one had written or read, herself. As if it were common—*normal.*

That frightened me more than the violence.

Despite my lukewarm reaction now, his smile didn't budge. Then his expression turned sympathetic. "I was so sorry to hear about your mom."

"Thank you," I said, forcing politeness. An awkward silence, and I gestured to my armload of clothes. "I'm working, Steff, I can't—"

"I know." He nodded, and his eyebrows went up. "But we need to talk when you're free. Your dad says you're in trouble."

"I'm fine." I picked up another stack of shirts.

"You still get off at eight?"

My gaze on a crack in the flooring, I sighed and nodded.

Fifteen minutes later, I clocked out, trying to ignore my nervous stomach. Steff followed me out the back exit.

"So." I pulled on my coat as the door shut behind us. "What do you want?"

He shrugged, his grin easy and affable. "I thought I'd walk you home. Wherever home is now."

"I don't think so." I turned away, heading for the sidewalk.

"Hey, hold on." He laughed, and in two long strides he'd caught up to me, grabbing my arm. I twisted free, my mouth tightening, and he held up both hands placatingly. "Relax, okay? I just want to talk."

"Last time you just wanted to talk, you nearly knocked my head off my shoulders." I spat the words.

"Well, don't make me mad." He spread his hands, his tone reasonable.

I rolled my eyes and kept walking.

He fell into step beside me. "Look, I miss you, Mer. You're a great girl, and I think you'll be a terrific wife. You'll make gorgeous babies. Ray says you don't want to live with him anymore, so . . . you can come home with me."

*He didn't waste any time calling you, I see.* I stopped and unleashed my glare. "Are you out of your mind? You know that would finish my reputation and dishonor my family."

Steffan smiled, shook his head as if I were being deliberately obtuse. "You missed the fact that I just proposed."

I bit back a laugh. *That was a proposal? How romantic.*

"Come home with me as my wife." He crossed his arms, flexing his biceps. "Ray gave his consent. We could go before Prinister Horchak tomorrow. Or I'll call your guy—what's his name, Severs? At St. Mike's?"

My eyes dropped to the sidewalk. Prinister Severs was the last person I wanted to see right now.

"I'll take care of you." Steff's voice gentled, oozed persuasion. "You won't have to worry about food, or a place to live. Heck, you won't even have to work if you don't want to."

*I wouldn't have to work.* My stomach wove itself into a thousand knots. *How am I going to buy groceries? I can't even afford the hotel.* My pause was a bit too long, and my teeth mashed my lip. Blood flavored my reply. "I like my job." I started up the sidewalk again, and he jogged to catch up.

"Okay, fine, keep your job. Just make sure dinner's on the table when I get home—you can do whatever you want." He caught my arm again, turning me toward him. "Hey, what's your problem?" His eyes met mine, but his tone was prosaic, not romantic. "I know you love me. You told me once—remember?"

My sigh was a half-laugh. "Steffan, I was sixteen! I didn't know what love was! And I'm not sure you do, even now."

"I do." Instead of getting mad, he pulled me to him. I resisted, but he cupped my face, his thumb stroking my cheekbone. "I've missed you. Come home with me. Be Mrs. Steffan Hagen. Let's start a family."

*A family. What do you know about children? Will you hit them, too?* Anger rose, shouldering aside temptation. "Let go of me."

His hand dropped to my arm, tightened. "Girl, you owe this to your father! I don't know what happened between you, but he's out of his mind with worry. Isn't it enough that he's lost his wife? Now he has to watch his daughter's reputation get dragged through the mud?"

Despite my anger, I knew he was right. One night away from home could be forgiven, covered up with a convenient excuse of emergency or illness; two nights or more invited gossip and would sully the family name. My absence could jeopardize Ray's job. I blinked back tears.

"Dammit, Meryn, what do you want? You want me on one knee? Fine." He released me and dropped to the sidewalk. "Here. Two knees. Just marry me, okay?"

I regarded him for a long moment. *It's a way out. And I would never have to worry about having enough to eat, a safe place to sleep . . .* Then the memory of Steff's fist connecting with my cheek sent a shock of fear through me—and in my mind's eye I saw Mom lying on the bedroom floor, the bloody pillow . . . I backed away, wary apprehension clutching my guts. "Leave me alone, Steffan."

"Meryn, I'm not going to leave you here on the street!" He started to his feet, and I broke into a run. "Meryn!"

Stifling sobs, I ran all the way to the sub station, relieved not to hear footfalls in pursuit. I made it to the car, slipping through just as the doors hissed shut, but once inside I could no longer stop the tears. *Oh, Mom! You didn't want this for me . . . or yourself.*

A woman in the second seat looked up, and I gulped, desperate to compose my expression.

Crying in public was a social solecism. The RD considered it a violation of the scripture that exhorts us to do everything "decently and in order," meaning no negative emotion should be displayed at church or anywhere else. Tears could get me arrested, which would cost me my job—no questions asked—and send me right back to Ray.

Settling into a seat, I smiled and blotted my face as if I'd just run a little too hard, ignoring surreptitious glances from other passengers. But my roiled emotions hadn't abated. A Guard came through from the adjoining car, and I averted my eyes, focusing out the window. As his footsteps approached, I closed my eyes, trembling, fear thwarting my struggle to keep more tears at bay. *God, I'm in trouble! Help me, please!*

The car was silent, as if everyone were waiting for the unfolding drama. I cursed inwardly; that helped. A little.

"Excuse me, Guardian?" A male voice. "Do you know how far we are from the Getts sub station? I'm afraid I'm new to Silvermine and I'm not sure where I am."

My mouth puckered. Liquid gathered at the corner of my left eye, crept down my cheek. *Stop. Stop it!*

The footsteps paused, turned. "You're not far, sir. Just six more stops."

"Thank you so much! Do you happen to know anything about the entertainments in this city? I have a whole glorious weekend with nothing to do."

Footsteps again, but away from me. The Guard engaged the man in quiet conversation, and I exhaled, opening my eyes. Casual, I propped my head in my left hand and my glove absorbed the tear, but the trembling didn't stop. A woman across the aisle smiled slightly and nodded. Biting my swollen lip, I looked away.

Ten minutes later, when the sub stopped at my station, I'd regained control. I disembarked with a half-dozen other passengers and headed up the street.

Pulling my hood forward to block the wind, I wondered why Ray had called Steffan. I supposed he figured Steff was his best chance to marry me off before I besmirched the family name. I snorted annoyance, but I understood Ray's position. My thoughts drifted to Mom, and her enforced stay at home after she'd become pregnant with me, and I wondered how Gampa Flint had managed to broker her marriage to Ray. I should've been a dealbreaker. Tears threatened again, and my mouth tightened. *I'm usually better at controlling—*

"Rough day?" a male voice said gently. I recognized the voice from the sub.

Startled, I stopped, and the man stepped up next to me. He must have exited the sub at the same time I did, but I hadn't noticed he'd been matching my steps. I castigated myself for my inattention.

Older and about my height, hair graying at the temples, he wore formal business attire, including a hat and expensive overcoat. Before I looked away, his eyes on mine were kind and a trifle worried. A green Caste Ring fitted neatly over his leather gloves. Although he had not addressed me in Mid-Caste Formal, I chose not to be offended.

Forcing a smile, I folded my hands in front of my chest. "You honor me in my distress, right honorable, distinguished sir! Before God, I am very well. I thank you most kindly for your generous concern."

He chuckled, his voice a reassuring baritone. "Well, the Guards can be too officious. No point in letting them take an honorable young lady to the station just because she had a difficult afternoon."

His informal speech gave me permission to drop to Mid-Caste Casual. I nodded, my eyes on the sidewalk. "Not a place I'd like to spend the night."

"No, I've heard too many stories of the evils that happen in such places." He gestured up the street. "I'm on my way to the hotel. May I escort you?"

Bravely, I met his eyes. My hesitation was so brief, he couldn't have caught it. "You may. Thank you."

He touched his hand to his hat brim, and we started up the street together. "You are staying there, as well?"

*How did he know that?* I paused, wary, but he turned to me with a disarming grin. "We must have exited our rooms at the same time this morning; you were ahead of me in the queue to the sub." I started forward again, and he fell into step beside me. A hovercar floated past us and up the street as he chatted on in a charming fashion. "It's not exactly the best hotel in the city, is it? Foolish me—I booked it without reading the reviews. Could you recommend someplace more, ah, genteel?"

*He's a businessman. In town for a meeting, or something.* I smiled. "I'm afraid I'm not familiar with the hotels in Silvermine, but I've heard the Temple Mount is one of the best."

"Ah!" He spread his hands. "Just the person to ask! I'll have to try it tomorrow. But tonight, I'll put up with the smelly room and the dirty bedspread."

I laughed, and he joined in.

"My business requires a substantial amount of travel, but taking bedbugs home is insufficient tradeoff for trying to save on the expense account. Are you from out of town also?" The freezing wind buffeted us, whipping his coat around his legs. "Perhaps visiting friends?"

"I, uh—" I fumbled, trying to remember what I'd told the clerk. "I live in Silvermine, but our heat is out. I had to make do."

"Oh, those wretched furnaces. Yes, yes, it happens." He pulled his coat tighter, as if feeling the chill of an unheated room. "Good thinking on your part to get out. Too many foolish people freeze every winter." We walked in silence for a few minutes, our footsteps in unison on the pavement. "Have you eaten? I miss my family, and you're good company. Would you perhaps join me at *Le Steak Petit* up the street?"

For a split second, I was tempted. Hunger warred with caution. *Since he's Management Caste, I might be safe.*

Caution won. "I'm sorry, sir, but I've had dinner." My stomach rumbled; I prayed he didn't hear it.

"Ah, my loss, then." His smile embodied regret. "You're about my daughter's age."

*You're being silly, Meryn. He's a very nice man. And free dinner . . . that isn't ramen . . .*

*I'm silly, yes. I'm not stupid.*

Just outside the hotel's lobby door, I turned. "I cannot sufficiently express my undying gratitude for your kind escort." I used the appropriate high-caste verbiage, putting my hands together in front of my chest and giving a slight bow, my eyes lowered. "You are most chivalrous, good sir."

"Not at all," he said. "You're in 145, yes?"

Startled, I stepped back.

"I'm in 150." He smiled. "I'll just walk you to your door."

Biting my lip, I turned up the walkway, and he joined me. *Should I be worried? He just came out his door this morning when I did, that's all. Of course.*

"So you have a career, I see?" he said.

"I do." Despite the cold, my hands were sweaty. *Don't tell him where you work.* "I, uh, work in retail."

"A good position"—he nodded—"although retail doesn't pay much. Especially for a young woman. And only thirty-two hours a week? Who can live on that?"

I chuckled without mirth. "No one I know."

"There are opportunities that pay more, you know." Our footfalls echoed softly on the concrete. "Especially for a lovely young lady such as yourself. And here we are."

We stopped in front of my door. My heart pounded. *Please just let me go. Let me go.* "Thank you for the escort, good sir."

"Mr. Josephus is my name," he said. Fishing in his pocket, he handed me a business card. "If you should need anything at all, please don't hesitate to call me. I am alone in town, and your gracious company would be most welcome if you would condescend to escort me to the Temple Mount. I will compensate you for your time, of course."

*He's propositioning me!* I'd heard of men who did such things, but I never expected to be on the receiving end. My stomach contracted.

Taking my nerveless right hand in his, he pressed my wrist to the door plate. It beeped, and he opened the door and stepped back. With a touch of his hand to his hat, he said, "Think about it, Miss Flint."

*But I didn't—* My jaw dropped. *He has an implant? And he scanned my chip? How DARE he?* It was the ultimate invasion of privacy. Fear warred with fury and I opened my mouth to speak, but he'd already turned up the walkway. I dove inside my room and slammed the door.

# 5. PRICE

For the longest time, I didn't turn on the lights. I stood at the window, watching wisps of fog from the bay curl and dance around the streetlights, willing my heart to slow. I wondered if the man had gone to his room, or if he was out there again, looking for another girl like me—another girl, alone, desperate. I wondered how many girls he found, and what he did with them. And if I refused him, would he contact Ray, or turn me over to the Guards, or follow me to my job? Fear shuddered through my bones, turning me cold.

Far down the street, beneath a distant light, a feminine shape hurried in the other direction. Moments later, she vanished in the gloom.

The way she moved reminded me of Mom. And then something—like a strong, muscular Guard at the doorway of my mind—turned my thoughts away from those homey memories and sent them marching in the opposite direction. I blinked. *Wow. I must be tired.*

"Sounds like you passed up a lucrative gig."

I stiffened. Slowly I reached for the light switch.

"Don't." The desk clerk moved from the shadowed bathroom into the small patch of illumination from the window. His hand grasped mine and lowered it away from the switch plate.

My heart pounded; my free hand slipped into my pocket. "Who's minding the desk?" I tried to make it sound conversational.

He chuckled, his fingers lacing into mine. "Don't you worry your pretty little head about the desk." His other hand lifted to my face, caressed my cheek. "You should've known I'd come back."

I swallowed; his thumb ran across my Adam's apple.

"You know what I think? I think you're on the run from your mean daddy or your mean husband." His hand dropped to my collarbone, fingers playing with my lace collar, and he chuckled. "Or both. But you see, darlin', I'm not mean.

"Now don't be nervous. I'll make it good for you, too. Or . . ." He paused. "You'll vacate the room. Tonight."

Outrage infiltrated my voice. "I paid for—"

"Oh, you'll get your money back." His hand released mine and dropped to his belt. I heard it clink.

"So you want me to . . ." My hands shook, remembering Ray.

"Yes," he whispered, his thumb stroking my neck as his arm brushed my bosom. "Make it good. I want to feel those pretty little lips of yours."

The silence stretched as I fought fear and anger, desperately praying for words. "I think we should try something else," I said.

His eyebrows lifted. "Oh? What did you have in mind?" His hand tightened around my throat.

"You go back to your office." I felt my pulse pounding against his thumb, too fast. "And I go to sleep, right here in the room I paid for."

He blinked. Then his lips curved, and he let out a laugh. "You really want to sleep in the gutter tonight, don't you? Why should I do that?"

I withdrew my hand from my pocket and held up my phone. "Because if you don't, your boss will find this whole conversation fascinating listening."

His eyes darted to the phone. I steeled myself for anger, but his face didn't alter. He shrugged, and a shivering filled my stomach. "You think my boss would care? He'll probably bend you over the bed just to teach you a lesson about tattling. He always gets first dibs, but if I'm lucky, he'll let me watch. What do you think, Joe? You want to take turns with this little morsel? After all, I found her." In the light from the window, his smile was shadowed, menacing. "Send your recording. His card's in the foyer."

My mouth dried to a sand desert. He buckled his pants and slipped through the door with the casual ease of someone on a social visit, closing it noiselessly behind him.

I fastened the lock, closed the drapes, and turned on the light. My heart was still galloping as I set the phone on the bedside table. *Would he . . .? No. No. Of course not. The manager wouldn't . . . would he?*

"I'm safe tonight," I whispered. Tears leaked from my eyes, and my mouth tightened. I dragged one of the battered chairs to the door and propped it under the knob. *It works in the movies. I hope it works.*

Without undressing, I climbed into bed. A sob burst from my throat. "Stop it!" I growled, frowning. "Just stop, Meryn. The door is locked and braced. Tonight, you have shelter." I said it out loud, the words reassuring me. "God is here. And everything is okay. Don't think about tomorrow." *Tomorrow. My last night at the hotel. When I'll have to decide. If I can even sleep here anymore, after what just happened. How can I stay? But how can I go?*

I stared at the water stain on the ceiling, unaware of time passing, unable to shut off the light, unable to close my eyes. I was too afraid of what might happen in the dark.

~

That whole next day at work, I flitted from one workstation to another, expecting Steffan to come charging out of the aisles, demanding I marry him. I caught Mary-Sarah regarding me with an odd expression, but I just smiled and tried to focus on my work. It wasn't easy; worry overlaid every moment of my shift, making my hands shake. My eyes were scratchy from lack of sleep. Twice I dropped garments on their hangers.

That afternoon, I retreated to the break room and dug my water bottle out of the fridge. Sinking down at a table, I folded my hands, uncertain. *God. I don't know if You're even listening to me anymore. I haven't been very faithful. But I'm out of options. I can't marry Steffan. And I can't stay at the hotel. So I suppose . . . I have to go home?*

Condensation from my cold water pooled beneath the bottle, and I used a fingertip to push the water around a brown stain on the tabletop, circling, circling. I don't know what I was waiting for—maybe an angel to appear in front of me and hand me enough money to live on my own until I found a better job, or a good husband. Maybe a stroke of brilliance that would show me another option.

Nothing happened.

*This is stupid. Life doesn't work that way. Prayer doesn't work that way.* I tried to tamp down my anger. *I guess I wasn't hearing God, after all. Okay, fine. It isn't what Mom wanted, but I don't have a choice. I'll go home tonight.* I sighed, blotting the tears that always seemed to hover just behind my eyes. *Family comes first. That's what God wants. Prinister Severs says it all the time. At least at home, I won't have to worry about some man—* I cut off the thought. It was a lie, and I knew it.

I didn't like the decision, but now that I'd made it, I felt confident. Purposeful. The dithering was over, and I knew what to do. *I have a direction. Good.* I just wished I felt happier about it.

~

My shift ended at four, and I returned to the hotel and packed my few things. To my relief, I didn't see the desk clerk. As I picked up my Bible, something fluttered to the floor.

Mom's holo.

Slowly I retrieved it, studying our smiles, remembering that day, remembering Mom . . . Biting my lip, I set the square of plastic on the little table and tapped the small red dot on the holo's frame. At once the image bloomed to full size in front of me: the two of us standing on a holographic beach in our swimsuits, arms around each other, smiling. A susurrus of waves oozed through the tiny speaker, birds calling in the background; Mom smiled at me, her expression peaceful. "Such a fun day," she said, and I nodded, pressing my cheek for a moment against hers.

"You're a fish, Mom," I said, and we laughed together, sounding like each other. "I didn't know you were such a good swimmer."

I smiled at the wonder in my younger self's voice. Back then, I thought I knew everything about Mom.

I thought I knew everything.

My smile faded.

"My father taught me when I was a little girl. He was a good swimmer, too." Mom reddened and shyly looked at the camera, waved a hand. "Oh, honey, that's enough. These are expensive." The image vanished, but I couldn't move. I stood in the middle of the room, staring at the plastic square, my thoughts swirling.

Mom told me once, it took courage to be a woman. Courage, to live in our society. She said asking God for courage every morning was the smartest thing I could do. I didn't understand what she meant, then. Why would I need courage if men took care of everything?

Now, I understood. *God, is it too late to ask?* Impatient then, I sighed, pushing the prayer away. *Too late. For too many things.*

"I'm sorry, Mom," I whispered. "I just—I can't do this. I thought I could. But I can't." Clenching my jaw, I pushed the holo into my Bible and stuffed the book in my tote.

It was impossible to ask for a refund; the last thing I wanted to do was confront the greasy-haired clerk. Resigned to the loss, I quit the room and headed for the sub stop.

The whole way home, I prayed. *Please help me work things out with Ray. I'll perform my Family Duty and I won't even complain, I promise. But I can't marry Steffan. I just can't. Thank You that I can go home.*

A hiss of door, and a Guard came through from the adjoining car, his face shield down. His head swung from side to side, which meant he was reading chips as he walked. My stomach tightened, and I looked out the window at the red access-door lights flashing by.

The Guard stopped by my seat. I looked up, trying not to let fear show, trying not to seem guilty of anything, even though his attention made me feel guilty.

His nightstick tapped his leg. "On your way home from work, Miss Flint?"

I tried to swallow, but my throat was dry. "Yes, sir." It came out a whisper.

"Unescorted, I see."

I cleared my throat. "I am single, sir, and my father works also."

I could see nothing of his expression through the faceplate—only the reflection of my nervous face, distorted. The silence lengthened.

*What does he want?* "I, uh . . . I just got off work. I'm on my way home, sir." I tried not to wince. *Never offer information. That's what Bree told me.*

"See that you get there, Miss Flint." He leaned over me. "And find a husband. Soon."

"Yes, sir."

He moved on, but my pulse refused to slow. Five minutes later the sub arrived at my stop, and I bolted through the doors and ran up the stairs to the bus stop, coughing out the filthy air, my heart pounding in my chest.

Riding the bus helped; Guards rarely patrolled the buses, especially in our section of town. After a few minutes the bus turned onto Stone Avenue. I opened my phone, touched the button on the Silvermine Transit Authority app, and the big vehicle slowed and stopped. The doors wheezed open.

Oddly slow, I stepped off, taking in the familiar neighborhood with its dirty apartment blocks and narrow streets. The bus roared away behind me, but I couldn't move. *What's wrong with me? I've made my decision! Family comes first!*

"Go home, Meryn!" I hissed. I forced one leg forward, then the other. Down the sidewalk. Past the pricey brownstone where I'd played with my childhood friend, Debbie, skipping rope and drawing chalk messages on the sidewalk. *God Loves You!* and *Jesus Will Always Be There* with flowers and curlicues and crosses. I heard an echo of a child's laughter in my memory. *"The rock landed on the four! You have to skip the four! You can do it!"* Neither of us saw the dark clouds on the horizon, that young. So young.

The walk became easier, my stride more fluid. I walked past the tree skeletons, all of them dead from some fungal infestation decades before, bark peeled from what was left of their trunks, branches broken off for firewood.

*"Meryn! Time for dinner!"* Mom always went to the end of the walkway on the second floor of our Worker Caste apartment building, leaning way out over the railing to call me home. *She's up there right now, crumbling tofu in a frying pan, and she'll smile at me when I come through the door. I'll start the rice—*

"Welcome home, Meryn!" Mrs. Kittiwax waved from her second-floor window as I opened the gate to our courtyard. I lifted a hand, forced a smile. Trust Mrs. Kittiwax to keep an eye on what was happening in our community. *Does she know I've been gone? Probably, but I hope not.* To my surprise, it felt comforting to be back to the familiar places and people I'd grown up with. I didn't realize how much I'd missed them. I waved at old Mr. Cook, who sat in front of his apartment on his chipped plastic lawn chair, wrapped in a worn, holey tan blanket, his long gray hair losing its combover in the wind. He was always there, regular as clockwork, no matter the weather, his apartment window open to the cold so he could hear DNN's broadcast through the screen.

He waved back and grinned. "Hey, girlie girl!"

This time, my smile wasn't forced.

I crossed the yard, out of Mrs. Kittiwax's sight, and climbed the stairs, finally at peace with the idea of staying with Ray. *Thank You, God. Maybe You needed to show me what I had before I could truly appreciate it.*

Still smiling, I reached the landing, looked down the walkway to our apartment—and froze. Some thirty feet ahead, his back to me, Ray was walking toward our apartment door. But he wasn't alone. His arm circled a woman's waist.

For a split second, my brain tried to tell me it was Mom, but this woman was too short and the hair color was wrong—and I remembered that something had happened to Mom so it couldn't be her anyway, and my mouth dropped open. *He's seeing someone! And that means Mom is—*

My peace shattered, childhood memories falling into a million random pieces on the concrete at my feet.

Ray and the woman paused at the door, and she simpered up at him as he pressed his thumb to the lock. Her eyes drifted toward me. I spun in place as if someone had forcibly turned me around. Not caring if anyone saw or heard, I ran to the stairs, clattered down to the courtyard, and bolted to the bus stop.

I cried the whole way back to the hotel, and no one even looked at me.

~

Long after I'd returned to my room and the sobs wound down, I sat on the dirty bedspread, my face buried in a towel, trying not to panic, trying to think. The room screen was blaring, DNN's evening anchors running through the evening news headlines with metronomic precision. But thoughts ping-ponged through my brain in a random scatter.

I thought again about the graffiti I'd seen in the subway—*LIBERTÉ!*— and a memory surfaced. The clandestine organization wasn't just apostate; it actively worked to overthrow the government. I'd heard of it only in whispers, mostly from my school friend, Connie. I smiled.

She and I didn't get along at first. All through grammar school, the girl was snarky, superior and sometimes downright mean. I wasn't the only target, especially once she discovered she couldn't bait me.

But when we started ninth grade, something changed. She came to school nice—congenial. I was forgiving, and we struck up a friendship. We were assigned as lab partners in biology, and often I would stay after school with her, helping her work through scientific concepts.

She loved the science of biology but hated lab work. When we had to dissect a frog, she threw up. I swallowed hard and finished the project, even though I had tears in my eyes for the poor frog.

"Where do you get the frogs, Mrs. Hopkins?" Ani Maher had asked.

Our teacher, a kind, intelligent woman with wavy brown hair, looked startled. "From a lab," she said, setting down a stack of petri dishes. "They're grown for us."

I looked down at the carcass on the lab table, my heart breaking for the poor frog that had never known a lake or a creek. I leaned down close, formaldehyde a tang in my nostrils.

"I'm sorry," I whispered, so softly that even the girls across the table couldn't hear. "You deserved better."

"Look!" Fanny Evert yelled. "Meryn's kissing her frog!"

The other girls laughed, and I straightened up, flushing. "I was not!" I retorted. "I was looking at his, uh, blood vessels."

"Use your magnifier, Meryn," Mrs. Hopkins said, and I complied.

It was almost dinnertime when I stepped back from the magnifier. The rest of the lab was quiet and dark. Connie typed at a rapid pace in her tablet, looking from diagram to screen and back again.

"Does it make more sense now?" I rubbed the crick in my back.

She looked up at me, gratitude writ large. "It does, thank you! The part about circulation is *sooo* complicated. And you add in the skeleton and the nerves . . ."

"Imagine how much more complicated it all is in your much more complicated body," I said.

She rolled her eyes. "I'm glad we don't have to study that. I'd be barfing all day!"

We laughed as we gathered our things and headed toward the door. Five minutes later we stood in the glassed-in foyer, waiting for Ray. Yawning, I let my tote slide to the floor.

Connie stared out at the parking lot as if searching for something she'd lost. A moment later she spoke, her speech low and wooden. "I trust you, Meryn." She didn't look at me. "I—I knew there was something different about you, even way back."

My scalp prickled. "Different?"

She nodded and smiled at the glass. "In a good way."

"I'm not different." I grasped the door's push bar and leaned back, stretching my arms. "I'm just like the other girls." My eyes skittered to the camera just inside the main doors. Even if the audio was active, it couldn't record our conversation in the foyer. Could it?

Connie shook her head, her body angled so the camera couldn't pick up the movement of her lips. "No, *Meryn Athena*. If you'd changed your name to Mary Athaliah, we wouldn't be having this conversation."

I gave a low laugh and angled my body away from the camera, too. "Okay, maybe a little different." *Wow, am I paranoid.*

She smiled, her eyes tracking a car as it pulled through the lot and onto the street. "I knew it. I've watched you in class. I've listened. You don't think like the rest of the girls."

"So?" Even to myself I sounded defensive. "It isn't like I'm a radical, or anything."

For a long moment, she didn't speak. When she did, her voice was almost a whisper. "I am."

"What?"

"A radical. I am radically against this unbiblical indoctrination of all of us." At last she turned, her back to the camera, and her eyes startled me with their intensity. "Meryn, if you tell anyone about this conversation, they'll kill me."

I wasn't sure I'd heard right, and a nervous laugh bubbled out. "C'mon, Connie . . ."

She hissed, her eyes a warning. "Keep it down. This 'Christianity' they're forcing on us isn't faith. It's fascism. I think you understand this, don't you?" I had to strain to hear her whisper. "We follow their rules, or we don't survive? Women being forced to marry? To have kids, or else? What kind of love is that, Meryn? What kind of faith? It isn't!"

I bit my lip, her questions kindling an unease in my mind.

She didn't let me respond but plunged ahead. "You . . . may need help someday, Meryn. The things you've said in class, the ways you've challenged our teachers . . . can't you see how they look at you? How worried they are? *You're not toeing the line!* Don't you see how dangerous that is? If you ever find yourself in trouble"—her cold hand grasped my arm—"call me. I know people. Non-RD people who believe that what the government is doing is wrong and are trying to fix it. They'll understand you. They can help. Okay? Don't forget. And for God's sake, *don't tell!*"

Before I could respond to Connie's astonishing revelation, a horn sounded outside, and Ray's car pulled to a stop at the concrete apron. I screwed my eyes closed and cursed under my breath. Connie threw herself against the crash bar, pelted out to the car as if chased by demons and dove into the back seat. I followed, climbing into the front.

"How was school, girls?" Ray smiled, and we chatted inconsequentialities the whole way to Connie's, the conversation so normal I almost forgot my friend's odd behavior in the foyer.

But as we pulled up to Connie's apartment building, I felt a tap on my shoulder from the back seat. "Remember, Meryn," she said, low and urgent. "And stay away from Joy Calumet." Then cheerfully to Ray, "Thanks, Mr. Esselin!" And she jumped out of the car, slammed the door and went flying up the stairs, pack bobbing on her back.

"Remember what?" Ray pulled back into traffic. "And what's wrong with Joy?"

*Why is he so interested?* "Oh, we have a biology test on Friday. And Joy's a gossip," I said, noncommittal. *Wait. Did I lie? No. We do have a test coming up. That's what Connie was talking about, surely.* I didn't expand on my answer about Joy. I knew what Connie meant, because there were rumors about such classmates: Joy was an RD mole who would turn me in if I stepped too far out of line. I wondered if Connie knew anything more. I wanted to ask, but where could we talk unobserved?

Connie didn't mention our conversation again, but I couldn't get it out of my head. "Non-RD people"? What did she mean? The people our Civil Society teacher called "the riffraff—the lepers, liars and lechers living on the fringes of society"? How could they help me?

And why would I need help? *I'm a good girl, aren't I? Don't I go to church? Work hard in school? Why does Connie think I'm not toeing the line? Do I ask too many questions? Challenge too many ambiguous points?*

Without meaning to, I looked at Connie, sitting across from me at the lab table. She was laughing with Pris Komplie over some illustration in the biology text. Connie caught my gaze, and I jerked my face down to the microscope.

*Fascism.* I'd looked up the term to make sure I had the precise definition. It talked about "dictatorial power." Was our popresident a dictator? Did Humboldt suppress his opposition? We had free elections. That's what our political science teacher told us. How could we have a dictatorship if we had elections? And the restrictions on women work-ing—wasn't that what our society wanted, to keep families strong?

Joy sat on a stool across the lab, typing in her tab, her hair coiled into a neat bun. Pious, easygoing Joy Calumet, who never wore makeup, never spoke up in class. I counted her a friend. Would she really turn me in for disagreeing with too many points?

I fiddled with the microscope control, trying to focus. *Control.* Was that so bad—having an ordered society, peaceful under the rule of law? Didn't we need Guards to keep the peace?

I tried to keep my attention on my lab work, vowing to ask Mom about the whole thing when I got home from school.

~

My question was quiet, but Mom bolted to the screen and turned on DNN's afternoon programming—some praise team doing a poorly executed version of "Jesus is Victor"—and turned it up loud. She led me back into the kitchen, where we'd been fixing soup for dinner.

"You're changing lab partners," Mom said, quiet but firm. As my eyes rounded in astonishment, she added, "I mean it, Meryn. Go talk to Mrs. Hopkins tomorrow."

"I can't, Mom." I held on to my patience. "It will affect my grade."

"Better your grade than your life!" It came in a harsh whisper. Mom's face flushed red, then went white. For the first time in my life, I regretted bringing my thoughts to her.

"Mom, come on! Connie isn't the issue here!"

"Connie is very much the issue here." Mom sat at the table, taking a deep breath. I turned the heat down under the soup and joined her, scared. Mom never got mad at me—not like this.

"So this group really exists," I whispered. I'd been half-hoping it was a myth.

Mom nodded, her eyes wary. "It's called Liberté, and they are known for active rebellion against the RD. That's all I know. And just knowing about it is enough to destroy your future."

*That* got my attention. "Now I understand why Connie told me not to tell anyone," I whispered. "How did you find out about it?"

For a long moment, Mom was silent, her eyes on the tabletop. "A friend, just like you did." Her chin quivered, and she looked up. "When I was carrying you. She knew I needed help, that your father had . . . well . . . so she offered. She asked me to think about it, and she'd get back to me." She pressed her lips together, as if debating whether to say more.

"What happened?"

Mom swallowed. "Before we spoke again, my friend . . . disappeared. Along with her entire family. Food left on the table, dog in the backyard, car in the garage, purses on the counter, everything right there as if the family had just . . . walked next door." Her hands twisted in her lap. A tear fell on her right thumb. "No one ever heard from them again."

"How do you know they didn't move?" I asked, shrugging. "Maybe they'd been tipped off that the Guards were coming, and—"

Mom raised her eyes to mine. "The dog." She continued as if I hadn't spoken, her voice a dull monotone. "She barked fiercely, nonstop, for hours. A neighbor, Mrs. Carlin, had a key because she took care of Muffin when my friend's family went on vacation. So she let herself in the house . . . to check on her, because no one had seen . . . and she decided to get dog food . . ." Mom's voice broke. "She'd fed Muffin and planned to leave a note, explaining, and that's when she saw . . . them." Tears were running unheeded down Mom's face.

"Saw what?" My mouth was open, my heart thudding in my chest. I hadn't expected this.

"The chips, Meryn. The family's chips."

Breath left me in a rush.

Mom dissolved into sobs. "They were laid out on the dining table, clean and pure . . . like little diamonds, she said. The parents' chips first, my friend's chip, the toddler's tiny chip, and it didn't matter that they were Governance Caste, didn't matter . . ." Mom buried her face in her hands.

My stomach heaved. "Someone cut out the chips of Governance—"

Mom shook her head and wiped her face with her handkerchief. "Not someone, Meryn," she said, her voice too loud with the effort to control her tears. Impatient, she reached forward and seized my arm with a cold hand, her grip tight and painful, her voice a hoarse whisper. "Guards. Only the Reformation Directorate can remove a person's chip with that kind of surgical precision."

"But why?" I tried to hold firm to logic, to shut out the storm of Mom's emotion. "How do you know—"

"To send a message." Mom's eyes were hopeless. "A very clear message not to defy the RD. It's one thing to argue the occasional theological point with your Bible teacher. It's something else entirely to associate with a group working to overthrow the government. And it's getting worse. Ever since Humboldt was elected—" She bit off her sentence.

I sat thinking, trying to reconcile this new view of the RD with what I'd been told in school, in church, by friends. "How very Christian of them." I didn't edit my sarcasm, staring at the table, seeing Ray's chip lying there, Mom's, mine . . . Tearing my eyes away from the scarred laminate surface, I looked at Mom, who hiccupped softly. "Are you sure they were—" I broke off, my eyes begging her not to say the word: *killed*.

Mom nodded, releasing me. "We're sure," she whispered. "You can't live in this world without a chip. The message was that the family wouldn't be needing theirs anymore."

"Not even the baby," I whispered, tears cutting a path down my face.

Mom took my hand in her usual gentle way, and we sat in silence for a very long time, while "I've Got the Joy in Jesus" played cheerfully in the background.

~

"Well, ordinarily I wouldn't expect this from you, Meryn," Mrs. Hopkins said, looking up from her desk, "but I know you've been working overtime helping Connie, and I don't want you burning out."

*How do you know that?* My stomach tightened. *And what else do you know?*

Mrs. Hopkins tapped her tablet, scrolling through names. "I'll pair you with . . . Naomi Thatcher."

I heaved a silent sigh of relief. Brilliant and as inoffensive as milk pudding, Naomi had worked with me on a group project for English. "Thank you, Mrs. Hopkins."

She looked at me over her glasses. "Under these circumstances, I won't dock your grade. I appreciate your willingness to work with Connie. It was generous of you."

*I didn't mind,* I thought, but I said, "Connie is a hard worker, and she genuinely enjoys biology." I bit my lip, struck by a sudden thought. "I hope this won't affect *her* grade?"

Mrs. Hopkins smiled. She didn't do so often, and it always transformed her face. "Not this time. I'll tell Connie I'm concerned about you burning out. I'm sure she'll understand."

Connie collared me after the next lab session, her face a mask of guilt. "Meryn, I'm so sorry! I didn't realize . . ."

I smiled reassurance. "It's okay; I'm fine. I never minded helping you."

"That's what Mrs. Hopkins said. And . . . Ruth Hernandez is great, but I miss you."

"I miss you, too," I said, surprised that I meant it.

She gave me a hug and peered at me intently for a long moment; then we headed off to our next class.

Over the ensuing months, I sometimes considered asking Connie for more information about Liberté. But fear kept me silent, and she never brought it up again. A year later, just eight months before we were due to graduate, she was caught in the janitor's closet making out with Jerusha Gunderson. The girls were dragged out, screaming, pleading, and crying, and the school's Guard let them drop to their knees and beg forgiveness of God and man before he executed them, right there in the hallway. The entire incident was recorded on security cameras, and the principal called a school assembly to preach on the evils of homosexual obscenity and show us the video. When it got to the place where Connie and Jerusha were shot, several girls screamed. My hands flew to my mouth, and black spots reeled through my vision, but somehow I held it together. Those who were still crying when the assembly adjourned received detentions. I managed to wait until I got home, then I fell apart.

The janitorial staff wasn't allowed to clean up the mess for three days. We all got the message.

~

Now, alone in the hotel room, I sighed. *I wish Connie were still alive. Maybe she could help me now.* I had no idea how to get in touch with

Liberté on my own, and asking around was far too dangerous. But I needed help.

A gentle tap at the motel-room door interrupted my thoughts; anger cleared my head. *What is this, the downtown bus station?* Lowering the towel, I rose. "Who is it." My tone wasn't remotely civil, and I didn't care.

"It's Mr. Josephus, Meryn. Do you have a moment?"

Clenching my jaw, I yanked the door open.

Dressed in the same immaculate fashion as the previous evening, the man removed his hat, a kind smile softening his eyes. "Please forgive the intrusion, my dear." For a moment his eyes traced the cracked sidewalk, and I tried not to grind my teeth. Finally, his gaze met mine, and this time I didn't look away. "I am moving to the Temple Mount tonight, but I wanted to check on you before I left. Something about your situation—" He paused, his expression frank. "Well, I'm worried about you."

"I'm fine," I said, but I'd cried so hard my nose was clogged, and it came out "I'b fide."

His smile was brief, but not cynical. "Your red eyes tell me otherwise." He took a breath, his eyebrows lifting. "Meryn, I wasn't kidding when I said you remind me of my daughter. She—" He looked away. "Well, her life has not been as . . . my wife and I had hoped. I am somewhat to blame for that." He shrugged. "The traveling, I suppose. Unavoidable, but still." For the first time, I noticed the odd, ice-blue color of his eyes. "I don't want to see anything bad happen to you. You are a lovely young woman, alone in Silvermine, and there are too many . . . well, unsavory characters in this town who might want to take advantage."

*Is he kidding?* I frowned. "Sir, last night I—well, I thought you—"

Wincing, he waved me to silence. "I'm a fool. I never should have read your chip." His eyebrows lifted, trusting. "Will you forgive me?"

*Wow. Maybe I misjudged him.* An unexpected hope bloomed inside, and I essayed a smile. "I forgive you, sir."

His smile transformed his face. "Oh, none of this 'sir,' business. Call me Mr. Josephus."

I chuckled, awkward. "Okay."

The silence lengthened while I examined the dented door sweep, and the strong bay wind emptied my room of warmth. He sighed. "Look, you have my card, yes?"

I nodded.

"If you need anything—and I do mean anything—please don't hesitate to call. Food, shelter, a work reference—whatever."

*Is he serious? He really wants to help me?*

He shifted his hat to his other hand and stepped forward, his hand cupping my cheek. Startled, my eyes met his, and I sucked in a breath. But his warm skin and comforting aftershave reminded me of Ray when I was a little girl—when I felt safe. I aborted my step backward.

"I'm not asking questions." His voice was gentle. "But if you can't go home, Meryn, call me. For God's sake, don't sleep on the street. At the very least I can make sure you have a safe place to stay for a while, and food in your stomach." His eyes crinkled with his smile. "Okay?"

I smiled. "Okay, sir." My face went hot, and I chuckled embarrassment. "I mean, Mr. Josephus."

"Okay." He patted my face gently, then stepped back and put on his hat. "Don't forget to lock that door," he said, and headed down the sidewalk toward the street.

I closed the door and locked it, smiling in wonderment. It seemed I'd just made a terrific new friend.

Or an enormous mistake.

# 6. CHANGING

"Miss, can I *please* get a changing room sometime this year?"

"Yes, ma'am—right away!" I turned to Steffan. "Will you go away and let me work?" I hissed, my eyes narrowing.

"I want your answer!"

I headed toward the changing area. Steffan grabbed my arm, and I twisted away.

"Flirt with your boyfriend later!" the woman yelled, her face furrowed with impatience. Giving Steffan a murderous glare, I crossed to where she waited, holding an armful of clothes.

"He isn't my boyfriend and I'm not flirting," I said, keeping my voice even with effort.

"Well, that's how it looks!"

*You're not wearing an MT. Why don't you flirt with him, honey? Take him off my hands.* I unlocked the door to a changing room, relieved to be out of Steffan's sight. "Here you are, miss. If you are unhappy with my performance, you may complain to my manager. Her name is Mary-Sarah." *Please do. Please tell her about this idiot who won't leave me alone!*

Her eyes rolling, the woman slammed the door in my face. I sighed and gathered garments from the return rack.

"Meryn." Mary-Sarah met me at the entrance to the changing area, her expression drawn and anxious. "I'm getting complaints about you today. If you can't focus on your job, I will be forced to call security and have your boyfriend removed."

I smiled for the first time that morning. "Please do! He's driving me nuts."

"You shouldn't encourage him to meet you here." Her manner starchy, she turned to the wall phone and dialed. "You know the policy." I opened my mouth to protest, but she was still speaking. "Yes, Mr. Millhouse, it's Mary-Sarah in women's. I have an employee violation."

My wrist buzzed. I looked at Mary-Sarah, who caught my gaze and lifted her eyebrows. "I'm going on break," I whispered, and she nodded.

I tried to slip out of the changing area, but Steff was waiting. "Meryn—" he began, and I rounded on him.

"My boss is calling security to have you removed," I said, my voice icy. "If you want to talk to me, you will have to wait until after my shift. Do you understand?"

"Come on." Steff's tone was jocular. "It isn't like you have a real job, anyway! What do you call this?" He motioned around at the women browsing. "You're just playing at work."

A woman perusing a sale rack nearby looked up, then turned away, reddening.

"You're a fine one to talk," I said, and he laughed. Steff had never held a job—the balance in his trust fund ensured he'd never have to work. I folded my arms. "I'm going on break. That includes a break from you. Come and see me at five."

I turned away, and he grabbed my arm again.

Anger lit my tone. "Steffan! I—"

"Miss." The store's security officer stood in the aisle, arms crossed. "Your manager has undoubtedly told you it's a violation of company policy for employees to flirt or carry on personal business while on the clock."

I smiled and poured honey into my response. "Sir, I'm trying my best to focus on my job. If you will kindly escort Mr. Hagen out of the store, I'll be able to resume my work."

The man turned to Steffan, his eyes twinkling. "Pretty little thing, isn't she, sir? I can see why you're gone on her. Let me get you a cup of coffee up at the mall so she can play pattycake with the customers. You know she's not going anywhere."

The resentful expression on Steffan's face didn't change. "Five o' clock," he said, turning and pointing at my nose. "Don't try to skate out of here without me."

Deferentially, the guard motioned for Steffan to precede him, and the two men headed down the main aisle, Steff muttering under his breath.

~

The call was from Ray. I sat at a table in the break room and took a deep breath, dialed.

"I don't have to tell you what this absence is doing to your reputation." His tone was unequivocal.

*MY reputation?* I opened my mouth, but a voice in my head interrupted. *Don't talk about the woman.*

I shifted mental gears. "Did you unleash Steffan on me?" My tone wasn't anywhere near polite and I didn't care. "He won't leave me alone, Ray! He's jeopardizing my job!"

"Your behavior is jeopardizing my job, young miss! Or had you forgotten that? So marry the man!"

"Ray, I don't love him! How hard is that for you to understand? Why should I—"

"Because you need protection! I shouldn't have to explain this." A pause, and a sigh. "Look, I understand that you're grieving. You're not in your right mind. But this wild, independent fling of yours is threatening this family, and you need to shut it down. *Now.* I want you back in this apartment by five-thirty tonight. Or I want to hear from Steffan that he's taken you before a prinister. Understand? The two of you have until six to call me." His voice briefly dropped to a mutter. "He won't last longer than that, young as he is. You hear me? SIX. Or I call the Guards."

"But Ray—" I heard the disconnect, which meant Ray had slammed down his phone.

Mine slipped from my fingers and clattered to the table. *Lord, help me! What am I going to do?* Then a sudden anger intruded my thoughts, and my hands clenched. *Where was God when Ray hit Mom? When Ray came home with another woman? When I nearly froze to death in my hotel room because I wouldn't have sex with the manager? When I couldn't stop crying on the sub? What makes me think God would care about me now?* For the second time in as many days, sobs burst through my control, and I put my head down, resting my arms on the table. I didn't even care if someone came in.

A thought surfaced. *Mr. Josephus is a nice man. Maybe I'll talk to him for a few minutes. He might even have some ideas.* Despite a lingering hesitancy, I picked up the phone and fumbled in my pocket for his card.

At that moment, my wrist buzzed.

*Oh, will everyone just leave me alone!* Wiping my eyes with the heel of my hand, I looked at the display.

Bree.

Taking a deep breath, I connected. "Hey."

"Wow." I could hear her surprise at reaching me. "Mer, I hate to bug you at work, but I just had this feeling I should check on you. How are you holding up?"

Her kind concern shattered my wall, and the whole horrible story poured out in gasping whispers, while I tried—without success—to stop crying. ". . . and I'm so afraid Steffan will follow me back to the hotel tonight, and that awful clerk might—"

"A hotel?" Bree's tone was sharp. "Mer, you're not at home?"

"No, I—well, I had to—"

A mild oath. "Why didn't you tell me?"

I opened my mouth, groped for words. "Well, you . . . you have enough on your plate, with your engagement, and work, and—"

"And you think I'm so self-absorbed I wouldn't care that my best friend is homeless?" Now she was angry.

"No, I—Bree, what am I going do? I can't marry Steffan. But how can I possibly live with Ray? Now that he's—I'll have to walk by that room every single time I—that room where Mom—I can't—" Tears crowded into my throat, impeding words.

A long moment of silence; her sigh was audible.

"It's all right. Where are you supposed to meet Steffan?"

I rubbed my nose on my sleeve, grimaced. "The back employee exit. Unless security lets him in the front, but they're not supposed to because he was escorted out. All the other doors are alarmed."

"Okay. Go out the front," she ordered. "Avoid the main walkways; use the sale racks for cover, just in case. I'll be waiting with an MT, okay? We'll disappear into the mall until he gives up."

Wearing an MT, I'd blend in with the crowd. I smiled at Bree's cleverness, tried to squelch a surge of hope. "Okay. Okay."

"And don't worry." Her tone was bracing. "We'll figure out where you can stay. I have an idea."

~

"I'm clocking out, Mary-Sarah."

The woman looked up from where she was putting away a new shipment of toddler clothes. "Sure, Meryn." Her face turned sympathetic, and she set down a stack of tiny shirts. "Dear, I was . . . overly hard on you today. Your young man is a little enthusiastic, I think."

"You could say that." I kept my face professional. "Thank you for your help."

She smiled, flapped a blue-ringed hand in my direction. "Go. Have fun with him."

I tried not to run to the time clock. Gritting my teeth, I waved my arm in front of the dial, waiting for the beep, then darted into a changing room and regarded myself in the mirror. Short of buying a whole new outfit, I could do nothing about my work uniform, and I didn't have the money or the time. I held up my purple coat, frowned. *Steff would recognize this from across Miners Stadium.* Then I caught sight of the dark blue liner. *Perfect.* I turned the coat inside out and donned it, then twisted my hair up into a bun.

My reflection in the mirror still looked like me. I sighed. Well, at least the neon orange blouse was covered. *Jesus, help me! Keep me hidden!*

Shouldering my tote and trying to ignore a fluttering in my stomach, I stole into the store. Steff was nowhere in sight. I hurried to the outer wall, where tall sale racks of dresses would shelter me from the main walkway. My heart pounded, and I tried to act normally. *What if Steff is in the store? Worse—what if he's waiting out front?* I likely wouldn't see him before he saw me.

A quiet voice came. *Don't worry about what you can't change. I am with you.*

The front doors were within sight, and my heart rate quickened as I moved along the last sale rack in the row. *Almost there—*

The doors opened and Steffan strode into the store. He wore a cap and his head was down, his eyes on his phone, but the arrogant swagger was unmistakable. Suppressing a shriek, I ducked into a dress rack as footsteps echoed along the walkway, just feet away. *Steffan? Someone else?* Several sets of footsteps. My nose brushed a long maroon dress, and I tried not to breathe. Gently I parted the garments, tried to peer— a hanger screeched. I froze.

*Go. Now.*

I didn't question; I moved into the walkway, resisting the urge to run for the doors. Several women were leaving the store, talking and laughing in their blue MTs, and I tried to blend in with them, keeping my steps measured. I didn't dare look back. Adrenaline pounded my veins. *Don't see me. I'm not here.* No one yelled, no one grabbed me as I pushed the door open and moved into the vestibule. Took two steps, then four.

"Merynnnn!" The ominous shout echoed through the store. Someone laughed.

Without permission, my feet took off, hurling my body through the outer doors. Frantic, I scanned the parking area as Bree burst from where she was hiding behind a bush just yards away.

"He knows!" I gasped. "He's coming!"

"Here!" She threw a light blue MT over my head, pulling me along the sidewalk as I fought to get my arms into the sleeves. The new garment reeked of plastic and starch. As soon as my head cleared the top opening, she jammed a wool hat on my head. She was clad in a dark blue MT, and with her blonde hair tucked under a wide-brimmed navy hat, she looked totally unlike herself.

I shook out the garment around my legs and broke into a run, and she yanked me back—no small feat, since Bree is about a foot shorter than me.

"No! He'll make you!" she hissed. "You're a matron, I'm your blind mother. Guide me!" She whipped my arm around her back and bent over as we both dropped into a shuffle. Aside from another pair of women who strolled toward the mall some distance ahead, we had the sidewalk to ourselves. *Is it enough? Are we too obvious?*

A sudden commotion behind us—a spate of screams.

"*Merynnn!*" The voice echoed; he was in the vestibule. Then the echo stopped, and I knew he was outside. He couldn't have been more than thirty or forty feet away. My back burned.

His voice was a raw howl, livid and menacing. "Where are you, gutter slut? I'll find you. You can't hide from me!"

The starch tickled my nose; I coughed, trying to keep it soft. *God, help us—don't let him see us!*

"It's okay," Bree whispered. "It's okay. You're doing fine." She patted my back, but I felt her body tremble under my arm.

Taking a deep breath, I matched tiny steps to hers.

"Don't think you can do this to me! I'll make your life hell! Do you hear me, bitch? I'll call your father—*your prinister! I'll ruin you, Jezebel! Whore! Meryn Flint is a whore!*"

This time, my gasp ended with a whimper.

A man in the parking lot yelled something unintelligible, and several people laughed.

Step by shuffling step, with an agonizing slowness Bree and I made our way up the sidewalk to the Silvermine Mall. My ears strained for the slightest sound behind us, but I heard nothing. The distance to the huge building had never seemed so great. At one point a man hurried past us from behind, and I nearly jumped out of my skin, but it wasn't Steffan. By the time the imposing, two-story doors parted to admit us, I was shaking so violently I needed Bree's arm to keep me upright.

We stopped just inside, and Bree let out a huge sigh. "Good job, Meryn. Perfect!"

She hugged me, and I tried to smile. The second set of doors opened, and Bree strode through, but I couldn't move.

"Bree—I can't—"

She turned, her face drawn with concern. "We can't stop, Mer. He might come this way. The sub station—"

"I know. My legs—I can't stop trembling." I didn't tell her I'd skipped lunch, nauseated from the stress.

Wrapping an arm around me, she supported me through the throngs of people until we found an empty bench, where I collapsed with a sigh. Through the noise of shoppers, the mall's PA was playing "Jesus, Show Me My Black'ning Sin." A young man down the walkway was singing along, loudly, his friends laughing and casting furtive glances about, looking for the mall Guards. Women brushed past us in their multihued MTs, carrying totes and babies. A child's piercing wail cut through the music as Bree settled next to me, digging through her tote. She pulled something out and handed it to me: a tiny wrapped candy.

"I need more than candy, my blood sugar's—"

"Put it under your tongue," she ordered, her eyes darting across the crowd, back in the direction we'd come. "It's a Coffee Drop."

Concentrated caffeine, sugar, and chemical stimulant, Coffee Drops were popular with the higher castes. I didn't ask how she could afford it; meekly I unwrapped the candy and popped it into my mouth.

"Expensive, I know, but this is an emergency," she said, as I felt the drop dissolve. A moment later the shaking stopped, and new energy raced along my limbs, clearing my head and draining away fatigue. "Better?"

"Holy wasabi," I whispered, and she laughed, rising, and pulled me to my feet.

"It'll support you for another hour or so. Let's go!"

Now I had no trouble keeping up as Bree darted through the throngs of people, making for the exit that led to the sub station. Every few minutes I looked back, but there was no sign of pursuit.

It wasn't until the sub doors closed behind us that I let myself relax. As the car jerked into motion, heading in the opposite direction of my normal commute, Bree grabbed a bar next to me. She pulled off her hat, her hair cascading to her waist, and fanned herself with its brim. "Whew. That was too close."

"What will I do now?" It came out a wail. Biting my lip, I looked around, but the car was loud with clacking from the rails and people talking. My voice dropped so only she could hear. "I can't go back to the hotel; I'm out of money."

"And you can't go home?" My friend's face was sober. A man across the car regarded her, his expression admiring, but she ignored him. Skin downy as a baby's, eyes as green as Mom's, Bree also had gorgeous blonde curls that turned men's heads, no matter what their age. I felt sure she must be GM, but she was tiny. She barely came up to my shoulder. Bree's parents were deceased, and she lived with her gamma, but I had never pressed her for details.

I shook my head. "I know it's a violation of Family Duty, but how could I go back? After what happened? How can I ever trust Ray? And to walk past Mom's room every single day—" I broke off, tears incipient.

Bree stared at the floor for a long moment, then met my eyes. "For tonight, you're coming home with me," Bree said in a tone that brooked no argument. "I called Gamma, and she said you could."

In spite of my desire not to be a burden, relief nearly made me weep. "Bree, I—are you sure? You told me your Gamma's place is tiny. I would be imposing. I shouldn't. I—"

"Well, it's your choice," Bree said. "But Meryn, I don't want you on the street."

"Neither do I." My laugh was mirthless. "But maybe there's another option. I—I met this man," I said, tentative. Bree's eyes widened, but I rushed on. "And he was really nice. A gentleman—Management Caste. He offered to put me up for a few days until I can get back on my feet, and help—"

"And you believed him?" She looked at me like I'd lost my mind. "Meryn, that's just how men find women like us to pimp out."

"No, it wasn't like that! He was genuinely concerned for me. He said I reminded him of his daughter, and—"

She rolled her eyes. "Well, I guess desperation can turn the brightest girl dim." I must have glowered, because she gave a tiny smile. "You didn't give him your number, did you?"

"Of course not!" I felt stupid, naïve.

"So you need a place to stay." Bree squeezed my arm in tacit apology. "Yes, you're right: we live in a tiny house, and there's not much room. But there are . . . options . . . in our neighborhood." Her tone turned prosaic. "Look, come just for tonight. Get some sleep, get a hot meal or two, and tomorrow you can check it out. If it isn't for you"—she shrugged—"we'll come up with something else."

I caved, and a huge weight slid off my shoulders. "Thanks, Bree. I do need time to think." I couldn't think at the hotel. I'd spent my time there sleeping or watching the screen, trying to forget what had happened to Mom, trying to forget I was running out of money—

"Of course you do." She gave a sharp nod. "You shouldn't be wasting what little income you have on a hotel." Her voice dropped. "Mer. Do you think Ray will turn you in?"

I bit my lip, and we traded sober glances. Even though I'd graduated high school with my diploma LT (Limited Training) at sixteen, I was still legally under his protection until I married; if he reported me as a runaway, the Guards wouldn't have to look any farther than my workplace.

"I don't know." I pushed back a lock of hair, anxious. "I asked him not to. But he told me I had to either come home tonight or marry Steffan. I'm supposed to call him by six. I don't know what he'll do when I don't. We'll just have to hope for the best."

Bree opened her mouth to reply, but a Guard entered from the adjoining car, and we turned our eyes to the floor and said nothing more.

# 7. HOPE

The bus groaned and pulled away from the stop, chuffing noxious fumes into our faces. Coughing, I blotted my streaming eyes.

We stood in a cold pool of light in one of Silvermine's oldest neighborhoods. The sun was long gone. Feeble, spitting streetlights revealed potholed streets and slouching gray houses, tired and crumbling. I bit my lip, hoping my friend wouldn't sense my uncertainty.

"This way," Bree whispered.

As we headed down the sidewalk, she withdrew something from her pocket: a tiny can of SecureSpray. A combination of assault-stop chemical and UV dye, the stuff was nasty . . . and effective. Or so I'd heard.

She grinned at my reaction. "Doesn't hurt to be prepared."

"Isn't that illegal?" My voice squeaked, and I cleared my throat. I wondered how she'd gotten it.

She nodded. "What's the scumbag gonna do? Call the Guards?"

*Good point,* I thought.

But I was more than a little surprised about this new facet to my friend—someone willing to break the law to defend herself. She gestured left, and we turned, crossing the street. A man walked, hands in his pockets, far ahead of us; I hoped he wasn't coming in our direction.

Bree gave a low warning, indicating a large break in the sidewalk just in time. I stepped across and stumbled a bit from fatigue. The effects of the Coffee Drop were dissipating.

"Almost there." She gave me an encouraging smile.

To our right, a well-lit area beckoned: a community of tiny houses. Bree guided me down the long driveway, past house after house, each perched on wheels, porch lights illuminating our way. I saw only a couple vehicles—old and battered, with internal combustion engines. Where the driveway curved away to the left, Bree stopped.

"Here we are," she said, turning to a house on the right. Quivering with fatigue, I followed Bree up the four steps (the third one creaked under my weight), through a screen door, and across the porch. The front door opened from inside, and light flooded out.

"Come in! Come in!" A woman's voice. We stepped into the tiny house, and I blinked in the sudden warmth. I'd heard of tiny houses on wheels but had never been inside one. It *was* tiny—and utterly adorable.

We stood on a multihued, handwoven rug in the living room. A worn, comfortable-looking futon draped with an inviting, crocheted red throw sat along the wall opposite the door. To the left was a small but functional kitchen with warm wood cabinets and a fold-out dining table. To the right of the door, a gentle fire crackled in a miniature woodstove. The whole interior was finished with wood—which astonished me because wood was rare and priced out of reach for all but the highest castes. Above the kitchen, a white curtain with cheerful red trim screened a loft from view; to my right was a short hallway. I glimpsed a bathroom and what looked like a bedroom before Bree turned to me.

"Meryn, meet my gamma, Magdalena McCafferty."

"Please call me Mags," the woman said in a pleasant alto, crossing her hands over her collarbones. Mags was as tiny as Bree, with curly silver hair that brushed her shoulders. Green eyes crinkled with her smile. She was open and kind and welcoming, and I trusted her at once.

I folded my hands over my chest and bowed lower than necessary to convey my respect. "It is a great honor to make your acquaintance, Mags."

"You grace us with your pleasant company. Be welcome in our home," she said, appropriately formal, and drew me into the kitchen, Bree following. "I just put on a pot for tea. Would you like a warming cup before you turn in, Meryn? Something to chase the chill?"

"Tea sounds delightful, but I'm afraid it might keep me awake." I'd been sparing with my allergy medicine; the stuff was pricey.

"I'm thinking something herbal," she said, pulling one, then two metal canisters out of a cupboard.

"Do you have a soporific?" I asked. "I—I'm not remotely sleepy." It was true: fatigue dragged at my bones, but my mind was a live wire, recording every moment with video clarity. I wondered if it was a side effect of the Coffee Drop.

She gave me a candid look that reminded me of Bree. "I do. If you're interested, I have an herbal tincture that will help relax you."

"It's good stuff," Bree put in, and smiled reassurance.

"Please, have a seat." Mags gestured toward the table. "You both look exhausted."

We complied. Mags's spotless kitchen was just like her—practical but cheerful, with herbs growing in tiny orange window pots, red towels splashing color and friendly, handmade pottery mugs depending from small hooks under a cupboard. The difference from the hotel room was profound and comforting.

She unhooked three mugs, placing one at each setting, and set a little jar, pitcher and dropper bottle in the center of the table. Bree took the lid off the jar and spooned precious sugar into her mug.

"Milk or sugar, Meryn?" Mags asked, with a sideways look at Bree.

"No, thank you," I said, just as Bree said, "She doesn't take sugar, Gamma." We smiled at each other.

The kettle started to shriek. As Mags crossed to shut off the burner, Bree tapped the tiny bottle. "Gamma makes these herbal tinctures herself. They have medicinal properties and they're very effective."

"I had to do something when Will died because I no longer had his insurance." Mags poured hot water into my mug, then Bree's.

My eyebrows crawled into my hairline. "You live here by yourself?"

"Well, not exactly by myself." She laughed. "We're full up.

"Anyway, I started researching herbs and flowers and their properties. This"—she topped off her mug and nodded at the dropper bottle—"is a mix of extracts with both physical and mental effects. It relaxes the muscles but also soothes the mind."

"Will it make me forget these last three days?" I blurted before I thought.

Mags set the teapot on a trivet. To my surprise, her eyes filled with tears of compassion, and I fixed my gaze on my mug, my embarrassment for her mixing with gratitude. "No, child. No herb or tincture can ease that pain. But someday the memory of this horrible time will be eased by the recollection of a thousand joyful yesterdays."

The silence lingered, until I managed a raspy, "I hope so."

"Time is a healer," Mags said, dunking tea balls in each mug and settling next to Bree, "although sometimes it seems as if a million years could never be distance enough to heal the pain."

"Hear, hear." Bree's voice was bitter. My eyes widened; I'd never seen her express emotion about the loss of her parents. Mags reached over and grasped her hand, and Bree forced a smile.

"I'd like to try your elixir, if I may," I said. "And thank you, Mags."

"It's my pleasure." Mags unscrewed the dropper and held it over my mug. "Let's start with a small dose—this stuff is pretty potent." She measured five drops into the mug and handed me a spoon.

Bree cradled her tea, warming her hands. As soon as I set down the spoon, she lifted her mug in a toast. "Here's to us. We did it, Mer!"

I raised my mug to hers, Mags joining in, somehow in full understanding, and the three of us clinked our mugs and laughed. Mine came out a trifle high and hysterical, but it felt good and broke the tension.

"Oh, Steffan." Smiling, Bree shook her head and blew on her tea. "Why do guys think being obnoxious and possessive is the way to win a girl's heart?"

"I don't think Steff is interested in my heart." I took a breath, trying to mitigate my bitter tone.

"Well, you have a point." She sipped, winced against the heat. "Mostly they just seem to want our bodies. Except for Kilte, of course." Her voice was proud. "He's a gem."

Mags smiled at her granddaughter.

Gingerly, I tested my tea. It was cool enough, and I drank, grateful. "I don't know how to thank you." I turned to Mags. "Both of you."

"No need." Mags reached across the small table and squeezed my hand, her face kind. "I hope you will forgive the breach of privacy, but Bree took the liberty of filling me in on your situation. Meryn, I know the conundrum you're facing with Family Duty, but given what happened, it doesn't seem safe for you to return to your stepfather."

I shook my head and a flush crept up my neck, my eyes going to the table. "I can't. He . . . I . . ."

The memory stopped my words: me, just thirteen, coming back to my room after a shower and finding Ray sitting on my bed. His offer to "make me feel more comfortable on my wedding night." Me, pulling away in a panic, twisting out of my robe as he grabbed me, running away nude, terrified and furious that I was giving Ray exactly what he wanted—a glimpse of my naked body. I ran to the bathroom, barely getting the door locked in time, sobbing while he stood outside, demanding I come out. I didn't come out until Mom returned home. I never told her what happened, but after that I felt torn, as if I had betrayed her somehow.

Now, fighting tears, I wondered if she had known. If she'd noticed that Ray and I stopped touching, stopped hugging. *Was that why she saved her mad money?*

Bree and Mags exchanged an unreadable look, and Mags spoke. "We will help you find a solution. You are welcome to stay here tonight, Meryn. Tomorrow we'll show you around. But then I think it would be best for you to go home."

"Gamma—" Bree began. The older woman silenced her with a look.

Disappointment soured the tea in my mouth, and something in my gut sank through the floorboards. "But I thought—" My thoughts flew to Ray, what he had done, what he might do. "I can't—"

Bree took a deep breath, choosing her words carefully. "It may seem safe here. But for someone in your situation, that's not entirely true."

What she said didn't penetrate my hurt and anger. "I will leave now," I said shortly, and rose.

Bree's eyes hardened. "Sit down."

I crossed my arms. "It's obvious you don't want me here."

"That isn't the case at all." Her mouth flattened in exasperation. "Stop being an infant—"

"Leaving now wouldn't be wise," Mags interrupted gently, as if she knew my feelings. "Please trust us, Meryn. We have a way to help you, but it will take time."

I sank into my seat. "Time is what I don't have." I grasped at straws. "If you could just give me a loan—just for a few days, I—"

Bree let out a cynical laugh. "A loan? Look around you, Mer! Do you think we have money to spare for a hotel?"

"And you may wish to consider finding a new position." Mags picked up her mug, her eyes thoughtful. "It doesn't sound like On the Mark is safe for you anymore."

My mouth dropped open as the truth of that observation sank in. "So I'm screwed." Tears forced past my resolve, and I buried my face in my hands, not even relieved that neither Mags nor Bree seemed offended at my profanity.

Warm hands patted my hair, my back. "Oh Meryn," Mags said softly. "How I wish it could be different." Bree slid in next to me, wrapped me in her arms and murmured comforting words as I sobbed. But all I heard were my thoughts. *Mom is gone, Ray is a monster, and I am alone with nowhere to go . . .*

Some long time later, I straightened up, weak and spent. "I'm so sorry." My face flushed. "I don't know why—"

"Tears help us cope with stress and fear, and you've had too much of both lately," Mags said. Her face, and Bree's, reflected only kind concern. "Please, no apologies. Emotion is never condemned in this house."

*Mom used to say the same thing.* I wiped my eyes, tried to smile.

"You're not screwed, although right now it may seem that way," Mags said, and I blinked resentment. *Easy for you to say.*

"Look, I don't blame you for not wanting to go home," Bree said. "But you do have the ability to defend yourself."

I winced. I'd told her about my self-defense training, but the reminder didn't help. What if I had to defend myself against Ray, but ended up taking it a little too far? Self-defense wouldn't work as a legal excuse—I'd likely be jailed, at the very least—but worse, I would have to live with knowing I'd injured or killed my stepfather.

Tears threatened again, and I suppressed the thought, taking a long drink of my tea. My knotted muscles relaxed as the elixir took hold.

Bree opened her mouth to say something just as the front door opened, and a gust of cold air hit my back. Two young men entered, making the tiny house seem even tinier.

"Ah!" Mags rose. "Perfect timing. Boys, come and meet Meryn. She's a friend of Bree's."

I got to my feet, swallowing the last of my tea. The young man closest to me was my height, clean shaven, with sharp eyes and sandy blond hair covered by a battered Silvermine Miners baseball cap. He carried an armload of kindling that he dropped noisily into the wood box. "Hi, gorgeous," he said, his voice a laughing tenor. "I'm Kilte. Meryn." His nose wrinkled. "That's an odd one. Not biblical. Not Mary or Deborah or Sarah, huh?" He snorted a chuckle. "Does your mother not like you?"

It hit like a punch in the stomach, and my eyes dropped to the floor. I heard Bree's intake of breath.

"Kilte—" Mags began.

But I looked up boldly, rudely, my narrowed eyes meeting his, my unhealed pain stripping away courtesy, the whiplash of his insult stinging me to response. Mom used to tell me when I got mad, my gray eyes looked like storm clouds. I hoped they did now. "Maybe she called yours and asked for advice."

His face froze over. Bree and Mags stood motionless, and I tried not to gasp. *Meryn, you idiot, you just put yourself out on the street.*

The big man broke the silence, smothering a laugh as he hit his friend on the arm. "She got you there."

Kilte gave the man a frosty glare; a moment later he forced a chuckle and shook his head. "Fair enough."

*"A lady never looks at a man directly." Maybe I can salvage this.* I smiled and put my hands together in front of my chest, gave the standard bow of greeting, my eyes on the floor. "Mr. Harris, it is a great pleasure to finally meet you. Bree mentions you often."

A silence; then he spoke. "Well, I should hope so," he said, and laughed. I risked a glance at him, and his eyes were no longer wary. "Since I'm going to be her husband!"

Bree relaxed. "I think Meryn's tired of me talking about you."

"Never." My smile at her was equal parts affection and relief, and I turned to her fiancé. "When you proposed, she floated for weeks. I should've known you from her photos." I couldn't hide my chagrin.

"It's the cap," he said, pulling it off and tousling his hair to life. "I could rob a bank wearing this thing and nobody'd ever recognize me."

I joined Bree's laughter.

"Meryn," Mags said, "the tall fellow is Walker."

Mags's omission of full names startled me, until I realized it was deliberate—likely I wasn't the first runaway she'd offered tea. I bowed, and unlike Kilte, he pressed his palms and bowed formally in return. Walker *was* tall, at least a head above me, with a brown mustache and beard. His dark brown hair was woven into a double handful of narrow braids compressed under a digger's hat. Both men smelled faintly of oily fuel, wood, and sweat.

"Walker and Kilte have a landscaping business," Mags said, a touch of pride in her voice.

"How do you pay the taxes?" It was out before I thought.

Kilte grinned, touched his nose. "Let's just say the RD thinks we're a couple of miscreants for not making more than we do."

"Oh," I said. *They're not reporting their whole income? But that's—*

Mags's smile was understanding. "Would you boys like tea?"

"Tea?" Kilte coughed, still with that grin. "No, thanks. Now if you have a jot of something stronger . . ."

Walker shook his head. "We had to finish clearing that tree lot for the Fletchers," the tall man said in a gruff, light baritone, setting a metal lunchbox on the table. "That's why we're so late. Lunch was terrific, Mom—thank you."

"You cut *wood?*" I couldn't keep the shock out of my tone. *Shut up, Meryn!*

Walker nodded, grimacing as if sharing my sentiment. Then he shrugged. "Rich people don't worry about that law."

"Made us a tidy profit." Kilte winked. "And we get to keep the fuel, long as we keep it under wraps." I bit my lip, then thought of my own recent moral missteps and looked away.

"Hate to hi/bye," he went on, "but now that I've dropped off your firing for the night, my home—and my bed—are calling. Goodnight, sweet princess," he called over my shoulder to Bree. She blew him a kiss.

I was in the way. "Mags," I said, turning, "maybe I . . . oh . . ." To my surprise, the room tilted. I flailed, recovered.

Mags gasped. "I miscalculated! Kilte—"

I opened my mouth to speak, but the room wobbled again, and my knees buckled. Strong arms caught me as I spiraled down into a sleep that could not be evaded.

~

My wrist buzzed. Warmth wrapped me, but even in my sleep I knew I wasn't home. My eyes blinked open to darkness. *What? Where—not the hotel?* I sat up, and memory rushed back.

I was lying on the futon in Mags's living room, covered with a comforter. *Oh, thank You, God!* My wrist buzzed again. Someone had put my tote next to the futon, and I dove for my phone without checking the display, answering before the override turned on the ringer. "Hello?" I whispered.

"Tell me you're married." Ray, his words slurred.

*Crap. Ray, stop calling me in the middle of the night!*

"I'll call you in the morning, okay? I'm asleep."

"You're not asleep if you're talking to me. Put Steffan on the phone."

I prayed for patience. "He's not here."

Ray's volume increased. "Then you get your fanny home, *now!*"

"Ray, I'm fine. I'll talk to you in the morning. Shutting off my phone now. Goodnight."

"Darn it Meryn! You—"

I disconnected. Sighing, I powered down the phone, tucked it in my bag and rolled over on the futon, trying to get comfortable. It didn't work. My anger at Ray was firing from several directions: for what he did to Mom, for taking up with another woman just moments after they carried Mom out of the apartment, for blocking my return home, and for waking me up when I was sleeping peacefully, the dreamless sleep I'd been craving for three days.

"Lord," I whispered. "Please help me sleep. Please?" I started to ask God if He would help me forgive Ray, but I couldn't bring myself to do it. Forgiving Ray meant letting him off the hook for what he'd done to my mother, and I would never do that. *Never.*

# 8. WAKIПG

*Clink. Click.*

A whisper. "Shh. You'll wake her up."

Another whisper. "No, I won't. YOU will."

"Be quiet."

"YOU be quiet!"

I could smell breakfast cooking. Something very appetizing . . . something salty . . . couldn't be . . . *bacon?*

That stiffened my spine, and I sat straight up in bed. Sunlight flooded into the tiny house, dancing through the cheery curtains behind me and warming my bed. "Bacon?" I said to the air, astonishment coloring my tone.

Mags laughed. "I knew that would get her up, Bree!"

I tossed back the comforter and twisted toward the kitchen, where Mags and Bree worked in elaborate choreography, as if reading each other's minds. Mags gave me a smile, and Bree chuckled at my wide-eyed expression. Two girls—perhaps about ten years old, with ebony braids and liquid eyes—stared at me from their seats at the table. Mags set glasses of an orange drink in front of them, patting one girl's shoulder to get her attention. It worked; the girl looked up at her with a rueful smile.

I got to my feet, realizing I'd slept in my clothing, which was now a rumpled mess.

"Good morning, Meryn!" Bree called, as she carried three steaming mugs to the table.

"Good morning!" I jumped forward. "Can I help?"

"Sure." Bree set down two mugs and handed the third to me. "You can drink this."

I cocked an eyebrow at her.

"It's just tea." Mags came up behind Bree. "I promise." As I sipped, cautiously because of the heat, she continued, "I'm so sorry about last night, Meryn. I rarely miscalculate a dosage." Her face was furrowed with concern, her eyes frank.

"It wasn't your fault, Gamma," Bree said, penitent, setting the mug on the table. "I didn't tell you I gave Meryn a Coffee Drop to get her through the mall. She was fading."

"And I should've warned you." I squeezed her arm with my free hand. "I'm sometimes sensitive to medications. I just didn't think of it."

"Of course not, tired as you were." Mags smiled. "Hungry?" She returned to the stove.

"For bacon?" I said. "Always!" Everyone laughed.

"I thought we should celebrate your liberation from Steffan." Using tongs, she lifted cooked bacon slices from the pan. "After breakfast we'll go over your options." Deftly she transferred the bacon to a rack at the back of the stove; a dish set beneath the rack collected the drippings.

I approved. No one sensible wasted precious bacon fat. I took a moment to duck down the hall to the bathroom, where I washed my face, the girl in the mirror looking puzzled at me. *They're so friendly this morning. Did I mistake last night? They're sending me away? No . . . wait. I have to go home, Mags said, but she also said something about options, and it would take time.*

Sighing, I tried to smooth wrinkles out of my clothes and hoped Mags would offer a viable option to my living at home. I returned to the table as Bree set a plate of bacon and fried potatoes in front of one of the girls.

"Meryn," Bree said, "I'd like you to meet my aunts."

"What?" My eyebrows climbed. The girls giggled and Mags laughed.

"It's true." Grinning, Bree put a hand on one girl's head. "This is Aunt Elijah. Ellie, this is my friend Meryn."

"Pleased to meet you," Ellie said politely. She picked up a slice of bacon and took a big bite, chewing while she took in my rumpled appearance.

"And this"—Bree gestured to the other girl—"is Aunt Elisha."

"Call me Lisha," she said, and I blinked, finally realizing the girls were twins. "I am sorry to be so rude as to eat in front of you, Miss

Meryn," she said in a very mature fashion and with a glare for her sister, "but we have a bus to catch."

*A bus?* A horrific memory nearly shattered my new composure. "It's a pleasure to meet you both."

"Sit," Bree said, pushing me onto a folding stool next to Lisha. Bemused, I sipped my tea. It was clear that one tea bag had been used to make all three mugs, but I didn't mind—Mom used to do the same thing.

"How can you be Bree's aunts?" I asked the girls. "Do you have some magic skin cream that keeps you looking so young?"

The girls giggled again. "Yes, and I invented it," Ellie said archly. Lisha stuck out her tongue at her sibling.

"Where *are* the boys?" Mags murmured, peering out the window.

"We're Mags's daughters." Lisha stabbed potatoes with her fork. "She adopted us from the orphanage because it was horrible there."

"It was," Ellie said, serious now. "Mom saved our lives."

I'd heard the stories. RD orphanages were dirty, the house parents overwhelmed and understaffed. Kids suffered rampant illness, abuse, and untreated injuries, and orphan girls often became pregnant. The girls were jailed, their babies taken from them and put into the very same orphanage, and the horrific cycle continued, ignored by the RD. I eyed Mags with renewed respect.

"We're not supposed to talk about the orphanage with strangers," Lisha said, picking up her plate, "but you're here so you're not a stranger so it's okay."

I smiled at young logic as Ellie licked bacon grease from her plate.

Mags smiled and reached over to take Lisha's plate. "Thank you, sweetie," she said. "Ellie, stop that. It isn't polite."

Ellie sat up and handed Mags her plate with a disarming grin. "Sorry, Mom. It's just so yummy!"

At the sound of a truck engine, Lisha's eyes swiveled to the window. "They're here!" she hollered. "Ellie! Bus!" She ran into the back bedroom as Ellie scrambled up from her seat.

The door opened, letting in a blast of chilly air, and Kilte and Walker entered, shaking the cold from their clothes.

"Boys!" Mags called. "I have your lunch."

"Good morning, princess," Kilte said, kissing Bree.

"Morning, Meryn," Walker said. "You feel better today?"

"Just fine, thank you."

"What? Bacon?" Kilte eyed me. "Wow, you rate."

"We had bacon for you, if you recall," Mags said, handing him the metal lunchbox.

*Bacon . . . they do this every time they have an overnight guest? Surely not.* I didn't let my puzzlement show on my face.

The girls came pounding out of the bedroom, jackets on, shrugging into backpacks.

"Now, you share that lunch with Walker," Mags admonished Kilte.

"What? This isn't all for me? I'm a growing boy. This fella's already grown." Kilte poked the tall man in the ribs. Walker chuckled.

Mags shook her head. "There's plenty for both. Go on with you, now."

"Bye, Mom! Bye, Bree! Bye, Meryn!" The girls darted out the front door and clambered into the truck bed, settling on their backpacks.

"Girls!" Walker yelled. "Don't get that motor oil on your clothes!" He tipped his hat to me and headed out the door.

"The bus?" I asked Bree.

"That's what they call it." She grinned. "And I have to go catch mine."

Mags looked at the wall clock in surprise. "You're opening?"

She moved toward the bathroom. "Britt called in sick and Carole's beside herself," she said over her shoulder.

Mags spooned Bree's breakfast into a container, wrapped it tightly with plastic and tucked it into her tote.

"Hey," I said to Kilte, "thanks for the catch last night."

"Kilte! Let's roll!" Walker hollered from outside. "Gotta get these babies to school!" He climbed behind the wheel.

"We're not babies!" Ellie yelled back, her voice tiny and young in the cold, thin air.

Kilte bowed to me with mock gallantry. "Much as I'd like to, I can't take credit for another man's labors. That was Walker's hero moment, not mine." I blinked in surprise, and he grinned and strode out the door, slamming it behind him.

As the truck pulled away, Bree came out of the back bedroom carrying her jacket. She grabbed her tote and smiled. "Mer, I'll think about where you might apply for a new position. Don't worry; we'll find you something. See you this afternoon."

Gratitude warmed me, driving away fear.

"Don't eat that on the bus," Mags cautioned her.

"Too right—I'll get mobbed!" She laughed and was gone, hurrying down the pebble driveway.

"Hoo! Now the chaos is over, come and eat, Meryn," Mags said, shutting the door. She fed a piece of Kilte's kindling to the tiny wood-stove as I settled at the table.

"Is every morning like this?"

"Pretty much." She set plates of steaming food at our places and sat, giving me Bree's impish grin. "Well, except for the bacon. The boys leave around four thirty or five to plow folks out or do whatever odd job they have in this cold, and they come back to grab breakfast and pick up the girls before going to their next gig. Do you mind if I say grace?"

"Please do," I said, and we bowed our heads and Mags thanked God for His provision and for my presence at the table.

The moment she said, "Amen," I dug in. *Meat!* It was a rare treat for anyone not Governance Caste or above. From the way Mags devoured her bacon and potatoes, it was a treat for her, too. We ate in silence for several minutes, and then I rolled my eyes, took a breath, and said through another bite, "Mags, this is heavenly. Thank you."

She chuckled. "You're quite welcome."

I swallowed my mouthful. "You called Kilte and Walker your boys?"

She smiled. "Walker is my son, and Kilte will be soon."

"How did he and Bree meet?" I asked, spearing more potatoes on my fork. "She's never said."

Mags took a sip of her cooling tea, her elbows propped on the table. "Kilte was a street kid. Walker brought him home one day. They were both eight at the time. The boy was sleeping on a bench over on Sweet Street. So"—she shrugged—"we made room. Couldn't very well leave the waif on the street. Especially not *that* street."

"Where is Sweet?" I knew Silvermine, but that name eluded me.

"It's a half mile west of here." Mags gestured in the opposite direction from where Bree and I had gotten off the bus.

"Oh! It's near Main?" Main was one of the oldest streets in the city.

"It is Main. But the locals call it Sweet because it's run by the Sweet brothers." She gave me a piercing look. "Don't go there at night, Meryn."

I nodded soberly, appreciating the warning, realizing how little I knew about this area of town.

She set down her mug and took a bite of bacony potatoes. "Kilte and Walker have been friends for a long time. Kilte endured a lot before he came to us." She chewed and swallowed before continuing. "He hides it with humor."

"But you said Kilte isn't your son yet," I said, and she shook her head.

"Kilte didn't want to be adopted, even though I offered." Her lips thinned, and she rolled her eyes. "More than offered. But he's always had that rebellious streak. And I wasn't going to force the issue. Made it a nightmare trying to take care of the kid because of legal issues, but we managed."

"I can't imagine." I shook my head. "And the girls, too?"

Mags laughed. "The girls are a walk in the park compared to the boys! Ellie is the cutup and Lisha is a pleaser. They're both doing so well," she said with obvious pride. "Top of their class."

As I scraped together my last bit of breakfast, her eyes dropped to my plate, her brow wrinkling. "Did you have enough to eat?"

"Oh, a gracious plenty, Mags," I said hastily. "Thank you." I smiled. "I'm like Ellie—I don't want to leave even the flavor on the plate!"

She smiled, her eyes crinkling. "Let it never be said anyone starved at my table."

We sipped our tea in the friendly, sun-warmed kitchen, the late autumn birds chirping outside, and I felt myself relax just a little.

"Bree said you graduated two years ago," Mags said.

"I did. And then I went to work."

Mags caught my tiny frown. "You were unhappy with that choice?" she asked, her eyes gentle.

"Not the job." I shrugged. "I just . . . I didn't want to stop."

Comprehension smoothed her face. "You wanted a full four-year diploma," she said, and I nodded. "You couldn't find a sponsor?"

"I had the grades." I stirred my tea for no reason, watching the liquid swirl in the mug, trying to squelch the still painful memory. "I didn't have the right connections, I guess." Finding someone willing to foot the tuition bill for a Worker Caste student like me had turned out to be impossible.

"I am sorry to hear that." Mags's forehead wrinkled. "I hate to see potential wasted. The cost of those last two years is too much for most of us. Were you considering college?"

*Dying to go.* I pressed my lips together. "I don't let myself think about it."

"Of course," Mags said in quick apology. She sighed, too, and took a swallow of tea. "I worry about the girls. Both of them are smart enough to go on to college, but . . ." she trailed off.

*College? Two women? Impossible.* We shared an understanding smile, then I sighed, looking around the warm kitchen, needing to leave, not wanting to leave. "I should go."

"I know this is hard," Mags said. Her eyes on mine were candid. "And I know you don't understand. But not staying here really is the safest thing for you right now."

I stifled resentment, and she went on. "But what we can do is help you find your own place to live."

Startled, I sat up straight. "What?"

Her smile was warm. "I'll show you what I mean, if you're interested."

I smiled back, shoving aside my complex emotions. "I am." I drained my tea, and she rose and set both mugs on the sideboard.

"Let me show you our place, first. We'll fuss with the dishes later. You've seen most of it already," and we both chuckled.

She led me to the hall and paused at the bathroom, small but efficiently laid out. "Since you and Bree are friends, you'll be in and out of here a lot. I'm sure you noticed the toilet's a composter," she said. "We don't formally limit toilet paper use, but we ask all the girls to try to stay under ten squares a day. Washer/dryer—" She touched the appliance. "We schedule the laundry and showers. Calendar's on the back of the door; we'll work you in. We try to limit each shower to eight minutes. It's 10GP per shower."

"That's fair," I agreed. Water was expensive.

She ushered me into the bedroom. "This is the girls' room. Originally it was Bree's, then Walker and Kilte's." I smiled at the tiny space. A twin bed with drawers beneath snugged against the far wall. A narrow shelf attached to the wall served as a bedside table. Someone had installed a bunk above the bed and created a ladder from raw plastic two-by-fours, smudged and darkened from use. Both beds were neatly made with blue-and-white coverlets, and blue-trimmed calico curtains covered the single window. A closet filled the space next to the door. The walls displayed several childish drawings clipped to a horizontal string, a few family photos, and a marvelous pencil drawing of Mags in full laugh.

The real Mags gestured toward the beds. "When Kilte joined us, we added the bunk—Walker's first construction project."

"Where do the guys sleep? On the roof?"

Mags laughed, looking just like her sketch. "We considered that! No, we came up with something better—it's my idea for you, too. I'll show you in a minute."

As we turned back to the hallway, my eye fell on a framed photo collage hanging on the wall between closet and bed. "Mags . . . is this you?" I asked, smiling at a happy couple.

"It is!" She stepped forward, her face wistful, her finger tracing the photo frame. "Will and me on our wedding day. And this is Bree as a baby, with David and Lisbet."

I looked at the beaming parents, proudly holding their infant, and my heart twisted for Bree. I wanted to ask what had happened but didn't dare. Bree had her father's smile and Lisbet's curly blonde hair.

"We lost David in a mass shooting—that bad one on the sub in Stone Lagoon neighborhood a couple decades back," Mags said, touching the glass with gentle fingers. "We moved Lisbet and Bree in here right away, of course. But Lisbet . . ." The older woman sighed, her mobile face settling into sad lines. "Well, she was fragile. She never recovered from David's death. Two years later she developed breast cancer. We took her to a clinic, but there wasn't much they could do—by then she was Stage Four, and of course she had no insurance." Mags shook her head. "She just wouldn't fight. I'd say she died as much from a broken heart as from the cancer."

I was silent for a moment. "She doesn't talk about it," I said, meaning Bree.

"No." Mags studied the infant in the photo. "Not even with me. Of course," she went on briskly, "I don't talk about Will much, either." She gave me a brief, quiet smile. "Grief is a very personal burden. Except it's so darned public."

I nodded, realizing how little I knew. Mom's absence was surreal—a raw, searing wound in my heart, one I couldn't bear to even look at.

"Does it ever heal?" I asked. *Oh, that was rude, Meryn.* Instantly I wished I could take the question back.

Mags didn't seem bothered. "Not completely." She tilted her head. "It's like . . . learning to walk with a limp. A part of you just doesn't . . . work . . . quite like it used to. That's once you get past the screaming." She shook her head and smiled. "Let me show you where the boys sleep." I followed her down the hall. We donned jackets and stepped out into the cold morning.

# 9. SHADY DELL

In the daylight, the porch looked bigger than I remembered from the night before. Screened on three sides, it ran the full length of the tiny house. At the far end, a porch swing with a faded, red floral cushion swayed in the light breeze. A white plastic patio chair perched next to it.

"I've had people sleep out here, but only when the weather's clement," Mags said as we descended the steps into the morning sun. "Can't leave it unlocked at night, or we end up with a host of homeless folks in the morning. Not that I'd mind, but I can't shelter all of Silvermine, and some of the neighbors here get annoyed."

The air was cold but moderate, the bowl overhead a sparkling cerulean. Silverminers lived for days like this—they didn't come often—when the onshore breeze chased away the smog and reminded us what the sky looked like. A playful wind rattled the bare tree branches and sent dead leaves scurrying across the pebble driveway, and Mags pulled up her hood.

In the daylight, I could better appreciate the scope of the community. Fifteen tiny houses on wheels—known as THOWs—lined the U-shaped drive. Parked end to end, each house had a generous front and back yard. Mags's was the fifth house on the driveway's east arm.

"This is Shady Dell," Mags said as we strolled the carefully tended driveway, where round stones framed the edges and delineated the walkways. "It was lovely when it was first built."

Mature trees punctuated the space. Although now they were bare of leaves, I could easily imagine how pretty the place must be in the summer. The tiny homes were painted or sided in a variety of colors and finishes; while some paint had faded, not one of the houses was rickety or in need of obvious repair. The community was loved, and it showed.

"We're doing our best to keep the place up," Mags went on as we paused at the center of the U. "This is the firepit." She gestured toward a circle of large, blackened stones, with a few charred sawdust logs in the center. "We have a fire most every weekend and it's usually an informal Shady Dell town meeting. If you stay, I'll introduce you around. We have a few families and some single guys, but mostly it's women—older chicks like me, or young ones like yourself with no place to go."

*Women live here alone?* The concept was foreign to me. Despite its proximity to Sweet Street, the community was quiet, and I sighed, drinking in the peace. "It's nice here."

"For its age," Mags said, turning back to her house. "Will paid our place off early. He wanted to make sure I would never be out on the street." She pointed to the roof. "I have solar panels up there for power, and a rain catchment system behind."

"You pay the fee?" I asked in surprise. Off-grid homes were legal, but the high taxes and fees pushed them out of reach for most people.

"Our community is grandfathered." Mags's smile was proud. "We fought the Reformation Directorate on that and—God is good—we won."

I shook my head, astonished. "You won against the RD."

She was nodding. "Right? We call it the Shady Dell Miracle. Not everyone here is off-grid, but it's nice to have the option. I'm also attached to city water—I needed a fallback when the droughts hit."

"And this is a place for more houses?" I motioned to the large space in front of the firepit, between the arms of the driveway. Trees filled part of it, but the rest was open, with one section covered by an elevated tarp.

"No, that's our insurance—our garden. In a few months we'll start working on it again. Yes, it's illegal, but so is letting people starve, in our opinion." She looked at me, gauging my reaction.

A nervous shiver straightened my back. A visible garden could bring down the full wrath of the RD. They claimed it was because gardens were water intensive, and because of droughts and rationing, a garden wouldn't survive long.

"Now I understand why Bree never just casually invited me over," I said slowly. Mom and I used to take meals to the shut-ins living in our apartment community, but this was a whole nother level. *They're actually risking arrest to help their neighbors. Maybe that's why—* I shook my head, not sure if I was impressed or afraid.

"We have to be very careful." Mags nodded, silver curls bobbing on her shoulders. "So far the RD has turned a blind eye, I think because feeding people helps keep the peace."

"And the homeless?"

"It's a problem," Mags admitted. "They like to help themselves to our apples and tomatoes. But how do you turn away hungry people?" She sighed, then gestured across the drive. "That one's Emily's place. We call it the Widow House because three of her friends moved in with her when they lost their husbands. The next house south is Marian's. She's a widow and has *four* other women with her. If not for the garden and our help, these women would starve."

Most widows had a difficult time. A man's retirement pension was discontinued when he passed away. His wife's ability to survive totally depended on what she and her husband had saved during his lifetime, as all his assets outside of savings—including the family home, if it was still mortgaged—devolved to the RD. And for mid- and low-caste workers, saving money was a laughable impossibility. The RD claimed it was the family's responsibility to "remember widows and orphans in their distress." But every winter increasing numbers of homeless old women froze to death on the street—the evidence sat outside the sub stations every day, even though the RD never shared the actual statistics.

I shook my head, trying not to show my frustration. "What about their families?" I asked, but in my mind's eye I saw Charity and her friends, their blue hands outstretched, their eyes desperate.

Mags's eyebrows lifted, and she shrugged. "Emily has no children. Her brother says he has his own family to provide for. Marian is on the outs with her son, and her two sisters—they live somewhere in the state of Zion—are barely hanging on. The others I'm not sure about and haven't wanted to pry. I know Marian has a small income from her husband's savings—she's like me that way. But it only stretches so far." In a change of mood, she gestured, her eyes twinkling. "Come see where the boys live."

She led me between two houses at the base of the U. As we rounded the corner, I stopped with a little gasp of surprise. Row upon row of small, corrugated tin sheds marched in an orderly fashion behind the five THOWs.

"Sheds?" I said.

"Houses," Mags said, her face merry. "The residents call it Tin Town."

She led me along the rows. The muddy board sidewalk beneath our feet ran the length of the town, its sections uneven and cracked. I could hear someone shaking out a rug, and dust rose into the air a couple aisles over. A door slammed, its metallic screech harsh in the morning air. I caught the reek of stale beer and "kitty," a synthetic (and illegal) *khat* drug popular with the Indigent Caste, but I made no comment.

"The first hipster houses were thrown together," Mags said. "Some didn't have floors or even rudimentary sanitation. As you can imagine"—she grimaced—"it got pretty bad. People died of various diseases, and we lost two old widows to the cold one winter. The community called an emergency meeting, and most people demanded we take the hipsters out. But some of us stood up and said no, we have the space, let's do this right." She sighed. "We were voted down."

"What?" I stopped walking.

Mags's smile was wry. "Yeah. The community dismantled the houses, moved the people into their THOWs and tried to go back to normal."

I nodded, trying to hide my cynicism. "It didn't work," I said flatly.

"Nope. All this"—she gestured toward the high fences surrounding the hipsters on three sides—"was just sitting here."

I looked up, aware of the space for the first time. "What . . . *is* this?"

"You're standing on an old tennis court." Mags grinned at my surprise. "Grass surface. Back in the day, Shady Dell had quite the amenity package. When we put in the garden out front, we had to crack out most of the concrete decking around the old swimming pool and spa, which we now use to store rainwater for the garden. We're careful to cover them up."

"A swimming pool?" My eyes widened. "You mean—for people? How did they afford the water?"

"That was before the weather changed. And our needs changed." Mags shrugged as we resumed our trek. "So when this space opened up, the vagrants on Sweet Street moved in. It was too irresistible. The community had another meeting and decided to go with our plan. It would require the homeless to build their own hipster if they wanted to stay." Sighing, she squinted at a row of houses. "Besides, the THOWs were overloaded. Fights broke out. It got pretty ugly."

"And you couldn't exactly call the Guards to come and oust the vagrants," I said.

She nodded. "Not with that illegal garden out front. They had us over a barrel, and they knew it." We turned down another board walkway, stopping at the second house, its door decorated with stunning artwork of a hawk in flight. It looked as if the image had been burned into the wood, and I marveled at the skill it must have taken to get every line just right.

Mags smiled. "This is Walker's place. He knows I'm showing it to you." She pressed her thumb to the lock. The display clicked green, and she opened the door, flipping on the light. I hesitated, uncomfortable with seeing a single man's home, but at Mags's encouraging smile, I joined her inside.

The house was truly tiny, maybe a dozen feet along each wall. We stood on a floor of unfinished plastic strips, its center covered with a brown-and-tan handwoven rug. A single bed occupied space to the left of the door, and a plastic shipping box served as a bedside table. Atop the box perched a tiny electric lamp and, to my surprise, two books. An antique chest of drawers with a cracked mirror stood along the right-hand wall. It held another stack of books, a container of hand sanitizer and a small mug warmer. A composting toilet sat in one corner, a curtain hung beside it for privacy. The place was spotless, odorless and reflected a neat, organized occupant—quite unlike the frat-house atmosphere I had expected. Shame washed my cheeks.

"Books?" I blurted and then winced inside. Why should I be surprised that Walker liked books?

"Oh, yes." Mags's face was proud. "Walker's always been an avid reader. Right now, he's into Reformation history. I hoped he'd go on for more schooling, but . . ." She trailed off, sighing.

"Print books are rare," I said, careful not to sound condemning. Literature had to be church approved and was only available online or through Sanctioned Libraries so that the RD could track their use. While not exactly illegal, print books were considered subversive and potentially dangerous. The RD frowned on book ownership.

"I have a few, myself." Mags tossed that off as if she were talking about shades of eyeshadow. "A screen is . . . urgent, somehow. Paper lets you slow down and think." She gently ushered me out of Walker's house, and we headed back toward the U.

"I had never considered that," I confessed. "I have a book, too."

Mags smiled. "You do?"

I nodded. "Mom . . ." My throat closed, and I trailed off.

"Temperature's dropping," Mags observed. Low clouds wiped the face of the sky from the west, obscuring the sun, and I pulled my hood tighter against the freshening wind as we climbed Mags's steps. "It's a challenge, this many people living in each other's pockets. But it keeps folks off the street, even though everyone knows their neighbor's business. It's hard to keep a secret at Shady Dell."

"I can imagine," I said, thinking of the rampant gossip at our apartment community. Inside the THOW, I greedily stretched my cold-reddened hands over the woodstove's warmth as Mags closed the door.

"I kept my books partly because they belonged to Will. But mostly, I love to read." The older woman hung her coat on a peg by the door and settled on the futon. "You're welcome to borrow them, if you wish. They're out of sight in the bedroom."

"That's prudent." I took a breath, holding firmly to my patience. "Mags, I appreciate the tour, but I don't understand how this helps me."

She gave me a candid look. "Meryn, I'll be linear with you. We're barely hanging on here. You can join our community, but you'll have to build your own tiny tin house."

"Build? My own house?" I hung up my coat to cover my shock. Until that moment, I hadn't fully understood that she was proposing I live by myself. "But I'm a woman. How can I possibly live alone?"

"Well, that's a decision only you can make," she said evenly, her eyes on mine. "But if you're uncomfortable living without a man's supervision, you're right back to deciding whether to live with your stepfather or marry your boyfriend." She chuckled. "As I'm sure you've noticed, no men live in this house."

I blinked as that hit me for the first time, and I sat next to her, turning over the ramifications in my mind. Mags sat quietly, letting me think. After a few moments, my eyes met hers. "Do you think it would be acceptable to God?"

"I do," she said gently. "In itself, a woman living alone is not immoral. But I ask no woman to go against her conscience." Then she smiled. "I believe you have sufficient maturity to live on your own. It's the societal pressure that may cause you problems. And the potential legal jeopardy, of course."

I blew out a breath, thinking. "I'd like some time to pray about it, but I'm open to the idea."

Mags nodded. "Walker and Kilte can help with labor, but you'll need something to trade. That's how it's done. If you don't stay, I've just taken an enormous risk by sharing all of this." She shrugged. "It's an open secret—anyone who flies over can see Tin Town—but we try to be as careful as we can." Her smile was warm. "Bree vouched for you."

I shook my head, cognizant of the risk Bree had taken. "I am honored to have earned her trust," I said formally. Then I touched Mags's hand. "Even if I don't stay, your secret is safe with me."

Mags's expression turned serene, as if I'd confirmed something she already knew.

I didn't push, but changed the subject. "I didn't notice a kitchen in Walker's place."

She nodded. "Some hipsters have hotplates and water, but—"

"Why do you call them hipsters?" I interrupted.

Mags waved a hand. "The first houses were affixed to the THOWs: literally 'hipped on.' We run power to them. And, in my case, I offer kitchen and bathroom privileges." She quirked a smile. "Someone called them 'hipsters,' and it stuck. Attaching the hipsters didn't work out— they sometimes damaged the main house in a freeze or a storm—so we made them freestanding."

"So meals and cooking?" I asked. "You mentioned a schedule."

"Come, I'll show you how we work the kitchen." Launching herself from the futon with the ease of a much younger woman, she led me to the tiny pantry. A schedule of chores was taped inside the door. Name tags designated shelves: *Bree, Walker, Kilte, Tamar.* Every shelf was at capacity.

"It's five GP a month for five inches' width," Mags said. "It's expensive because a lot of our space here gets used for garden truck. I have jars of preserves all over the house. I'd rather everyone store their own food at home, but that isn't always practical."

"Who's Tamar?" I asked. If my stuff would be in the same cabinet, I reasoned, I had a right to know.

Mags didn't blink. "She lives in Walker's row. She's been here about three years. A good person—she has a job and a little girl."

My mouth dropped open. "A child? In one of those . . ."

Mags nodded as if she shared my ambivalence. "She insulated her place and keeps it warm for Priscilla. She built an addition, so Pris has her own little space, and they have a lavatory and sink and some storage. Her husband died three years ago—she hasn't said how. A month later she and Pris were out on the street."

"How old is Pris?" I asked.

"She's eleven. Takes the bus to school, smart as a whip."

"Takes the bus?" It came out more angrily than I intended.

For a moment Mags said nothing, her expression neutral. "You can talk about it, you know. If you want."

"It's . . ." I tried to say "nothing," but it wasn't nothing and my mouth refused to say the word. I hadn't discussed the incident with anyone except Mom since it happened. "I was twelve." The words came haltingly. "I sat with my friend Debbie Delaney on the school bus. Every day. And one day the boys . . ." Tears pricked my eyes. "They lured her to the back of the bus, and they raped her."

Mags's eyes went wide, then watered. "And no one did anything?"

I shook my head. "I spoke to the principal. He said since I hadn't actually witnessed the crime, there was nothing he could do, especially since Debbie's father chose not to report it.

"He forbade me to talk about it." Bitterness poisoned my tone and I didn't bother to mask it. "He said it would frighten the other girls and unnecessarily upset the parents, and I could face disciplinary action for 'spreading rumors shameful to my caste.'"

Mags nodded. "So you kept quiet."

"I kept quiet." I took a deep breath. "I've always wondered if this happened to some other girl. If my silence—"

"Meryn, you were twelve!" Mags leaned forward, her eyes intent. "It wasn't your responsibility to see those boys brought to justice. And you know how few rape cases actually make it to court."

I grimaced. "I do. But that doesn't make me feel better."

"I will mention this to Tamar." Mags shook her head. "Maybe Walker can add Pris to his morning run."

"Anything to keep her off a school bus." I blotted my eyes.

What I didn't tell Mags was that Mom had immediately enrolled me in karate classes at the Y, even though they were supposedly restricted to boys. I don't know exactly what Ray said to the instructor, but within a week I was joining the boys at the dojo. They were resentful, but that didn't stop me; I was the fastest, most motivated learner in the class.

We were still standing in the tiny kitchen, and I changed the subject, shaking off the memory. "So . . . can I have a little fridge space, too?"

"Absolutely," Mags replied, opening the door for a moment to show me the size. "Same price." She shut the door and smiled.

"So how do we do this?" I shrugged. "If I want to live here, I mean."

She tapped her lip with an index finger. "Well, I would let the boys know you need a house, and they'll start planning. There's still room in my row—the row attached to my THOW—so that's where we'd put you. And you'll have to schedule with them to get your materials and help with the labor. You can do that through Bree, but be careful what you text. We have to assume your stepfather is monitoring your phone."

My eyes widened, but she went on, "If you wish, you can bring some things while you're building—clothes and such—and store them up in the loft until your place is finished, as long as there's nothing with your name on it. That way you're not too obviously moving out of your stepfather's house."

"That's very generous of you." I looked at the floor, trying not to let irony taint my tone.

She nodded. "We try to help where we can. Meryn."

I met her eyes.

"There's something you need to understand. You are welcome to join our community. But Shady Dell isn't a paradise, and we're not immune from the Guards." She paused. "You are still an unattached woman. Some unscrupulous types here may turn you in for the bounty, if your stepfather takes it that far."

I gasped, and she nodded, her expression grim.

"It's happened. You may be in just as much danger here as you would be at home."

"Ray's apartment isn't my home." Blood pounded in my ears, an unrelenting boombox, as I sorted options, parsed alternatives. It didn't take long. "But if I live here, it will be my danger, Mags. *My* choice."

Her nod was slow, respectful, and her crooked smile acknowledged my pain. Then she straightened. "I need to run to the market this afternoon. You are welcome to join me, if you wish."

My gaze skirted the countertop, trailed across the cheerful window pots. "I'd like that. But first, I need to go back to Ray's." I said it slowly, trying not to shudder at a memory. "He's going to punish me."

She was silent for a long moment. "In that case"—she extended her hands—"may I pray for you?"

*As if that will help.* The thought was bitter, but I took her hands in mine.

# 10. HOMECOMING

Heart pounding, I pressed my wrist to the apartment door. It clicked and the light turned green—Ray hadn't deprogrammed it, after all. I took a deep breath and went inside.

Wearing shorts and a stained, off-white wife beater, his hair in greasy gray spikes, Ray sat slouched at the dining table, one thick hand curled around a mug, the other propping up his head. He looked up as I entered. "Well, well. Look what the dog dragged in." His words slurred, and I could smell beer from across the room. "Who'd you shack with last night?"

"Nice to see you, too, Ray," I said, dropping my tote on the carpet and closing the door. My eyes wandered the apartment—familiar, yet now somehow alien—and I realized I was looking for Mom. Tears pricked my eyes, and I cleared my throat. "I know you find this hard to believe, but some of us are perfectly fine sleeping alone."

"Liar." Wincing, he pushed to his feet. "I put it out there that you've been spending time with relatives in Zion state. That old biddy Kittiwax didn't buy it, but at least she hasn't called the Guards yet."

A hint of relief loosened my gut. "After three days? That must be some kind of record. Maybe she's getting dementia."

*Was that a smile I just saw?* I thought. *No, couldn't be.* "So what's my punishment?" I shifted from one foot to the other.

His arms crossed. "You sound awful eager. And it isn't punishment. Your disobedience must be met with appropriate discipline."

"You sound like Prinister Severs." I spat it. "Whatever homily you want to clothe it in, let's get it over with."

"I haven't decided, okay?" He rubbed his eyes, his hand stained with something yellow. I caught a whiff of *khat*. "I should probably consult him."

"You should probably figure out how to be a decent father without having to talk to the church first." My stomach quailed. *Meryn, stop it. Don't make him madder.*

"I should probably let him handle it." My stomach turned to ice, and he scrubbed at his scalp. "I'm going to take a shower."

I stood in the living room for several minutes after he retreated to the bathroom. The sound of water running provided an oddly homey counterpoint to my anxiety, while my eyes examined the sofa and the chair, darted through the dining area, looking for any evidence of the woman I'd seen. When Ray started whistling, I lifted my tote and slowly headed down the hall to my old bedroom, turning my head away as I passed the room where Mom died. Collapsing on my bed, I caught my reflection in the mirror. She looked bitter, angry, hopeless. "Well, we tried," I whispered, and her mouth curled in a mirthless smile.

~

I met Mags at Jesus Saves, where I picked up a package of undies and two T-shirts on the cheap. Mags, wearing a brown Caste Ring and a tan MT, reminded me faintly of my Gamma Flint, so for a couple of hours I could almost pretend everything was normal. Realizing I would need toiletries at my new place, I purchased waterless cleanser and dry shampoo. I hated the stuff—it gave me dandruff—but it was better than being dirty.

We were careful to stand in the checkout lane for the Indigent Caste, even though the line there was long, while the green Management Caste lane was deserted. "So," I asked Mags, my eyes on the bored checkout clerk, "when I leave and I'm no longer with Ray, will I be Indigent Caste?"

Her gaze on mine was briefly sharp. "So you'll be joining us?"

"I'm—praying about it." *What other option do I have? But then Ray will turn me in, and I'll be in even more trouble than I am now.*

"You'll be in a gray area," she answered, setting a package of girls' socks on the belt. "Technically you should go down to City Hall and register your altered status, because you're right—since you're not under Ray's roof and you don't make enough money to qualify for Worker Caste on your own, you're now Indigent like me."

She sighed, smiled. "But since you can't register without getting arrested, I think it's safest that you continue to pretend you're Worker

Caste. If you were to wear an Indigent Caste Ring, a Guard could pick you up for Caste Deception."

Over my objections, Mags shared with me the cold lunch she'd tucked in her tote, and then we took the bus to Gambit's Grocery. With crowds of women bustling around us in their brown and blue MTs, I bought a few groceries for myself and for the house. And that was the end of my paycheck.

As Mags paid for her purchases, I realized her suggestion to go shopping was deliberate; she knew I'd come to them with only what would fit in my tote. "I do some shopping online," she was saying, putting her packages in a fold-up wheeled carrier, "but I get tired of being scammed or drone-jacked."

I nodded. "We tried that, too. We—" I was about to say *Mom*— "constantly had to send things back and pay the shipping and restocking fees. And the jackers were making a good living off us. So we stopped."

The lights went out, eliciting groans from the shoppers behind us. "So much for that," a woman muttered.

Silvermine's unpredictable blackouts stopped everything: commerce, subs, school. The reasons were opaque; blackouts were just a part of life, something I'd been accustomed to since I was a kid. I'd heard rumors they were caused by an inconsistency in coal shipments to the power plants.

The store manager propped open the door, and we all exited, those who were still in line leaving their goods behind. "I always feel so sorry for the ones who can't check out," Mags said. I tried to ignore my shame that we'd made it.

By the time we got back to Mags's, pulling her cart from the bus stop, Walker's truck sat parked in front of the tiny house; all the blinds were closed.

As we came into the porch, he opened the door and relieved Mags of the totes looped over her shoulders. "The girls are doing homework," he said, nodding a hello to me.

"Time got away from me." Mags's eyes crinkled in a merry fashion. "Meryn and I had such fun shopping."

Walker's expression darkened.

"I just got paid," I said in an apologetic tone, "And I do need clothes."

His face cleared. "Of course."

I appreciated his sentiment. *He's probably seen too many people try to take advantage of Mags.* Looking around the warm, well-lit room, I offered a silent prayer of thanks for Mags's solar panels.

"Yeah, you had to bolt practically naked, didn't ya?" Ellie piped up from the table, her eyes curious.

"Ellie, that's unkind." Mags crossed her arms. "Come and help with the groceries."

"I'm doing my homework," she said with the airy manner of a child in possession of a legitimate excuse.

Mags blinked, lifted an eyebrow at her daughter. "You need a break."

Ellie set down her tablet—I recognized it as school-issue—and set to helping Mags willingly enough. Lisha sat on the futon, using her tab to work from the house screen.

All homes were required by law to have some form of communications screen to receive official RD news and programs. Mags's was older but excellent quality—a Chinese model from before the embargo. Her family must have purchased it right after the Reformation. The latest screens created holo projections that required no wall or desk space, or so I read. The technology was luminano-based, but I didn't know how it worked. The Chinese were very proprietary about their technology, something Popresident Humboldt grumbled about constantly, even though China wasn't one of our trading partners. It didn't make sense to me.

Walker sat on a storage hassock next to Lisha, guiding her through history homework. The screen displayed a series of formal head shots I recognized at once: the Founders of the Christian States of America. She was groaning, "Who *cares* who the architects of the American Reformation were?"

"It's important to understand this stuff," Walker said quietly.

"Why?" she asked, with just a touch of her sister's spirit. "Look at them! They're all white men. I'll bet every one of them was a GM purist, and they had every single African gene clipped out of their kids!"

"That's a lot of clipping," Ellie murmured as she came by, tossing me an amused look.

"That's why the Exalted Caste keep having idiots—they intermarry way too much. Don't any of them study genetics?"

"It isn't just that," Ellie said. "It's all the gene therapy they use on their kids. I heard from Sarah who heard from Peace that therapy introduces genetic similarities because they keep using the same gene bank."

"We don't make those kinds of assumptions, girls," Mags remonstrated from the kitchen. "Meryn, thank you for the fresh broccoli, but you didn't have to go to such expense."

She said that for Walker's benefit, I knew, because she had already thanked me in the store. Ellie folded the empty shopping cart and tucked it next to the fridge.

"Fresh broccoli?" Lisha said in astonishment, craning her neck to see around Walker's bulk.

"I get the stems!" Ellie yelled.

I laughed. The peeled stem was the best part.

"Here's what I have so far." Lisha read, *"The American Reformation sprang from a dramatic move of God, paving the way to create a nation honoring His name. Too many former Americans had turned their backs on God, and on the founding principles of our God-fearing nation. But our noble founders held firm to these ideals and invited the other states to leave and form their own godless nation. After the exodus, a new nation known as the Christian States of America was born.*

*"The godless states formed a loose coalition they called the Democratic Republic of the United States, or DRUSA. Walls were erected, treaties signed, and constitutions amended or rewritten. Except for the occasional skirmish where DRUSA factions grew arrogant, such as at the Battle of Chicago and the Portland Pagan Riots, the Reformation was free of violence. The new government redrew the states' borders to ensure citizens had fair and balanced representation, and every state in the CSA was given a new name to honor the holiness of the new nation."*

I smiled at the memory of civics. The state of Paradise, where Silvermine was located, comprised sections of more than one state from the former U.S., but I didn't know what the states were called before the Reformation. We weren't taught that.

Lisha was still reading. *"The CSA is governed by the Reformation Directorate, informally known as the RD. Church leaders are the foundation of our governance: from the city council, whose candidates are appointed by the church, to the bishor (or bishop mayor), the carvenor (cardinal governor) and the popresident. Such leaders govern wisely because God appoints and guides every one of them. Even our RD's motto reflects this piety:* Guided by the Hand of God."

"That's a good synopsis, Lisha." Mags set a pot on the stove.

"I have to expand on the treaties." Lisha scrolled up, reading. "Can I put that in a different section?"

"You can." Walker leaned forward and tapped the pad's display. "For your first section, I recommend you itemize the Founders, starting with Kyle Weeks. He used personal charisma to great effect in rallying other leaders to his position, even those who opposed his platform."

"Charisma, or something else," I muttered, thinking of Weeks's autocratic and heavy-handed techniques, and Walker's eyebrows lifted. I bit my lip. *Shut up, Meryn.*

"Our teacher says Christianity would have died out completely in the pre-Reformation United States if it wasn't for Weeks," Lisha said. "She—"

"Mom says God is quite capable of keeping His church alive and growing, even under the most oppressive circumstances," Ellie broke in. "She's told us all about underground churches in the old Soviet Union and China and North Korea and other ungodly places."

"I know," Lisha said, a trifle testy. "I go to Bible study, too."

"Then you can cover the treaties. And in the economics section," Walker went on, "touch on how imports come only from nations that honor our religious convictions."

I wondered if the Chinese went nuts from their brain implants, or if they'd improved them somehow. All our technology was imported from New Korea. *No, I'm sure they're the same.*

"Meryn, are you going to join us for Bible study?" Ellie asked, her eyes earnest. She wasn't being rude.

"Meryn may not be interested," Mags said hastily from where she was putting away clean dishes. She hung a mug from its hook and looked at me. "It isn't a requirement to join the community."

I bit my lip.

Bible studies were perilous. Either they were RD-Sanctioned and leaned heavily into an approved list of dos and don'ts—which I'd had a gutful of at St. Mike's—or they were considered subversive, which made them illegal and dangerous.

"Well, you believe in God, don't you?" Ellie went on.

That one was easy, and I smiled. "I do."

"Well," Ellie said, as if that settled it. "We hold class here every Wednesday night."

"Walker, it's okay," Mags said. Walker had stood and was pulling Ellie over by her sister.

*There is an undercurrent here*, I thought, using one of Mom's ocean metaphors. *A strong one. That bodes well.* Despite our congenial conversation earlier in the day, I wasn't sure of Mags's position on the Bible. And of course it was impossible to ask. The thought flitted through my head that Mags could be an RD plant, and Shady Dell just a cover. Then I bit my lip, repentant at thinking such a thing about the woman who was helping me.

"It's just that sometimes I have to work," I said to Ellie.

"Oh, of course," she said, now very adult. "Like Bree."

I smiled at the girl. "Walker," I said, "when you have time, could we talk about tiny tin house construction? Mags showed me your place, but I'm not sure I can do it. Actually, I'm quite sure I can't."

"Does this mean you're staying?" Ellie clapped.

"I'm thinking about it." I kept my smile in place, but my stomach twisted.

"We can go now." A corner of Walker's mouth turned up, and he reached for his coat. "When we get back, Lisha, I'll want to read your first draft. I expect to see each of the founders listed by name, along with their role in the Reformation."

Lisha's eyes met mine, her expression desperate.

"You can do it," I encouraged her. "Do you have your outline?"

She nodded, doubt etched on her face.

I caught Mags's smile from the kitchen, where she was pressing tofu with a checkered cloth.

"Then just start filling in what you know," I said. "It doesn't have to sound pretty yet."

Walker was whispering to Ellie. Her face was a study in hurt.

I knew I wasn't supposed to hear, so I focused on Lisha. "You have a great intro and you can write the closing paragraphs later."

"I don't have to do it start to finish?" Her eyes widened, and I shook my head.

"You'll have a better paper if you don't."

Relief cleared her face of desperation. "Really? That makes it so much easier, Meryn! Thank you!"

"You're welcome. And if you run into trouble, I'll be happy to help."

Ellie piped up, "What grade did *you* get in history, Meryn?"

Lisha turned and hit her sister on the arm. "Rude, why don't you?"

"Ow!" Ellie rubbed it, glaring at her twin. Walker moved behind me, taking my coat off the rack by the door.

"I got an A," I said, letting myself grin.

"Ellie, come finish your homework," Mags said.

Ellie gave me a mournful look. "Do you have any tips for algebra? We started a new module today and I can't figure it out. It's weird."

I stifled a laugh, remembering my frustration with the module system.

"Girls," Mags said, "Meryn is not your private tutor." Ellie's expression turned penitent, and she bent to her homework.

Walker smiled and held out my coat. "Ready?"

Lisha was already typing. "What good this does anyway," she muttered, "since all this information is online."

As I moved toward the door, Mags said, "It teaches you how to understand, connect and process that information, child. Data by itself is meaningless unless you know how and why it influences and relates to other—"

The door closed behind us, cutting off Mags's voice.

Walker chuckled in the sudden silence. "Mom has mellowed."

"That's mellow?" I arched an eyebrow, and he laughed.

"Mom homeschooled me." He opened the screen door for me. "She's a good teacher, but yeah, she can be exacting." We clomped down the steps and turned toward Tin Town. The scudding clouds had lowered, threatening snow, and I zipped my coat against the cold.

"You must've gotten in under the wire." Homeschooling was illegal.

He nodded. "I graduated the year before they banned it. Mom still teaches the girls more than they get in class. The schools don't cover enough, especially in topics like history. Ellie complains that she has two teachers to satisfy."

I chuckled as we crossed behind the THOWs to where the tiny tin houses marched in neat rows.

"This used to be a slum." Walker bypassed his house, leading me to the end of the row. He turned and gestured back at Tin Town. "People put up houses here because—Meryn."

My eyes lifted to his, then darted to the ground.

"Meryn. Look at me."

I did, and my breath caught in my throat. Walker's eyes were intent on mine. It was unnerving, and my stomach tightened.

He smiled. "I understand what they teach you in school," he said. "But it isn't a sin to look at someone."

"It's forward." I bit my lip, my eyes flitting from one tiny tin house to the next.

"Well, in this family," he said, "looking at someone when they speak is considered good manners. And since you are moving into our row, you're a part of our family now." Dropping the subject, he gestured at the closest house. "Come on," he said, and to my surprise he touched my arm with his gloved hand, his eyes warm, amused. "Let me show you how we'll build this house you say you can't build."

~

"The way Walker explained it makes it seem doable," I told Bree, Mags, and the girls over a dinner of dal and chapatis. I didn't mention that Walker had touched me. Of Kilte there was no sign.

"He and Kilte have it down to a science," Bree said, tearing her chapati in half. Mags poured Lisha more tea.

After Walker and I parted, I'd taken a walk up the U and along Oak Street, thinking and praying. Saying yes seemed logical, especially since Ray seemed inclined to throw me on the mercy of Prinister Severs. And I already knew mercy wasn't a trait Severs had in abundance. But Mags was right—living at Shady Dell wasn't a guarantee of my safety, either. *Ultimately, it could make things worse for me.* I sighed. *Lord, I need help. Some guidance.*

A mile or so up Oak Street, I turned around. No sense in getting lost in a new area where I didn't yet know the hazards, especially since the neighborhood seemed to deteriorate as I got farther from Shady Dell. The broken windows, stained curtains and peeling paint reflected an abject poverty and pervasive hopelessness that seemed to claw at my mind, trying to pull me in. An old man sitting on a sagging front porch glared with rank suspicion as I walked toward his place. I took the hint and turned around.

As I headed back up the street, fighting a cold wind, I still didn't have my answer. With Mom gone, Mags's suggestion was my best hope—my only hope.

I approached the head of the U, my eyes tracing the ancient wood sign with its carved letters spelling out *Shady Dell*. As I watched, a bird flew from a nearby tree, alighting on the sign. It chirped at me, angling its head in a quizzical fashion.

A sparrow.

I stopped. In my memory, I heard the ticking of Gampa Flint's clock, the echo of a hymn in the courtyard of our apartment complex . . . *His eye is on the sparrow, and I know He watches me . . .* The wind coaxed tears from my eyes and blew them in cold rills down my face.

The little bird chirped once, twice, hopping toward me, then flew up the U into Shady Dell. It alighted in a garden tree and sang merrily as I walked up to Mags's THOW. Perplexed, uncertain, I paused at the screen door, my eyes on the sparrow. The chirp that came was authoritative, as if saying, "Go on!" In spite of my tears, I chuckled.

Now, sitting in the warm tiny house with my new friends, I studied their expectant faces. "I've decided I'm staying," I said, my voice hesitant. "I'm going to build, and as soon as my house is finished, I'll move here."

Mags set down her spoon and beamed at me while Lisha and Bree cheered.

Ellie just shrugged and nodded as if my news were no surprise.

I sighed, smiled. "I just hope I'm up to the challenge. The idea of building a house is pretty intimidating, even though Walker's system seems foolproof."

"Is he going to help you, Meryn?" Lisha's tone was coy.

"He said he would," I replied. I didn't mention the relief that had flooded me when he'd tendered the offer.

"Maybe he thinks you're pretty," Ellie said, trying to hide a grin.

"Maybe he thinks he's in looooove," Lisha said in the same exact tone, and both girls giggled.

Bree's expression reflected a strained forbearance. "You both know he's seeing Tamar."

*He is?* An odd disappointment made me focus on stirring my dal.

To my surprise, Ellie made a face. "She's no good for him. She's a snob."

"As if," Lisha said, "she has any reason to be lofty. She lives here, doesn't she?"

"Girls, gossip," Mags murmured.

Both girls deflated.

"Oh." Lisha curled around her bowl. "Sorry, Mom."

"Is it gossip if it's true?" Ellie asked, straightening up and frowning.

"You know full well it is," Bree snapped with the impatience of someone rehearsing an old argument.

Ellie crossed her arms, and her face went defiant. She shot back, "And where is *your* fiancé, sis? Out whoring?"

Bree dropped her spoon as Mags reached across the tiny table and grabbed Ellie's wrist. "You are one breath away from a time-out, young lady." Mags's voice was iron. "I never want to hear that word in this house again. Especially not in reference to a member of this family. Do you understand me?"

Bree's face flushed red, her eyes narrowing to furious slits. An embarrassed heat rose in my own cheeks.

Ellie's gaze locked on her soup, her teeth digging into her lower lip. "Yes, Mom," she whispered.

"Now," Mags said, "you owe an apology to this table."

Ellie didn't look up. "I—I'm sorry, everyone." It came out a whisper.

"I can't hear you." Mags's voice was firm.

Ellie cleared her throat and lifted her head, meeting our eyes in turn. "I'm sorry for what I said. Please forgive me."

"Thank you, Ellie." Mags turned to her granddaughter, but Bree picked up her water and drank, not looking at anyone.

"Well, I forgive you," Lisha said, scooping more dal onto a chapati.

"So do I," I said.

Ellie darted a glance at Bree, who set down her mug.

"Bree?" Mags said it gently.

Her face set in anger, Bree rose, seized her coat and slammed out of the house.

For a minute or two, no one said anything. Ellie looked at me with liquid eyes, and I gave her what I hoped was a reassuring smile. "Sometimes forgiveness takes a little time," I said softly. Then I remembered it was one of Mom's sayings, and a fierce pain in my chest made me wince.

Mags turned to the girl. "Where on earth did you pick up that word?"

Ellie blinked. "School."

"What?" Mags set down her spoon with a *clink*.

Lisha nodded, ebony braids bouncing. "We get all kinds of sex ed from the older girls," she said with the air of someone being helpful.

Mags's mouth dropped open.

"What . . . kind of sex ed do you get, exactly?" I asked, my eyes traveling to Mags.

"Oh, nothing bad." Lisha's words crowded each other in her haste to reassure. "They don't *do* anything to us. They just tell us stuff. 'Cause our teachers tell us nothing."

Mags's face turned severe. "I think we need to have a discussion after dinner."

"Are we in trouble?" Ellie asked piteously.

Mags's anger vanished. "No, sweetie," and she smiled. "And thank you for the apology—you did it well. But the older girls at school are pushing up my timetable a bit and I want to make sure you get factual information."

I put the last bite of chapati in my mouth, rose and started carrying dishes to the sink.

"It's my turn," Lisha protested.

"It is." I said it around my mouthful, picking up her bowl. "But you have a lot to do tonight so I'll do it this once."

"Aw, thanks, Meryn."

As I cleared away mugs, Mags said, "Let's start with this new word, whore. Do you understand what it means?"

"Yeah," Lisha said. "It's a woman who will sleep with any guy 'cause she likes it."

"Like Merica," Ellie said with a touch of her usual impudence, and the girls giggled.

"Merica?" I asked, returning to the table for empty bowls.

"Yeah, she lives in Tin Town and she's really pretty. The guys love her. They say she's called that 'cause she's been with every guy in America," Lisha said.

*One of our neighbors is a Sweet Pea?* I pressed my lips together and smiled at Mags, who looked a bit overwhelmed. "I'll just go see what the garden is growing."

She smiled, and I sensed her relief. "Thank you, Meryn." As I shrugged into my coat, she turned her attention to the twins. "First, there is no such thing as a whore. That is a term used by people of limited understanding. You remember how some children in the orphanage had been badly injured by the people who were supposed to protect them?"

The girls nodded, their faces sober. I slipped out and eased the door shut.

# II. UΠSEᵀᵀLED

Bree was nowhere in sight as I descended the steps. A few houses away, a girl and boy wearing heavy coats tossed a faded beach ball back and forth in the dying light. The ball bounced off the boy's hand, and he gave chase while the girl laughed. Dishes clinked in the house next door, and conversation filtered through the closed window. *No wonder everybody knows everybody else's business.* Across the U, a flickering video screen reflected through the windows of a tiny house—someone watching the RD evening programming, no doubt. From three houses away came the echo of someone singing, *sometimes I feel like a motherless child,* on and on in a voice raspy and soulful, and something inside me twisted, my heart a cap of razor wire over a well of pain. Traffic noise drifted over from Sweet Street.

I knew I had to get home before Ray found me gone, but the razor wire kept me moving toward the other side of the U, glad of the chance to get a closer look at the tiny houses. The air felt less smoggy than usual, and I picked up my pace. I wondered if the neighborhood had a safe place where I could run, or practice my *katas*, the self-defense moves I'd learned at the Y. I wasn't familiar with this area of Silvermine, but I missed the release of my workout.

As I passed house after house, I wondered about the people inside. Were they all Indigent? Did they have hopes and dreams for their future, or had they—like so many of my classmates—given up on any real ambition? Job opportunities in Silvermine were limited, as China had taken much of our industry. Humboldt had ridden to his re-election on promises to "get tough with China," but we hadn't seen any improvement yet.

Most girls in my class had gotten married right after they graduated at sixteen, some taking care of husbands still in school. All of us knew the clock was ticking, and our future depended on who we married. My classmates—Worker Caste—had mostly married tin miners; their husbands spent weeks in undersea mines off the coast. Grimacing, I shoved that thought away.

Our first year in high school, we were required to take Biblical Womanhood. The class focused on how to find a husband and keep him happy. Beyond the instructions on housekeeping—cooking, cleaning, sewing and other domestic skills—we were taught how to defer to one's spouse, how to keep one's voice low and melodic (even in an argument), how to serve a formal tea or dinner (in case we married up), how to walk gracefully, how to cross one's ankles in public (and *never* cross one's legs), how to apply makeup and perfume with precision (and never overdo), and so on.

We dutifully memorized the rote responses necessary for socially acceptable interaction with those in the Management, Governance, and Exalted Castes, and were cautioned not to use low-caste, hasher language when speaking with any other caste. We learned how to pick up a teacup properly, and how to set it in its saucer with the handle positioned so as not to offend. We were taught the proper way to use all the accoutrements of a high-caste event.

We learned to hold ourselves erect, shoulders back, spine straight, even while sitting. We were instructed never to lean back in the presence of those of a higher caste. Comfort, I supposed, being reserved only for the wealthy.

The class provided no actual sex education ("ask your mother," we were told), with one exception: we were to please our husbands at all cost, and whatever he asked us to do in bed we were to do, without hesitation and with a smile, no matter our personal abhorrence for the act.

Our teacher, an ample woman with gray hair pulled back in a severe bun, pinned us with a gimlet stare. "Girls, he has the right before God to use every orifice in your body for his pleasure. You will not deny him." Several girls gasped as the import sank in. Davida broke down in uncontrollable weeping, and our teacher sent her to the nurse's office. My friend Connie and I traded grim looks.

"Is it any wonder most of us left that class in shock?" Bree had commented after I shared my ambivalence about the instruction. "They expect us to be ladies in the living room and know exactly how to serve formal tea, and Sweet Peas in the bedroom and know exactly how to go down on a guy—but they give us zero instruction in *that*."

I was fourteen at the time and more than a little shocked by her raw language. Later I learned—through older girlfriends—what the act entailed. While it wasn't enough to put me off marriage entirely, I couldn't imagine loving any man enough to want to do . . . *that*. I took a moment to wonder if husbands reciprocated, but then I decided the act would be far too messy and repellent for the guys I knew.

Bree had also been my lifeline when the RD summoned me for my first state-mandated pelvic exam just a month later. "This makes *no* sense!" I told her, fear bluing my tone.

"They want to test your fertility and ensure you're ready for marriage," she explained, patient. "They also want to make sure you're a virgin."

"But why can't Mom come?" Tears choked the words in my throat. "I can't take off my clothes in front of some man I've never even met!"

"Their logic is that your mother won't be with you on your wedding night. It's stupid, I know. I'll be right there in the waiting room." Bree gripped my hands soothingly. "I was just as upset when it was my turn, and a friend came with me, too. But if you want to graduate, you need the doctor's approval."

It was worse than I expected. The pain I experienced during the procedure was new and frightening. The doctor—an older, balding man with a manner so clinical I felt like a frog undergoing dissection—told me nothing about what he was doing to my body, or why. Feeling alone and incredibly vulnerable, I sobbed, my hands pressed over my eyes, while he probed and prodded every part of me with his hands and his instruments and his hands again. At one point, a stab of pain made me yelp, and he glared at me from between my knees. "Stop it," he barked. "You can't possibly feel that."

My head snapped up and I glared at him, my cheeks tearstained. "My body says otherwise!" He got even rougher after that, and I had to bite my lip, hard, to keep from planting a foot in his face. I wanted to beg him to stop, but my pride wouldn't let me. All I could do was endure.

When it was over, he turned away, ordering me to take my clothes and dress in the hall. He did not look at me again. Cold, humiliated, I obeyed, while male medAngels down the hall watched and laughed, whistling and clapping as if I were putting on a show.

I didn't find out until much later that he was supposed to wear gloves.

I bled on my panties for the next three days.

~

Movement in my peripheral vision intruded my reflections. Bree strode up the U, and I smiled slightly, testing her mood. The wry grin she gave me in response didn't hide her pain.

We met in the middle.

"Ellie can be such a snot sometimes," she said by way of greeting.

"She's a child." I shrugged. "Kids try to provoke."

"Why would she think Kilte would ever do such a thing?" She twisted her plain steel engagement band around and around on her finger, color rising in her cheeks.

"Of course, he wouldn't," I said.

"Sometimes he works late." Her tone was defensive.

*Stays at the job site without Walker?* I thought. But I said, "He has a marriage to save for," and smiled.

Bree's eyes locked on mine, probing. Then her tension dissolved, and she gave me her familiar impish grin. "He does! And if he thinks I'm cheap, he's in for a surprise!"

We laughed. It broke the tension, and I was glad, but then her gaze shifted to a spot over my left shoulder and her expression darkened. I turned to see Ellie approaching, wrapped in Mags's oversized coat.

Bravely she strode right up to us. "Aunt Bree," she said, and I realized that this was the true relationship between them, all joking aside. "Mom told me to wait, but I had to come and find you and apologize."

"I'll go check Lisha's history paper," I said, and turned back to the house. By the time I got inside, the afternoon light was dimming, and I was chilled to the bone. *The temperature must be dropping again.*

As I collected my tote and left for Ray's, there was still no sign of Kilte.

~

"Where the hell have you been?" Ray demanded, standing in the living room. He was still in his work clothes, but an open bottle of beer sat on the side table next to his recliner.

"You're home early." Wary, I closed the door, trying to keep my tone casual and light.

"Answer my question."

I took a careful breath. "I went to thank my friends for their kindness, and we talked for a while."

"You do not have permission to leave the house."

My mouth dropped open. "What?" Ray had never done such a thing.

He folded his arms, color rising in his face, and my breath sucked in; I knew that look. "If I didn't make it clear this morning, you are confined."

"Ray, I'm eighteen!"

"I don't care if you're eighty. You're still under my roof, under my jurisdiction, and you will not leave this house until I say you may. Is that understood?"

My stomach dropped, and nausea bittered my saliva. *If he won't let me leave the apartment, I can't work on my house, I can't prepare my escape!* "But—"

"I have not yet decided on your punishment, and—"

"Confining me isn't enough?" The moment the words were out, I regretted them—and my scathing tone. I bit my lip and dipped my head in submission, trying to form an apology. "Ray, I—"

"I think I will discuss this with Prinister Severs, after all." His eyes narrowed. "Clearly you learned nothing from your little adventure."

I let that pass, although even the mention of Severs's name made my blood run cold. "I do have a job, Ray. I have to work. In fact, I have to work tomorrow." It was a flat-out lie, but Ray didn't know that.

"You will clock in and out here just as you do at your workplace. I will purchase a chip reader for the door. If you leave early or return home late, I will know about it and you will be punished accordingly. Am I understood?"

*A chip reader?* I swallowed, struggling to contain my fear. "You are."

"You are, *what?*"

"You are, sir."

~

The next morning I dressed for work and told Ray I'd be back when my shift was over. The skies were still dark when I found a seat on the bus. As it pulled away from the stop, I called Mary-Sarah at On the Mark to resign my position. I knew I couldn't go back, even if I couldn't find anything else; I couldn't risk Steffan following me to Shady Dell.

At my words, Mary-Sarah made a regretful sound. "Well, I will miss you, Meryn. You're a good worker and the customers like you. If you don't mind my saying so, you might want to tell your boyfriend. He's been—"

"He isn't my boyfriend, Mary-Sarah." It came out harsh, and I winced.

A long moment of silence, broken only by the roar of the bus and the murmuring conversation of other passengers. I had opened my mouth to apologize when she spoke. "In that case, I will tell him that you are no longer with the company, and he will have to find another way to impress you."

I hoped the sound of my teeth grinding wasn't picked up by the phone's mic. "Thank you. I'm sure once he knows I'm not coming back, he'll leave you alone."

We disconnected, and I blew out a breath, letting the seat hold me up, trying not to let fear in. *This could go so bad so quickly. All Ray has to do is call me at work. Lord help me.*

When I got to Mags's, Kilte was back, joking and flirting with Bree. She'd regained her usual cheerful demeanor and she was helping Mags fix pancakes, the two of them moving in spontaneous dance around the tiny kitchen and elbowing Kilte out of the way with a laugh or a kind word. My friend caught my eye and pointed at the full woodbox; he must have brought home a load of kindling the previous night. *So that's what kept him.* I smiled, and she grinned and rolled her eyes.

We'd had to take the dawn on faith; thick clouds covered the sky, and someone had turned on the kitchen lights so we could see to work.

Mags fixed everyone "toast coffee"—hot water dripped through dark-toasted stale bread. She said it didn't taste at all like the real thing, but it was cheap, hot, and good, and we could use the leftover bread for pudding later.

As Bree rose to clear the table, the door opened and Walker blew in, slamming the door against the wind.

"Breakfast, honey?" Mags asked.

Walker shook his head. "Thanks, Mom, I've eaten." His eyes shifted to me. "Meryn, glad you're here. Mom told me you're staying, and today would be a perfect day to get building materials. Kilte and I are free."

I swallowed a mouthful of coffee, my gut tightening inexplicably. "Oh! Of course. I don't know how much I can afford, though."

"We'll do some scrounging," Walker said with a quiet half grin. "The whole idea is to keep this cheap."

Encouraged, I rose from the table, pushing the last bites of pancake into my mouth.

"Don't let me interrupt your breakfast," he said hastily.

"Not a' all," I said through a mouthful. "'s almost done." I set my plate in the sink, chewing, and whirled back to the living room to grab my coat. Throwing it on, I followed Walker out into the frigid morning.

"Kilte's not coming?" I asked.

"He'll help with the unloading—we won't need him till then," Walker said, coming around the side of the truck to open my door for me. I didn't show my surprise at the unexpected courtesy.

"Thank you," I said, and he slammed the door. I hoped it was due to a stiff hinge rather than some suppressed anger. A moment later he climbed behind the wheel and started the truck, flicking on the headlights as we drove up the U. "Have you ever had coffee?" I asked, raising my voice over the noise of the engine. "Real coffee, I mean."

"Once," he said. "Kilte and I were landscaping for a wedding, and the lady of the house came out and gave us each a cup." He turned left onto Oak Street. Traffic choked the streets—people trying to get errands done before the weather worsened.

"Is it good?" I asked.

He lifted a shoulder. "It's bitter. I guess it's easier to drink if you put sugar in it. Some people even put in cream—can you imagine? Wasting real cream in coffee? But I liked it." Then he laughed. "We got that yard done in record time!"

I chuckled. "So how long have you guys been in business?"

"Since graduation." He glanced my way. "Couldn't go to college, so we had to find a way to make a living. We're not rich, but it's working out."

I remembered Mags's comment about Walker's intelligence, and I wondered if he'd given up on college because of Kilte. I didn't dare ask.

"Besides," he said. "College only helps if you've got connections."

My eyebrows lifted. "But they teach us—"

"—that everyone has the same opportunity," he finished for me, then gave a chuckle. "Yeah, not in the real. Unless your best friend or your sponsor is Governance Caste, college doesn't help. You can get a job all right, but you'll spend thirty years in the same spot. And that's if you're lucky." He shrugged. "Why waste the money?"

*That's cynical. I wonder if it's true.*

We chatted in a companionable fashion as the truck bumped and shuddered over rutted roads to the industrial part of town. I briefly wondered what Ray would think if he saw me, then I shoved the thought away. After a few red lights, Walker pulled into a business that read *Turner's Ironworks.*

"Stop one," Walker said. "Hallie's great. We'll see what she's got."

He drove around to the side of a large warehouse, where sheets of corrugated metal and other oddments lay in neat stacks along the exterior wall. Before I could even grasp the door handle, he was out of the truck and striding to the first stack.

As I opened my door, a blast of freezing wind caught it, nearly wrenching it off its hinges. I climbed out and closed it, but it bounced open and the wind struck it again, pushing me off balance. Annoyed, I slammed it, hard; this time it stayed shut.

"The sign says ironworks, but Hallie has everything: aluminum siding, steel, pipes, you name it," Walker called over the wind. "If it's metal, she trades in it."

The building's side door opened, and a heavyset, balding, red-faced man came out, lurching from side to side as if walking on a tossing ship. "Walker!" he called. "Good to see you." He wore a T-shirt and no coat. His arms were blotchy, but he didn't look a bit cold. I envied him. The wind knifed through my coat, but my shaking had nothing to do with the cold. *Ray would kill me if he saw me here. Then he would kill Walker.*

"Philip, likewise." Walker stepped back from the pile. "How's your mom?"

"Ohh, ornery as always," Philip said in a gruff bass, but he was looking me up and down, his eyes obscured behind a tangled briar patch of eyebrows. I chewed my lip, then recognized what I was doing and forced a smile. *Does Walker know how risky this is for him? Does Philip?*

"This is Meryn," Walker said.

"Pleased to meet you, little lady," Philip said, touching a scarred hand to a nonexistent cap.

I folded my hands, bowed. "The pleasure is mine, sir." As quickly as I could without being rude, I shoved my freezing hands in my pockets.

"What can we do for you, Walker?" Philip turned back to him. "The little girl here need shelter?"

*Little girl? Really?* But I hid my indignant thought behind a smile.

"Yes, we're building a hipster." Walker snugged down his cap against the wind.

Philip coughed up a mouthful of phlegm and spat, then hastily begged my pardon as the spittle froze to the ground. "You want a mansion or a hut?"

I tore my eyes away from the yellowish blob and looked questions at Walker, who smiled. "We'll start small," he said.

"A hut, then." Philip moved one or two pieces of metal off the stack. To my astonishment, he then picked up several large metal sheets as if they were tinfoil and placed them in the truck bed.

Walker was looking at me, his eyes twinkling. "You want a hand there, Philip?"

"Nah, I got it." Philip picked up several more pieces, dropping them atop the others with a crash, then went back for more until he'd filled the bed. "That'll get you started," he said to me, dusting off his hands.

Again I bowed, this time low, as I would to the high caste. "Words cannot adequately express my heartfelt appreciation for your kind generosity, good sir," I said. "What manner of recompense do you require?"

"Not a thing, Miss Meryn." He looked at the ground. "You live long and well in your little house." Abruptly he turned and lurched his way to the warehouse door. Before it clanged shut, I heard someone shout his name.

I only noticed my mouth had dropped open when the cold air rattled my tonsils. *Free? Who gives away building materials?*

Walker was tossing lengths of pipe in the back of the truck, but his eyes were on me, so I closed my mouth and swallowed.

He smiled. "Ready?"

I nodded, and he climbed behind the wheel. This time, I got into the truck on my own. As we pulled out of the parking lot, I said, "I don't get it. Why does he give the stuff away?"

"It's Hallie's policy," he said. "I don't know the details, but she and her mother lived on the street for a time, and her mother froze to death one winter. Hallie's on a cane—missing some toes, maybe from the same incident." The truck fishtailed on a patch of ice as we rounded a corner. "She married Hank Turner, and he left her the business when he passed. The State of Paradise tried to seize it because it isn't legal for a woman to own a business, you know, but the Turners had a good lawyer and he put the place in Philip's name. She runs it, though. Everybody knows who the boss is."

A spurt of envy. *A woman, owning and running her own business!* I wondered how she was able to manage the men. Maybe Philip did it for her. "So we make the house out of those steel panels," I said.

"Tinplate." Walker nodded. "Galvanized steel is too expensive. So we use the cheap stuff. It's not as long-lasting, but it keeps the weather out." He gestured through the windshield as we drove by warehouses and industrial installations. "Ironic that we still call this place Silvermine."

"They did mine silver here, though, didn't they?" Briefly, I closed my eyes, trying to recall my history lessons. "Way back, before the Reformation."

His laugh was ironic. "Mostly bronze, actually. The silver played out fast, if it was even here at all. But 'Bronzemine' didn't have quite the same expensive ring to it. Now it's tin they're finding, mostly off the coast." A light ahead flipped to red, and he eased the truck to a stop.

I nodded, remembering a class presentation I'd made. "Right. One of our main exports." I looked at him sideways. "You didn't want to mine?" Mining was one of the few good-paying jobs in the state.

He smiled, not unkindly. "Well, I've been breathing for awhile now. I kinda like the habit." The light changed, and he stepped on the gas.

I thought about my classmates, and the tin widows at the sub station. I knew what he meant; the job was dangerous, the shifts long, and men ended up with severed limbs or compromised lungs if they worked the underwater mines for more than a handful of years. Often men drowned or succumbed to hypothermia if their wetside suits malfunctioned. Miners called it "shiver death."

A few minutes later, Walker stopped the truck at the rear of an old brick building—Silvermine Shipping—where dozens of pallets, both wood and plastic, sat stacked in rows. "You stay here," he said. "It's getting colder and those clouds look like snow."

"I can help," I said, trying not to let my anger show. *I'm not useless! Or why did you even bring me?*

He grinned. "You can, but I know what I'm looking for and you'll just slow me down. No offense."

He climbed out of the truck. When I saw the rapid way he selected pallets I knew he was right, but that didn't improve my mood. Tossing them into the bed, he hopped into the cab and jammed the truck into reverse, backing out fast and swinging onto the road. A light snow skittered across the windshield, and he turned on the wipers.

"They don't mind folks picking up a few pallets here and there," he explained, "but they're not as friendly about it as Hallie. I try not to impose on their hospitality."

"We're not . . . stealing or anything, are we?" I chewed my lip.

Walker glanced at me, his face impassive. "No," he said. "We don't steal. That would shut us down right quick."

"Of course." My laugh was embarrassed, and I looked out through the windshield as the wipers swept it clean. "I'm sorry."

"No, you're legit," he said. "When people see other people taking things, they figure it's all free. I have permission and I know what is okay to take and what isn't. Now, we'll get this first load home."

I glanced at him. His profile seemed contented, and I felt my stomach soften.

Obtaining the metal panels and pallets we needed consumed the rest of the day. After a quick lunch Kilte joined us, helping Walker with the heavy lifting while I stayed in the cab, gunning the engine to keep the heat going. Each time he climbed back in the truck, Walker couldn't avoid bumping into me. I was oddly conscious of his presence in a way I wasn't with Kilte. Was it because Walker was so big? I wasn't sure, but I couldn't edge away from Walker without edging closer to Kilte, which might give him the wrong idea, so I just tried to keep myself scrunched narrow to avoid touching either of them.

When we got back to Mags's, daylight was retreating behind the lowering sky, and the morning's sporadic snowflakes had morphed into a wet, heavy snowfall. I gasped when I looked at the time on my phone. *I'm too late. Ray's going to—I have to get home!*

"You hop out," Walker suggested as the truck groaned to a stop. "We'll cover the load and be right in." I smiled my thanks.

"Hey, I'm cold, too," Kilte objected, but he gave me his lopsided grin and jumped out of the truck to let me out. I wasted no time getting into the warm house.

Bree looked up from the stove as I entered. "I can't stay," I gasped. "Ray thinks I'm at work." Quickly I outlined what had happened the night before.

"He's a piece of work, that one," she said, throwing a potato into the pot. Water splashed out, sizzling on the stovetop.

"I don't know how I'm going to do this, Bree." I rapidly rewound my scarf, preparing for the walk to the bus stop. "I won't be able to deceive him forever."

She turned to hug me, her expression concerned. "It won't be forever. Just until we get your house finished. I'll tell the guys to expedite. And if you can, come to church with us tomorrow. It'll do your spirit good. Gamma said it was okay, and I should ask you. We leave here at nine."

*Church! The last thing I want right now is church!* I sighed. "I'll try."

~

I sat straight up in bed, startled. I could have sworn someone called my name. Moonlight filtered through the window of my room. Down the hall, Ray snorted and tossed in his sleep.

I lay back and pulled up the covers and tried to identify what had woken me. *A noise? Did my wrist tingle?* I checked my phone; two in the morning, but I had no messages. The only sound was the bubbling of my fish tank, but it seemed I could feel the press of people around me, their thoughts almost audible, with all their demands and hopes and needs and dreams, so close it was overwhelming. What would it be like to live at Shady Dell, where everyone lived jammed so close together?

*God, I don't like Shady Dell. I don't want to live there. I want to be right here in my own bed, Mom sitting on the edge, holding my hands as we whisper our evening prayers together. Is Shady Dell really what you want for me? I miss her so much! I can't . . . I just . . .*

For the rest of the night, I lay awake in my dusky room, hot tears staining my pillow, wondering how it was possible to be so surrounded by people and yet feel so profoundly alone.

# 12. CHURCH

"Church with your friends?" Ray turned from the coffeepot to glare at me. Still dressed in my pajamas, I fixed my eyes on my cereal bowl, pushing the mush around and around with my spoon. "You are confined," he said hoarsely. "That is non-negotiable."

"I just thought—"

"Yeah, that's the problem." He crossed to the table and set his mug down, hard. Coffee splashed his bare hand and he cursed, his volume ramping up with the pain. "Women don't think. You weren't made to *think*. You were—"

"So that's why you sent me to school, so I wouldn't think?" I knew I was pushing it, but anger drove me. "Sounds like a waste of my time and your oh-so-important tax dollars."

"Women were made to obey. Do you understand me?" He sat, sucking on the burn. "We're going to St. Mike's this morning. Period."

*Some things never change.* "Funny how you didn't want to go to St. Mike's until Mom started insisting on it." That wasn't entirely true, but I went on, anyway, my spoon clattering into the bowl. "Is that why you killed Mom? Because she wouldn't *obey?*"

Ray shot to his feet and lurched across the table, his face inches from mine. The table skidded under his weight, pinning me to my chair. "Don't you ever—*ever*—speak about her!" His spittle flecked my face, his eyes devoid of reason. "Do you hear me? Don't you ever say her name!" Kicking over his chair, he yanked his coat off its peg and strode from the apartment.

And I sat, shaking, not because of what had just happened, but of his threat to take me to St. Mike's. I'd heard the stories—how girls and women were taken to a room in the basement if they were deemed "uncooperative" or "rebellious." No one talked about what was done there. Men scoffed at the tales, claiming they would never do such a thing to their wives or children, and I'd believed them.

Now I wasn't so sure.

I didn't wait for Ray's return. Running to my bedroom, I tossed clothes and makeup in my tote and tied on my coat. As I hurried past Ray's room, my eyes glanced in, and I stopped dead in the hallway. Slowly, I crept to the door, my eyes on the bed.

The covers were thrown back, as always, with complete disregard for neatness. Ray's pillow bore a yellowing circle in the center. But it was the pillow next to his—Mom's—that held my attention. Obviously the bedding hadn't been washed since she died, and a rust-colored splotch still marred the pillowcase. The room reeked of body odor, copper and *Rose Is*, the perfume Ray had gifted Mom as a wedding present.

"Dear Jesus," I whispered. *How could he bring that other woman . . .* Fighting tears and an overwhelming revulsion, I quit the apartment and bolted for the bus to Shady Dell.

~

Bree and I stood in the kitchen, elbow to elbow, washing and drying breakfast dishes. When I'd arrived, everyone was still eating, so I'd ducked into the back bedroom to change before the guys could see me in my pajamas. (I was more than lucky to have missed getting caught by the Guards.) Now the twins bantered as they bounced around the room getting ready for church, drowning out Mags's soft singing in the bathroom. As soon as breakfast was over, Kilte and Walker had headed out into the cold.

"I've heard that, too." Bree turned away to set a clean cereal bowl in its spot in the cupboard. "It's a new form of discipline. Of course, there's never any proof, but . . ."

I swirled soapy water in the oatmeal pan. "I don't know if I want to find out the hard way, just to know for sure."

"But then you would have a testimony. You could go to court." She plunged the pan into the rinse water while I started scrubbing flatware. After a moment of silence, she said, "So . . . what have you heard?"

"I don't want to talk about it." And was it really illegal, what happened to women in those basement rooms? And if it was, what would happen to me if I actually pursued a lawsuit against my prinister? *No. No way.*

DNN nattered, background noise. St. Peter Anderson, the latest mass shooter, murdered 315 people at a Miners game and somehow got away scot-free. Unlike most shooters, he hadn't killed himself or waited for the Guards to take him out. Commentators were saying he'd escaped to a private place to kill himself. I disagreed. Why work so hard to give yourself an out, just to gladhand with the demons later? It didn't make sense.

I dropped my handful of flatware noisily into rinse water, trying to drown out the broadcast so Bree wouldn't hear.

"Go on." She jerked her head at the loft. "I'll finish up here."

I smiled my thanks. On my way to the bathroom, I hit the mute button.

Mags had described their church as a quiet, unsanctioned gathering. She'd also been forthright about the home-based Bible studies. "We don't use a study guide," she said. "We just read the Bible and discuss it." That gave me the reassurance I needed to feel comfortable attending.

I dug through my tote for Mom's coral bead necklace and looped it over my head twice. The coral made a nice accent to my church outfit: a full-length navy skirt with pink and coral swirls (with a pair of jeans underneath for warmth), and navy blouse with coral jacket. I realized my palms were sweating. Nerves.

If you wanted to be a part of Christian States society—get a job, make friends, attend school, start a business—you had to be a member of an RD-Sanctioned Church. When I applied at On the Mark, Mary-Sarah asked about my church membership and followed up with a phone call to the church office to verify my attendance. A few days later, Prinister Severs had filed an approval for me to work.

Mom and I had been a part of St. Michael's Community Church (everyone called it St. Mike's) for as long as I could remember, attending services and classes, going to confession once a week. Ray attended too, but for many years he came infrequently and under duress. He had an easy excuse because his job kept him on call over the weekend. But his lack of attendance was noticed by Prinister Severs and church leadership, and Mom and I never quite fit in because of it. "And where is Raymond today, Mrs. Esselin?" was the morning's first hymn.

Crossing the living room with makeup bag in hand, I sighed. I hoped Mags had finished in the bathroom.

The door was closed. As I raised my hand to tap it, I heard a male voice. I paused. *Walker? Walker is in with Mags?*

"It's dangerous, Mom!" he was saying, his voice earnest and low. "You just don't know—"

"But I do, dear boy." Her tone was normal, gentle.

"She could be a plant! She could turn the whole church over to the RD!"

*He's talking about me.* Astonishment and anger prickled my scalp. *I thought he trusted me now that I'm staying?*

"She isn't and she won't," Mags said, her tone confident. "Otherwise, I never would have taken her in. And our conversation is no longer private."

The door jerked open. Walker filled the doorway, frowning down at me, and I glared right back. *You wanted to meet my eyes? Well, here you go.* He muttered an oath, pushed by and slammed out the front door.

"Of course you may use the restroom, Meryn, dear." Mags had finished her preparations, her hair styled and held in a loose net that matched her natural gray. "It *is* the only place in the house to have a private conversation. Now, don't fret," she continued, stepping close to me and dropping her voice. "Walker worries about me, but sometimes he worries a bit too much. Sons, you know!" She laughed and slipped by me, squeezing my forearm.

I stepped into the bathroom, smiling, and started on my makeup. As I drew a line around my lips, someone pounded on the closed door. My hand jerked, arcing red lip liner across my cheek. Fuming, I slid the door open. Ellie giggled when she saw my face. "Are you done, Meryn? I gotta pee."

"I am now." I reached back for my makeup bag and marched to the living room. Having to finish the job in my tiny compact mirror just made me madder.

~

To my surprise, Bree said, "This is it!"

The truck had stopped in an abandoned industrial park. The uneven concrete parking lot looked long unused, dead weeds poking up through wide cracks, oddments of rusting machinery occupying parking spots. A light snowfall covered random shapes that on closer inspection turned out to be the husks of old cars and cast-off refrigerators. Nearby, something metal clanged noisily in the cold wind. But two pickup trucks and a small, rusting school bus were parked close to the warehouse door, and someone had swept the sidewalk clean of snow.

The dozen people we'd picked up on the way sat crowded in with me and Bree, Walker, and the twins. The group turned out to be a blessing; only my face and my legs felt the cold. To my relief, Walker insisted Mags ride in the cab with Kilte, who was driving, and two other women carrying babies. Two young men—we hadn't bothered with introductions in the cold—jumped out of our truck bed and lowered the tailgate for the rest of us.

Our group hurried through the door. Cracked concrete riven with white salts covered the floor beneath my feet. Two stories overhead, a maze of ancient girders, piping and metal trusses supported rusted metal panels that somehow kept the snow out. The trusses held a revolting mix of old cobwebs and decades of oily dust that seemed poised to drop on the crowd below. I hoped nothing would shake the building during service. To my right, the morning light struggled through a bank of cracked and grimy windows sealed shut by years of rust and layers of chipping paint. Six battery-powered lanterns sat on shelves or dangled from hooks in random places around the room. Their light was insufficient, but better than nothing—then I realized the dimness was deliberate.

An eclectic mix of chairs and benches marched in neat rows through the center of the space. At the far end behind an old wood lectern, a walled-off area with wide windows might have once served as an office. I wondered what the warehouse had been used for originally. I wondered where people went for confession in this makeshift church. The only heat came from the three-dozen people gathered in groups, chatting, holding steaming cups of ersatz coffee or tea.

A woman perhaps Mags's age glided toward us, radiating warmth and joy. "Welcome!" she called, her voice clear and melodic. Bundled in a blue MT and a thick blue parka, she crossed her hands—clad in fingerless black gloves—over her chest. White curls peeked out from her raspberry-red beret. "Welcome to Our Lord's Church! I am Clare Nelson Dixon."

"I am Meryn Flint," I said, bowing. "Meeting you brings joy to the coldest morning, right honorable Goodwife Dixon."

"It makes our joy complete that one of such stature in the eyes of God has graced us with her presence on this Lord's Day," she said, formal in turn. Her eyes were a serene brown, and her countenance so peaceful it seemed she'd stepped out of the pages of the Bible. *Yeah, she has no problems,* I thought. She gestured across the room to a white-haired man who was greeting Walker and Kilte with hugs. "That is my husband, St. Peter Dixon. Our son, Hamilton, is here somewhere."

"Right here, Mom." A man appeared next to me bearing a steaming cup. "It's just toast coffee," he said with a smile of apology, "but it's hot."

"It's wonderful." I was careful as I took the cup with a gloved hand. The warmth oozing through the paper thawed my frozen fingers, and my other hand curled greedily around it. "Thank you. I'm Meryn Flint."

"Hamilton Dixon," the man said. "Call me Hamil. It's a pleasure."

"Mags!" Clare gathered Mags into a hug. "You brought us a guest! God bless you!"

"As many and as often as I can, Clare!" Mags responded. "Happy Lord's Day!"

Others crowded around, greeting us. Chatting, Mags and Clare crossed to the lectern, as Bree engaged Hamil in conversation.

Exhaling, I could see my breath. But I appreciated the wisdom of not generating heat. The RD religiously hunted unsanctioned churches, and the penalties were severe. *So what am I doing here? I must be nuts.*

The building had just one entrance that I could see: if the RD raided the service, they'd come in through that door, cutting off our escape route. *Isn't there another exit somewhere?* I wondered if any of the good people drinking coffee were RD plants. My pulse hammered in my throat and my eyes darted around the warehouse. *Maybe we could break windows to get out. Would we be arrested? Or would they just execute us on the spot?* I'd heard of such things happening, horrific rumors from school friends. I could imagine the neat rows of chairs tumbled in disarray as people tried to flee, blood staining the salted floor, Clare's cap—

Bree touched my arm, and I turned to her, grateful for the interruption. "The girls and I will go save us some seats. You come when you're ready, Meryn." She took a cup of coffee, smiled her thanks at Hamil, and moved away.

"Is this your first time here?" Hamil's eyes were as serene as Clare's.

"It is." I hoped my smile didn't seem forced. "Your mom is lovely."

"That she is," he agreed. His curly dark hair was graying at the temples, and he wore a pair of round-framed glasses, an oddity in our GM society. "She's always delighted to see new faces."

"Do you get a lot of new people?" I sipped my coffee, trying to calm my nervous stomach.

Hamil shook his head. "But we are always grateful to God when we do," he said, his smile crinkling his eyes. "We might do things a bit differently from what you're used to, but we all worship the same God."

"Different is good." I tried not to let my tone go caustic. Other parishioners glanced at me, curious, but no one was overtly hostile. Walker and Kilte stood with a group of young men across the room. Walker glanced in my direction; when our eyes met, his darted away.

My anger at him melted. *He's worried about the same thing I am: a raid. His whole family is here—his whole world. He doesn't want to lose that.* I felt tears rising. *But I no longer have a family. Different is not always good, I guess.*

Hamil was looking toward the lectern. Clare nodded. She touched the arm of the woman next to her and gestured toward the chairs, and Hamil turned to me. "We're about to start, but later I'll be happy to introduce you around." If he noticed my moist eyes, he didn't let on. "You'll be sitting with Mags?"

I nodded, trying to find her in the crowd, as Clare moved behind the lectern, shuffling notes. I blinked. "Your mom is the *prinister?*" I said, louder than I intended. Several people nearby chuckled.

I flushed, but Hamil just smiled. "The pastor. She is. Ah yes, Mags is in the third row, right in front of Mom."

Following his gaze, I found Mags's silver curls and thanked him. People moved about, finding seats, conversations thinning.

"This way, Mer." Bree appeared at my side. We moved to where Mags and the twins were seated, and settled into two empty chairs next to Kilte. Mine was cold and a bit rickety, but it held my weight. Walker strode forward and dropped into a chair on the other side of Mags.

*How is this possible? A woman prini—pastor, I mean?* If there was a raid, Clare would be the first person executed, and my blood ran cold. *Stop it, Meryn. They do this every Sunday. The odds are good it's safe.*

*Until that one Sunday it isn't. We will be executed for sitting under a woman's teaching, every one of us. I've heard rumors. They won't even have to clear out the bodies, this place is so remote. Just shut the door and walk away, and no one will ever—*

Clare raised her arms. "Welcome, everyone! Welcome to Our Lord's Church. Happy Sunday!"

People called out greetings, then quieted respectfully. I looked around at the shining faces, wondering if anyone else felt afraid here. Did they just pretend not to feel it, or was I the only faithless Christian in the place?

"Let us begin with a song." Clare blew into a pitch tuner and led us in "Amazing Grace" in a rich, sweet soprano.

Something surged in me at the familiar hymn—my fear that someone might hear us dissolved into an unexpected comfort. Joy swelled and rose through the congregation, driving away my dark thoughts.

Singing gave me a pang of nostalgia for the praise team at St. Mike's—but only for a moment.

# 13. DOUBT

In grammar school, every student sang in the school choir, even the ones who couldn't carry a tune with a grav-lift. My teachers told me I had a pretty little voice and should use it for God's glory, so when I was eight I joined the Children's Choir at St. Mike's. We sang services only on Christmas and Easter, but I loved being involved, feeling like a part of the church, like I was doing something special for God.

At sixteen (the minimum age), I tried out for the praise team. They needed a good alto and by then I'd been singing harmonies for three years. The worship leader, Saint Bartholomew, accepted me on the spot. The other vocalists—a soprano and tenor, both in their twenties—were less enthusiastic.

"Why'd you saddle us with that kid?" I overheard John, the tenor, ask Bart one night after practice.

"She's good," Bart said mildly, settling his guitar in its case. "Her voice blends well with us."

"Jobette Gunderson is—"

"Jobette's a lovely girl," Bart broke in, "but she sings flat and loud, John. She pulled the whole team off pitch at tryouts because she doesn't know how to back off and blend. Meryn does. And did you notice, I almost never have to hammer out the part for her? And how fast she picks up lyrics? Give the girl a chance, willya?"

John grumbled, and I slipped away before they caught me listening.

Despite that, I loved the praise team. Bart was a stickler for technical perfection, and I worked hard to make sure my standards matched his. I was careful to be on time and have my harmonies down cold. I watched the guys run sound, and I even prepped the audience Dynamic Display on occasion if our AV guy was out. The whole process fascinated me.

But for all our technical skill and hard work, after a few months I started to feel as if something was missing.

I brought it up to Mom one night after rehearsal. The hour was late, the sun long gone. Ray wasn't home; I suspected he was at the local speakeasy, but by then I'd learned not to ask.

"But you've been so happy on the praise team," Mom said, bringing two cups of steaming mint tea to the table and setting them in saucers. Mom grew the mint on the kitchen windowsill and dried it for later use.

She fetched the carafe of soymilk and added a splash to my tea. I swirled the milky clouds with a spoon. "I feel awful, bringing this up. Being on the team is such a blessing! Other girls would give their left arm . . . and here I am, complaining . . ." I trailed off, chewing my lip.

"Is it Bart?" Mom poured a generous dash of soymilk in her own cup and settled into her chair.

I shook my head. "Bart's great. DeeDee is nice now and John's backed off. It's more . . ." I groped for words. "We're so focused on technical perfection, sometimes I feel like we're almost . . . ignoring God. It's just . . . What are we doing, exactly?"

"You are leading worship," Mom said gently. "You are leading people into the presence of God."

My spoon clattered into its saucer. "Are we?" I asked, quiet but blunt. "How dare we think that we, in our paltry humanity, can do such a thing? Isn't that arrogance? And are we 'leading people into the presence of God,' or are we just feeding our own egos?"

Mom sipped her tea, placid. "Is that why you're up there, Meryn? To feed your ego?"

"No! —maybe! I don't know!" Heat rushed into my face. I launched myself from my chair to pace the kitchen.

"Okay." Mom placed her cup in its saucer. "Tell me why you joined the praise team."

I flipped my hair over my shoulder, annoyed—not at Mom, but at something I couldn't identify. "I love singing to God."

"And is that the only time you sing to God? Sunday morning?"

"No, of course not. I sing to Him during rehearsals, too, and—"

Mom smiled. "And in the shower, and in the car with the radio on, and when we dance around the living room together . . ."

I chuckled, leaning against the counter, but I couldn't keep smiling. "I enjoy singing. But sometimes I wonder if I enjoy it too much. I like my voice."

Mom's eyes widened. "Why shouldn't you? Do you think God wants you to hate your voice, to hate your service to Him? Must everything we do for God be clothed in wailing and sackcloth?"

"Well, Prinister Severs says—"

"Prinister Severs," Mom interrupted, loud and harsh. My eyebrows crawled up to my hairline.

She bit her lip, her eyes darting around the room before meeting mine, and her voice dropped to a whisper. "I've been wanting to talk about this, and of course I can't bring it up in front of Ray. Sweetheart, do you remember Prinister Severs's sermon last Sunday?"

I blinked, moving closer so I could hear. "Um, it was about obedience. Obedience to God."

"And the church. How we must strive to live our lives in a manner the Sanctioned Church would approve, from the minute we rise in the morning until our eyes close at night." She paused. "It's been the focus of his whole series, these past months. That the Sanctioned Church has a right to observe and correct the behavior of Her parishioners."

"Yeah. He was speaking metaphorically," I said.

"I'm not sure he was."

My mouth dropped open. "You think Prinister Severs is proposing that the church, what—*spy* on us?" I laughed; I couldn't help it.

Mom said nothing. Sighing, she looked at her hands in her lap, and my smile melted away.

"You're not kidding. Why would God want that kind of control?"

"Please keep your voice down, darling." Mom shook her head, her normal gentle expression replaced by an odd intensity. "Not God. *The church.*"

I sank into my chair. "But the church is the bride of Christ, God's body on earth," I whispered.

"It is." Mom nodded, stirred her tea. "But the church is like any other group of people. She is flawed because people are flawed, faith and good intentions notwithstanding." She released the spoon, her eyes on mine. "We must never forget that."

Wheels were turning in my head. "Well, what does the church gain—or Prinister Severs, what does he gain—out of controlling us?"

Mom tried to smile. "Prinister Severs believes that he has an obligation to present his church to God 'without spot or blemish.'"

She shrugged, but I could tell she was choosing her words with care. "Sometimes I wonder if he gets a bit . . . carried away. And because the church is tied to our governing bodies, the church—and our attendance there—is the controlling authority in every area of our lives."

"Well, yeah." I gave a little laugh. "We learned that in Godly Society & Governance class."

The lights flickered and went out, and the automatic night light in the kitchen blinked on. Sighing, Mom rose and went to the sideboard, struck a match, and lit the two oil lamps there.

When I was little, Mom used to say that magical things happened in the dark. It was a time when God could sneak in and heal a sick child, or send an angel to help someone in trouble, or leave an unexpected 20CD note where just the right person would find it. It's the main reason I was never afraid of the dark. But she hadn't said that in a long time. I wondered if she still believed it.

As she carried a lamp to the table, her face wrinkled. "Some people believe the Sanctioned Church is reaching into areas of our lives where She has no business going."

That stunned me to silence. Mom had just challenged everything I'd been taught—in church and school. I knew enough about civics to know if anyone outside of our apartment heard her, she'd go to prison. A frisson of cold ran up my spine, and I picked up my teacup and drank, sorting my thoughts.

"Mom," I began in a whisper, and then the words revised themselves in my head. "Prinister Severs says every aspect of our lives is spiritual. Our work, our play, school, home life—they all are, or should be, governed by God."

"By God." Mom folded her hands in her lap. "Not the church."

I blew out a breath. "Is that why Ray doesn't go?" I knew how Ray felt about being controlled—he made his feelings clear at the dinner table whenever he'd had a run-in with his boss.

"That, among other reasons. But his choice in that regard may be ending." She sipped her tea, her eyes dark and troubled over the cup's rim.

"What do you mean?"

She was silent for a moment as if debating whether to answer, lamplight casting odd shadows across her face. When she did, her voice was so low, I had to strain to hear. "Priscilla Conyers told me that she and Dave received a summons to appear before Prinister Severs and the Board."

"Oh, no." Like Ray, Dave Conyers wasn't at church much.

Mom set her cup in its saucer. "Prinister Severs told them—not in so many words—that if Dave wants to keep his job, he has to improve his church attendance. Go to confession. Join the men's group. Be involved."

We looked at each other with grim expressions.

"Ray's time is running out?" My eyes were bleak.

She nodded. "They've given him a break because he's frequently on call with the city. But I'm afraid he's taxed their patience."

Anger launched me to my feet. "Mom, that isn't right!" I paced the kitchen, conflicted, my motion making the lamplight flicker. I'd always wanted Ray to come to church with us, but only if he had the desire to. "Isn't it like that verse in Corinthians that tells us to give cheerfully, not under compulsion? Shouldn't that be true about to going to church, too?"

Mom pressed her lips together. "I think so. And I'm glad you see it. But I think you can also see, darling, why it's so important for you to stay on the praise team right now."

"So Ray can keep his job?" I swallowed hard, keeping sarcasm out of my voice. "If we toe the line, that gives him a little slack? Is that why you volunteer at the church bookstore?"

Mom shook her head. "I enjoy it, sweetie. Just like you enjoy the praise team. And if it reaps us other benefits, well"—she shrugged—"I don't think that upsets God." She smiled, but her smile faded when she saw my expression.

"I do," I said, and my voice was hard.

Ray cornered me two days later after school. "All right," he said the moment my car door closed. "What did you say to your mother?"

"What?" He'd caught me off guard.

"You know what I'm talking about." He was impatient, pulling into traffic. "She thinks you're going to turn us over to the RD."

"What?"

"Right. So what did you say?"

"I—" I was sorting through my memory of our conversation, trying to figure out what could have given Mom such a crazy idea.

"Well, what were you talking about?" Ray prompted.

"My ambivalence about the praise team, and—" I gulped. We'd been discussing Ray. I shook my head.

"Well, something you said got her scared." Ray turned onto Millhouse Road and glanced at me, curious. "What's wrong with the praise team?"

I sighed inwardly. "Nothing's wrong, exactly. I'm just . . . questioning my motives, I guess."

Ray's eyebrows shot up. "Good." Rain spattered the windshield, and he turned on the wipers.

I looked at him, eyes wide. "Good?"

"Yeah. When people get complacent in their service for God, they get sanctimonious." He glanced in the rearview mirror and changed lanes. "You're better than that."

My mouth dropped open.

Ray glanced over at my expression and chuckled. "Didn't expect that out of your ol' apostate dad, didja?"

I shook my head, and he laughed.

"Well, I wasn't always." He sobered. "I used to be a regular little choirboy."

"You?" Amazement colored my tone, and he grinned at my reaction.

"You are looking at the record holder for the most Bible verses memorized in the fifth-grade boys' Bible study at St. Matthew's Church," he said with mock pride.

I laughed, and he laughed with me. "So . . . what happened?" I kept my tone gentle, not leaking any of my avid curiosity. "Why'd you leave?"

"Ahhh." He looked away, out the driver's side window. "I saw the church ruin too many good people, me included."

I stayed silent, not wanting to interrupt Ray in this unusual confessional mood, the only sound the *thunk-squee* of the windshield wipers.

"Too many guys started buying the religious BS about being in charge. Too many church leaders believing their own press releases." He stopped.

"What do you mean?"

A hovercar flew above us in our lane and pulled ahead, its wash spattering our car. Ray gestured out the windshield. "See that guy?"

"Yeah," I said, my laugh a bit puzzled. We saw hovercars all the time.

"That's how the church leaders are. They're lofty, pursuing lofty ideals, and they forget about those of us down here on the ground, having to slog through the crap." Ray slowed for a car braking in front of us, and the hovercar left us behind. "They're happy to condemn us when we sin, but when the shoe's on the other foot they start yelling about how they're being persecuted, and 'Oooh, don't touch the Lord's anointed!'" Ray sounded bitter. "Even when the Lord's anointed is touching little boys."

I rolled my eyes at the window. "Come on—does that really happen?"

Ray's laugh was cynical. "Sure, it happens. But you'll never hear about it, except in whispers. You sure won't hear it on DNN. And gossip is a sin, you know," his voice taking on the cadence of a prinister, "gossip is an affront to Almighty Gawwd, and will land you in the pit—the very pit of hell!"

He glanced at me. I was stifling laughter because he sounded just like Prinister Severs when he was on a roll, but I'd been taught never to mock a man of God. Then Ray chuckled, and we both started laughing.

Ray pulled up to a stoplight and turned to face me. My laughter died when I saw the pain in his eyes. "They wanna pull me back into that den of snakes, Mer, and I won't have it. I won't go to church every Sunday just to satisfy their ideal of what a 'godly family' looks like, or improve my social standing, or even keep my job. I won't do it."

A bit of fear shot through me. *Not even for his job? For us?* Somebody behind us honked; the light had changed. Ray waved a hasty apology and hit the gas.

"When we get home," he said, "Let's talk to your mom and see what bat's flying around in her belfry."

I seized on the distraction. "Ray, I would never turn Mom over to the RD, even if I could think of a good reason, which I can't."

"I know, Mer," he said. "I can't imagine it was anything you said."

A thought struck me. "It isn't! It was something *she* said!"

When we walked in, Mom was vacuuming the living room. She smiled a welcome, but her smile faded when Ray shut the machine off.

"Let's talk," Ray said with no preamble. Perplexed, she nodded and settled on the sofa. I joined her. Ray lowered himself into his chair, wincing. "Rose, let's discuss what's troubling you."

Her cheeks bloomed a delicate pink, and she bit her lip and turned to me. "It isn't you, Meryn."

"Well, that's a relief." I gave a little laugh; my stomach unknotted.

Mom sighed. "It's just that during our talk the other night—"

A chime interrupted us.

"Oh, for Pete's sake!" Ray swore as the wall screen chimed again and brightened. The RD logo came up, swooping across the screen and into the DNN newsroom where Chastity Chisholm, one of DNN's "Faces to the World," stared gravely into the camera. She delivered the morning news—always featuring prinisters and RD thought leaders—and hosted a morning talk show, *Chatting with Chastity.*

Even in a world of GM perfection, Chastity was a standout. Not a hair out of place. Eyebrows groomed to the ideal arch. Nose fit for a film star. Mouth like a bow with perfect symmetry. If you cut a photo of her face in half lengthwise and held it up sideways to a mirror, her perfect face stared back at you. She was so flawless she didn't seem human. I often wondered if she'd had surgery to achieve that symmetry, or if it had been done *in utero*. My eyes were slightly uneven, my nose a bit crooked, and I thanked God for the imperfection every time I saw Chastity onscreen.

I wouldn't have minded her so much, but the syrupy tone she used to deliver every pronouncement made my skin crawl. She sounded like a grandmother speaking to six-year-olds.

"Well, here's our token female." Ray's expression was surly. "Lousy timing, Chatty!"

Chastity gave us her on-air smile. "Hello and God bless, fellow citizens of the Kingdom! We have some important information to share with you today!

"Effective immediately, Popresident Humboldt's Office of Morality Maintenance has made an urgent change to the women's public dress code."

"Office of Morality Maintenance?" I frowned. "I don't remember studying that one."

"It's new," Mom said. "Popresident Humboldt has been working hard to return our society to the purity our founders intended."

She sounded serious and I opened my mouth, but the screen cut to Humboldt, standing at a lectern that bore the popresidential seal. His face was weighted with solemn gravity, his tone ponderous. "For decades, our Reformation Directorate has been criminally remiss. We have abdicated our most sacred duty: Shepherding the lives of American citizens, to keep their feet on the path to life everlasting. God has called me to this divine position as your popresident to renew that shepherding, to reject the rampant liberalism of the last two administrations and return us to the basics our Founders enshrined in the Holy Constitution.

"The Reformers were wise. They knew that for men to effectively accomplish the tasks that God has set for them, they must not be distracted by the presence of a woman's figure. So they shrouded their women in mystery, which is as it should be. Allowing women to dress in an alluring manner smacks of hedonism and defiles the marriage bed by encouraging lust of thy neighbor's wife. It also causes envy and strife among our women as they covet each other's clothing. That is not what God wants for our families. No, married women must attire themselves with modesty and honor, as befits daughters of the King.

"Girls, even though you are exempt from this rule, that does not mean you have license to be seductive temptresses. If you cannot comport yourselves with appropriate modesty, you too will be covered."

I bit my lip as the screen switched back to Chastity.

"Popresident Humboldt's solution is brilliant in its simplicity," she said breathlessly, her hands describing impressive arcs. "All married ladies will now wear a standardized garment over their street clothes. Implementing this regulation should cut down on the many unintended code violations."

"A what?" I said. Mom shushed me; Chastity was still speaking.

"Many women found the dress code to be *sooo* confusing," she went on, still in that honey-sweet tone. "And too many of our moms were being detained at Guard stations, instead of getting home to their husbands and children where they belong. This innovative garment will solve the problem. This"—and the display cut away from Chastity to show a plump, smiling woman modeling the dress—"is what we call the 'married topper,' or 'MT,' for short."

"It's a sack!" Ray hooted.

I agreed. The dress—if one could call it that—buttoned up to a high, faux-lace collar under the chin. The long sleeves ended in elastic gathers at the wrists, and the bottom hem brushed the tops of the model's shoes. The dress had no waist, nor even darts to suggest a female shape. Its sole redeeming factor was its color—a pretty sky blue.

"This practical and charming topper," Chastity said, "will make it possible for you to be in compliance with modesty laws, no matter what you may be wearing when you leave the house." The camera shifted to a view of a large vending station, where smiling, modestly attired women presented their wrists to the sensors. The machine disgorged dress after dress in varying colors, each folded in a plastic package.

"You can purchase the garment at any subway or bus station kiosk. And the MT is effortless to use." A smiling woman tore open the package and, letting the plastic drop to the floor, shook out the dress and tossed it over her head. "Just button up"—the smiling woman did—"and you're ready to go! Whether you're off to meet the girls"—and the picture shifted to a shot of several young women wearing blue MTs, talking animatedly and bouncing babies on their laps—"or stepping out for a night on the town"—a woman in a merlot-red MT and wearing a large diamond wedding ring beamed as her tuxedo-clad husband escorted her into a swanky restaurant—"the MT will get you there in style and without any bothersome delays."

The camera shifted back to a smiling Chastity. "Remember, ladies, it's the new must-have for this season's wardrobe. And it's the law. So don't be caught without it!" She waggled a finger at the camera.

"And make sure you catch the DNN evening report tonight at five-thirty. We'll give you all the deets then. For your hubby, Knit Tucker will report on Popresident Humboldt's proposed tax reform legislation. As always, remember to pray for your Reformation Directorate: *Guided by the Hand of God*. Thank you for watching, and God bless. Ta!" The screen faded to black.

Ray roared with laughter, pounding his chair arm. "What a piece of junk!"

"It isn't funny." Mom didn't smile. She and I exchanged a look; her face was worried.

He wound down to a chuckle. "I know. It's just so stupid, it's hilarious. What woman would want to go 'out on the town' in that getup? And now we have to buy those things . . . like we can afford one more regulation . . ."

"Well, at least you don't have to buy one for me," I said.

Mom nodded and motioned to the darkened screen. "Chastity said it's for married women. Single women are exempt, I guess because you're still looking for husbands."

"You still have to obey the dress code," Ray said. "But yeah, you can flaunt it until I walk you down the aisle. Then you gotta cover it up."

"Well, of course I'll obey the dress code," I said, irritation creeping into my voice. "This whole thing is ridiculous! Who wants to violate the dress code and get detained by the Guards?"

"Some women like the attention," Ray said.

Mom and I both looked at him and I rolled my eyes. "Ray," Mom began, her eyes closing in what I knew was a silent prayer for patience.

"I'm not saying you do!" he protested. "But some women, you know, they're not getting it good at home, so maybe the attentions of a Guard are preferable to not getting it at all. We hear about them on the news, like that chick in Belmont who said she got raped, and it turned out it wasn't rape at all, and she ended up going to jail for bearing false witness?"

My memory flashed on Debbie Delaney, raped on the school bus when she was twelve, and I shook my head in disgust. "Just because she couldn't prove it doesn't mean she wasn't raped, Ray." I gave him a trenchant look, remembering the time he'd tried to force his attentions on me, but he turned away. My mouth thinned. "I have schoolwork."

Rising, I grabbed my book bag. After a few minutes I had to close my bedroom door to shut out the sound of Mom and Ray arguing.

We didn't find out until later that the MTs were color-coded by caste and wearing the wrong color could land a woman in jail. Mom was careful to purchase several MTs in light and dark shades of blue, appropriate for the Worker Caste. The Indigent Caste were required to wear brown or tan; Management Caste wore shades of green; Governance Caste were clothed in pink/red/orange, and the Exalted Caste in purple or lavender—although I never saw a woman in a lavender MT, and I didn't know anyone who did.

Shortly after the RD mandated the use of MTs for married women, they created Caste Rings for us girls. Sometime later, the requirement to wear Caste Rings was expanded to include everyone.

We never finished our conversation with Mom.

# 14. SURPRISE

I pulled my attention back to the service as Pastor Clare began her sermon. The cold crept up my legs and numbed my fingers, but I hardly noticed. An excellent teacher, Clare kept her exegesis firmly anchored in the Bible, but unlike Prinister Severs, she didn't use it in a coercive way. I wasn't the only one enthralled—Lisha was jotting notes in her tab.

"So you see," Clare said, "If you belong to Christ, no one can snatch you out of his hand. No matter what you have done in your life. No matter how badly you think you have sinned, or fallen from what others may consider the true path, He still walks beside you. He will never forsake you. You are His, and you are safe."

The words touched a core of fear inside me, warming and melting it. *So I'm not going to hell for leaving home? For violating my Family Duty?*

"All things work together for good," she said. Her eyes rested on me. "*All* things. Not just the stuff we think of as holy, not just the touching moments in prayer, not just our Bible reading or our obedience—all things. Our lack of ability. Our unfaithfulness. Our homelessness. Our poverty. God uses it all." A pause, and she smiled around. "Let's pray."

We bowed our heads. She named those who had needs due to illness or financial difficulty, and then she went silent, allowing the congregation time to pray. My eyebrows lifted in surprise; Prinister Severs had never done such a thing at St. Mike's. I looked at the others nearby without moving my head, then closed my eyes.

*God, please keep me out of the discipline rooms at St. Mike's. Please protect me. If they're even real. I pray they're not real, God. Please.*

When we stood to sing the closing song, I glanced at my phone, startled—the service had gone on far longer than I'd thought.

People rose, gathering their things and talking. Hamil passed out cups of still-warm coffee to those who approached the beverage table.

"Ellie, Lisha, come on!" A little girl with red hair stopped next to us, and the twins squeezed past me. The three ran off, giggling.

Bree turned to me, her eyes sparkling. "Did you like the service?"

I grinned. "I did! Mom'll love—" I stopped. Tears welled, unbidden. Bree's smile dimmed, and she bit her lip.

"I'm sure she would have." Mags touched my arm with quiet sympathy. "The Master leads us according to His grace. We have but to listen."

I forced tears away and seized on what she had said. "But how do we hear God?"

Her gaze was distant, her smile full of mystery. "Get to know Him. Spend time with Him, just as you would with a friend. Prayer and meditation, and baptism of the Holy Spirit."

"The Holy Spirit? I thought that was just for the early church," I said.

Mags nodded. "Many people believe that." The girls pelted by, and she called, "Ellie! Lisha! Come help now!"

She followed the girls past parishioners who still lingered, chatting, some busy folding chairs and stacking them against a wall.

I turned to Bree. "I don't see a confessional here."

"We don't do confessions much." She said it casually, and I blinked. "But—"

"The Sanctioned Churches do, but Pastor Clare considers it a form of control," Bree said, and my mind immediately veered to my conversation with Mom. "She says she's always happy to hear confessions one on one, if someone feels led, but it isn't church policy."

Walker and Kilte began herding people toward the door. Mags, Pastor Clare and the twins stood huddled, talking to the two mothers we'd brought in the cab. Mags cooed at one of the babies while Lisha handed a small bag to each mother. "It's bottom balm for diaper rash," the girl said, her smile wide and proud. "Mom taught us how to make it."

The woman thanked her, and her eyes went wide as Pastor Clare gave each woman a large shopping bag. "Rags and pins for diapers, Celestia," she said.

"Oh, thank you!" Celestia said, her relief transparent.

I turned to Bree, my voice low. "So the church helps . . ."

"Every Sunday." She nodded. "Tuesday mornings, Clare sends out a group text of needs. That gives the church time to collect food or diapers or bus passes or whatever by Sunday morning."

I stayed silent, not wanting to mention I'd never seen anything like this at St. Mike's. Only Mom, and her work helping the widowers. I made a mental note to look up more Bible verses about poverty when I got back to Mags's.

~

The trip home was frigid. I dreaded every stop; even though my back pressed against the cab, every time a passenger got out, that was one less person to add warmth. The minute space opened up in the cab, Kilte bundled the twins in next to Mags. He and I did our best to shelter Bree. By the time we got home, I was stiff with cold and shaking. Kilte had to help me down from the tailgate. "Let's get you warmed up inside," he said, low, his arm around my back.

Discomfort made me shudder. "Thank you," I said politely. He winked and turned away, and I bit my lip. *Does he do this with all of his female friends? Or just me?* My eyes darted to Bree, who was helping the girls out of the cab. She hadn't seen the exchange. *Should I ask her?*

"Come inside, everyone!" Mags called. "I have ginger-squash soup on the back burner!"

We piled into the warm tiny house, where Walker stirred up the fire and added a stick of fuel.

"Kilte, would you set the table, please?"

The young man grabbed spoons, napkins and mugs without complaint. Walker folded out the table and the twins hung everyone's coats where they belonged, putting Walker's and Kilte's on hooks by the door. Every day I saw more clearly that the tiny house worked on an organized system: everyone pitching in, everything in its place.

"Meryn, would you pull out chairs, please?" she asked, and I smiled and complied. The "chairs" were folding stools that tucked away behind the futon. I'd straightened up and was stepping back from setting a stool in place when I felt a warm hand on my shoulder blade. I turned in surprise, expecting Bree or Mags.

Walker was setting a carafe of oil on the table for the bread. I'd almost backed into him. "Careful," he whispered, with a tiny smile. It was the first he'd spoken to me since the bathroom incident.

"Sorry," I said, keeping my tone kind.

He patted my back and stepped away.

*Does that mean he's forgiven me? Or is he just making nice so he can keep an eye on me?*

Mags ladled steaming soup into bowls and brought them to the table while Kilte swiveled by her, bearing the heaping platter of toast.

We stood in a circle to pray. Bree and Kilte clasped hands; a split second later, everyone was holding hands. *What? We touch each other when we pray? Men and women, together?* Lisha stood on my left, her hand tiny and cold in mine. Without warning, a warm, callused hand took my right.

*Walker!*

My breath caught in my throat, and I squeezed my eyes shut. I didn't dare look at him. It took every ounce of control I possessed to keep my hand from trembling. Walker's hand was so big it enveloped mine. Wasn't he gripping me too tightly? How would I even know? I'd never held hands for prayer before; aside from Steffan, I'd never held hands with a man at all. I swallowed and focused on Mags's prayer.

". . . and Lord, we thank You for the opportunity to worship you this morning in Your church, with Your people. Thank you that we can serve them with Your hands and love them with Your love. Thank You for Your generous provision. We . . ."

I peeked through my eyelashes at Walker's hand, strong and brown. *Is that his pulse I feel? Or mine? Lord, how am I supposed to focus on You?* This was frightening. Intimate. My heart was pounding so hard I suspected everyone in the circle could hear it. I reminded myself that Walker didn't trust me. Probably didn't like me. That in his eyes, I was a burden. An imposition. A risk to everything he held dear.

"Amen," Mags said.

"Amen!" we echoed.

We released hands, and I released a breath, trying to keep it silent *so no one will know how I—*

"Dig in, everyone!" she said with a laugh. "This'll warm you up!"

The rich squash soup was thick with onion and some kind of bitter greens, and redolent with ginger and a hint of spice. Walker handed me a bowl and a plate with two slices of toast soaked in an herb-infused oil. I thanked him and he nodded, avoiding my eyes.

*Ohhh, he's still angry. Would he have spoken to me if I hadn't nearly backed into him? Why did he stand next to me for prayer? Well, that's his usual spot to sit. Of course, he could've found an excuse to stay in the kitchen and take Mags's hand.* Heat rose in my cheeks, and I sighed, impatient. *Why am I even thinking about this?*

Walker's eyes flicked in my direction. I locked my eyes on my bowl.

Bree was telling Kilte about her schedule for the coming week, and the girls regaled us with a list of who was—and was not—in the morning's service. Walker ate with single-minded intensity, his eyes unfocused. I forced myself not to look at him. The soup was too hot, so I started with my toast. The bread was amazing—fresher and more delicious than anything we'd gotten from the store.

"Merrr-ryn?" Bree said in a singsong voice, and I realized she'd been talking to me. I blinked apology, and she grinned. "Carole texted this morning. Eva quit last night, and we're in a real bind."

I swallowed, astonished. "There's an opening at Mrs@18?"

Bree nodded. "Carole said she'd love to meet you tomorrow. I gave her your number."

Mags laughed, delighted. "See? God's taking care of you!"

Bree's grin was smug, but I couldn't blame her. "I said you have solid experience in retail, and she's very interested. Would you touch base with her today and let her know what time works for you? I'll text you her contact info."

"I will!" I said, euphoric. "Thank you so much, Bree! I'll do it right now." I twisted around to find my purse, and Lisha piped up, "Mom says no phones at the table, please."

"Oh!" My face flushed. "Of course." I felt again the spiky discomfort of being where I didn't belong, where I didn't know the rules, didn't know the people.

"Meryn couldn't know. It *is* a house policy." Mags's smile was rueful, as if she understood what I was thinking.

"That's why Tamar never eats with us." Ellie dunked a slice of bread in her soup. "She's always on her phone, even at meals."

"She doesn't talk to Pris?" I seized on the new topic.

Lisha shook her head. "We don't know *who* she's texting with."

"We think she has a secret lover," Ellie added, and the girls giggled.

I looked at Walker out of the corner of my eye while Mags said, "Girls, gossip," but he seemed unconcerned.

"We can't talk about anybody," Ellie complained.

"That's the point," Bree said.

Lisha set down her spoon and tipped the bowl up to her mouth.

"How are we supposed to find out if someone might be dangerous, or an RD informant, or something?" her sister asked, chomping her toast.

I used my toast to scrape the last bite of soup from my bowl, letting the food's warmth and the normalcy of eating assuage my discomfort.

"More, Meryn?" Bree offered.

"Another spoonful would be welcome." I smiled. "And another slice of that incredible bread, if there's enough."

"There's always enough." Bree grinned and extended the toast plate across the table. I smiled my thanks.

"Gossip is more than an exchange of information," Mags said.

Bree poked Kilte in the ribs, startling him. "What?"

"You're closest to the stove," she said.

"Oh." He reached across the table for my bowl and headed for the soup pot—a trifle resentfully, it seemed. *Am I an imposition? I guess so. One more mouth to feed. One more body to find room for, around a table already too small. I know there isn't "always enough." I shouldn't have asked for more.* A flush warmed my cheeks again, and I took a big bite of toast.

"And information is not for entertainment," Mags continued. "Your comments about Tamar were spiteful and unnecessary."

"Oh," Lisha said. She looked penitent.

"But it's true." Ellie sobered, frowned. "I think it's important to know who might be ratting on us to the RD."

"Here you go." Kilte handed me the bowl, and I thanked him.

Lisha looked at her sister, wide-eyed. "Do you think Tamar would—"

Mags interrupted. "That isn't a discussion you're ever likely to have. And if someone brings it up, you're to halt the conversation and inform me at once. Such people could be dangerous. As for Tamar, she is a friend of this house and we do not speak disrespectfully of her."

An uneasy memory stirred in my mind, and I turned my attention to my soup.

"Yes, Mom," Lisha said.

"Maybe Tamar's just avoiding talking to you," Bree said to Ellie.

Kilte let out a yelp of laughter and Ellie rolled her eyes at him. "Anybody else want more soup while I'm up?" he asked cheerfully.

~

After lunch, I bolted to the bus stop. On the way home, I checked my phone. My wrist had tingled during service, so I knew I'd received a text, and my stomach churned with a mixture of anger and dread.

I had two. The first was Carole, inviting me to come in the following morning to chat about a potential position—obviously Bree had beaten me to the punch. I texted back at once.

The second was from Bree; she'd sent me a link. When I clicked on it, it took me to the *Silvermine Sentinel*. The obituary page.

Mom's obituary.

Silently I took in Mom's smiling face (her high school graduation photo) and read the facts of her life laid out in short paragraphs. The funeral information: date, time, location. Bree had written a brief note. *I'm so very sorry, Mer. I'm always here if you need to talk.*

My face twisted. I shut my phone off before the other passengers could see my expression.

A moment later, my wrist buzzed again. This time it was Ray.

*You'd better be home when I get there.*

Fiercely I bit my lip, trying to keep the tears at bay, trying to ignore the lead in my gut, trying desperately to pray as the anger inside turned to an unrelenting blackness I couldn't confess.

# 15. MRS

"Miss Meryn Flint, it is my great honor to present you to my supervisor, our manager here at Mrs@18, the right honorable Miss Carole Stilwell." Bree was careful to use the expected gestures with her caste-appropriate introduction, which immediately told me Carole was also Worker Caste. My stomach relaxed, and I folded my hands, bowed.

"Miss Stilwell, please greet my dear friend, the right honorable Miss Meryn Flint." Giving me an encouraging smile, Bree finished with the requisite formal bow and retreated to the back of the store.

I'd visited Bree at her job a time or two and had declared myself impressed with the stunning clothes and ideal, second-level mall location, but I'd never met her boss.

Carole returned my bow and immediately dropped into Mid-Caste Casual. "The pleasure's all mine! Welcome to Mrs@18, Meryn." She was as tall as me, with vibrant blond hair and a confident smile. "Thank you for considering us in your employment search. May I scan your chip?"

I held out my arm, and she completed the formality.

Smiling, I gestured around. "You have a beautiful shop." *That's an understatement. This makes Mark look like a garage sale.* "The clothes are excellent quality, and your marketing materials are impressive. I also like the stability of your parent company, and its commitment to bringing couples together in godly relationships."

Carole's eyebrows went up. "You've done your homework."

I let myself smile. "I like to know who I'm working for."

She nodded, gestured to the store's walkway. "Let's take a stroll, shall we?"

For the next hour we perused the shop, discussing fit, fabrics, and customer service standards. Thanks to my work at On the Mark, I felt comfortable answering questions and offering ideas.

"Our whole focus is helping a woman find that special man God has ordained for her," Carole said, her arm sweeping to encompass an entire wall of date-ready outfits. "We want to empower her to bring out the beauty in herself for the world to see. So our tagline is, *Welcome to Mrs@18. How can I help you find a husband today?* When you're working the floor, you'll greet every woman who walks through the door with those words.

"This position can be fast and high-pressure. We don't have a big budget for staff, so you may have to juggle a half-dozen clients at a time, all with a smile."

"I think On the Mark was the perfect training ground," I said. "Often a coworker would call in sick and I'd have to cover more than one section, sometimes managing a dozen customers." I smiled. "I actually prefer that to a slow shift."

Carole stopped by a mannequin. Was that approval in her expression? "As I'm sure you know, most mall employees are Worker Caste," she said. "Have you had much contact with the higher castes?"

A stab of nerves. "Most of our clients at Mark wore blue rings," I said, and she nodded. I didn't have to tell her that some stores—including On the Mark—were never patronized by anyone above Worker Caste. The more upscale stores often posted prominent notices prohibiting the lower castes from entering.

"While we do have some low-caste clients at Mrs, you'll find we serve predominantly higher-caste women," Carole said, her tone prosaic. "We're allowed to address the castes above us—Management, Governance and Exalted—out of necessity. We don't often see the Indigent Caste. They can't afford to shop here, and they're often escorted from the premises by the mall's Guardian Angels before they even get upstairs.

"Most of the time, Management Caste women are easy to serve; they moved up from Worker Caste or have friends or family in it. We do have clients from Governance Caste. They can be difficult, and we must be very careful in our interactions with them. A single inappropriate word from a salesgirl can result in a Caste Insult charge being filed against her at the Guard's station." Carole's face was frank.

My eyes widened. I bit my lip, and she gave me a smile. "For your first six months at Mrs, Bree or I would handle all Governance clients while you watch, and we'll instruct you on how to do so safely. Of course, we know each client's caste by the color of her MT or Caste Ring: blues for Workers, light and dark green for Management, and red or pink for Governance. Unmarried women don't often come in without their mothers, but any woman not wearing an MT we treat as Governance Caste." She lifted a shoulder, and her grin turned wry. "If she's not high caste, she'll let us know right away by how she speaks.

"Of course, we don't have to worry about serving the Exalteds. Their staff do it for them."

Relief relaxed me. "I had Elocution and Caste Ethics in high school," I said. "I remember the lessons."

Carole's face didn't soften. "I have to be candid with you, Meryn: I don't generally hire unmarried women. I'm tired of training girl after girl, just to have her quit the moment she gets engaged." A chill brushed my skin.

"I can't predict the future, Miss Stilwell, but I can tell you I'm not involved, and I have no desire to marry anytime in the near future." I held her eyes with mine and smiled. "And even if I were to marry, I would still want to keep my job. I enjoy working."

She regarded me for a long moment while my insides did cartwheels. Then she glanced at her phone. "Well, I'm willing to take a chance on you. I think you're well suited to a position with our company," she said, and a surge of euphoria made me feel like floating up to the ceiling. "Your chip records are clear, and prinister approval for employment is current on your file. When could you start?"

*Oh, thank You God, thank You God!* If Ray had discussed my punishment with Severs, my employment clearance would have been the first thing the church revoked.

"As soon as you need me," I said promptly.

Visibly pleased, Carole nodded and motioned me toward the checkout counter. "Welcome aboard. Let's get your personnel file set up." As we walked, she offered an hourly rate that made me bite my cheek, hard, to keep from screaming with joy. *On this salary, I might be able to buy all my own food after I move out!*

Carole was still talking. "And if you have a little time this afternoon, you could help Bree with the windows. That will help you become familiar with our new line.

"You'll need to purchase two outfits to wear during your shifts." Even though Bree had warned me, I gave a slight gasp now as I did the mental math. Carole smiled. "We understand that most of our employees can't afford to purchase two outfits right out of the gate. What we can do is rent them to you and take the fee out of your paycheck. It isn't much, and when the new lines come in, you may purchase your old uniforms at half price."

My smile didn't waver. The clothes were worth it, and the salary Carole quoted me was double what I could earn at any other retail store.

She handed me a Mrs name tag, which immediately read my chip and displayed my name before I'd even attached it to my blouse. As Carole turned to the computer, I shot Bree a wide-eyed look and smiled my euphoria. She grinned and gave me a thumbs-up.

At my first break, I slipped into the stockroom and texted Ray that I had to work late, and I'd be home by eight-thirty. He didn't have to know I had a new job.

~

By closing time at eight, we'd redone both display windows, dressing the voluptuous live-quins in clothes from next season's line and reprogramming the holo backdrops to reflect the change. We switched on the last live-quin, the one we'd just dressed in an outfit from the intimates line: a white lace wedding outfit, complete with sheer robe, sequined bra and thong panties, and tiny top hat.

"Pretty revealing," I murmured to Bree as we walked her into position. Powered by internal battery systems and covered with synth-skin, the live-quins looked human. We programmed them to move in sync with the holo backgrounds the graphics gurus sent in the marketing package. As the live-quins moved, the background changed with them, creating a realistic scene.

We stepped out into the walkway to study the effect.

The live-quins were in motion, smiling, waving, and flirting through the windows. Our bride met her husband at the front door. When he saw her, he dropped his briefcase, scooped her into his arms and carried her toward the bedroom while she laughed over his shoulder, winking at us.

The working girl, wearing a below-knee skirt, floral blouse with matching camisole, and sensible shoes, handed her male boss a sheaf of papers and got a kiss on the cheek as a reward. She hugged an armload of files and smiled dreamily as she returned to her desk.

Our active girl caught a football (wearing our ridiculously thin workout togs and so-called "athletic" shoes I wouldn't use to cross the street). A handsome jock grabbed her and spun her around, laughing, while their holographic friends cheered and clapped.

My stomach tightened as I reviewed the scenes. "The bride scene is awfully risqué," I whispered to Bree.

"This new line is for a girl's wedding night. We market to single women," she said, low, and shrugged. "The company is betting the RD turns a blind eye."

"Nice," Carole said. I had been so engrossed in our work I hadn't noticed her approach. "That should bring in some traffic. You made a good start today, Meryn. Tomorrow morning you'll unpack in the stockroom, and then I'll want you on the floor."

I smiled. "No problem."

"Bree, do you mind staying on for another half hour to reconcile today's receipts?"

Bree smiled an apology to me, and I headed for the stockroom to clock out. Carole lingered in the walkway, studying the windows, the light from the changing displays flickering over her face.

~

I didn't sleep much that night. I stared through my bedroom window at the stars as they winked and shivered in the cold, and tried to figure out why Ray hadn't taken me to St. Mike's yet. Did he forget? Unlikely. Was he playing a game with me? I wouldn't put it past him, but it wasn't really in character. Ray was a lot of things, but he wasn't a schemer. Since I had so flatly rejected Steffan, was Ray thinking of finding me another boyfriend?

Ray had chosen all my boyfriends, of course, according to church policy. The RD said it was biblical that girls should have no preference when it came to dating (although boys did). But Mom and Ray had always said they would never pair me with someone I didn't like. Still, it seemed Ray's main focus was finding me a young man from a wealthy family and a higher caste. Not an easy task.

Grimly I reminded myself that my boyfriends were *former* for a reason. Patronizing. Telling me how many babies they wanted, as if that would automatically open a path to my heart. Ray tried to be understanding as the suitors came and went . . . until the night I broke it off with Steffan, who promptly called Ray to complain about what he called my "selfish and unbiblical" behavior and demand my punishment.

To say my stepfather lost his temper is to do the term an injustice.

"I've never seen you do something so stupid!" His rage made the living room shrink. "That man is your security! Your future!"

"God is my security and my future," I told Ray, determined to keep my composure. I sat on the sofa with Mom, who was holding my hand. She looked at me sidelong; I knew she could feel my trembling.

Ray stopped pacing to glare at me. "And what makes you think that *God*"—he spat the word—"didn't bring Steffan into your life to be your husband? Huh? For pity's sake, Mer, the man's a *Hagen. Governance Caste!*" The Hagen family all but ran Silvermine. Of course, Ray could force the issue. All he had to do was call Prinister Severs.

Ray had been going to church with us for about a year at this point. Every Sunday he climbed into the same suit, put on a tie, and with a martyred expression that never changed, drove us to church, sat through service (in the men's section in front, of course) and brought us home. He never told us why he started going. But after St. Mike's began enforcing attendance, he'd come home from work one night, tight-lipped and pale. The very next Sunday he suited up.

His workplace also stopped putting him on call on the weekend. "They hired a kid for that," he grunted when Mom asked him about it. He was punctilious about ensuring the chip reader at the entrances caught all three of us, whether we were attending service or Bible study.

The downside was, the more he attended church on Sunday, the more he drank during the week. When I was fifteen, the RD instituted temperance laws, making alcohol illegal. It didn't matter. Bars went underground and became speakeasies, with passwords and hidden cameras. The price of booze skyrocketed. Ray's drinking went underground, too, and became heavier. Our food budget shrank. Mom lost weight, her gaunt shoulderblades jutting through her blouse; Ray didn't.

I looked at my stepfather—red capillaries on his face, yellowed eyes, thinning hair—and realized he was just worried about my future.

So was I. Despite my resolve, my voice shook. "God knows me well enough to know I will never marry a man who hits me."

"Well, that's a nice bit of circular logic." Glowering, Ray reached down to pull a flask from behind the plastic plant in the corner.

Mom forced a smile. "Darling," she began, "Should you really—"

"Don't you start with me, Rose," he snarled, taking a long pull. "And don't you"—he whirled, poking a stubby finger at me with his free hand—"ever ask me for a dime. You hear me? Not one bleeding dime!"

I got to my feet, disgusted. "Why don't you just auction me off to the highest bidder, Ray? And don't worry, I won't ever ask you for anything. I'm going to take care of myself!" I stalked down the hall to my room. *I'm going to have a career, and I'll never need a man for anything!* Even as the thoughts formed, I knew the utter impossibility of my desire.

"Take care of yourself?" Ray yelled at my retreating back. "You're Worker Caste! You're just a girl! You can't even take care of a few stupid fish!"

I slammed my bedroom door and caught my reflection in the mirror, tears of mingled hurt and grief glassing my face, remembering my beloved little fish that had died and livid that he would even bring it up.

This time, nothing could drown out the argument that raged in the living room after my departure.

Now, awash in the memory, I rolled from my left side to my back, trying not to cry, afraid I'd wake Ray. *Ray wanted Steffan. Who was supposed to be my "knight in shining armor."* I snorted softly. *No wonder I'm still single.*

After the argument, Mom had come to check on me, kind and sympathetic. But I'd unloaded my pain and anger on her. "Is this all God wants for me, Mom? Is getting married the grand ambition of my life? Because if that's all I have to look forward to, then I must not mean very much to Him." It was the only time I'd ever known my eloquent mother to be speechless—and then her eyes filled with tears, which made me feel worse.

The memory still smarted.

~

The next day, Carole had me on only until two. After that I was slated to work on my house with Walker, although from the look of the weather forecast, I wasn't sure if we'd be able to see, much less work—a huge weather system was rolling in off the bay. Still, I was determined to get my tiny house finished as quickly as possible. As I scrolled through Bree's texts about Walker's schedule, I encountered the link to Mom's service. Hastily I shut off my phone.

The bus was nearly empty. Closing my eyes, I forced myself to face the reality of going to Mom's funeral—and found myself fighting a rage so powerful, my hands nearly ripped a hole in my tote.

The truth was, the idea of going anywhere with Ray terrified me. Even being in the same apartment with him was almost more than I could stand. Every time I thought about him, I saw him with his arm around that blonde woman, and I wanted to scratch his eyes out.

That—and what he did to Mom—created a composite violation of trust I found impossible to forgive. On top of all that, now he planned to turn me over to the church for discipline.

And yet, somewhere deep inside, I missed him. He was the only father I'd ever had. But the day Mom died, Ray turned into someone I didn't know. He looked like Ray, he talked like Ray, but he'd become some kind of transformative monster who could leap out at any moment and kill without warning. This new Ray murdered my stepdad at the same moment he murdered my mom. I not only didn't want to live with him—I didn't even want to be in the same *ZIP* code.

I didn't know how I could love someone I was afraid of . . . and when that thought surfaced, I was forced to admit the truth: I was afraid of Ray. I feared his uncertain temper, his unthinking cruelty, his unwelcome sexual advance when I was barely into my teens, and my inability to cope with it all. And yet I still missed him. My eyes misted with tears. I knew he missed me; worse, somehow I knew he missed Mom.

When that thought presented itself, I rejected it. How could he miss her when he was the one responsible for her death? How could I love the man who had killed my mother? *I can't. I don't!* My thoughts chased my emotions around in my head until I was exhausted.

And I rode right past my stop.

Frantic, I jumped up and pushed my way to the front of the bus. "I missed my street!" I gasped. "I should have gotten off . . ."

The driver eyed me, his expression churlish, but the bus didn't slow. Instead, I was forced to debark with several others at the next stop. Main.

Sweet Street.

~

I stepped off the bus into a darkening swirl of snow, fully cognizant of Mags's warning, but also thinking I was probably safe since it was still midafternoon and I was surrounded by small group of people.

After a few moments, I wasn't so sure. One woman climbed into a hovercar waiting nearby; the man next to me hurried into the building on the corner. The noise and cooking odors told me it was a restaurant. A middle-aged couple walked across the street, going in the other direction. That left only two other people going my way.

Well, I had to get to Mags's. I headed up the street, fighting the icy wind, still lost in thoughts of Mom's funeral. Beyond the restaurant was a small pawnshop/payday cash store; the couple in front of me turned to go in, bypassing two men, homeless and dirty, who sat at the entrance. I didn't meet their eyes. From six feet away, through the wind, I could smell them. Their catcalls trailed me, but I ignored them. It always surprised me to see how filthy people could be in the midst of pristine snow, and I wondered if the cold killed the fleas and lice, or if the warmth of the men's bodies kept the parasites alive. A few vehicles nudged the curb. One—a black hovercar limousine—angled to take up three spaces. The license plate read SWEET B. I wondered if it belonged to one of the mythical Sweet brothers.

Beyond the pawnshop was—of all things—a candy store. As I drew closer, a young woman bolted through the door and ran right up to me. Her skin was so pale it seemed translucent, her delicate face capped with a head of fiery red hair that reminded me of Mom. She wore retro high-heeled boots, a skirt cut so short it revealed her thighs, and blouse that violated every dress code on the books, with only a thin sweater wrapped against the cold.

"Have you seen JoJo?" she asked, shaking, her brows puckering. "I have to get him my rent."

"I—I'm sorry," I said, taken aback. "You must have me confused with someone else."

"Oh!" She peered closer through the light coming from the candy store, and her eyes filled with tears. Was it the wind? She pushed her hair away from her face, yanking the sweater more tightly around her thin frame. "My God. You're not dung caste . . . go home, honey." Her hiss was urgent, her eyes white and round in a face reddening from the cold. "Now. Get off this street!"

"I am, I—" I began, but she turned and bolted down the sidewalk. A moment later, she ducked into the restaurant.

"Girl, you need a cheeseburger and a parka," I said under my breath, and resumed my trek toward Shady Dell—but now my pulse pounded with apprehension.

I didn't pay much attention to the next two stores or the buildings across the street because the wind had increased to a howl, whipping icy snow straight into my face. I pulled my hood forward, holding it in place to shield my eyes. Beyond the storefronts was an area ringed by a chain-link fence. As I got closer, the snow thinned, revealing a fire-gutted building set back from the street. The sign indicated it had once been a convenience store. Now the wind surged through shattered windows like an invading flood, flapping the melted signs advertising mild intoxicants, and driving snow along blackened timbers that sketched the caved-in roof. Disturbed snow and footprints surrounded the empty husk, and I wondered if the neighborhood kids were using it as a fort. I wondered if it was safe.

"Hey, baby."

I stopped, a chill sweeping through me that had nothing to do with the weather. A car sat by the curb just ahead, the passenger window down. I couldn't see the man's features in the gloom.

"Come get out of the snow, love. It's warrrm in here." A gloved hand came out of the window, gestured.

"No, thank you," I said politely, and began walking. *Don't get out of the car. Please. Don't get—*

"I'll make it worth your time." Behind me, the *click-squee* of a car door opening. I bit my lip. "I got a big ol' fat roll right here in my pants. We can party good, sister!"

*God, what do I do! What do I say?* My ingrained obedience to any request or order by a man warred with the awareness of my peril.

*Say nothing. Keep walking.*

"Hey, now, don't be that way! Come back, baby! I got the warmest lap in Silvermine!" A long pause. "Hey! I'm talking to you, whore!"

The sound of another car door opening. I gasped. *Dear Jesus! Help me!*

"What, you think you're Sarah Humboldt? You think you're some Exalted bitch, turning your back on me?"

I kept moving, my senses heightened, realizing the snow would muffle the man's footfalls if he was following me. Was he alone? Or had others gotten out of the car? There was no way to know without turning around.

Could I run? No. The pavement was too slick. I released my hood, put my hands in my pockets to slip off my gloves. The skin numbed within seconds, but now I could use them. The wind whistled past my ears. If he grabbed me, I had moves I could use in defense—my brain was sorting and discarding options at a rapid pace—but the slick footing was a factor, and his coat might present a problem, too. My coat was thigh length, easy to lift if I had to kick. My eyes scanned the cars ahead, then the fenced area, back and forth, back and forth, blinking away snow, desperate to see. My ears strained for any sound of pursuit.

"Hey!"

Fear morphed into anger, and I stopped walking and spun in place. Two men stood not eight feet behind me. *God, give me words, please.*

"Well?" I demanded. My heart was pounding so hard it threatened to burst through my chest. "Just how far do you want to push this?

Because I'm not going anywhere with you." *God, please don't let them be armed. Please don't—*

The tall man frowned. "Then give me your damn tote. Now!"

I laughed, not hiding my scorn. "You're a proper idiot if you think I'm carrying anything valuable on Sweet Street." The men hesitated, and I yelled, "Well?"

The shorter man turned to his companion and said something, low. The taller man's eyes widened, and his eyes dropped to my hands. He snarled something unintelligible but didn't resist when the shorter man pulled him toward the car. I waited until the doors closed, then resumed my trek. At each step my foot pillowed, then slid slightly. I dared not look around.

When I got to the corner, I glanced back. Sweet Street was veiled in swirling white dark, the only illumination from a single streetlight and windows of the few shops still open. I couldn't identify which car held the men, but no one was following me. Breathing a cautious sigh of relief, I turned onto Oak, slipping my numbed and frozen hands into my gloves.

By the time I arrived at Mags's, I was shaking from both the cold and the encounter. A gust of wind pushed me through the door, and I hurled my weight against it to slam it shut. For a moment, all I could do was breathe. Tears gathered in my eyes. *What if those men had—*

"Well! You do make an entrance."

# 16. STRAY

A twentysomething woman stood in the kitchen, pouring cups of tea. Her stylish tunic sweater and form-fitting leggings accented her slender, womanly figure, and her hair framed her face with a flawless curtain of gold. She set the teapot on the stove and carried cups to the table, placing one in front of a girl—maybe eleven—sitting in Ellie's spot.

Confused, I blinked back tears and dropped my shoulders. "I'm so sorry, I must have the wrong—"

"No, you're at Mags's, if that's the house you're looking for." The woman lifted her cup with a fine-boned hand. "You would be the new girl. Mags certainly is generous, the way she takes in strays."

*Hmm. Already a topic of conversation, I see.* My eyebrows rose, but she was still talking.

"I'm Tamar, and this is my daughter, Priscilla."

*This is the woman Walker's dating? Oh.* The casual introduction was like a slap, but ingrained courtesy overrode my pique. "It is my honor and pleasure to make your acquaintance," I said, bowing.

The girl rose. "The pleasure is mine, Miss Meryn." She bowed lower, conveying respect at my maturity.

Tamar did not bow. She was smiling at her daughter, and I wondered if the woman was being deliberately rude or if she was just focused on training Pris in appropriate greetings.

I chose to ignore the slight and smiled, pulling my hood away from my face. It crackled, and bits of ice sifted to the floor. "That's a good idea," I said, nodding at the tea and removing my hat, static making my hair fly and cling. "It's downright arctic out there." I knew my face was red from the cold, and I felt frowzy and unkempt.

"I can start you some hot water if you wish," Tamar said, tucking a neat strand of hair behind one shell-like ear, "but I'm afraid I'm out of tea."

"That would be most kind." I hung my coat on the hook. While she ran water in the kettle and set it on the stove, I rummaged through my supplies on the pantry shelf until I found a packet of miso soup powder.

"Where is everyone?" I asked, realizing I couldn't hear the twins. I'd never seen the tiny house empty.

"Not sure where Mags and the girls are." Tamar settled at the table, crossing her legs in an elegant fashion, and stirred her tea. "Kilte and Bree are off somewhere together"—she waved a vague hand—"and Walker is at his place, waiting for us."

"He's gonna teach me how to play backgammon," Pris said, her eyes crinkling.

"'He shall teach me,'" Tamar corrected. "You really mustn't talk like the natives, Priscilla." The girl hunched around her tea, and a flush spread up her neck.

I turned away so Tamar wouldn't see the look on my face, unhooked a mug and snagged a spoon from the drainboard. As I was tearing open the soup packet, Tamar said, "I was sorry to hear about your mom."

The world stopped, the only sound the stove's hissing. Firmly I reminded myself to breathe—in, then out. "Thank you," I said.

"Terrible thing, her being murdered like that."

I shook powder into the mug, ignoring my tightening solar plexus.

"And by your own stepfather! How awful!"

My spoon clattered to the counter. "Yes, and I don't care to discuss it," I said to the mug.

"Oh, I'm so sorry," Tamar said. "Forgive me, Meryn—I didn't mean to offend."

Her delivery struck me as odd, polished. I turned, but she was a picture of contrition. My frown melted. "I forgive you. I just can't talk about it. How was school, Pris?"

"It was fun, thank you." The girl smiled. "I enjoyed English class today! We started a new book. It's called *Mary's Journey of Obedience*."

Now Tamar frowned. "Sweetie, we shouldn't keep Walker waiting." She rose, picking up her mug. "Bring your tea and let's go play backgammon."

"Okay!" Bouncing to her feet, Pris shrugged on a coat. "Bye, Meryn!"

"Bye." I smiled.

A moment after the door closed, the teakettle whistled. I stirred the soup to life, trying not to be angry, not to be hurt, and failing.

I sat at the table, curling my fingers around the cup's welcome warmth, the soup's comforting umami pungency reminding me of Mom. *Who told Tamar? Walker? Mags? Does it matter? And what an awful thing to discuss in front of a child!*

*Stop being judgmental,* I told myself. *Word gets around. Especially here.*

I sipped my soup, trying to stifle anger. *Okay, God. I guess You want me here. Please help me make a new life. And help Ray do the same.* As soon as I'd prayed it, a surge of anger stopped my words. *Praying for the man who killed your mother, Meryn? The man now seeing another woman?* But then a new realization hit: Mom would've.

*Mom would've.* I sat motionless for a long moment as the shock of that truth settled into my bones. *Well, that was Mom. I can't. I—*

*You can do all things through Me.*

I took a deep breath, hating my discomfort with the still, small voice, hating the message, hating my resentment. *I don't resent God!*

*Don't you?*

*That* stopped me. *Do I?* I stirred my soup, forcing myself to face the question. *It seems like things with God always start great, but then sour somehow. It's been that way since I was little. God is love, but only if you obey. Jesus accepts you as you are, but loves you too much to leave you that way.* My prayers always felt fleeting and scrambled, and always mixed with guilt.

I hated the ambiguity: wanting to pray, but fearing God. Wanting God, but not the church. *Wait. Is it God I resent? Or the church?* My eyebrows rose, and for the first time I realized how much St. Mike's had shaped my perceptions of God. *The only time I ever really felt comfortable with God was when I sang on the praise team, and that didn't last long.*

~

My ambivalence about the team came to a head one summer when Bart was about to take a well-deserved vacation.

Usually, he called around to find a competent buddy to fill in during his absence. This was always a trial for the rest of us because we had to clue in the new guy to our procedures so we'd have the least amount of disruption for the congregation. But the canon of available worship music was enormous. Most of the time the sub didn't know our set, and we'd have to build a new set from his list on rehearsal night and teach it to the congregation Sunday morning.

The result was chaos.

During one of these late rehearsals, after our sixth run-through to "get it right," I had turned to DeeDee in frustration.

"You play keys," I'd whispered. "Why don't they just let you lead?"

She raised her eyebrows. "Women don't lead worship, Meryn," she chided. "It isn't biblical."

"Neither is this," I grumbled.

But this time was different.

All the men on the praise team were attending a weeklong men's retreat. Most of Silvermine's churches had decided to hold their retreats on the same week, at the same retreat center. The event was billed as "Empowering Warriors for God's Army."

It hadn't occurred to anyone that few men would be left behind to cover liturgical absences. Bart couldn't find a substitute, so he hit on a novel solution.

"Here," he said, brandishing his phone.

"You're going to lead worship over the phone?" Dee laughed.

Bart chuckled. "No. I've recorded the set. Syntyche will roll the vid of me playing and singing, and you girls will sing along."

As that sank in, I blinked. "You're kidding."

"No, it should work fine," Bart said, missing my tone. "You're solid on the songs. Let's give it a shot." He started toward the sound booth.

"Wait," I said.

He turned. "Is there a problem?"

My mouth was open. "Who's leading worship?"

"I am."

"From a recording." I tried to hide my disdain, but I could tell from the look on Bart's face that I failed.

He was patient. "It isn't ideal, Meryn, but it's the best we can do under the circumstances."

Something snapped, and I couldn't stand the whole stupid charade another minute. "We have a perfectly competent worship leader right here."

"Meryn—" Dee began.

"Who?" Bart asked, interested.

"DeeDee," I said. "She's great on keys, she knows the set and the congregation—"

The guys in the band dissolved in boisterous laughter.

"Couldn't you just see Prinister Severs' face?"

"That's a fumble! Somebody lost that football!"

"I don't see what's so funny!" My anger stilled the room.

James, the bass player, smirked at the drummer. John studied his shoes. Bart eyed me, wary, as if unexpectedly confronted by a wild animal. He turned to the band. "Guys," he said softly, "take a break."

Somebody whistled. With deliberate care, the guys set down their instruments and left the stage. As John sauntered past, he murmured, "See ya, Meryn."

*Oh no. What have I just done?* My blood cooled in my veins, but I forced my head up. DeeDee turned toward the steps.

Bart lifted his guitar over his head, set it on its stand. "No, Dee, you stay."

"Bart, I'm not—"

He held up a hand to quiet her, but he was looking at me. "Meryn," he said, "you are a valuable member of this team. But what just happened here is unacceptable. Do you understand the concept of biblical authority?"

"Of course," I said, my eyes focused on his shoes.

"So you understand that you just challenged my authority in front of the team."

*What?* "No Bart, I—"

"Yes, that's exactly what you did." He turned to DeeDee, crossing his arms. "Did you put her up to this?"

My jaw dropped.

Dee's eyes flew to me. "No, Bart," she whispered.

"She had nothing to do with this!" I said, my voice rising.

"Well, I know how girls are," Bart said. "You tend to stick together, against all logic and reason. And despite biblical injunctions, you just demonstrated this. This is why you need a man to guide you."

My mouth closed with a snap over what I wanted to say. Dee nodded, her head dropped forward, her light brown hair obscuring her face. For the first time, the submission of her posture struck me forcibly. *Is that what I look like when I don't meet a man's eyes? A cowed animal?*

"So you have one option here, Meryn." Bart's voice was a steel drum. "As a girl, you are in a subordinate position in this church and on this team. You will sing with the recording this Sunday. Period. If you push this issue, I will speak to your father. Then I will remand you to Prinister Severs and the Board for a disciplinary hearing. Do you understand me?"

*A hearing? Why is this escalating?* "Discipline over what?" I asked, keeping my tone even with effort. "Offering a viable option to solve a problem?"

Bart sighed. "You know as well as I do women don't hold leadership positions in the church."

"But we're not talking about preaching or teaching." *Why can't we discuss—* "I don't know of any verse in the Bible that says women cannot lead worship. Especially since all the men will be at the retreat. That is hardly—"

"Then clearly you need more study," Bart interrupted. "Even if I agreed with you—and I don't—what if the custodian is here on Sunday morning? If he so much as hears your voices echoing down the corridor during service, this church will be in disobedience to God."

*Women are that dangerous? That toxic?* Without realizing it, I shook my head, the pain in my heart pricking tears in my eyes. *Why did God even create us?* I looked at Dee, who was nodding. *Oh, of course. To have babies. But He could have given men wombs and eliminated women altogether.* My eyes went to Bart and I imagined him, big with child, and the humor of it helped drive away the tears. But his next words shattered my fragile equilibrium.

"We took you on too fast. Having girls on the team at all is a huge concession to modernity. The men like it, but frankly, I think you're a distraction." His face was cold, unmoving. "A man shouldn't be tormented by a woman's figure, especially during church. It's why we seat you in the back."

Dee covered her mouth with her hands, her eyes looking anywhere but at Bart. I bit my tongue, hard. *A distra—*

"And it strokes your ego too much, being up here. Just look at how willing you are to confront my God-ordained authority. You wouldn't have done that even three months ago. You're getting above yourself." His expression turned reflective, and he crossed his arms, tapping his chin with an index finger. "Perhaps it might not be a bad idea for you to chat with Prinister Severs about this matter. I'll give it some thought."

A flush spread up my neck, and I looked at my feet.

"In the meantime"—Bart spread his hands, struggling to make his tone conversational—"why don't you take a week or two off? You've been working pretty hard since you joined."

*Glad you noticed.* The thought was bitter, and I bit my lip in repentance. *God, forgive me, but this is—*

"Dee can manage on Sunday."

"Me? Alone?" Dee squeaked.

"No, I'll call Jobette." He turned to me and forced a smile. "I'll be in touch after the retreat, and we can talk about how you need to adjust your attitude so you can rejoin us."

*Adjust my attitude.* To my surprise, anger shouldered past my fear. I folded my arms and met his gaze. "Let me ask you something. Exactly why are you here, Bart?"

His eyes narrowed.

"Because I can tell you why I am," I went on, keeping my tone mild. "I'm here to worship God. God is my purpose, and my focus. I'm not standing up here without an MT to provide entertainment for the men in the congregation or to fulfill your 'concession to modernity.'"

Bart's face reddened and he opened his mouth, but something great and unknowable hovered over me, pulling me higher, pulling the words from a secret place inside of me, a place I never knew existed, driving away fear.

"If you have such low regard for the women on this team, then frankly, you don't deserve us. And this congregation—and God—deserve much better than the half-baked ignorance you've been supporting, and the technically perfect, self-promoting performances we've been giving." I set down my mic and picked up my tote.

Dee stood, silent tears streaming down her face, her eyes darting from me to Bart and back again.

I looked Bart in the eyes, my tone no longer cordial. "Don't bother calling until you get *your* priorities straight."

I turned on my heel and strode out of the sanctuary, never once bowing my head. In the foyer, the guys silently watched me go.

~

I couldn't stop sobbing, my tears pooling on the kitchen table. "Mom, what have I done?" I looked up, eyes hot and scratchy, seeking absolution. "What was I thinking?"

We were fixing dinner—or trying to—the evening after my walk-out. A bin of peas for split-pea soup sat on the table, pushed to one side. Mom sat next to me, stroking my hair.

The great unknowable truth I'd felt in the auditorium had vanished, leaving me with profound embarrassment, tainted with a lingering sense of dread. I straightened up and threw a hand in the air. "I'm off the team. That's it. And all because I couldn't keep my mouth shut."

Mom patted my hand where it rested on the table. "It sounds like this has been building up in you for a while."

"The way Bart treated us—me and DeeDee—it just made me feel so . . . worthless." My chin quivered. "As if we're only up there for the men to admire. As if all our hard work and dedication to God meant *nothing*."

"I don't think that's what he intended," Mom said in a consoling fashion. "Of course you're valuable to the team."

"I don't think so," I said, but my tone was thoughtful now, not bitter. "At least, not in Bart's eyes. He made that very clear. And he was so . . . *patronizing*. As if Dee and I were children."

"Sometimes men don't know how to show their appreciation to women." Mom shook her head. "I don't expect Ray to compliment me on every dinner. I just put it on the table. That's my job."

"That's different." I let the chair hold me up, the wood ribs digging into my back. "You and Ray don't cook together. You decide what to fix, and he eats it."

"Well, he tells me what he likes. And I'm happy to make it because I love him." Her face glowed—it always did when she talked about Ray.

"Well, I don't love Bart." I chewed my lip. The theoretical was becoming way too real, and I didn't like where my thoughts were going. "Is this how it's going to be, Mom? Is this how men are going to treat me for the rest of my life—including my husband? Like I'm some little girl who can't think for herself?"

"Unfortunately, some men are that way." Mom traced a scratch on the worn laminate tabletop with her finger. "They don't understand how to treat women with respect, as the weaker vessel. Both men and women have a place in God's design."

"Weaker." I snorted, crossed my arms. "I can put every single boy in my karate class on the floor. How does that make me weaker?"

Mom chuckled. "The Bible isn't talking about only physical strength. Men have strengths women don't. And women have nurturing capacities that men don't understand." Her hands described arcs in the air, came together. "God has given both our unique place, and when we obey Him, all relationships work together in harmony."

*Good grief. She sounds just like Prinister Severs.* "But only if the woman gives in." I groped for words. "Mom, when I'm at the dojo, I feel strong. Capable. Not just physically, but mentally." My hand on the table curled into a fist. "But the minute I walk into St. Mike's, I feel like . . . emotional mush. Like I couldn't cope with somebody throwing a frisbee, much less a punch. So which am I supposed to be? A strong woman? Competent? Or meek, subservient, demure?"

Mom nodded, decisive. "I think you can be a strong woman. As long as you remember who has final authority."

My laugh came out a croak, and my face drew into wrinkles, a pleading, trying to understand her, trying to understand myself. "Mom, if a man always has final authority, that means I can never be strong. I can never make a decision for myself—not with any finality. Every action that influences my life—every thought that comes through my mind—will have to be tested in the light of some man's approval. Are women really meant to be so servile? So . . . worthless?"

"Oh, sweetheart." Mom's expression reflected an odd pain. "Women don't measure our worth by the battles we win. It's a false calculation."

I sat, rubbing my temples, struggling to understand. "So I was disobedient when I confronted Bart."

Mom hesitated, choosing her words with care. "I think you taught Bart a very important lesson about being respectful to the women under his authority."

I chuckled, but it didn't feel funny. "You sound like you're trying to convince yourself."

This time, she didn't smile. "Meryn, there's something you need to understand. If you challenge a man on any issue of authority, you will lose. There are no exceptions to this; no caveats."

The silence hung between us like a shroud. "So what I did was stupid." My chin quivered. "I was going against God." *Men must matter more to God than we do. Well, I guess . . . He made men first, after all. That's what Prinister Severs says.* The realization of it sank into me, all of the tiny truths of the world coming together like a giant millstone around my neck: women sitting in the back of the church while the men sat in the front. Women prohibited from working a full-time job. Women forced to marry just so they could put food on the table.

My breath came in short gasps. I felt strangled. Second. *Less than.* "Should I repent to Bart and ask his forgiveness?" My voice slowed, and bile rose in my throat. *Lord, help me understand. Why would You make women this way?* "Should I confess to Prinister Severs?"

I hated confession. I hated having to share all my secrets, hated the sorrowful or smug or condescending looks I got from the prinisters, looks that made me think God must regard me the same way. I knew hating it was a sin—such correction was biblical, after all—but I'd never been able to bring myself to admit it to anyone, much less ask forgiveness. That made it seem worse: a darkness in my soul, hidden and black.

Mom studied her hands in her lap, silent. Finally, she met my eyes. "I should say yes." Her voice was very quiet. "It is always the woman's place to seek reconciliation. It is part of our ministry. And when we sin, we must confess."

My eyebrows lifted. "But?"

Mom pulled the bin of peas onto her lap and started sorting. "I've never mentioned this, but before you were born, your gampa used to attend Bible study with a man who trained dogs for the Exalted Caste."

*What? Where's this going?* "That sounds like fun," I said, and the strangling sensation eased. Dogs were rare; no one below Governance Caste could afford a pet.

"That's what your grandfather said." She smiled, her eyes twinkling. "They would go get a coffee together, and he would tell Gampa Flint all about the nuances of dog training.

"He once spoke about a client who brought him a dog that was almost impossible to train. The dog was frightened and would bark and lash out, urinate where it wasn't supposed to, all sorts of bad behavior. The trainer couldn't even pet the dog because it would try to bite him."

"What did he do?" I was fascinated. "I hope he didn't kill the dog."

Mom shook her head, tossed a bad pea in the trash. "Dogs are too valuable. No, he invested a lot of time in the dog. He would sit with it, talk to it and feed it by hand, trying to get the poor thing used to his presence. Finally, the dog relaxed. He petted it, and he was able to train it. He said it turned out to be a really good dog. He took it back to the owner, and the dog took one look at that man and hid behind the trainer. It took all the trainer's skill to get the dog to go home.

"A week later, the owner called with more complaints. The trainer couldn't figure out what was wrong. Well, long story short, he found out the owner was beating the dog. He took the dog home himself and told the man he should never get another."

"The trainer took the dog away from an Exalted Caste owner?" My mouth dropped open. "Mom! Was he arrested?"

Mom smiled. "He should have been, but no. The trainer said he would tell the judge all the cruel things the owner had done, so I suppose the owner dropped it. Anyway, the trainer found a safe home for the dog, and the dog was just good as gold after that.

"He told your father, 'You can't train a dog by hitting it. You'll break its spirit. You only train a dog through love and kindness. Meet the dog where it is in life and go from there.'

"Now, I didn't tell you this story because I'm comparing you to a dog." She sobered, her eyes on mine. "But I'm not going to demand you go to confession. Not this time. You're almost an adult, Meryn. It's time for you to take responsibility for your conscience before God."

I was stunned. For a long moment, I couldn't breathe.

This had ramifications far beyond just what might happen to me. Family Duty said Mom and Ray were held accountable for my behavior until I married, at which time that accountability would transfer to my husband. For Mom to abdicate that responsibility was unheard of. It indicated a level of trust that humbled me. She wanted me to do the right thing, and she expected that I would.

"Mom," I whispered, "have you discussed this with Ray?"

A slight smile played at the corners of Mom's lips, and she arched an eyebrow. "You think I should talk to Ray about this?"

I opened my mouth and closed it. As I was about to laugh, Mom sighed, her manner impatient, as if she was rethinking what she'd said. "Just understand that if you do not behave in a Christlike manner with men, your life will be much harder."

*Christlike. Did Christ treat women this way? I'll have to study more.* My eyes followed a crack in the linoleum at my feet. "I have to think about this." The words came slow. I looked up. "What if Bart reports me?"

Now her smile was easy. "It's unlikely, sweetheart. Bart's the one who chose you to join the team. He'll have to answer to Prinister Severs for that if he decides to file a complaint. I suspect he'll just say you were too immature for the position, and find someone else." She rose and went to the stove to stir the onions.

"I hope you're right." Relief covered the raw edges of my hurt. "He made me so mad, I really wasn't thinking before I spoke." I pulled the pea bin to my lap and stirred them idly with a finger, looking for rocks. *I suppose . . . I should go to confession. I should do what's right in God's eyes.* Something inside twisted in rebellion, and I thought about the strong Presence I'd felt when I was talking to Bart. I wondered if it was Satan.

"Mom," I blurted. "Can we find another church?"

"You want to leave St. Mike's?" She turned, taking in a breath, and blinked. "Well, I suppose we can discuss it." Mom was being brave; a lot of our friends attended, the church was congenial to the Worker Caste, and Ray was going now. Changing churches would not be a small thing for us.

I carried my pan of peas to the sink to rinse. "I don't know," I admitted, my back to her. "I can't see myself standing in the congregation, watching the team lead worship. And what do I tell Ruthie and Mary Celeste and Dinah about why I left the team? Do I lie? Tell them I'm a heretic?"

"You tell them you left for reasons you do not care to discuss," Mom said firmly.

I rolled my eyes a bit and nodded. It was the standard, churchy, no-gossip answer that did nothing to stop rampant speculation. I brought the peas to the stove and trickled them into the pot. Mom stirred in water, and we retreated to the table, Mom carrying the teakettle.

"They'll see right through that." I shrugged, settling into my chair. "They'll figure I was asked to leave."

"And that hurts *your* ego." Mom tried to suppress a smile, failed.

I blinked and let out a chuckle. "Yeah, I guess. But I have to admit that outside of the social aspect, I don't have a lot of desire to stay at St. Mike's." I struggled to put my thoughts into words. "It feels more like . . . school to me. Shouldn't church be . . . more reverent, somehow? It's as if God is an excuse for our party, instead of being the whole reason we live. Is this making any sense?"

Mom nodded, pouring hot water into our cups. "So how would you change St. Mike's, if you could?"

"Eeek," I said with a little laugh. "Changing a Sanctioned Church . . . isn't that heresy?"

We both knew the answer to that one.

"Hypothetically speaking." Her smile was gentle.

I pondered the question, my eyes on the cheery sunflower wallpaper. "I want to study the *whole* Bible, not just the passages that Prinister Severs uses for his sermons. I have to study whole books on my own. Which is okay, but context would be helpful. I mean, was Queen Esther just a beauty pageant winner? I think there's more to it."

"Now there's a good example," Mom said. "Esther saved the Jews, but only because she was obedient to Mordecai."

I grimaced, and Mom waved a hand.

"Ignore me," she said. "Tell me what else you're thinking."

"I want to dig into Jeremiah, and it's hardly ever mentioned." My enthusiasm built as I warmed to my topic. "Socializing should take a back seat to worship. And our worship should be . . ." I hurled myself out of my chair and paced the kitchen. "Open! Exuberant! Joyful! Not so regulated and stilted."

Mom smiled, and I blinked, surprised that she hadn't gently corrected my attitude.

Emboldened, I propped a thigh against the counter. "Remember two weeks ago when we were singing 'Wholly Unto Thee'?"

Mom nodded. "Bart kept looking at you."

"It's such a moving song! And it was like I could feel God smiling at me—like I could feel His joy, His love!" I gnawed my lip. "Mom, I almost started crying."

She gasped, her eyes rounding. "Right there on the platform?"

I nodded. "I managed to choke it back, but I couldn't control my pitch. And when we got back to the green room after the set, Bart told me my behavior was completely inappropriate. 'We're supposed to be moderately upbeat,' he said. 'Never give in to emotion during a set.' Like I chose to! And then he told me he might have to explain my actions to Prinister Severs and asked me if it were my 'time of blessed womanhood.' Like he could use that as an excuse."

"He didn't!"

"Why *can't* we cry during worship?" I asked. "Or dance, or laugh—whatever? God gave us our range of emotions; why is it heretical to display them in His presence? 'Moderately upbeat.'" I snorted.

"Sweetie, you won't find a Sanctioned Church anywhere that will allow that." Mom's face was a warning.

I flopped into my chair, sighing. "I know. But why not? What are they so afraid of?"

Mom didn't display any impatience as she set her cup in its saucer, idly rotating the handle. "They refer to the scripture that says things in the service must be done decently and in order. And as with all things from the Sanctioned Church, it has been applied to our society with a rather broad brush."

"In the service." My thoughts cartwheeled. *Who decided that meant—*

Mom was still talking. "The church teaches that unchained passions lead to sin. We mustn't be controlled by desire, whether for a spouse and children, material wealth, or even spiritual enlightenment." Mom gestured around the apartment. "We accept what God gives because all is a gift. Displaying emotion is a signature of desire, and so we must not—"

"—yield to emotion," I chimed in. "Yeah, I know, I've had the lessons. But it doesn't make sense to me that there's anything indecent about tears. The Bible itself tells us Jesus wept. Doesn't that mean that God not only understands emotion, but He also experiences it?"

"I agree," Mom said mildly.

I looked at her and blew out a breath. "I'm . . . venting."

She smiled and patted my hand. "You're allowed. Just keep it at home from now on."

That explained why she wasn't chastising me. We sat in silence while I sipped my tea, trying to calm down and cognizant of the irony. But the questions wouldn't go away. *God, I'm tired of being afraid of the church.* The thought startled me.

"You know what bugs me?" I said, setting my cup in its saucer. Mom nodded, encouraging, and that was all it took. The bitter, sinful words tumbled out, but I was so troubled, I didn't censor them. "I look at the elders and the deacons, Prinister Hernandez and Severs and the Sunday school teachers, and I think about that passage in Romans that says we should be transformed by the renewing of our minds. And I—Mom—" At last I let it out, my eyes on hers. "I don't . . . see that . . . in them."

Her eyebrows went up. "You know it isn't our job to judge anyone else's walk," she pointed out.

"Yeah, although I've noticed they're pretty quick to judge ours." I knew it wasn't my place to criticize the servants of God. I knew Mom would remonstrate with me. But I spoke the blasphemy aloud anyway, my eyes on the sunflower-patterned wallpaper. *If I have to go to confession anyway, might as well make it good.* "When I look at those people, Mom, I realize . . . I don't like them. And I don't want to *be* like them. They're mean. Cruel. Judgmental, and they wrap it all in Bible verses, like that makes it okay. I don't want my character transformed into *that.*"

The words were unbiblical, I knew. Judgmental in their own right. Worldly. The admission was painful, but it had been brewing for a long time. Mom might as well know what a horrible daughter she had. I couldn't meet her gaze. I sighed, focused on my hands in my lap, guilt raking my mind.

"Well then." Her voice was a loving caress and carried none of the shock or rebuke I expected. "Let us pray that God will transform you into who He wants you to be, not who anyone else wants you to be. And let's pray that if He wants us out of St. Mike's, He'll make a way to move us."

Astonishment drained my face of expression. She smiled, her eyebrows lifting, and a moment later we both burst out laughing. Why did my mother's understanding always surprise me? She always seemed to know me better than I knew myself.

And that became our prayer, just the two of us, every night for a long time.

It didn't occur to me then how dramatic God's answer might be.

# 17. CONSTRUCTION

"Meryn, come take a look," Walker called.

I stepped back from where I was nailing together pallet pieces, pulled off my tattered blue glove, and stuck my aching thumb in my mouth. My tiny house was almost complete, and Walker and Kilte had tasked me with starting the floor for another. That was their nice way of getting me out of the way so they could work. All I had succeeded in doing—in my opinion—was hammering my thumb. I hoped my paltry efforts wouldn't have to be redone. The severe cold had abated and the sun was shining, but it was still frigid work, pulling pallets apart and nailing them back together.

Happy for the break, I tossed down Walker's hammer and strode to the front of the tiny house where he stood, arms crossed and chin in hand, regarding his work.

My eyes opened wide. He and Kilte had just finished the roof, and my tiny house actually looked like a house! Well, a shed; they'd long since eschewed a traditional house roof in favor of the easier, cheaper, single-slant roof. I couldn't care less and did a joyful little dance. "Yes!" I cried. "Walker, it's a tiny tin house!"

He was grinning. "It's *your* tiny tin house, Miss Flint! You help us out on two more and your sweat equity is paid in full."

"You want my help?" I laughed, lifting my eyebrows. "You do want houses that don't fall over, right?"

"Your foundation's good and solid, Meryn," Kilte said, coming around from where I'd been working, slapping his gloves against his thigh. "Your labor's a little slow, which is understandable, but your floor work is well done."

Walker nodded at Kilte, looking at me. "See? There you go. The general contractor approves!"

"Thanks, Kilte," I said. "You guys taught me well."

"You picked it up quick," Kilte replied, pulling frozen dead grass and mud off his gloves. "It was nice not having to babysit for a change."

"If I may interrupt the mutual admiration," Walker said with a laugh, "Meryn, here are your keys." He handed them to me with a little bow.

A thumbprint lock was out of my budget, so I'd bought a traditional padlock. I accepted the keys with a sense of triumph.

Kilte swept off his cap as I came by, his grand, complex gesture toward the door more appropriate for someone of Governance Caste or higher. He looked so comical I couldn't help but laugh. In the days since I'd joined them for church, he'd been scrupulously appropriate in his behavior toward me. I hoped it would last.

Ray had started riding me about giving Steffan another chance. My stepdad didn't seem to understand that my *no* was non-negotiable.

Pushing those worries aside, I pulled aside the door catch—it gave a loud, metallic *clack!*—and opened the door.

The inside was unfinished, of course. The metal exterior covered a traditional wood frame. I'd blown most of my budget on a tiny wood-stove, with just enough left over to buy four precious glass panels for a small window by the front door. The house had no running water and no electricity, and the studs were exposed for all to see. But I didn't care. It was mine, and I loved it at once. Tears stung my eyes. *Mom . . . can you see this? My house!*

A quiet voice came from outside. Kilte. "Uh, may we come in?"

"Oh!" I dashed moisture from my cheeks and spun around, smiling. "Of course . . ."

Grinning, Kilte slapped Walker's arm with his gloves, and with only a touch of his usual conceit, stepped over the threshold and gave the place a casual once-over, nodding. "Nice, even if I do say so myself," he said in his jocular fashion. "Walk, whadda ya say?"

Walker's bulk dwarfed the door, darkening the room, and I stepped back to give him space, perplexed at how I couldn't seem to breathe properly whenever he was in close proximity.

"Thanks, dude. I can see now," Kilte joked, and I smiled at him, grateful for the interruption.

Walker was examining the joins and stability of the panels as if he hadn't just installed them. When he looked up to check the small trusses, he caught my expression and his eyes crinkled. "It's a fool who thinks his work is perfect the first go."

"Well then, call this fool hungry!" Kilte replied. "You won't get better than this, Meryn. Let's get some lunch."

I laughed. "I think the twins are whipping up something special. I heard them plotting with Mags in the kitchen this morning—"

"That's all I need to hear!" Two long steps and Kilte was out the door. Walker followed, taking a last quick look at the door frame before disappearing outside. I tried to squelch an unwelcome disappointment at his absence and looked around the room to distract from my growing guilt.

"The bed could go there," I murmured, pondering the space in front of the door. "Or . . . under the short wall. Yeah, and a bucket in the corner with a curtain." My thoughts excited me. "Maybe after another paycheck, I could—"

"Meryn!" Kilte roared from far outside. "Eat now, admire later!"

With a contented sigh, I exited, closing the door behind me and securing the lock. Then I ran the hundred feet or so to Mags's, where Walker held the door open.

A delicious smell wafting from the kitchen had me salivating before he even shut the door.

"All done?" Mags called.

"Another one bites the dust!" Kilte crowed. "Harris and Walker Construction strikes again!" Walker regarded his friend with amusement.

"Congratulations, Meryn!" Mags sang out. The twins stopped to applaud. Then Ellie went back to setting the table. Lisha was slicing bread.

"What is that wonderful smell?" I kept having to swallow.

"It's a surprise!" Lisha bounced on her heels.

"Mom, you didn't," Walker said, but he was smiling.

"Of course I did!" Mags opened the squeaky oven door and, with no small effort, lifted out a large baking dish full of something browned and bubbling. "It's a special occasion! It's Meryn's Independence Day!"

I'd never thought of it that way. As she set the casserole in the center of the table, I *ooohed* my appreciation.

"It's lasagna." Mags pulled off her red oven mitts and hung them on their hooks while Ellie bounced excitedly, looking over her shoulder. "We used canned tomatoes from last year's harvest, basil and oregano . . ."

"And cheese!" Ellie broke in.

"Real cheese?" Kilte asked, astonished.

"Yep!" Her smile was smug, and I couldn't blame her. "Lots and lots!"

"Oh, Mags!" I said, overwhelmed. *That's so expensive!*

"We may be eating rice and beans for the next six months, but today, let's celebrate!" Mags said. Ellie cut the casserole into even pieces. The first one she set on a plate, Mags promptly covered and put in the fridge. "This slice is for Bree, since she had to work. Sit down, everyone, and let's eat!"

"You better put it where I can't find it," Kilte joked as we took our seats.

"Don't be mean." Lisha turned from setting bread on the table and poked him.

After a quick grace, we dug in, and the tiny house grew quiet. I'd never had real lasagna—cheese was too expensive, and now I understood why. The flavor was incredible.

"I think I might just be guilty of gluttony." I put another bite in my mouth and rolled my eyes heavenward.

"Mmm," Ellie mumbled agreement. "Is it possible to lust after food?" Lisha laughed.

"This food, absolutely!" Kilte said through a mouthful. "That's it—I'm leaving Bree for a serving of lasagna." The twins giggled.

I forced a smile but said nothing. I was learning not to be offended by Kilte's offbeat sense of humor.

As we finished our portions, we all started digging into the empty casserole dish, looking for the last little bits, picking burnt cheese off the edges.

"Good thing I took Bree's portion out first." Mags arched an eyebrow, but she didn't chide any of us for our table manners.

Lisha burped. "'Scuse me."

Ellie giggled and rose, gathering our dirty plates.

"I should do that," I protested, but she shook her head.

"This is your party," she said, carrying them into the kitchen.

"I read somewhere that burping is a compliment to the cook," Walker said at the same time.

"Well, in that case . . ." Ellie set her stack of plates in the sink and belched louder, and everyone laughed.

"Thank you, Ellie!" Smiling, Mags shifted her attention to me. "Congratulations, dear."

"Thank you, Mags." Warm gratitude overwhelmed me as I looked around at these new friends whose generosity was keeping me alive. I tried not to think about Steffan. "And thank you, Walker and Kilte. Your work is stunning."

"Glad you like it, Meryn," Walker said.

"That's Kilte and Walker," Kilte put in.

Walker grinned and turned to Mags. "So what's on this afternoon?"

"We *are* having a town meeting!" Mags replied, rising and gathering mugs. "The temperature is supposed to drop later, so we decided to meet while the meeting is good."

Ellie was running hot water, filling the sink.

"No bonfire?" Lisha looked disappointed.

Mags laughed. "We'll have a bonfire, sweetie." She set the mugs on the drainboard and stroked Lisha's hair. "Just earlier than usual."

The girl brightened, and I remembered how anything out of the ordinary is an event when you're ten.

As the girls started the dishes, I slipped Mags my spare key, just on the off chance she would ever need access to my house. Then I climbed to the loft to assess my belongings and figure out what might go where in the tiny house. I would need some type of closet; I considered rigging a hanging rod from the roof trusses and planned to scrounge some boxes for undies and sweats.

Even though my tiny tin house was technically finished, it would be another two weeks before I could move in. Kilte and Walker had installed the woodstove, but I needed a bed of sorts and a couple pieces of improvised furniture to make the place livable. For that, I'd need a paycheck or two. So, two weeks.

I checked my bank balance and winced; my paychecks were going way too fast. Carole had me scheduled for twenty hours a week, which would have been fine when I was living at Ray's. But living on my own, my paycheck didn't stretch enough to cover my needs. I had no choice but to ask for more hours. "Not exactly the smartest move for a new employee," I murmured. *So I risk my job and ask for more hours, or I work what I'm given and starve. That's not much of—*

"Time for the meeting!" At Mags's call, Ellie shut off the water.

Pushing aside my worries, I grabbed my coat and followed Mags and the girls outside. People were coming out of tiny houses all up and down the U and gathering around the firepit. A balding, overweight man tossed logs made of hay and wax on the fire, building it up. He wore a filthy coat, grease-stained shorts, and sneakers with no socks or laces.

Ellie and Lisha ran toward the fire, moths to a flame.

"Girls, careful!" Mags called. "Don't get too close!"

Tamar and Pris approached, Tamar finding Walker and slipping her gloved hand under his arm. I noticed her gloves were new—and they looked like real leather. I wondered how she managed to afford them. Walker turned in surprise and smiled, bending to give her a peck on the cheek. Pris wrapped her arms around his waist.

The girl and boy I had seen tossing a ball my first week at Shady Dell weaved between the adults, laughing and shrieking. Happy for the distraction, I watched them play tag with Lisha and Ellie, well away from the fire. Lisha had told me their names were Iscah and Gabriel Owle. A gaggle of older women crowded around Mags, their faces furrowed and earnest. Kilte was flirting with a parka-clad young woman with a red cap who giggled every time he spoke. I tried not to frown. *Does he do this a lot when Bree's at work?* Across the firepit, a woman with straight, glossy black hair and olive skin watched them too, her expression reflecting detached amusement. I guessed her to be in her twenties.

The man with the shorts began turning in a circle, hitting a cowbell with a stick, and the talk thinned and died. Some people had brought chairs or stools, and others brushed the snow from large rocks set in proximity to the fire. Everyone else just pressed in close.

"Well, ain't it nice it warmed up," the man said to scattered laughter.

"We see you got the shorts out, Handy," a man called.

Handy chuckled. "Th' legs needed to breathe." He lifted first one thick leg, then the other, while several women watched, their expressions stony.

"Junia, y' wanna update us?" Handy asked, offering the cowbell to an older woman who had been chatting with Mags.

Junia's smooth gray hair was tucked up under a worn green hat, but she had the quiet, reserved manner of the high caste. She accepted the cowbell with a cordial nod. "I thank you, Handy," she said in a mellifluous alto. "First, God has answered our prayers: The RD released Josiah Morton from prison, and he is home with his father in Grove's Corner."

A smattering of applause, and a few people called out, "Praise God!"

"And several people have approached me with ideas to extend our growing season." She sobered. "There is some concern that this year's harvest won't see us through the winter, and even though we can forage when spring arrives—"

"Weeds for lunch! Yum, yum!" a thin, black-haired man yelled. Someone laughed. A woman grimaced and muttered something to the woman next to her, who shrugged and gave her a wry smile.

The crowd shifted, and I saw Kilte standing across the firepit, behind the first grouping of people. The girl was nowhere in sight.

Junia smiled, waved a hand. "While not universally accepted as a viable option, it is still food. And medicine. But some root vegetables to supplement it would be a great comfort to many of our families."

"Only the lazy hashers," a man behind me muttered. My eyes widened, but I didn't turn.

Junia didn't hear the quiet comment. "Clara suggested we build a greenhouse. The produce—"

"The RD would love that!" a red-haired man to my left interrupted.

"You don't have the bell, Tyler," Walker observed.

"I thought this was supposed to be a discussion," Tyler shot back.

"He and Judith are new," a voice murmured at my elbow, startling me. Mags. She gave me an apologetic smile.

"As the bell-ringer, I agree that Tyler has brought up a valid point," Junia said graciously. "Greenhouses are against the law. However, we're already in violation of the law with the garden, so we—"

"Two wrongs don't make a right," Tyler said, sticking out his chin.

Junia sobered. "You have not been recognized."

"Bell-ringer?" A thin woman with sallow skin raised her hand.

"Yes, Huldah?"

"We need the extra food security. The widows got very hungry last year, and so did many of our children. And while I'm not keen on breaking the law," she said with a sidelong glance at Tyler, "where can we put the thing where it won't attract attention?"

Kilte's eyes rested on me. I tried not to look at him.

"Good point," said a woman with salt-and-pepper hair. "That's the last thing we need—trouble with the RD." Her shoulders hunched and she darted nervous glances around the community, as if expecting Guards to burst out of hiding.

"We've studied this possibility," Mags said, loud enough that her voice would carry. "The only logical place is on the west side of Tin Town where we still have some room."

"Wait, our hipster is there!" a man called out in protest.

An older woman in a hand-knitted orange beanie cap waved her hand. "Where are we supposed to put new people?"

Protests erupted from all sides.

"New people? We can't even take care of the people we have!"

"This is crazy!"

"What, you *like* being hungry?" From somewhere behind me, the woman's voice trailed off into a horrible, wet hacking. She spat, and I tried not to grimace.

"My grandmother almost starved, and—"

I crossed my arms and hunched my back, wondering how close she was, if she was contagious.

"This is against the law! What do you people not understand—"

"I'm not going to let my little ones go hungry, you—"

"We have too many people as it is!"

Kilte rolled his eyes.

"I'm tired of worrying about food!"

Junia struck the cowbell until the babble died down. "Mags," she said, with a courteous nod.

Mags smiled her thanks. "It isn't ideal," she said. "We'll have to decide how big a structure we need, how much room it would take, and so on. Pete, we can move you and Tabitha, and Thad's hipster. We'll reroute your electricity."

"Move us?"

Walker raised his hand, and Junia nodded. "Pete," he said, turning toward the man. Tamar shifted to keep her hand on his arm, her lips tightening. "Moving a hipster is pretty easy because they're all one piece and the floors are solid. We hook it up with a tow chain and we're good to go. But my concern is power. We'll need to keep the greenhouse warm and light, so stuff grows. We all know how cold it gets here in winter."

"Bell-ringer?" A young teenage girl raised her hand.

"Yes, Katia?"

"Can I move into the greenhouse?"

Everyone laughed. An older man with graying black hair and a beard—her father?—tousled her hat, releasing her curly hair. She smiled and grabbed her hat before it fell.

"Bell-ringer?"

"Yes, Celeste?"

"Maybe we shouldn't build a greenhouse," the woman next to Mags said, twisting her wool cap in her hands. Her gray hair blew across her face. "Maybe we should build a shed with grow lights, so the neighbors can't see anything. Or the hover people."

A few people laughed. Tyler's face scrunched into a grimace.

"No, that's a good idea," Junia responded. "The lower the profile, the better."

"So how are we going to pay for all this?" Tyler asked.

"It would be an extension of our HOA dues—perhaps a special assessment," Junia replied. "We will come up with a couple of different options and put it to a vote."

The wind was coming in gusts now, chasing the fire out of the pit and sending smoke into my eyes, and I coughed. Walker glanced at me, his brow furrowing. When I met his eyes, his expression cleared, and he looked away.

"So, more taxes." Tyler folded his arms, belligerent.

"We do not *tax*, Mr. Eberhard," Junia said, and for the first time I heard a note of impatience in her voice.

"Sounds like it to me," he said in a surly tone.

"You may certainly sell or move your THOW elsewhere if you believe our governance is unfair." Junia turned away. A young blonde woman in a blue coat—I assumed it was Judith—pulled at Tyler's arm, whispering in his ear. Snarling, he jerked free.

Junia gave them no more attention. "Everyone who thinks we should proceed with a greenhouse, say aye."

A chorus of *ayes* responded.

"Those opposed, say nay."

A few people yelled *nay*, including Tyler. I noticed Judith kept silent.

Junia struck the cowbell once. "The *ayes* have it; the motion is carried." She looked around. "Any new business?"

A dark-skinned man spoke. "Bell-ringer, Faith and I would like to add two solar panels to our THOW. With the kids growing and Mom moving in, we need more power."

"You know the risk." Junia was grave.

From the corner of my eye, I saw Tamar whisper something to Walker. A moment later, she disappeared into the crowd.

"We do," he said. "That's why we're bringing it up to everyone."

"This isn't in the bylaws," Mags murmured, "but it might as well be. It's considered being neighborly."

"Does anyone object to Zechariah and Faith installing two more solar panels?" Junia asked, scanning the assembly.

This time, no one responded.

"Zeke, you and Faith may proceed, and may God bless your endeavor. Other new business?" Junia looked around the circle.

"We have a new neighbor," Mags called out. "Everyone, meet Meryn. She just finished her hipster today!"

"Welcome, Meryn!" Junia smiled warmly, and others called greetings.

The sudden press of faces and eyes unnerved me. I waved, shy. "Thank you. It's good to be here."

"If you need help finishing your interior, Meryn, just ask around," Junia told me. "We have several tradespeople here who can help make your place more comfortable."

I nodded and smiled my thanks. The wind gusted again, blowing sparks from the bonfire. Several people stepped back.

"Everyone, say hello to Meryn when you have the chance. Is there anything else?" Junia looked around the circle. "No? Then shall I motion to adjourn?"

"Seconded!" several people yelled.

Junia hit the cowbell. "Meeting adjourned!"

The relief was palpable. As if mocking the bonfire's warmth, a cold wind rose, and the crowd dispersed within moments, most people hurrying back to their houses. Walker had vanished, but I noticed Tamar slipping away from the older woman with salt-and-pepper hair.

*Is she looking at me?* I couldn't be sure, and several people approached, distracting me.

"It is such a pleasure to have you with us." A woman with white hair touched my arm. She wore several sweaters over a tan MT, and I wondered if she owned a coat. Although her face bore the lines of a difficult life, her countenance was peaceful, her manner gracious. "My name is Bernice—I'm a friend of Mags's. Please let me know if you need anything, and I'll be happy to help if I can. My THOW is right over there." She pointed.

"Thank you, Bernice," I said, and she smiled and stepped aside.

The older woman with salt-and-pepper hair strode up to Mags, frowning and motioning in my direction.

"Welcome to Shady Dell!" A short young woman bounded over from my right, wearing a purple parka. "I'm Hagar Calderón Espinosa. My kids are running around somewhere," and she waved a hand. "If they're skinny and have red hair, they're mine." She grinned, showing a broken front tooth and dimples. Frizzy red curls crowded out from under her hood.

"Nice to meet you," I said. "I promise, I'll forget your name at least twice."

She laughed. "Me too! I'm lousy with names. But 'Meryn' is unusual enough I think I might remember it. If you were another 'Debbie,' well, no guarantees." She pointed down the U. "We're in the blue house with the white picket fence."

"Oh, you have the fence! Your place is so charming! It's straight out of a storybook."

The older woman's voice intruded, her tone full of outrage. ". . . a runaway, rejected by her father's house! Not to mention the caste, which . . ."

"Marian—" I heard Mags say.

*Oh no.* I bit my lip as I turned my attention to Hagar.

She rolled her eyes at the older woman, then grinned. "Yeah, the kids insisted. 'We gotta have a picket fence, Mom!'"

"Did you get help with it?" I asked, and she nodded.

"Walker and Kilte put it up for me. I traded them two dozen quart jars of my famous tomato soup. If you can find something to trade or barter," she offered, "that'll make life here a lot easier."

"Hmmm." I wondered what on earth I could trade. "Thanks for the advice."

"Don't mention it. Us single chicks gotta stick together!" She sobered, glancing at the woman, who was still in mid-rant. "Don't pay any attention to Marian. She worries about the Guards." Hagar gave a long-suffering sigh. "Constantly. But we know—"

"Meryn!" Handy was striding toward me across the frozen ground.

"Oops!" Hagar pulled her hood around her face. "Stop in anytime, Meryn!" She scurried away as Handy strode up. He watched her retreat before turning to me.

"Name's Clarence Peters, but call me Handy." The man was as big as Walker, but heavier, with a belly that obscured his belt. Despite the cold, Handy exuded a sour smell. His eyes disappeared in the fleshy folds of his face, his greasy hair was combed to hide a bald spot, and a three-day growth of stained, gray beard covered his chin. Mom would have called him "unkempt."

*What a slob,* I thought.

"Anythin' y'need for your new house," Handy was saying. "Don't worry about the cost—you can pay me later. You want power? Plumbing? Handy's your man. I own The Handyman's Shop, y'see. I've got it all." He winked. "And I'm the best at putting it in."

"He charges too much." A woman's voice, cold.

Handy's eyes widened as the olive-skinned woman stopped next to me. She had the countenance of a Mayan queen, with clear, luminous skin and dark eyes. Her hot pink parka didn't hide her womanly figure, and she wore expensive pink snow boots.

Handy's expression turned amused. "You didn't seem to have any trouble paying, Merica."

Her gaze on him was like a knife, her tone glacial. "I didn't have much choice, did I?" Her attention shifted to me, and she looked me up and down, arching a perfectly groomed left eyebrow. "Do yourself a sterling favor, kitten," she said, and although her tone was warmer, it was still several degrees shy of friendly. "Find another handyman." Turning away, she strolled toward the hipsters.

Handy looked after her, chuckling. "Don't worry about her. She got all resentful when she couldn't pay, and we had to make other arrangements. But you"—he patted my shoulder—"I heard y' got a job, so you won't have any problem."

"Thank you, Handy," I said, stepping back. "I'll keep that in mind."

"You do that." His gaze traveled to my shoes, then rose, lingering on my hips, my chest, my mouth. "You do that very thing, kitten."

My tone went as icy as Merica's. "My name is Meryn."

"I know what your name is," he whispered, holding my eyes. Then he grinned and bellowed, "Taylor!" I jerked, and he turned away, following a startled man with black hair.

The woman I'd seen talking to Mags was striding in my direction. Ignoring Handy, she stopped in front of me, her face drawn into angry lines, her eyes clouded. "Why are you here?"

Blinking, perplexed, I took a small step backward. "I—I'm here because God brought me here."

Marian shook her head. "God didn't bring you here—disobedience did! Satan did!" She leaned in, her eyes intense, and gripped my arm. "You must repent! Repent, and go back to your father!"

My mouth dropped open, and I vacillated between anger at her presumption and wondering if she was right. "I . . . uh . . ." Words refused to come.

"Hello, Marian." Kilte stood behind her, his hands in his pockets. His stance was casual, but something hostile burned in his eyes.

She stiffened without turning, and her eyes narrowed, not leaving mine. "You don't belong here, little girl. You're Worker Caste. If you care about Mags and her family, go home. Before you hurt people."

I shook my head. "I don't mean to—" I began, but she wheeled away and marched toward a nearby THOW.

Feeling caught in a whirlwind, I turned to Kilte, who gave me a cynical smile, quite unlike his usual open grin. "Sorry I didn't get here sooner."

"Is this the usual initiation?" I asked, matching his pessimism.

"For women, yes. Especially since you haven't renounced your caste. Handy likes a challenge." Kilte looked past me to where the big man was chatting volubly with Taylor.

"Well, that sounds fair." A sudden rush of fury made me hot inside my jacket. *Just like Ray.*

Kilte turned sober. "It isn't. Marian's just a pain—nobody's going to call the Guards on you for wearing a blue ring—but Handy doesn't take no for an answer," he said, keeping his voice low. "I keep an eye out. You have any trouble, you let me or Walker know, okay? We'll take care of it."

"Do you charge too, Kilte?" I looked him in the eyes, not bothering to hide my anger at his own inappropriate behavior.

For the first time, I saw him redden. "Nah, Meryn," he replied, looking anywhere but at me. "Never." He pivoted and strode back to Mags's.

I followed, my pace slower, nodding to various people who said hello, wondering if I really was any safer at Shady Dell.

# 18. DAMAGE

When I opened the apartment door, Ray was standing in the living room with his coat on as if he'd been waiting for me.

Nerves wrapped tentacles around my throat. "Going out?" I said, struggling to keep my tone from sounding strangled. "If you're not interested in dinner, I can—"

"We both are," he interrupted. "We're going to St. Mike's. Now."

My eyes widened, and every bone in my body seemed to dissolve like limestone in acid. "I can't believe you're taking me there," I whispered, swaying in place. "After everything they did to us—"

"And they were right," Ray said, crossing to me. He put both hands on my shoulders. "Don't worry, Peanut. This is for the good of the family."

*The good of the*—My mouth dropped open. "How can you say that after what happened at the disciplinary hearing? Have you forgotten?"

That meeting marked a frightening new change in Ray's behavior and the beginning of the end of my allegiance to the Sanctioned Church.

It sprang from an incident that happened at St. Mike's several months after I'd left the praise team. I'd volunteered to help with the babies and toddlers that day because the nursery crew was down a person. My usual assignment was teaching the five- and six-year-olds, using a tablet to illustrate Bible stories. I discovered I loved teaching, loved working with kids. Every time a child memorized and recited a Bible verse correctly, she or he would receive a gold star.

I was keen to teach the girls. The boys were displaying arrogance even at that young age, so I made sure they didn't edge out the girls in class. Children were taught together until third grade, when they were segregated into separate classes like the adults.

First Service had finished, and I was walking to the sanctuary, which took me past the fenced play area. The five-and-older kids had been released into the playground to wait for their parents.

I was mentally reviewing my class, watching the kids with half my attention, when Jimmy Giff ran over to the swings. He yanked a little girl—it was Abigail Marino—out of a swing and screamed in her face, "This is my swing! *Mine!*" Her face twisting into a stubborn scowl, she clung to the plastic chains.

I looked around for the playground supervisor—it should have been Eli Hamilton—but saw no one. Taking a firm grip on my temper, I started toward the pair.

Jimmy didn't see me coming. He wrenched the swing out of Abigail's hands and, before she could move, punched her hard in the stomach. She screamed and fell to the ground, sobbing.

Cursing under my breath, I broke into a run and hurdled the fence. Jimmy wore new cowboy boots, and he kicked Abigail before I could reach him. He was just stepping back to kick her again when I grabbed a handful of his hair and yanked him away.

"Hey!" Face knotted with fury, the boy wheeled and threw a wild punch. I blocked him without thinking and twisted his arm up behind his back so he couldn't do it again. The other children stopped playing and crowded around, drawn by the drama.

"You know hitting is against the rules, Jimmy," I said mildly, while he struggled in my grip. Abigail lay motionless on the ground. I sucked in my breath at the nasty lump rising on her forehead, the blood seeping from gouges on her face. Abby attended my class; she wasn't more than five. Jimmy had just turned nine.

"Ow! You can't tell me what to do! You're a *girl!* Girls ain't nothin'! I have authority over you! Lemme go! I order you—"

"Not when you break the rules," I said. He tried to kick my shins, and I thrust him out of range. "Come on, we're going back inside. You need a time out." *And I need to take care of this little girl.* Behind me, the children muttered to each other.

"What's going on here?" a male voice demanded. Eli.

Jimmy screwed up his face and started bawling. "She hit me!" he wailed, pointing at me.

"No," I said, "but right now I really *want* to."

"Maureen, this isn't your assignment today." Eli's expression was reproving.

"I'm glad you're back, Eli. Here." I shoved Jimmy at Eli, who automatically took the boy's arm. Evading Jimmy's parting kick, I knelt next to Abigail. She wasn't crying, which frightened me, and her eyes wouldn't focus.

"Abby, shhh, sweetie. Come here," I said, trying to assess the damage. In addition to her forehead injury, her nose was bleeding and had doubled in size—either she fell on it, or Jimmy landed more than one kick. The little girl tried to get up, but she reeled. I caught her before she fell and rose with her in my arms. "She needs a doctor, Eli."

"Did she fall?" he asked, his eyebrows knitting.

"No," I said.

"Yes!" Jimmy yelled. Sarah Wilcox giggled.

"Jimmy pulled her out of the swing, punched her in the stomach and kicked her," I said, trying to keep my anger in check. "I didn't get over here fast enough."

"*Liar!*" Jimmy twisted in Eli's grip. "She's just a lying girl! You can't trust her!"

"She's not lying, you are!" an older girl yelled from the safety of the group.

"I'll find Abby's parents," I said. "Someone should call 911."

"Maureen, I should do that. I'm playground supervisor." Eli let go of Jimmy, who pushed past the other children and ran into the church.

"Very well." I handed Abby to him.

He set her down, and her legs buckled. He grabbed her by her dress and eased her to the ground.

I took a deep breath, trying not to grind my teeth. "She may have a head injury. Do you want me to keep her quiet while you call 911?"

"No, uh . . . I'll take care of it, thank you." He turned to Abigail. "Get up, Allie. We'll find your parents." He tried to pick her up by one arm, but she was limp. "Come on, stand up!"

*Oh, for Pete's sake!* Panic for Abby overwhelmed the sensible part of me, the part that said I was about to make a mistake. I gathered the girl into my arms again and pulled out my phone.

"Maureen—" Eli began.

I got a dispatch operator at once. "Yes, a little girl is badly hurt. She may have a head injury. No, an older boy struck and kicked her."

"Now, you don't know that," Eli temporized.

"Hold a moment, please," I told the operator. I turned to Eli. "Go find Abby's parents. The medAngels will need a parental release."

"You're not the parent?" the operator asked. "We'll need a man's authorization to—"

"Maureen, really—"

"No, sir," I said. "I'm a bystander." My patience snapped, and I put my phone against my shoulder. "For God's sake, Eli, do something! Go find her parents or I will!"

Eli's mouth dropped open, but he turned and hurried toward the church.

"Miss, we need a man's authorization to—"

"A little girl is hurt!" The words ground out of me like a cement block dragged over asphalt. "She needs—"

"Miss, you are wasting my time, and I will hang up if you don't—"

"Fine," I snarled into the phone. Whipping around, I found a boy in the gaggle of children, pointed. "You, Thomas—come here." He was only twelve, but his voice had changed; he'd do.

By the time Abby's worried parents had been located, the medAngels had arrived with an ambulance.

Abby's mom ran to her daughter. The medAngels were treating the bleeding and had put a cervical collar around the girl's neck. "What happened?" she asked, her face ashen. I remembered her name was Dorcas.

"She's pretty badly hurt, ma'am. We have to take her for a few tests," an Angel said.

The other turned to Abby's father. "Sir, if you'll present your wrist, we'll get the admission file started on the way," he said.

Without argument, the man held out his arm. As the tech scanned his chip, Mr. Marino turned to me. "Were you watching her when she fell?"

I shook my head. "She didn't fall, Mr. Marino. An older boy beat her up."

"What? Where is this boy?" He looked around the playground.

"I believe Jimmy Giff is inside the church," I said.

"I thought you nursery workers were supposed to prevent fights!" he said, his voice rising.

"One, two, three." The medAngels lifted Abby's gurney into the ambulance. Dorcas climbed in after them.

A monitor turned to Abby's father. "We're going to Silvermine Children's, sir, if you want to meet us there."

"Thank you," he said, then turned to glare at me. "You are not qualified to watch children, young lady, and I will take this up with Prinister Severs."

Eli folded his arms, his chin thrust out.

As Marino strode toward the parking lot, Eli headed back into the church. Looking after him, I saw Jimmy Giff watching from one of the classroom windows. He stuck out his tongue at me.

Furious, I stuck my tongue out right back.

~

On a humid, overcast evening three days later, Mom, Ray, and I found ourselves sitting in the church's boardroom with Prinister Severs and the Board, as well as Solomon Giff, Joseph Marino, and Eli.

I had immediately shared the incident with Mom and Ray. It didn't go over well. Ray launched a tirade about my "stupidity" for involving myself in an issue that didn't concern me, especially when a man was in authority, and when Mom tried to intervene, he accused her of always taking my side and stomped out of the apartment.

We received a summons the next day, which didn't improve Ray's temper. Over the following two days, the tension in the house was thick as pea soup, despite Mom's efforts to smooth things over. When we got to church that evening, Ray was still nursing a short fuse, I'd bitten my nails to the quick, and Mom was working to maintain a positive expression.

"Maybe it won't be so bad," she said in the car on our way over. "Maybe they'll just give us a warning."

Ray snorted.

"You raised Meryn to be thoughtful and kind," she reminded him. "She did protect and help a little girl. It might be helpful to keep that at the forefront of the conversation."

"As if they give a crap about some little girl," Ray muttered.

I'd never seen the boardroom at St. Mike's. With its elevated dais, it reminded me of da Vinci's *The Last Supper*; the twelve board members sat in padded chairs at a long table of carved wood. Prinister Severs's chair was centered behind a podium with an imposing frontispiece that bore a cross, the RD logo and the logo for St. Mike's. A black box was positioned at each seat, but I didn't know its function.

The effect was extremely intimidating.

Ushers led us to a row of rickety folding chairs, small and crowded too close together, facing the dais. Mom and Ray settled me between them. Eli, Giff and Marino pulled their chairs away from ours, Giff acting as if we might infect him with something vile. For a moment, I wished we could; then I bit my lip in repentance.

A bailiff standing to the side cracked a gavel. "Oyez, oyez, oyez, this hearing will now come to order," he said. "All rise."

Severs entered from a side door, his black judicial robes billowing.

"The right honorable, distinguished God-appointed Prinister Noah Severs, presiding," the bailiff said as Severs settled in the imposing center chair and slid his green ring on his forefinger. "You may be seated."

Severs scanned the room, his expression hard and commanding. His gaze stopped on Mom. "Mrs. Esselin's presence was *not* requested."

That startled me. Ray, sitting on my left, got to his feet. "This is a hearing of the utmost importance," he said, his hands folded and his chin down. "We felt that because of its critical nature, we should address it as a family."

"Interruptions of these proceedings by an emotional female will not be tolerated." Prinister Severs's voice was granite. "This Board must be held in the highest respect."

"Of course," Ray acknowledged, and sat.

Prinister Severs gave Ray a piercing look, as if trying to divine his veracity, then moved on. "We are here today to address an incident last Sunday that precipitated injury and injustice to two of our children."

I blinked. *Two?*

"We will also address the egregious breach of church policy that led to this unfortunate incident."

*That's encouraging,* I thought. Church policy stated that children were never to be left unsupervised on the playground.

"I want justice for my son!" Solomon Giff shot to his feet. A large, bear-like man with thick, silvering black hair and a full white beard, he looked and sounded like an Old Testament prophet. His heavy red hands clenched into fists.

Prinister Severs raised a placating hand. "That is why we are here, Brother Giff, I assure you. First," he turned to Eli, as Giff took his seat, "let us hear the sequence of events. Brother Hamilton?"

I lifted my hand. "Excuse me."

Prinister Severs gave me an angry glare and banged his gavel. "You are out of order, Miss Esselin!"

I bit my lip, and Ray stiffened.

"Honey," Mom whispered.

"I'm sorry, but how is Abigail?" I asked. We'd been praying for her but hadn't heard a thing since she was bundled into the ambulance.

Joseph Marino looked at me in surprise. "Well, she—"

"We will get to that, Mr. Marino," Prinister Severs said, and Marino sat back. "I will tolerate no further interruptions. Please continue, Brother Hamilton."

Several board members looked at me with expressions varying from disdain to overt hostility. I didn't let my puzzlement show on my face. *What are they so angry about?*

Nervous, Eli cleared his throat. "Uh, right. On the day in question, I was supervising the playground during and after First Service. Prudence Tincher was sick, so it was only me. I needed, um"—he glanced at Mom and reddened—"a bathroom break, so I appointed one of the older boys to watch the playground in my brief absence."

*Why didn't you go get Prinister Hernandez? He was right in the next room with the teens, and he was free.*

"And whom did you select?" Prinister Severs asked.

"James Giff. He has exhibited maturity and a keen interest in scripture, especially the letters of the Apostle Paul," Eli said.

*When you can get him to sit still and stop interrupting.* I sighed. I'd taught Jimmy's class on occasion.

"Most impressive," Prinister Severs said. Solomon Giff swelled a bit. "Go on. What did you see when you returned from your break?"

"Well, I saw this girl, Maureen"—he gestured toward me—"in the children's area. She had grabbed James Giff by the hair, and I believe she struck him."

My mouth dropped open. I felt Mom's fingers curl around mine.

"I see," Prinister Severs said. "And the little girl?"

"She was on the ground, crying like little girls do. I think she fell and skinned her knee."

I took in a breath to speak, but Mom squeezed my hand in warning.

"Uh . . . prinister?" Joseph Marino raised a tentative hand.

Severs shifted his gaze. "Brother Marino, you will get your turn." Marino subsided. "Go on, Brother Hamilton."

"Well, I took charge of the situation right away," he said, sounding more self-assured. "I forced Maureen to release the boy and asked him how badly he was hurt. He said he was fine—he's a tough young man— and he had been trying to help little Allie up after she fell off the swing, when Maureen attacked him."

That was *it*. "I did *not* attack him!"

"Meryn." Mom's whisper was urgent. "You mustn't—"

"Silence!" Prinister Severs bellowed, banging his gavel. "These proceedings will be respected!" Glaring at Ray for a long minute, he turned back to Eli. "Please go on."

"Well, the next thing I know, Maureen is calling the medAngels! I told her the child was fine and she should hang up, but she blatantly ignored my authority. I dismissed James to his father, as Brother Giff is generally prompt in picking him up after service, and then I went to find Brother Marino. I thought he should know that his daughter was about to take an unwelcome and expensive ambulance ride. It's a good thing I did, because when we got back, the medAngels had arrived and were bundling the little girl into an ambulance without a yea, nay or maybe." He looked at his hands.

*You having a hard time swallowing that one, Eli?* I bit my tongue, hard. *How can he lie like this? God, what's going on here?*

"And after that?" Prinister Severs prompted.

"Well, Mrs. Marino got into the ambulance with the little girl, and I believe Brother Marino followed in his car. I returned to the office to write up an incident report, per regulations." Eli nodded once, his chin lifting.

"I see," Prinister Severs said. "Very good, Brother Hamilton."

I looked around the chamber without moving my head. Green camera lights in the shadowed corners indicated that the whole session was being recorded from several angles.

"Do the gentlemen of the Board have questions for Brother Hamilton?" Prinister Severs asked.

A man with short-cropped, graying red hair pressed a switch, and a red light appeared on the black box in front of his chair. I recognized him but didn't know his name.

"The chair recognizes the distinguished member, Brother Deacon McAllen." The red light changed to green.

McAllen said, "Thank you, prinister. Brother Hamilton, how long have you worked with our children?"

"Six years," Eli replied. There was a murmur from the Board.

"Long time," Mom whispered, not moving her lips.

"And in that time, have you dealt with injuries or other conflicts such as these?"

Eli shrugged. "Kids get into arguments, but most kids at St. Mike's are pretty good. But I've never had a teen girl bully younger kids before. That's a new one."

My hand crushed Mom's. She stroked my thumb with hers, but her attempts to calm me weren't working.

McAllen nodded. He looked at me, and his lip curled. "No other questions, Prinister."

Prinister Severs asked, "Any other Board member?" After a moment of silence, Severs banged his gavel. "You may step down, Brother Hamilton."

Eli sat. He didn't look in my direction.

"The chair calls Brother Solomon Giff."

Giff rose.

"Brother Giff, would you share with us your understanding of the events last Sunday?"

"Of course." Giff had a sonorous voice and a polished delivery. "My son, James, came to me after service on Sunday, very upset. When I asked him what was wrong, at first he insisted there was nothing. But you understand," Giff raised an index finger, "I know my son. So I pressed him gently until the truth came out. He told me that Brother Hamilton had appointed him temporary playground supervisor—a great honor for such a young man—"

Prinister Severs was nodding. One of the Board members smiled.

"But he said that only minutes after Brother Hamilton left the playground, young Miss Marino fell out of her swing. He hurried over to render aid—she was crying, of course. As my vulnerable child was helping the little girl to her feet, he was brutally attacked from behind without warning. *This* woman"—Gill whipped around, extending his arm in a dramatic fashion to point at me—"seized him by the hair and struck him repeatedly!"

My hand gripped Mom's, hard. I took a deep breath, trying to control the panic rising in my gut. *Why are they—*

"And how did he get away?" Prinister Severs asked. Two Board members leaned forward in their chairs, leather creaking.

"I taught my little boy how to defend himself." Gill placed a hand on his chest, fingers splayed. "I never suspected that he might have to use the techniques at church, of all places, to defend himself from some insane woman. He was able to extricate himself from the grip of this—this *Jezebel*—and disable her further attempts to do him harm."

My incredulous huff came out louder than I intended. The whole fabrication was so insane, I didn't see how anyone could believe it.

Severs's mouth pinched, his gavel thudding with his fury. "Silence!" His gaze shifted to Ray. "This does not reflect well on your discipline, Mr. Esselin."

"For God's sake, Meryn," Ray hissed, *sotto voce*, "shut up!"

"Ray," I whispered, my eyes desperate on his, "they're lying about me—about everything!" *And why aren't you defending me?*

He murmured in my ear, "I know, but let it play out. We'll get our chance." He shifted to a normal tone. "Prinister Severs, please forgive the interruption."

Not looking at me, Severs gave him one more glare before turning back. "You may continue, Brother Giff."

*"Let it play out?" It's all going into the official record!* I remembered civics well enough to know that. And they couldn't recant their testimony without penalty.

"Well," Giff said. "James rendered her unable to move and continued to help little Miss Marino until Brother Hamilton returned and took charge of the situation. He then returned to the church and came to find me. Since the incident he has been most concerned about the little girl, asking me daily about her condition."

"And how is James?" Prinister Severs' face reflected concern.

"He sustained several bruises," Giff replied, "but he is recovering well, thank you."

I looked at Mom, hoping she'd caught the lie. Her lips compressed, and she nodded without looking at me.

Severs turned to the Board. "Questions for Brother Giff?"

No one said anything. A few of them shook their heads.

*I have dozens,* I thought. *Let's start with these supposed bruises and move on to that supposed training.*

"Very well, Brother Giff, you may be seated."

Giff sat, his chin in the air.

"Brother Marino," Severs said, "would you please share with us the condition of your daughter?"

"Yes, my son is most anxious to hear," Giff said from his chair.

Marino stood, shoulders hunched and hands together, his eyes darting from man to man. "Uh, Abby's improving. She's home now, but she has a broken nose and a lump on her forehead, as well as several cuts and severe bruising, especially on her stomach. The doctor said she has a slight concussion, so we're keeping her quiet."

Murmuring came from the Board members.

"I didn't know that James Giff was charged to watch her," Marino said, and now he looked at me.

I kept my expression neutral.

"You may sit down, Brother Marino," Prinister Severs said.

"Yes sir, but I am confused by the testimony I have heard tonight," Marino went on. "Abby told me quite definitively that James Giff pulled her out of the swing and then struck and kicked her. She's very afraid of him now." He paused, his hands whitening as his grip tightened. "She doesn't want to come back to church."

*Oh, thank You, God. Finally, the truth.*

Giff shot to his feet and rounded on the man. "You *dare* accuse my son of lying!"

"Now, now." Prinister Severs raised a benign hand, his face gentle. "Brother Marino, you stated that your young daughter suffered a head injury. That could make her recollection of the events faulty."

*Oh no. No.* My face went chill.

"Abby isn't prone to lying," Marino said.

"All children lie." Giff folded his arms and looked away.

"No one is accusing anyone of lying," Prinister Severs said, nodding, "but we all know that a head injury can leave anyone disoriented, especially a little girl. Please take your seat, Brother Marino."

"Prinister, the medAngels said her injuries were not consistent with simply falling out of—"

"Mr. Marino," Prinister Severs interrupted, smiling benevolently. "You're new to St. Michael's, aren't you?"

*No, he isn't—*

"My wife and I have attended here for five years. I don't see what—"

"Yes, you're new. Please take your seat."

Marino looked around uncertainly, but none of the Board members met his eyes. As he sat, I crushed Mom's hand again, a growing fury supplanting fear. *They didn't even listen to him! What's going on here?*

"Well." Severs's face fell into harsh lines, resolute and sorrowful. "We have heard all the details of this horrible incident. It is time to decide what action should be taken to discipline Miss Esselin for her role in the injury to our children."

*Action? Against me?* I sucked in a breath, and a wave of nausea made me grip my chair.

Severs went on. "Her actions on Sunday clearly violated church ethics and laws, and fly in the face of established Biblical hierarchy. Her failure to obey Brother Hamilton is a grave offense. As is manipulating an innocent young man to fraudulently call the medAngels."

I had just opened my mouth when Mom spoke. "Excuse me, Prinister Severs? With all respect, Meryn has not yet had opportunity to give her testimony."

My breath released. I couldn't let myself smile at Mom, but I thanked her with my eyes. Wary, I looked at the Board. *Lord, Mom is sticking her neck out for me. Please protect her.*

Severs looked at Mom, his eyes hooded. "Mrs. Esselin, your presence here is tolerated only by the grace of the Board. Please do not make things worse for your daughter or your family by drawing attention to your lack of discipline."

Mom didn't falter. "But she was there, prinister. The Board should hear her memory of the events."

Ray hissed, "For God's sake, Rose, shut up!"

"Mom is right," I said, keeping my voice calm and measured. "I have the legal, *constitutional right* to tell the truth of what happened."

The next thing I knew, the floor was rushing at my face. A loud buzzing filled my head on the left side—the side next to Ray—and for several long moments my body refused to obey my commands to rise. I felt Mom's hands on me, saw the concern on her face, but I couldn't hear a word she was saying.

Someone was lifting me from behind. *What? Who—* An usher. Two ushers. A vision of chairs passing. I realized they were removing me from the boardroom. "I have a right to speak!" I yelled, my voice a booming tympani inside my head. Behind me, Mom twisted in the grip of another usher.

"This is a farce, and you all know it!" I heard her scream. "You're lying to implicate my daughter! Take your hands off me this instant—how dare you touch me! Ray, he's—*ow!* Take your—filthy hands *off!*"

# 19. JUDGMENT

The men released me so abruptly I would have collapsed if Mom hadn't grabbed me. Blinking, I looked around in confusion; we were standing in the hallway outside the boardroom. The ushers returned to the chamber and closed the door.

"Sweetheart, are you all right? Can you hear me?"

"I can, Mom," I said. The fire on the left side of my head was subsiding to a throb, but I could hear nothing through that ear. "What happened?"

"Ray hit you." Mom's face was pinched with anxiety.

"Ray?" It came out a disbelieving whisper.

She took a deep breath, motioned. "Come, let's sit."

The hallway offered no chairs, so we settled on the floor, our backs against the wall, Mom spreading her light blue MT over her legs with careful modesty.

She took my hand, and I heard her sigh. "This is my fault. It's essential that the Board sees Ray in control of the family." She shook her head. "I never should've spoken up as I did."

"Well if you hadn't, I would've!" I retorted, my words slurring. "How could they do such a thing? Pre-empt our right to testify? I don't care if I am just a woman—this is a violation of my rights!"

"I don't know." Mom shook her head. "The law requires them to take your testimony."

"That's what they told us in civics." I sighed. "What now?"

"I suspect the Board members are discussing our punishment."

"Our punishment." I was so upset, my voice was flat. "For keeping a little girl from getting the crap kicked out of her by a bully."

Mom nodded, and our eyes met in mutual horror. "I . . . can't process this," she whispered. "The church has been illogical, foolish perhaps, but never willfully blind."

*Lord, how can they discipline me for trying to help a little girl? Is this justice? How can there be any good in this? And Mom—she didn't do anything wrong. Please protect her and Ray. I'll take my lumps if that's Your will, but please protect them. Well, Mom anyway.* Fury at Ray simmered beneath my surface fear.

"Are you praying?" Mom whispered.

I nodded.

"Me, too. Lord, we need you. Please help us. And please help little Abby. Heal her completely so she has no lingering injuries from Jimmy's attack."

"And no emotional effects, either," I said. "I pray she doesn't grow up in fear because of this."

And amidst my fuming anger and pain and fear came a tendril of peace. A brush of love, of all-rightness. It was as if Someone was standing in the hallway next to us, covering us both with a blanket of comfort. I hoped that meant I'd gotten off without punishment.

A few minutes later the door opened and Giff came out. When his eyes met mine, his lip curled in disdain, and he walked away. Marino came next; averting his gaze, he hurried down the hall. Ray emerged behind him. I got to my feet and helped Mom up as Eli slid past us.

"Let's go," was all Ray said.

I knew we wouldn't see Prinister Severs and the Board—they used a separate exit. So it was just the three of us heading out to the west parking lot as clouds obscured the sky. I had to move with care; my head still buzzed, and the distant thunder and gusting wind threw me off balance. Mom wrapped an arm around my waist, supporting me the rest of the way to the car. Eli, Giff, and Marino were long gone when Ray pressed his thumb to the door lock.

I couldn't hear too well on the way home because of the engine noise, and I ignored Ray's efforts to involve me in conversation. I caught a few snatches: our family was "on probation." They had assigned me two hundred hours of community service—which was a joke because I'd already put in that much hundreds of times over on my own. And we all had to attend a twelve-week *God's Design for the Family* class.

The punishment that I found most ironic and twisted was that we couldn't go to services. We were to be shunned for two months. Upon our return, I was not to go near the nursery or any of the children. My security clearance was revoked, and I would no longer be interacting with kids in any capacity. If I violated that rule, the church would consider me a danger and report me to the Guards.

That stung. I really loved kids, especially the kids in my class. I looked out the car window at the rainy night. I wondered if God was crying for me. I couldn't cry. I was numb.

We walked into the apartment with Ray going on about how he'd been informed that any further infractions by his family could jeopardize his job.

"Did they say that?" Mom gasped as she pulled off her MT.

"Not in so many words," Ray said, "but I got the message. We're all going to have to toe the line, especially *you*." He stabbed his index finger in my direction.

I raised an eyebrow, then turned my back and headed to my room. I sat on my bed, watching the goldfish hovering and darting in their tank, trying to ignore the low conversation in the master bedroom.

Sometime later, a knock on the door startled me out of my reflections. "Come in, Mom," I said, sighing. I knew it wasn't Ray.

Mom entered, shutting the door. She sat next to me and handed me an icepack.

I applied it to the lump on my head, hissing at the pain. "I take it Ray wasn't exactly gushing apologies." My tone was bitter.

"You guess correctly. Give that girl a gold star." We both smiled, mine a trifle sour. Her next words came out on a sigh. "He says hitting you saved his job."

My brow wrinkled. "You're kidding."

She shook her head, red curls slipping off her shoulder. "After they ejected us, Prinister Severs—"

"*Don't* dignify that godless, lying hypocrite with a title," I snarled, a bit appalled at the strength of my anger. "Not in my room."

Mom nodded, and her mouth quirked understanding. "Severs said to him, 'Well, Mr. Esselin, it's good to see you do impose some discipline, after all.'"

"He didn't!"

Mom nodded. "And he added, 'The Board will reexamine its initial recommendation.' And they took a short break to discuss it."

I indulged in a brief moment to wonder about that initial recommendation, then I shook my head. "Mom, I don't get this. Jimmy Giff beats the stuffing out of Abby Marino—a little girl half his size—in broad daylight, on church grounds, sends her to the hospital with a concussion, and all they can do is blame me?"

Mom's fingers tapped her right forearm. "The church has really been pushing this *Train Up Boys to Be Men* campaign."

I knew what she was referring to—a six-month Bible study by Grain of Wheat Press, a popular Sanctioned publisher of church literature. The women were studying *The Biblical Way of Marriage*. Its main focus was submission.

"Pushing what?" I asked, half joking. "Training boys to hit women?"

Mom's eyebrows lifted. "That may be a byproduct of the class. From what I've heard, there is also a 'spare the rod, spoil the child' emphasis."

"Too bad Giff doesn't take that one seriously," I said.

"Meryn, I think that's the message men are getting from the Bible study." Mom propped her chin on her knuckles, her brow furrowing. "Ray has alluded to it a couple of times."

"What?" Cold, I pulled the lavender and green bedspread around my shoulders. "You mean the boys are being taught that they have authority"—my memory flashed on Jimmy Giff's taunt—"not just over their future wives and families, but over *all* women."

"And the fathers are being taught that corporal punishment is biblical and will be supported by the church," Mom finished. We looked at each other, and her face was frightened. "I've always known that some men hit their wives and children. Sarah Lorrant, Mrs. Kelleher—"

I nodded. "I've seen the Lorrant kids with bruises. Prinister Hernandez brushed me off when I brought it up. But now the church is endorsing it?"

Mom looked at her hands, gripping each other in her lap. "This is *not* biblical," she whispered. "But if the curriculum is approved, it—"

"Came straight from the RD," I finished. "But that's why Ray hit me." I was silent a moment, lost in thought. "Mom, if he did it once, he'll do it again."

Mom shook her head. "He loves you, Meryn. I'm sure he feels terrible about it."

"I wish I were as sure." I was turning over the ramifications in my mind and I didn't like where my thoughts were going. "Mom, I . . . I want you to promise me something."

"Of course, if I can, sweetheart." Her face was kind.

I looked at her beautiful eyes, her fragile hands and slender figure, and something in my heart twisted. "Mom, promise me that if Ray ever hits you, we'll leave."

Mom looked startled.

"Please, Mama," I pleaded. I took her hand and put it on the uninjured side of my face.

Mom smiled, her tension dissolving. "Oh, my darling, please don't worry. Ray loves us. He would never hit me. Don't worry."

"Mom, this morning I would've said Ray would never hit *me*. I—" Tears overwhelmed my control.

"Shhh." Big as I was, she pulled me into her arms, stroking my hair. "Don't worry, Mer-child. Don't worry. Jesus is holding us both."

I finally cried, letting out all the hurt and frustration of the past several days, Mom rocking me to sleep as if I were still a little girl.

~

It was weird, not going to church. Mom and I improvised by creating our own worship services every Sunday morning. We took communion with crackers and grape juice, sang hymns and worship songs, prayed, and read sermons from RD literature.

Ray didn't join us. Ray drank.

Word had gotten around. The first week I got a couple of texts from friends—*Where were you Sunday?*—but after that, silence. None of Mom's friends called her. She held her head up and kept smiling, and I tried to follow her example.

The shunning didn't extend to work or school, but some of my classmates attended St. Mike's, so the news spread fast. In the halls, the girls ignored me or whispered and giggled as I passed. Someone taped a red "S" to my locker. Furious, I ripped it down. I tried to sit with friends at lunch, as usual; when they saw me coming, they got up and moved. Even teachers kept their distance, refusing to call on me in class or even meet my eyes. I felt invisible—unwanted. Worthless. I tried not to let it get under my skin, but it became harder to get up in the morning, to keep going.

Bree stuck by me. Even though she had graduated and was working full time, she started taking me out to lunch a couple times a week to get me away from the toxic atmosphere at school. We'd buy two soft drinks at an affable restaurant and sit and eat our home-packed lunches.

"They're children," Bree said one Thursday when I was particularly down. "What do you expect? They have no compassion, no maturity."

"What's Hannah's excuse?" I asked, my eyebrows rising. Hannah, one of our neighbors, had been Mom's best friend for years. They often visited shut-ins together, but we hadn't heard from Hannah since the shunning, and she didn't even attend our church. The shut-ins refused Mom's offers of food, as well; she had come home one day in tears, carrying the rejected bags with portions of soup, which I promptly put in the freezer.

"Hannah's a child, too," Bree said. "Seriously! The shunning is only supposed to apply at church. They know it's psychologically damaging, but they still let it spread."

"This isn't Christianity, Bree," I said.

Her eyes shifted to people at the tables nearby. "You know," she said, raising her voice, her tone conversational, "I've heard that women in the DRUSA are forced to testify in court cases. Can you imagine?"

I looked at my friend as if she'd lost her mind.

"We're so blessed that our Supreme Court protects the women of this country, ensuring we will never have to do such an awful thing." She took a bite of her sandwich. "I imagine you didn't hear about it," she said, chewing.

I shook my head.

"It just happened, and it wasn't on the news very long. Me, I'd proclaim it from the housetops." She shrugged, her eyes darting to a man sitting nearby. He seemed to study his phone, but he glanced at us and took out his earpiece.

*That's why the Board didn't take my testimony. They didn't have to.* I took the hint. "How awful of them. They really have no idea how to respect women, do they?"

She shook her head. "And if the women object, they're thrown in prison. So are their families. It's horrible."

My appetite deserted me. *Dear Jesus. Mom and Ray . . .* "I thought that was an urban legend," I said, keeping my voice low as I took a bite of my sandwich. It tasted like dust in my mouth.

Her voice dropped to a whisper. "It's not."

The man started typing on his phone.

"This restaurant is so great," I said. "Did you know it got five stars on Urban Legends?"

She nodded, and we went on to safer topics.

The man didn't look at us again. Five minutes later he left.

~

Ray came home tight-lipped and cranky every night. Mom and I stayed vigilant, careful not to do anything that might upset him. Mom fixed his favorite meals. I did laundry, helped clean up after dinner, and avoided him as much as possible.

We obediently attended our weekly classes, held in a musty room in the church's basement, and obediently listened to the teachings from Paul's and Peter's epistles about "God's Design for the Family." We smiled when the teacher, a Deacon Raven, told us how women were to be subservient to their husbands because men were the head of the household as Jesus was head of the church. We smiled when we were told that children—he motioned to me and one other young woman, also with her parents—should be subservient to their parents, seen but not heard.

We took the quizzes. We passed. Ray joined in the discussions. Mom and I sat appropriately quiet. The other young woman—her name was Jael—kept looking at me, and I at her. She wore a blue Caste Ring, so she was Worker Caste, like me. I wondered if she was as scared as she looked. I wondered if I looked that scared. I wondered if she believed everything she was hearing, or if, like me, she was hiding her confusion and fear.

"Meryn, are you listening?" Mr. Raven asked. Rail-thin, jaundiced, and balding—an impassive pedant—he wore a green Caste Ring. When he smiled, which wasn't often, he showed teeth cracking and stained from lack of hygiene.

I suppressed a gasp at being the sudden focus of attention. "Yes, sir."

"What did I just say?"

"You said that man is the image and glory of God, but woman is the glory of man," I recited obediently, hoping my voice wasn't shaking. "Because of this, a woman should array herself appropriately both in public and in private, so her husband receives the glory he is due: in public, from others, and in private, from his wife."

"Very good, little Worker Bee! You *have* been paying attention!" Raven favored me with a rare smile, his sallow skin pulling across his emaciated face, giving him the appearance of a leering skull. The smile never touched his cold eyes. "And chapter and verse?"

"First Corinthians, chapter eleven, sir. You're teaching based partly on the first ten verses." I winced inside at the word "partly," but I couldn't lie—in my opinion, Raven was stretching scripture. For the first time in my life, I didn't repent for questioning a Bible teacher, even in my mind. I wondered if I was going to hell.

He either didn't hear or let it pass. "Very good. Mrs. Esselin, give me the rest of that passage, verses eight and nine."

"'For man was not made from woman, but woman from man,'" Mom quoted. Her voice was raspy, and my heart ached for her. "'Neither was man created for woman, but woman for man.'"

"And what does this mean in the context of your relationship to Ray?"

"I was created for him: for his pleasure, his success, and his joy. I am fully responsible for his pleasure, success and joy."

"And if Ray has no pleasure, fails at work or does not show the joy of the Lord in his life?" Raven pressed.

"Then I have failed, and I must try harder," Mom whispered. She looked at her hands, twisted together in her lap.

Hidden in my jacket sleeves, my hands curled into fists.

"*Very* good, Mrs. Esselin." Raven allowed himself a look of satisfaction. He turned to Ray. "Now, Brother Esselin, if your wife fails you, what are you to do?"

"Well, I can punish her," Ray said.

"Not *can*, Brother Esselin—*should*. The husband has an obligation before God to keep the wife and children on the road to life everlasting. If the wife falters, the husband must discipline her to work a spiritual correction in her life. It is the same with children. The father must lead the whole family, or the spiritual order breaks down."

"Don't the wife and children contribute to the spiritual order of the family?" Ray asked.

"Very good question! Indeed they do, through their obedience to you and to the church."

"What I meant was, don't husbands learn from their wives?"

"Ray." Raven's voice was kind. "It's such a blessing that you and your family are here in this class, so we can all learn the answers to these questions together. Brother Dodson." He motioned to another man in the class, a black-haired fellow much younger than Ray, sitting across from us with his wife. "How would you answer that question?"

"That men learn from the church, and women learn from their husbands at home, in all submission," Dodson said quickly.

"There you have it, Ray." Raven spread his hands. "Men learn at church; women learn at home."

"Deacon Raven?" Dodson raised his hand. "Why are women allowed to attend church at all?"

Several women gasped, including Mom. Mrs. Dodson, who couldn't have been much older than me, smiled gently as befit an obedient wife. I schooled my face into a blank expression and froze it there. *He can't be serious!*

Raven nodded. "A valid question, since it is well known that women lack the basic intellectual capacity to understand scripture."

Someone coughed, and I bit my tongue, hard. *I'll show you intellectual capacity, you Scripture-ignorant toady!* Several other adjectives that I was sure would send me to hell without a trial warred for space in my head. I decided I didn't care if I went to hell. On the heels of that thought, I felt a wash of remorse and looked at a torn spot in the green linoleum floor.

"This question has been explored many times by Bible scholars greater than I. The best answer I can give you is that women are social creatures, and it would be cruel to deny them the companionship of like-minded females. Look at them." He motioned to Mom and me. "Look at how this shunning has affected them. Can you not see the pallor, the evidence of insomnia, the wounded, broken expressions?"

Dodson regarded us as one might look at a display of preserved animal specimens, raised his eyebrows and nodded at Raven. "Indeed."

I toyed with a momentary fantasy of felling Raven with a kick. *Which would be more effective: a straight kick to the gut or a roundhouse to the mouth? Would a kick to the gut be less of a sin?*

"Women need the company of other women," Raven continued. "They are weak creatures. In addition, if they are at church, the husband knows where they are and what they are doing. Church attendance gives them less opportunity to become rebellious and divisive."

*The mouth,* I decided, sitting up straighter. *Definitely the mouth.* I wondered if he would still consider me "weak," and I smiled at the thought.

Then my eyes traveled to Mom. At the weariness on her face, I sank into my chair. *I'm being childish. This is killing Mom. Ray's right; I need to toe the line. For her sake.*

"And it is to be hoped," he said, "that such instruction as they do receive—and comprehend—will be salutary."

"But isn't that dangerous?" Dodson seemed to be enjoying his role as instructor foil. "I mean, won't they get arrogant and vain from knowledge of scripture?"

"Ah." Raven lifted a finger. "That is where you, the husband, come in. It is your job to discipline her, ensuring your wife stays humble and gracious, as befits a godly woman."

"I can't believe this!" A woman's voice.

All our heads snapped around.

It was Jael.

"Now, Miss Wilton." Raven was severe. "You know the rules. You are here to learn. Children must be—"

"—seen and not heard," she interrupted, "yeah, I know the litany of 'shoulds' and 'should nots.' But this is not biblical!" She stood. Her mother seized her arm, trying to quiet her, but Jael shook her off and turned to the rest of us. "And you all sit here like it's okay, passively accepting this . . . this . . . *demonic distortion* of God's glorious scripture!"

"Brother Wilton," Raven said delicately.

Without a word her father rose, turned, and backhanded her across the face. She whirled in place, the sound of the blow blending with Mrs. Wilton's scream and reverberating around the hollow room. Jael crumpled to the floor, and the older woman fell to her knees beside her daughter and looked up at her husband, her eyes brimming with horror.

My heart dropped into my stomach, my memory flashing to the moment when Ray's fist connected with my temple. Tears sprang to my eyes.

The room erupted.

"Now, Wilton—" one of the men began.

"Discipline was indicated—"

"That's a little—"

I moved to get up, to go to the girl. Quick as a cat, Mom's hand clamped on my forearm. "Don't move," she hissed, her whisper lost in the noise and chaos of the moment.

I couldn't believe what I was hearing. "Mom!" I whispered. "She—"

"Don't you *move*, Meryn!" Her hand was a vise, holding me in place. I sank into my chair, my heart pounding. Raven's face shifted from impassivity to a slight frown, and the room went deathly silent, the only sound Mrs. Wilton's sobbing.

The demonstration of control made my blood run cold. I bit my lip, looking at Mom, but her eyes were on Raven. To anyone else, her face would have seemed impassive, almost bored—but I clearly saw Mom's fear. Without moving my head, I tried to look at Ray, but I couldn't discern his expression.

Jael lay motionless on the floor, a broken doll.

"Brother and Mrs. Wilton, you are excused from the rest of this class so you may take your intractable daughter home." Raven's emotionless voice scraped the walls, making me shudder.

"We'll be back next week," Wilton said earnestly, looking up from where he knelt beside the girl. She moaned, and Mrs. Wilton gulped back sobs, speaking gentle mother-words.

"Yes." Raven gave him a thin smile. "I know you will."

As the Wiltons carried Jael out of the room, Raven turned back to us, his eyes dead pools in his bloodless face. "Let's revisit the role of discipline in raising children, shall we? Open your Bibles to the book of Proverbs, please . . ."

~

Now, standing in the living room, ready to take me to St. Mike's, Ray crossed his arms. His conciliatory manner vanished. "What, you think I'm soft in the head? Of course I haven't forgotten. But that incident was very instructive for the entire family. And no real damage was done."

"No damage!" It came out a gasp. Before I could protest further, Ray had taken me by the arm and was hauling me toward the door.

I jerked away, and he whipped me around, his face inches from mine, his breath beer-foul in my nose. "You gonna hit me, Meryn?" A harsh whisper. "I may not know any of those fancy moves and didoes you learned in your class, but I can still hit back."

His words felt like a bucket of icewater poured over my head, but I didn't break my gaze. "Yeah, Ray." It came out high, strangled. "I know exactly how good you are at hitting people."

Dropping my arm, he jerked away as if I had actually struck him. A rush of emotions fought for prominence on his face. While I searched for any indication of repentance or shame, his expression settled into impassivity. A moment later, he headed to the car.

Disappointment weighted my shoulders, and I followed, resigned.

Normally taciturn, Ray chattered the whole way to St. Mike's, which told me he was far more stressed than he let on, but my mind was a tangle, his words like sandpaper on my raw nerves. By the time he pulled up to the front door, I was mashing my lip with my teeth to keep from screaming. He put the car in park but made no move to get out. "You go in alone," he said, his eyes skittering across the marble steps, lifting to the maple tree, bare of leaves. "That's the deal. You're an adult now, so you take your chastisement as an adult."

It was as if all the air emptied from the car. *If I'm an adult, should I need chastisement at all?* I thought, but Ray leaned across me and unlatched the door, shoving it open. "Severs said your chat shouldn't take long."

*Our 'chat'?* My eyebrows lifted.

Some twenty yards up the street, the church receptionist was spelling out the title for Sunday's sermon on the letterboard: "The Freedom We Have In Christ."

Ray nodded. "He agreed to waive the virginity check, for now."

My heart crowded into my throat. I had heard the church performed virginity checks on wayward women, but I never thought about that when I ran away. Heat prickled my scalp, and tears threatened.

"Go on." My stepfather wouldn't meet my eyes. "I'll be in the parking lot when you're done."

The world turned, wordless, not even a birdcall breaking the silence. My legs felt like bags of concrete, but I forced them out of the car and I stood. I could feel Ray's eyes on my back, watching me, just watching, as if he were waiting for me to run, as if I were a deer or a rabbit. I could hear my breathing, ragged, and something that sounded like the neurons rubbing together in my brain, and I wondered if he could hear them, too.

I don't remember climbing the steps. Just inside the front door stood a deacon—Stevens, I remembered. I'd known him for years. *Should I be reassured? Would a stranger seem less menacing?* "This way, Miss Esselin," he said, his voice dry, a dead leaf.

We headed toward the administrative section of the building, my shoes squeaking on the marble floor. An odd odor invaded my nose, made me turn my head—*bleach. That's it.* A tiny sound passed my lips—a whimper? Bypassing the boardroom, Stevens led me through a door at the end of the hall and down a long staircase.

"I don't—" It came out a whisper. I cleared my throat. "Wait. I don't understand. Why aren't—"

"Your case has already been adjudicated, Miss." He stopped in front of a blank metal door. "And here we are."

*No hearing?* "But I haven't—"

The hinges creaked as the door swung open, the smell of bleach much stronger now, almost a physical force. In front of me waited a chair, bolted to the floor, its padding cracked and stained, plastic straps attached to its arm rests. A gasp—*Was that me?*—I turned, tried to back away, but two men had me by the arms, forcing me forward.

The door slammed, the sound hollow and painful, like a cavity, like a tomb.

# 20. PRICE

"Stop being such a baby. It isn't like they spanked you. You just got a talking to." Ray's words rattled around the room until they lost all meaning. I lay on my stomach on my bed, fighting nausea.

"Some kind of bug . . . Ray, I . . ."

The slam of a door, room shaking. *I hate him.* I didn't even try to repent for the thought. Moments later I lost the battle with my stomach and vomited into my bedside wastebasket. With a groan, I wiped my mouth with a rag, already rough with dried fluid. I longed for the release of tears, but weeping would only increase my misery. Some time later—*hours? days?*—I lifted my head. Quickly, before another wave hit, I texted Carole, telling her I was sick, then shut off my phone. The room reeked; the sun poked dirty fingers through the broken plastic window blinds. Even with them closed, the room was painfully bright. Slow and cautious, I pushed until I was more or less sitting up, and set my feet on the floor. It rocked like the deck of a ship. "Oh Jesus," I whispered, "no more. Please."

Frowning, I regarded the tiny pinpricks in my arm. How long had I languished in the basement of the church? An hour? A week? Someone had carried me out to Ray's car. Told him I'd fainted from the stress. Laughed. "Did her good, that little chat." Ray's voice. Him thanking the man. *Thanking him. Betrayer!*

*What made me think Ray might actually be sympathetic?* Blinking sand from my eyes, I regarded the woman in the mirror. She looked as bad as I felt: complexion green, eyes bloodshot with puffy, dark rims. *What did they give me? What the hell did they do?* I felt no shock at the profanity, but nausea rose again, like a persistent toothache. Memories of my discipline session floated through my brain, flailing, sinking, bobbing indistinct. Severs's voice. Pain. Noises?

The door opened, startling me; wincing, I lifted a hand in protest, unable to focus. *Just . . . stop. Everything stop. Please.*

"I'm going to work. Get your butt in the shower. You stink. You told me you had a shift this morning."

*Too loud. God—* "I—can't. I—"

A hand, callused, grasping my chin. Pain made me flinch. "You can and you will. I installed that chip reader on the door. If you're still here at lunchtime I'm taking you back to St. Mike's, and this time they'll really put the fear of God into you. Are you reading me, young lady?"

*No! Not again!* Nausea pushed me, and I gasped. "Yes. Yes, I'll—"

"Good." The hand released me. "And I want your schedule from now on. Every week. Tell Mary-Carol to get it to me today." Door closed—softer this time. Footsteps. Front door, open—close.

*Oh no. No.* Hopelessness overwhelmed me, and I leaned my head against the dresser, eyes shut tight. *I can't stay here. Have to work on—*

Another wave of nausea struck. Unable to get to the wastebasket in time, I threw up all over Mom's beautiful lavender-and-green quilt.

~

Head whirling, I stepped down, slow and careful, gripping the bus railing with a gloved hand. I'd barely managed to stabilize myself before the doors slammed and the bus roared away, wrapping me in a stench of exhaust that made my stomach turn somersaults, but there was nothing left to vomit. Hunching my back against the cramping, the lacy orange top itching my neck under my coat, I made my way to the sub station, people flowing past. Every time someone bumped me, my stomach heaved again. Step by step, I tried to focus on the sidewalk—the ice patches, dirty with coal dust. Coughed. Something red veered into my field of vision. *A red . . . hat? On the ground? No. On . . . a woman. Sitting. Charity?*

*My name? Someone said my name?* A face, in front of me. Eyes, concerned. My name.

I opened my mouth. "I'm late. I have to—" A blackness flirted with my vision, and I heard Charity's voice. "Keturah! Prudence! Quick—" and I knew nothing more.

~

I roused. Something wet on my forehead, but warm; the rest of me, cold. My eyes blinked open, shut.

"I see you're back with us, Meryn."

My stomach replied with a groan that morphed into a high-pitched squeal.

"Aye, did a number on you, didn't they?"

My eyes opened on a blue glow: the underside of a tarp. Charity sat next to me, wrapped in her usual rags. A crackling of fire; an odd, chemical odor. My nose wrinkled, and my mind flashed back to the church basement—

"I know, a plastic fire's not the best thing for someone who's been poisoned, but we had to get you warm."

"Poisoned?" It came out a croak. "Saint . . . Mike's?"

Someone sitting close by laughed without mirth.

"Now, Keturah, she's just a child. Of course she wouldn't know."

"Figures." A strange voice.

"Well, it's not the flu. Shh, here now. Drink." I blinked; Charity held a spoon to my lips. "It's just warm water, child. But it will help." She dribbled water into my mouth, and I swallowed. My stomach grumbled. "It isn't likely to come back up. Here, a bit more now."

She was right; the warm water felt good going down, and it eased the raw tissues in my mouth and throat.

Someone curled up behind me, and I jerked, startled.

"It's just me," Keturah said, no friendliness in her voice. "We sleep together. It keeps us from freezing." She pulled a rough blanket up to my face, covering us both, and my stomach recoiled at the stench.

"What's that smell?"

"Eula. The goat."

"You have a goat?"

"We had a goat," Charity corrected. "She kept us warm, nights."

"What happened to her?" Keturah's warmth soaked into me, and the world dimmed.

"Someone ate her when we were at the sub station. Sleep, Meryn."

Without permission, darkness closed over me again.

~

"Tomorrow I'll take you to Lois's."

Charity sat by the fire, sipping heated snow-water from a metal cup. I half-sat, half-lay against a wall, rags padded between me and the cold brick. Snow pocked the tarp overhead and swirled, hissing, into the fire. My feet and hands ached with cold. "Hold this," she said abruptly, handing me the cup. "And drink. You need fluids."

Greedily my hands curled around the cup's warmth. Steam teased my nose. "Who is Lois?" My voice still rasped harsh.

"My daughter." Charity gave me her toothless grin. "Her husband might be all Mister High and Mighty with his green ring, but she remembers her mother. Here." The woman rummaged through her rags, pulled something from a pocket. It crinkled. She handed it to me.

Crackers. My mouth watered, but I tried to hand it back. "Charity, I—"

"No, no." She held up a hand. "I can get more. I'll show you how."

Restraint gone, I tore open the package.

"Slow and easy now." Her eyes went sharp, cautious. "You haven't eaten in three days."

"Three days?" I stared, food forgotten.

"They're getting more reckless, Charity."

I blinked at the form across the fire. Another woman I'd seen begging in Charity's row—she had a sharp, angular face and intense brown eyes—nodded a greeting. "Yeah, your Severs, he's got some lofty ambitions, that one. Won't be happy with the green, not while he lives."

*She must be Keturah.* "You said they poisoned me."

Charity nodded. "Let me guess. You threw up every time you thought about disobeying? Every time you got angry or resentful?" When my mouth dropped open, she smiled. "It's pretty effective. Classical conditioning. You learn to associate disobedient thoughts with the vomiting, which makes you avoid disobedient thoughts."

I sifted my memory. Psychology class. Mrs. Piper. "But how—I wasn't at church long enough for them to—" Nausea fluttered closer.

"Oh, they programmed it into your chip via nanoinjection," she said. "Doesn't take long at all. And I'm sure they added a few choice injuries to drive the point home."

"I have . . . welts on my calves." My stomach tightened like a twisted towel, and she nodded.

"Right where no one will see them and you can generally act normally. Your stepfather wouldn't notice a thing."

*Three days. Ray!* Realization flooded me, and I felt my chip vibrate. *Or did I imagine it?* "I have to get home. I have to leave right now!"

Charity leaned forward. "The next twenty-four hours are going to be pretty hard on you, Meryn. But if you don't want to go home, we can help you."

My stomach roused. *I want—I—* Nausea pulled at me, and she lifted a hand. "Don't say anything. Don't even think it. Just hang on until tomorrow, and we'll be able to talk. Okay?"

Fluid gathered in my mouth, and the world tilted. "Charity . . . I don't think I can . . ."

She drew a syringe from her rags. "Do you trust me, dear? I promise, it's as clean as I can make it."

My eyes widened. Did I? I had no idea. I didn't know this woman—not really. But every moment I resisted getting to my feet and heading for the bus, the torment worsened. I nodded.

She put the needle to my arm, and I spiraled down into blackness.

~

"Are you mad, bringing her here?" A whispered hiss. The woman, carefully coiffed and perfectly clean, shot panicked looks at Charity and Keturah as they supported me into an elegant sunroom at the back of a large house. "No, no. Mother, stay right here. Julia!" She hurried out of sight. "No, leave that, get yourself to the market, now. And don't forget the cheese." A long silence; I forced my head up to look at Charity, who gave me a reassuring smile. The woman's voice. "Yes, now! Out the side door with you!"

A squeak, a slam, and a moment later she was back. "Come. Get her on the kitchen table. What—?"

"Nanotoxin, of course," Charity said, navigating me up the steps. "She's been disciplined." As the older women settled me onto a hard surface, Lois stood, her hands fluttering beneath her chin. "Can she find her way back here? Do you think she—"

"Lois!" Charity rounded on her daughter. "Get the sedative and the nanocide. Now!"

Hurried steps. I closed my eyes. The moment the sedative wore off and I'd woken two hours earlier, nausea stalked me like a living thing, making every movement a misery. I felt Keturah slip my arm out of my coat, her fingers tracking the injection sites. "Sweet Jesus, how much did they give her?"

"Enough for a three-hundred-pound man." Charity's voice was grim. "This wasn't chastisement; this was punishment. This was a prinister's revenge."

Someone tucked a pillow under my head, and I coughed. My throat felt like I'd drunk acid. "I don't know where we are. I promise I won't—"

"Shut up." Keturah's voice, a hiss in my ear.

"Meryn." I forced eyes open, and Charity's face swam into view. "Are you sure this is what you want? When the RD finds out you—"

I seized her jacket in both hands, my uncooperative mind reeling, stomach a volcano pit, and forced the words out. "I want my *mind back!*" Exhausted, panting, I released her. A warm hand patted my arm.

Steps approaching, self-important heels on marble. "Here." A cold swabbing on my arm. "Really, Mother, you could have killed her using that unsanitary—"

"Enough," Charity said. "It saved her life. She was puking her guts out." Her grip on my arm was too tight; a pinch. Something cold entered my veins. A brightness behind my eyes began to dim. *How did I not even notice—* "Severs is mad, what he's doing. And those lackeys of his. He gets a lift, so do they. Neat little club they have there." Her sarcasm made me smile inside.

Slowly, the nausea eased. My sigh of relief became a moan.

"Better, dear? No, don't open your eyes. Give it a minute."

"Die, you little bastards." Keturah.

"What did she do? Who is this girl that you would risk—"

"She's one of us, Lois!" Charity's voice was an uncompromising rock. "She's blue, and she's in need, and that is enough."

"Blue." A sniff.

I felt Charity's arm encircle my upper back. "Can you sit up now, Meryn dear?"

I curled upward, my gut muscles protesting every move.

"Yes, you'll be sore for awhile. You were vomiting even in your sleep."

"Charity stayed up with you, keeping you rolled on your side so you wouldn't drown." Keturah's voice, carefully neutral.

*My God . . .*

"Mother, when is the last time you checked your toes? Can you still feel them?"

Charity didn't answer. I blinked; her face came into focus. Everything was too bright, and I winced.

"Don't you want to give her the sedative?" The younger woman, standing behind Charity, hands wringing. She'd stopped at some point to veil her face. "Shouldn't you give her the sedative? Mother?"

"She's been sedated for too long as it is." Charity sighed. "We can't carry her back to the alleyways, Lois. It was all we could do to get her here without notice."

Lois's voice rose an octave. "But . . . she'll recognize the house! She'll know how to get back here! She could—"

Charity released me to round on her daughter, Keturah grabbing me before I could fall. "This young woman has more integrity and concern than anyone who's ever helped me! You should be thanking her, not insulting her." Turning to help me off the table, Charity tossed over her shoulder, "We'll blindfold her on the way out. No one will jeopardize your precious standing in Silvermine society."

~

"I can't believe she won't do more to help you."

They'd removed the blindfold once we were on the bus. With my hood pulled forward, no one knew I wasn't a little old lady being helped by friends. We'd debarked on Jordan Avenue in downtown Silvermine, and the women led me to an alley crowded with other homeless women, guiding me through a maze of tarps and improvised sheds and piles of frozen excrement until we'd arrived at the spot I'd spent the past four days. Nothing had been disturbed or taken, and I gratefully curled up on my pallet.

Now Charity crouched over the fire, stirring something in a pot. "I know she seems harsh, Meryn. But Lois actually helps me quite a bit. So does Keturah's daughter. No, get your feet over here, closer to the fire."

Adjusting as directed, I knew she was right, and I shouldn't judge. Homeless family members could be a burden and sometimes a risk, especially if they were under condemnation of the Sanctioned Church.

"She actually lets us shower in her house," Keturah put in, "so long as we don't stay more than an hour or two."

*A hot shower . . . when's the last time . . .*

"Are you going to tell your stepfather where you are?" Striking the spoon on the pot rim, Charity sat back, settling next to me beneath the tarp. "I've felt your chip vibrating."

I shook my head. To my relief, no nausea replied to the rebellious thought. "I have to call him, though. I'm sure he's already contacted the Guards to report me missing." Fury at Ray pulsed along my veins.

Keturah's eyes flickered to Charity.

I knew that expression. "Look, I've already jeopardized you enough," I said, gathering my tote. "I should—"

"Stop getting your knickers in a knot, Kettie." The look Charity turned on her friend was trenchant, then the older woman pushed me back against the wall. I was still so weak I couldn't resist. "Child, you need to eat. Don't worry about us; we're already on the outs with the

Guards, so turning you out won't help us. But it would piss off God, and *that* I'd rather not do. Here." Removing the pot from its stones, she set the hot cereal carefully on the ground in front of me and handed me their spoon. "Eat."

I didn't argue.

~

Hours later, a painful yank on my arm pulled me from the warm cocoon I shared with Charity and Keturah. I groaned a protest, and my muscles refused to cooperate. Disoriented, I forced my eyes open.

"Ohh yeah, nice and fresh, she is." *A man's voice. Who—*

Before I could gather my wits, a flash of blade, a masculine howl, and the grip on my arm vanished. I fell onto Charity and heard her grunt. Blinking, I climbed off her as a homeless man reeled across the alley, crashing hard into the wall.

"Try again." Keturah stood, holding the knife. "We'll just put you in tomorrow's stew."

Cursing. A chorus of shouts and chuckles down the alley. The sound of footsteps running away, and Keturah settled again. Charity patted my arm. "You didn't hurt me, dear. Go to sleep now. He won't be back."

~

"Where have you been?" Bree hissed, her green eyes wide with concern. "We haven't seen you in days!"

"I texted you I was sick," I said, feigning surprise.

That morning we'd gone to Keturah's daughter's house, dressed as a cleaning crew and pushing a cart. Although I never saw the woman, I'd taken a glorious shower that thawed my hands and feet to painful tingles, then I changed into my work uniform. I left my rank clothes with Keturah, who promised to wash them with hers and Charity's. The two women told me I could stay with them in their little alcove for as long as I needed. I'd met some of the other homeless women I'd helped in the past—most of them lived in the same alley where they could watch out for each other and share food and other assets.

"That must have been some bug," Bree muttered.

"I wouldn't wish it on anyone." *Truer words never spoken.* I hung my coat on its hook in the stockroom and tossed my tote on the shelf.

My painful, swollen feet forced me into slower movement the whole day, but it felt good to be back at work. That afternoon I took my break and sat in the stockroom, shoes kicked off, rubbing my toes. My wrist buzzed, and I checked my phone.

Ray.

Whispering a silent prayer, I picked up.

"Where the *hell* have you been?" His volume carried across the room. I sucked in a breath, hoping no one in the main store heard him.

"I have been very sick, Ray. I needed someone to take care of—"

"You get yourself home, *now!*"

"No." I surprised myself with the calm response, and how quickly it came. "No, Ray, you abdicated your parental responsibility when you delivered me to St. Mike's. Just know that I'm fine, and I'm taking care of myself."

A long, ominous silence . . . then Ray disconnected.

Bree entered the stockroom, and hurriedly I slipped on my shoes before she could see my feet. "I just wanted to remind you," she said, settling next to me with a sigh, "that you'll need to put in for a day off so you can go to your mother's funeral."

I looked at the phone in my hands, silently acknowledging the utter impossibility—I could never go where Ray could so easily find me. I had no doubt he would take me right back to St. Mike's.

And I would never let that happen again.

# 21. INSULATION

On a Saturday evening four days later, I stood in my tiny house, admiring.

My bed was just a pallet on the floor, but I'd put up my clothing rod, and my uniforms now hung clean and wrinkle-free. I'd cadged a few plastic shipping boxes from the trash bin at work; stacked on their sides, they made terrific cubbies for undies, sweats and socks. I'd used another box as an improvised bedside table. A battery-powered camping lantern provided light.

The previous day I'd taken a trip to the dump with Walker and Kilte. While they and a couple dozen other pickers scavenged for wood, wiring and other sources of salable materials, I went hunting for usable items for my house. An old lawn chair was a grand find; although the frame was a bit rusted, it was sturdy enough to hold my weight. It would serve nicely as a loo.

"You can't move in just yet," Kilte had mentioned when I showed it to him. "Your place isn't insulated."

And I nodded and smiled and went straight to my tiny tin house and kept working. I knew he was right—a layer of tin was no proof against the cold, any more than the tarp was that I slept under every night, Charity and Keturah tucked beside me—but I had to get my place habitable.

So I removed the plastic webbing and sanded off the rust, and spent precious paycheck money on a new, cheap toilet seat (I couldn't bear to use one from the dump) and affixed it to the frame. I'd scrubbed out an old five-gallon paint bucket; it was a simple matter to line it with small plastic bags and set it under my improvised toilet. I noticed several people digging ashes out of the firepit for use in their toilets, and I did the same, hoping no one would mind. Every time I used the loo, I added a scoop of ash, twisted the bag shut and pitched it with the community's trash.

A curtain across the far-left corner screened the toilet from view, and a pitcher and bowl provided a rudimentary sink (although I had to carry water from Mags's). I put a bottle of hand sanitizer next to it.

I gazed around the house with great satisfaction and no small amount of pride. It was rude and primitive, but it was clean, and it was mine.

Walker suggested positioning my washing station right next to the tiny stove so its heat could help warm the water and dry the towel, and I felt both grateful and resentful for the thoughtful suggestion as I washed my face in the bowl, grimacing as my ablutions turned the water brown. Grateful because it made sense; resentful because I was annoyed at how much space Walker was taking up in my head, and I wanted it to stop. He was dating Tamar—I didn't want to think about him anymore. And then I found myself wondering if he was thinking about me, and that made me even madder.

A hollow tap rattled the metal door. Thinking it was Mags or Bree, I opened it.

Handy stood outside, too close. I took a reflexive step backward, and he smiled. "Just wanted to, ah, check in on ya," he said, trying to peer around my body.

I didn't move. "I'm fine, Handy. Thank you." Smiling, I tried to close the door, but Handy shoved his foot in the gap. The door bounced open, and my blood ran cold.

"Now, I know you'll be needin' things, Miss Meryn," he said. "To insulate, and such." His eyes traveled down my coat to my worn boots. "Things only I can give you. Things you best not be getting from anybody else."

Anger spiked; my smile vanished. "And who are you to make that decision for me? *I* choose my contractors, Mr. Peters. If I decide I want your services, I know where you live and how to find you." My tone went from polite to icy. "In the meantime, this is *my house*. Get out!"

Nodding a bit, Handy stepped back, his eyes calculating. "Don't you forget, Miss Meryn. Don't you forget about ol' Handy."

The sound of my slamming door could've been heard on Sweet Street. Through the ringing in my ears, I heard the crunch of his footsteps over the icy path, and I took a deep breath.

Carefully (because my muscles were cold), I stretched, syncopating my breath with movement, trying to dispel the fury and adrenaline. My *sensei* drilled us on the importance of breath, and how it worked with the movements he was teaching—to the point he would force us to do a sequence again if even one student had his breathing wrong. I'd brought it up to him one evening after class, when the other students were heading out the door, chatting and wrapping themselves in scarves and coats.

"Why do you keep hammering us on breath?" I asked. "I mean, I understand that it's important, but—"

"The *kokyu ho* is more than important," he said, his hands spreading. "Breath is the foundation of life. It's a direct connection between your body"—his hands touched his chest—"and your mind"—they rose to touch his forehead—"and so it is the foundation of everything you will do and learn in this class." His hands lowered. "If you can't master your breath, you will never master the *kihon*, the essential moves."

Later, as my comfort level with *katas* rose, I began to understand. "It's like a wall," I told him after class some months later, as I picked up my tote. "It's almost like it's part of me, but it's outside of me. Like some kind of force—a life force." I bit my lip. "Does that sound weird?"

He smiled. "Not weird at all. You're getting it." His eyes went to the door, where John Rezner was exiting, the last student. He waited until the door closed before speaking again, his voice low. "We once knew much more. You're right about the force. There's a relationship between you, me"—he motioned toward the window—"the trees. The birds. All of it."

I was intrigued. "Can you teach me?"

His expression shuttered. "Too dangerous. The RD thinks it's a pagan religion. They're afraid." He looked at the mat, then met my gaze. "*Karateka*. I have taught you much, and you learn well. Learn this." He stepped forward, demonstrating a strike. "This must be used by men only."

"By men?" I blinked. It was the first time *sensei* had made any distinction between me and the boys, and it filled me with disappointment and an odd foreboding. "I don't understand. I know the sequence—"

"You must unlearn. The move is intended to disable. It can kill." He touched my neck at the base of the throat. "You must never kill."

I bowed. "This is true. You teach us the way of karate is not to kill."

"It is not what we do. You know how to disable and defend. It's too easy to move to the next step."

I shook my head. *This makes no sense.* "Why are you telling me to unlearn, *sensei?*"

His dark eyes met mine. "*Karateka*, you are a woman. If Rezner-Kun were to kill a man in self-defense, the Guardian Angels would not blink. But you—" He shook his head. "If you kill a man, Miss Flint—no matter the reason—they will find a deep hole. And they will drop you in it. And you will never again see the light of day." Turning away, he bent to pick up discarded practice mitts.

I opened my mouth and closed it, cold fear congealing my guts. *Dear God. I can never escape. Not even here.*

Before I could move, he straightened, and his eyes pinned me. "Pursue the path. God will lead you beyond the physical. I cannot. And I will deny we ever had this conversation." This time the dismissal was final; mitts in hand, he retreated to his office and shut the door.

Now, finishing my *katas*, I frowned, wondering what had brought that memory to mind. *Am I really that mad at Handy? Am I that afraid? Or is this even about Handy at all?* I blew out a breath.

Maybe there was good reason for the *sensei* to be afraid—maybe the philosophy behind the moves was indeed pagan. "Then why would God have led me to the dojo?" I said aloud.

During construction, I'd discovered the space behind my house row was large enough for me to do a full series of *katas* out of sight of the rest of Tin Town. I still hadn't found a place to run, but I was considering taking the bus back to my old school a couple days a week to use the track. Exercise was the only thing that calmed my mind. But tonight, the *katas* were not enough. I started the sequence again, cycling through the moves until I panted, dripping with sweat, my muscles trembling with fatigue.

After finishing my stretches, I lingered over the warmth of my tiny stove, rubbing my hair until it was thoroughly dry. Then I bundled up and headed back to Charity's tarp.

~

"So how is the house coming?" Mags asked the next morning over our breakfast of plain hot rice cereal.

"Cold." I left it at that, not mentioning the stiffness in my legs and arms, the constant swelling of my hands and feet, my scratchy eyes.

"This—" Bree seized my hand with its reddened fingers, and my spoon clattered to the table. "You didn't get this swelling working on your house." Her eyes lifted to mine, accusing. "Meryn, are you sleeping on the street?"

For a long moment, I couldn't speak, as the wind whistled under the eaves, and the cookstove hissed hot. "The church disciplined me," I said, my eyes on the table. "I couldn't—"

"Tell us!" Bree's demand was unequivocal.

Mags sucked in a breath. "Oh, he didn't—"

I kept the narrative brief, focusing on the help I'd received. "And I've been staying with them," I whispered, forcing a smile. "They have a tarp in an alley . . . it's actually quite—"

"Well, you're staying here as of right now," Bree said, her tone brooking no argument. Her glare shifted to her gamma, who looked as if she had aged a decade.

"Meryn, I am so sorry. Yes, of course you must stay here now."

"I could just move into my house—" I began, but both Mags and Bree were shaking their heads.

"You must recover from the cold, first." Mags's eyes were still anguished, but she sipped her tea. "You need your fingers and toes, dear. In fact—" She went to the cupboard and returned with an ointment blend in a metal jar. Ignoring my grimace, she set it in front of me. "Rub it in. Twice a day for a week. It's a bit malodorous, but it will help."

I nodded, penitent, and unscrewed the jar.

"And we have to get your place insulated," Bree said, her voice sharp with unexpressed anger. She would not quickly forgive me for not telling her about St. Mike's.

"With what?" I asked, trying not to sound desperate.

"Well, clothes work." Mags set down her mug.

"Clothes?" I blinked. "Like . . . a house parka?"

At last, Bree chuckled, and I felt muscles unstiffen. "Old stuff that isn't wearable," she said, gesturing at the walls with her spoon. "Blankets, old jackets, whatever you can find."

"You chop the clothes fine and fill the space between the tin and your wallboard," Mags explained.

"I saw something like that when you showed me Walker's." I closed my eyes, trying to visualize the interior of his tiny tin house as I rubbed Mags's salve into my hands. "What was it he used for wallboard?"

"Thinwall," Mags said, and my eyes popped open and I winced. Thinwall was expensive. But then, Walker had a dependable business.

"But people use cheaper options," Mags went on. "Tamar nailed sections of upholstery cloth over her insulation. Sometimes people just hang blankets over their walls, although that isn't as effective."

"What about packing boxes?" Bree asked, cocking her head. "Those plastic ones we get at work. Cut them apart." She unfolded her hands as if opening a box. "Use the pieces like Thinwall. Screw them into place."

My eyes widened. "That's a great idea! They'll help insulate, too." Then I deflated; the boxes we used at work were sent back to the warehouse. "Where will I find enough on such short notice?"

"You might find a few on the cheap at City Trade." As if she hadn't just dropped a bombshell, Mags stirred her tea. Bree's gaze flew to her gamma, her eyebrows climbing into her hairline.

To cover my shock, I picked up my mug and took a long drink.

City Trade was Silvermine's largest illegal flea market. The location rotated every week to avoid detection. Flea markets, garage sales and the like required a permit, enabling the city to tax the profits—and taxes priced the merchandise out of reach for the Indigent or Worker Caste, the bulk of Silvermine's population. So City Trade flourished, kept moving, and maintained an active and interested clientele.

Or so I'd heard. I'd never been there. "Sure, but how do we find it?" I asked. Its location was a well-guarded secret.

Bree cocked an eyebrow at her gamma, who grinned. "I'm a member of Liberté," Mags said with no preamble.

Adrenaline flooded me. I opened my mouth in shock, shut it. *And I've been worried about compromising HER?*

Bree laughed. "You really didn't know!"

"But that's—" I closed my mouth.

"Illegal," Mags finished for me. "Yes, it is. That's why we couldn't let you move in when Bree first brought you home—it would have been far too dangerous for you if I were caught."

My mouth dropped open, and shame flooded my cheeks. This whole time, I'd thought they were being selfish, when they were just trying to protect me. *God, forgive me—*

Mags was still speaking, her eyes frank. "Once you're in your house, if we're arrested, you have plausible deniability. Are we friends? Sure. You work with my granddaughter. But that's all you know. I'm a harmless little old lady who dabbles in her herbs and grows veggies for her neighbors. You'll have a night or two in a Guard station and be on your way."

"And you?" I asked, trying to take it in.

She shrugged. "I'll likely be executed. I just don't want to take people with me. The twins don't even know—not really. They know we go to City Trade, but not about Liberté. So please don't mention it to them."

We sat in silence for a moment while I digested this news. Mags sipped her tea, serene. Bree darted glances at me while eating her cereal.

*Liberté*. I winced at the memory of Connie's death. My friend Connie, who had been executed right there in school supposedly for being a sexual deviant—*Or was she? Did they find out she was a part of Liberté? And just didn't want the rest of us to know?*

The mortifying truth was, after the shock, my first emotion had been relief. My connection with Liberté was severed, the threat removed, and I was safe. Mom and Ray were safe. I shook my head. *God, forgive me! I reacted exactly the way the RD wanted.*

Her face serene, Mags sipped her tea. Bree dropped her spoon in the bowl with a loud *clink*. "Well?" she demanded. "Are you going to tell?"

My stomach tightened, but so did my jaw. "Tell what?" I retorted, cocking an eyebrow. "That some crazy old lady claims she knows something about Liberté? And tell who? The Guards? The first thing they'll do is read my chip. No." I picked up my tea, now tepid. "I won't tell." I shifted my gaze to Mags. "And I'd like to see what I can find at City Trade, if that's okay."

As I spoke, adrenaline surged—I'd just committed a reckless endorsement of rebellion against the RD. On its heels, a brief wondering what Ray would think (old habits die hard); then a hard grin. *I may be only a woman, but I trust these people far more than I trust Ray, the Sanctioned Church, or the RD.*

"Of course it is," Mags said, her tone brisk. "We'll go Saturday, early."

"We don't have a choice." Bree's expression was grim. "We don't have enough food to make it through winter."

~

I crouched by Charity, stirring the miso soup. "I don't know how to thank you for taking care of me." My smile was tentative, frank. "You saved my life."

She pushed her red cap back from her eyes, her brow crimpling with concern. "Moving in with friends is dangerous. For all of you. Do they know?"

"They do." *More than I ever did.* I didn't elaborate. "Charity, Keturah, I . . . I will have a place to live. It's just a little shed, and it isn't finished yet. But when it is, I want you to come live with me. There isn't much room, but you'll be out of the elements. You'll be able to stay warm. You'll be safe."

Keturah's eyes danced to Charity's, her mouth curling in a slight smile, and I took that as encouragement. I ladled soup into the two extra tin cups I'd brought for them, steam teasing the rims.

"As soon as I've finished insulating, we can get you shifted."

Charity lifted a hand in protest, her face turning away as if she smelled something foul. "Oh, my dear Meryn. Please don't tell me any more. I cannot take the temptation."

*What?* My smile faded, and she sighed.

"Now, child, that was such a generous offer. So Christlike of you. But we cannot come."

Keturah shook her head.

I sat back abruptly, my eyes on hers a stunned question.

Charity's smile brought a hint of spring to the frigid, swimming blue space beneath the tarp. "Oh Meryn, don't you see? This is where Jesus has us. For a reason. If we go with you, who will help the next poisoned girl as she rushes to the sub? Every week, there is a new need." She gestured at the alley beyond. "Who will bring food and clothing to these women? No, child."

I thought of her blackened toes, her frostbitten hands. "Please," I whispered. "Charity, please."

She folded those swollen hands around her mug and sipped, savoring the soup before continuing. And I let her, because I had no words, no further argument to make. "We are right where we need to be. But now you know the need, we know you'll be back. And that is enough, dear girl." She patted my arm, her hand warm now. "That is enough."

# 22. TRADE

City Trade fascinated me. Clandestine location—an old convention center—password to enter, the whole bit. I felt as if I were in a spy vid about DRUSA agents infiltrating the RD.

"Is there a secret handshake?" I asked Mags softly once we'd passed the entrance.

Bree heard me over the general clamor and rolled her eyes, but Mags, clad in a brown MT, just laughed. "I wouldn't be surprised if they implement that someday. It's a big risk, this"—she gestured around at the throngs of people selling and buying—"but it's a necessity. Trading helps so many of us who are barely hanging on."

"How do they keep this private?" I asked, trying not to show my nervousness. "Half of Silvermine is here."

Bree raised an eyebrow. "Nobody wants to go to jail."

I found that answer simplistic, but I kept silent.

Kilte followed with the girls, who pulled a large red wagon with tall plastic sides, filled to the brim with knitting: scarves, mittens, and sweaters, all in myriad colors. He touched my shoulder, pointed. "There."

I followed his gaze to a middle-aged couple stacking boxes next to a folding table. A young woman set out a handmade sign: *Office Supplies*.

"They probably pitch that after every market day," Kilte observed. "It's safer than a professionally made sign if they're raided."

Bree clued me in to bring untraceable scrip; most sellers wouldn't risk chip purchases. My fingers found the small roll of bills in my pocket, and I turned toward the building materials, but Mags touched my arm.

"Let's get food first," she said.

"I can't just—"

"We stick together," Bree explained. "If there's a raid, we don't want to be separated."

"Oh!" *A raid? Lord!* I wondered if raids happened often, but I was too nervous to ask. Humbled, I followed Mags, who paused to give me an encouraging grin.

"You'll get the hang of it."

We passed a booth where a man of indeterminate age was chewing a well-worn stick of something pungent and setting out metal tools, wheels, and gears. I couldn't tell if the rank odor came from him or his wares. As we passed, he doffed his cap and gave me a toothless grin, his mouth black. I nodded, swallowing against revulsion. Tucked in a nook festooned with multicolored lights and gauzy scarves, a young woman strummed a guitar. I suspected she employed some sort of portable amplification; her song about Guard brutality and abuse of power carried easily over the general clamor.

At the next booth, a woman called out, "Meds, bandages, syringes, gauze! All guaranteed unused, fresh, and sterile! Meds, bandages . . ."

"Sabine works in a clinic," Bree murmured. "Gamma has traded for some of her stuff. It's clean."

*But doesn't she steal—* I thought. *Or maybe not. Don't judge, Meryn.*

Across from Sabine, a young man with a giant iridescent cross tattooed on his shaved scalp moved back and forth, setting out small cages. I looked closer. He wasn't selling . . . birds? My stomach twisted.

"Best protein anywhere," he called out. "Fresh and fine for grilling or roasting!"

My head jerked away, and I caught Kilte's expression. He winked and grinned.

Bree groaned, her complexion ashen. "I wish he wouldn't do that."

"What?" Kilte teased. "You don't want pigeon for lunch?"

Bree hit him hard on the arm, swallowing several times.

I whispered, "You okay?" hoping she could hear over the din, and she nodded. Digging in her purse, she pulled something out and popped it in her mouth. I caught the sharp, clean smell of ginger.

Next to the bird man, a woman and two young girls showed passersby their handmade mugs, plates, and bowls. The crockery looked well made and I longed to examine it, but Kilte linked his arm in mine and steered me after Mags. I gave him a penitent look.

We passed two more booths and a young man performing juggling tricks, throwing balls in the air. I paused, fascinated. A hat sat in front of him, upside down, with a piece of cardboard that read *thanx 4 tipps*. A man tossed a scrip bill in the hat, and the young man smiled his thanks, keeping the balls going. I caught Kilte's understanding grin and I lengthened my stride to keep up, but everything I saw made me think of Charity and Keturah and the women in the alley, how little they would need to see such an improvement in their conditions . . .

Mags stopped in front of a large sign that read *Fresh Produce*. A sharp-eyed woman with black dreadlocks turned from where she was stacking bags of turnips. "Potatoes toward the front, Roddy," she told a young boy, pointing. Then she saw us, and a grin lit her face. "Mags!"

"Hello, Keziah!" Mags leaned over the battered table to give the woman a hug and a kiss on the cheek. "How are the boys?"

"Rascals, as always!" Keziah said with a raucous laugh. "Hello, Bree! Kilte finally making an honest woman of you?"

To my surprise, Bree flushed and dropped her eyes.

"Now, Keziah." Kilte gave her an injured look, but she just grinned. Then she bent down so she was eye level with the twins.

"Girls, I found something for you." Her expression confided secrecy as she reached under the table and handed each astonished girl a fist-sized fruit the color of sunrise. "They're just now ripe."

"Mangoes?" Ellie exclaimed, her eyes rounding. "Real mangoes? I've only seen pictures!"

"Oh, Keziah!" Lisha's eyes fixed on the fruit in her hand.

"What do you say, girls?" Mags prompted gently.

"Thank you!" they chorused, and Keziah beamed.

"Their reactions were thanks enough!" she told Mags.

"You're too generous." Mags smiled, but silently I agreed. Scarce and expensive, mangoes couldn't be grown anywhere in the CSA. I'd enjoyed one once—a Christmas gift from Ray. I squelched a quick stab of envy.

Mags asked, "So what's fresh?"

Keziah shrugged. "It's winter, but the potatoes and turnips are still good."

"One hundred fifty pounds of each, please," Mags said, and I couldn't hide my astonishment.

"We have a long cold season ahead," Kilte said in my ear, "and who knows what she'll still have in February?"

"This won't get us through to spring," Bree murmured, catching our exchange. "We have six to eight people at every meal—sometimes more." Kilte made a wry face.

"Now, what have you been—oooh! Sweaters!" Keziah's face lit up at the marled blue sweater Mags lifted out of the wagon. The older woman spread it on the table and Keziah fingered the perfect stitch. "Impeccable work, as always, Mags."

"And one for Pete." Mags laid another large sweater on the table, this one green, as Bree tucked the rest of the knitted items in her tote.

"Deal. Pete!" Keziah called. A lanky young man pulled aside the curtain behind the booth. "One-fifty each of russet and turnips, please."

He disappeared and returned a moment later hefting two plastic burlap sacks under one arm, and another over his shoulder. An older man bearing the same sharp eyes and black hair carried three sacks of turnips as if they held feathers. The men came around the front table where Bree and Keziah stood chatting, and loaded the bags into the girls' wagon. The men brought more bags until the wagon was full. Kilte and Bree each picked up a bag, Kilte balancing his on one shoulder. I took the hint and grabbed a bag of turnips.

"Thank you, Peter," Lisha said in her sweetest tone. Ellie giggled.

"You're welcome, girls," Pete said in a fine baritone, tousling Lisha's braids. Fleetingly I wondered if he sang. Her eyes got big and for a moment I thought she was going to swoon. He headed back behind the curtain and Ellie pinched her sister's arm.

"Ow!" Lisha glared.

Mags set a big basket of beets atop the wagon. "No greens at all?"

Keziah pursed her lips in sympathy but shook her head. "Pirates got most of my collards. Try Hogla," she said as she folded the sweaters away under the table. "I heard she canned her whole crop of spinach."

Ellie made gagging noises. Bree frowned at the girl.

"Thank you, I will!" Mags handed Keziah two pairs of mittens and nodded her thanks, and we started down the walkway. Kilte immediately relieved me of my bag of turnips and took the wagon away from the twins. He headed for the door, balancing a bag of potatoes on his shoulder.

The thickening crowds flowed by. A couple passed us, the woman holding a baby, a burping cloth draped over her shoulder. The infant's blue eyes fixed on me, and I smiled.

"He's dreamy," a little voice beside me said wistfully.

I looked down at Lisha and smiled. "Pete?"

The girl nodded. "He likes me better than Ellie."

"You can have him," Ellie retorted.

"He's too old for both of you," Bree put in, but she was trying to hide a grin.

"Not for me." Lisha sighed. "I like older men."

I laughed. Two boys ran past us, their misshapen legs propelling them as fast as possible along the walkway. Mags watched them go, her face pitying. "Too many babies with rickets," she murmured.

"Don't you, Meryn?" Lisha asked, looking up at me.

I waggled my hand. "Older men have their merits, but I've noticed they treat their wives as if they're little girls."

"I'm never getting married," Ellie vowed. "Men are silly!"

An MT-clad woman buying "Genuine Coffee Drops" at a booth nearby overheard her and laughed.

"Why, thank you," Kilte said in an injured tone, rejoining us.

Each time the little wagon filled, we took our purchases out to the truck, locked them in the cab and returned. And each time the crowds grew thicker, until we had to wait in line to reach the stall selling packing boxes. Wary, I eyed the press of people that seemed more suited to a Miners game than a clandestine flea market.

"This is taking too long," Mags murmured to Bree, who nodded, her eyes darting from booth to booth, her face wrinkled.

"Should we just go?" I tried not to sound worried.

Mags turned. "No, there's—"

"The voice of God!" an old woman's voice called from somewhere off to my left. Out of the swirling crowd, she appeared at my side.

"Not now, Zipporah." Kilte's face darkened, and Bree ducked to the other side of him as if trying to hide.

"Time is a river." In her dirty blue fingers, gnarled with age, the old woman held what looked like a necklace of polished beads with an oddly shaped cross hanging off one end. "Most do not know how to swim."

The line shifted, and we moved forward, the old woman matching our steps.

Her garment was a mass of rags sewn into a semblance of dress or tunic, her white hair tied back with a worn strip of red cloth. On her nose perched a pair of odd glasses with double metal rims, but no lenses. She peered up at me, her light amber eyes not a bit rheumy or cloudy. I'd never seen that shade before. *This strange old woman is GM?* I paused and the crowd moved forward again, pushing me along.

"Aye," she said, pointing at me with a crooked finger. "You know, Mer-child. You know I have the sight."

I stopped dead in my tracks, staring, blood draining from my face. The only person who'd ever called me that was Mom; no one outside our family knew my nickname, not even Bree. "Have we met?" I knew we hadn't. I knew I'd never seen her before.

"You know what you need to know. You know my sisters. Oh, the knowing . . . it's been your rock, hasn't it, mermaid? A rock in an angry ocean, the waves of faithful and faithless trying to swamp your only safe place."

Mags and the others had stopped by now. Sober, Mags dug in her pocket and handed the woman a coin.

"Zipporah," Bree began, "leave her—"

Zipporah held up a hand. To my surprise, Bree fell silent.

"But still a wee babe." The old woman clucked. Her hands blurred; the coin vanished into a fold of her garment. "Still helpless, kicking in your blood. I say to you, *live!* The rock will shift to sand beneath your feet." She stuffed away the necklace, whispering inaudibly. Pulling a thin slice of purple crystal from a hidden pocket, she slid it into her glasses frame so it obscured the lens on the right side, and lifted her eyes to mine. Her left eye narrowed shrewdly.

"Ohhh, dive deep, mermaid. You drift too close to the shallows. The shoals are unseen, dangerous. The sharks circle and deceive, hiding their teeth. You fear the ocean, but you must dive deep if you want the sky to open. Drop the gem. Trust the puppet master who pulls hidden strings." She paused, her words coming slow, cold molasses. "The lost tribe will follow you through the path of the sea, through the mighty waters. Only on this path will your footprints never vanish. The flame-haired one leads, now she is free. She knows the paths through the waters; mark them well, child. But she—" Zipporah's face grew quizzical. "The dark one pursues, and she fades. The flame flickers. The flame . . . is gone."

Closing her paper-thin eyelids as if exhausted, the odd old woman removed her glasses. We stood in an island of silence, the crowds chattering and swirling past us. Swaying, she stumbled forward and seized my arm with a cold hand, her grip painful, eyes the color of sunset riveted on mine.

"You must find the ancient path and forge it anew. Only your song will complete the symphony. In the darkest depths, none sees but one. Mermaid." It came a harsh whisper, her breath wafting an odd sweetness in my face, like the smell of mildewed flowers. "The walk begins, but be careful where you step. When blood is in the water, the fish don't care what they eat."

Abruptly she whirled away into the crowd and disappeared.

And I gasped for air, my body remembering the need to breathe. Tears threatened; my pulse pounded in my ears.

"Meryn." A woman's voice. Too loud, an echoing drumbeat in my head. "Meryn."

I turned, blinking, uncertain, haunted.

Mags handed me an open vial. "Sniff. Easy does it."

Mechanically, I lifted it to my nose. The powerful tincture invaded my tissues like a slap in the face, and I gasped and coughed. At once my head cleared. Tears coursed down my face—whether from the tincture or the encounter, I wasn't sure—and I wiped them away, impatient. Concern filtered the faces around me. Ellie frowned, her hands gripping her arms, body tense with suppressed anger, her eyes darting across the crowds. Kilte wore a skeptical expression.

"I'm sorry," I said, but it came out a whisper. Irritated, I shook my head and cleared my throat. "I'm sorry."

"You have nothing to apologize for." Kilte looked after Zipporah, his face wrinkled in annoyance. "Crazy old bat."

"She can be unsettling," Mags said gently, taking her vial and tucking it away without looking, her eyes worried on my face. "Are you okay?"

If I opened my mouth, I'd blubber like a fool. I nodded, fighting emotion. *How did she know . . . No, later. Focus!* The tears retreated. "Is she always that way?" I managed to get it out, my tone casual.

Bree and Ellie relaxed.

"Pretty much." Mags's mouth quirked. "She's often very accurate."

"And always a pain in the butt," Kilte said, his tone bitter. I wondered what Zipporah had told him.

"But what did she mean?" The intensity of her words unsettled me, like sand shifting under my feet. "I'm not sure I understand."

"What I recommend to anyone who receives a prophecy is that you pray about it." Mags's eyes were kind. "Prophecy can be a double-edged sword. God will reveal the truth in His time."

*Prophecy?* I nodded, still confused. *Isn't that Old Testament—*

"She's muddled." Bree said, indignant. "She told me a long time ago that I would 'walk alone'."

"Well, she was wrong about that," Kilte said, hugging her close with his left arm. "She's just loony. I'm amazed anyone listens to her drivel."

"But—" I began.

"Let's go." Bree looked over her shoulder and licked her lips. "She could come back."

Kilte snorted, but Bree's worried expression didn't alter. Before we could leave, the people in front of us moved away from the booth selling my boxes.

To my relief, the transaction was quick. I was elated. It looked like I had enough construction material to finish my entire interior, and it had cost me almost nothing.

"The focus has shifted," Mags mused as Bree and the girls stacked the boxes, flattened for ease of transport, on the little wagon. Only I was close enough to hear her.

"What?" Bree twisted around.

"Bree," Mags said, low, "Take the girls and prep to leave. Now."

Bree's eyes widened. "But you—"

"Do as I say!"

At her tone, my eyebrows lifted, and an odd frisson of fear crawled up my back. My friend's mouth closed with a snap, and she turned to the twins. "Let's go. Go!" Grabbing the wagon handle, she strode briskly toward the exit, the girls balancing the tall load and looking questions at each other.

I heard Lisha say, "Aunt Bree, what—" and then her voice was lost in the clamor of the crowd.

Kilte turned to follow, but Mags caught his arm. "Stay, Kilte? And you, Meryn. I have to see someone."

Kilte and I exchanged a puzzled glance, but we followed Mags as she moved up the walkway, weaving around slower knots of people and passing booth after booth until we were nearly at the other end of the building. Because my feet were still healing, I moved slower, and I found myself paying closer attention to the kind of tiny details that used to flow past me: that woman, wearing the tan MT of the Indigent Caste and yelling at a running child; the big man with black hair who watched me approach, then turned back to where his tall companion was dickering over a pair of gloves.

In my heightened awareness, I noticed that Kilte was marking the exits. He looked at one door in particular and nodded. Perplexed, I tried to look closer without turning my head, but the door had no signage indicating its purpose. I opened my mouth to ask—

—and a loud siren pierced the air, cutting through the sounds of buying and selling. Screams echoed through the building. Before I could react, Kilte had me by the arm and was dragging me toward the unmarked door.

"Kilte, what—"

He glared, severe, as if I were being obtuse. "Raid!"

At that, I ran with him, ignoring the pain in my feet.

"Guard raid." To my surprise, Mags was right next to me. She uttered a mild oath. "They'll have the building surrounded. I hope the girls—"

"They had time," Kilte tossed over his shoulder. He pushed through a crowd of screaming, crying women in MTs, and turned to be sure we were still with him. Staccato popping erupted from behind us.

"They're—" *Shooting?* A vision of Connie and Jerusha flashed through my memory, and icy fingers clawed my spine.

"This way!" Kilte pulled us through the nondescript door, into a long hallway. Others followed, running, their panicked cries and footsteps echoing.

Mags pulled out her phone, pressed a single button. "She knows where to meet us."

"Damn noisy crowd," Kilte muttered. Mags nodded.

At the end of the hallway we pushed through a set of double doors, coming out into a parking garage. I turned toward the daylit entrance, but Kilte pulled me in the opposite direction, following Mags as she took off up the ramp, its concrete broken and jagged from age, gaps showing rusted hunks of rebar. As I turned to follow, another hand grabbed my arm, whipping me around. A tall man pulled me to him, his face implacable. Fear chilled my blood, and my eyes widened.

"Insurance," he muttered, low. "C'mon, sweet."

His companion, the black-haired heavyset man I'd seen watching me, chuckled. "Meryn ain't with her daddy."

*They read my chip!* Fury spiked my fear. Without thinking, I spit in the tall man's face. As he reared back in revulsion, I struck his hands away and slammed the heel of my right hand into his nose. He bellowed, his head snapping back, hands flying to his face.

The other man lunged at me, snarling curses. Flush with an odd euphoria, I came around with a defensive strike, but my eye caught a blur of steel, moving so fast I barely had time to register it was Kilte; I yanked my hand away. A squeal of pain, a spray of blood across pavement, and Kilte had me by the arm, hauling me up the ramp so fast I stumbled as I ran.

*Did Kilte just—*

People boiled out of the doors behind us, streaming toward the entrance, their muted sobs and muttered curses echoing. I looked back just long enough to ensure the men weren't following us, and caught a glimpse of them helping each other toward the entrance, one gripping his arm.

We rounded a corner, taking us out of sight of the crowd. A split second later, angry yells came from down below. Guards must have surrounded the parking area, too, expecting people to make a break for it. *How will we—*

A voice through a bullhorn. "You're under arrest! On the ground, hands on your head!" A staccato of gunfire, a spate of screams.

I gasped, bit back a scream of my own.

"Keep it together," Mags whispered, tugging me to the right, toward the concrete barricade where sunlight streamed in. Her eyes reflected serene understanding. "They haven't seen us."

The sound of running feet, and a young couple pelted around the corner behind us, the woman holding her MT around her waist, her legs bare. "Run!" she gasped out as they bolted past, her eyes wide with terror. *"Run!"*

Two more people came dashing after them as Kilte sidled up to a pylon. He held up a hand, darting glances outside while Mags pulled her MT to her waist and knotted it. Under the dress, she wore rubber-soled shoes and jeans. *Smart.*

More people ran past us, the open expanse of concrete drive leaving us horribly exposed, and I bit my lip, my heart pounding. *All it will take is one Guard coming around that bend—God, don't let them come this way, please, God help us, God please—*

"Okay," Kilte whispered, hoarse. "Come on!"

*What? Jump? Is he nuts?*

He climbed over the concrete half-wall as Mags pulled me forward. My eyes widened. Kilte clung to an overgrown tree on the other side of the pylon, his free hand reaching for Mags.

"Mags, how can you possibly—"

But the older woman was already moving, stepping onto a large branch while Kilte held her arm. The tree grew from the other side of a fenced alley that paralleled the parking enclosure, but the long branch reached us easily, and someone had pruned away smaller shoots to facilitate escape. Mags headed for the trunk, and Kilte turned to me, his face lined with urgency. "Come on!"

Shouts and the sound of jackbooted feet pounding up the ramp gave me all the incentive I needed. I threw myself over the barrier, the branch shaking as I ran. Mags reached the trunk and started down, and the moment her hands left the branch below I followed, fear robbing my breath. I shifted around the trunk so Kilte could follow more quickly. Below us in the alley was Walker's truck, Bree behind the wheel, her face pale and anxious through the glass.

I glanced up; someone was following Kilte and for a moment it was all I could do not to scream; but it was a woman, pulling her blue MT above her knees and helping a little girl, who was crying.

I dropped to the truck bed next to Mags, and Kilte thumped beside me. As soon as Kilte's feet touched the bed, Bree hit the gas. He flailed, caught the side of the truck, recovered. I glimpsed Lisha through the back window, her eyes wide and panicked, her mouth a round *O*.

"Lie down," Mags ordered. I complied, my back flattening against storage boxes.

"There's a little girl—" I began.

"We can't help her," Kilte said, dropping and pulling a tarp over the three of us. A moment later the truck bounced over something—a curb?—and the bullhorn came again.

"Stop! Stop or we'll shoot!"

The truck took a sharp turn, Kilte's weight all but crushing me against Mags, and we flew into the air again as the truck took another rough dip. A fusillade of gunfire; Bree screamed a curse, and I screwed my eyes shut, the tarp a blue glow in my brain, my heart pounding. *Dear Jesus! Help us!*

We heard nothing more from the bullhorn, and we lay there, my heart so high in my throat it nearly choked me, while the truck shuddered and jinked over Silvermine's roads, taking us away from City Trade, away from the screams and shouting, the bullets and the dying.

"They're killing people!" My whisper was a shriek echoing under the tarp. "How can they just be killing people!"

Hovercars screamed overhead and I gasped, wondered if they were Guard cars. Guard cars used infrared. I couldn't look; tears blinded me.

Kilte squeezed my arm in warning, his reply harsh. "Put it in a box, Meryn. We'll do a post later."

I bit my lip just as the truck went over a bump; I tasted blood. *When we get home? Is that where she's taking us? Lord, what if we can't go home? What will happen to that woman and her little girl? What now? What NOW?*

# 23. BASEMENT

"I knew they were cruel." It came out a raspy whisper. "I had no idea—" My hands shook, the mug rattling hard against the table. A wave of tea scalded my thumb.

We sat in the kitchen, stunned and exhausted. The moment we'd gotten back to Mags's, the older woman had brewed a fresh pot, adding liberal doses of tincture to each mug.

"Drink," Mags commanded, setting the kettle on the stove. I obeyed, the liquid stinging my ballooning lip as I willed the tincture to work.

"We don't have anything stronger than tea?" Kilte asked, his voice thick with fatigue.

"Trust me, this is better for us right now." She settled at the table. "Drink, sweetie," she urged Lisha, proffering a mug, and the girl complied. A moment later Lisha set it on the table and collapsed against her mother, sobbing. Mags rocked her, shushing, consoling.

"Good thing we had a plan." Bree swilled her tea.

"Walker's idea." Kilte glanced at the clock. "He should be home soon."

"How'd you know where the exit was?" I asked.

"City Trade uses about a half dozen locations; they just rotate." He stirred a generous spoonful of sugar into his mug. "Walk and I scoped 'em out. We trimmed that tree back just a couple months ago. Good thing we weren't at the Eli Brothers Port warehouse. They'd have taken us for sure."

Lisha looked at him with wide eyes, her sobs breaking out afresh. "Mamaaaa, they could have . . . they could have . . ." She broke off, gulping.

"They didn't," Mags said firmly.

"But . . . but what if you hadn't come?" Tears brimmed her eyes again. "And Aunt Bree . . . they could've . . ."

"If we had been taken, I would've let Bree know at once." Mags stroked her daughter's hair. "There's a special button on my phone, and she would've had you and Ellie safely away before the Guards found you." Her eyes flicked to Bree, and my friend nodded, her face white. I wondered just what kind of emergency plan they had in place.

Ellie turned to Bree, who smiled brightly at the girl. "You were both so brave!" Bree said, hugging her shoulders. "You did exactly what I told you without arguing. Moved all those potatoes and turnips in record time. Thank you!"

"We lost a bag of onions." Kilte's face was grim.

"But . . . *Mommy* . . ." Lisha buried her face in Mags's shoulder, weeping piteously.

"I'm here, sweetie. We're safe." Mags rocked, soothing her, gentle.

"We're fine," Ellie said, but her skin was ashen. Her mouth firmed and she sat up straighter, looked at Kilte. "No problem. We got away, and that's the important thing. I want to learn how to plan like that, Uncle Kilte. That was awesome."

He nodded, and his eyes held the look of pride in a kindred spirit.

"And we got food and the stuff we needed." Ellie shrugged. "Win-win."

"It wasn't a win for the people who got hurt," Lisha said, wrenching around to glare at her twin. She looked at Mags, and her chin trembled. "Mommy, was anyone . . . do you think Pete and Keziah . . ."

"We don't know if anyone was killed." Mags sighed. "But let's pray that didn't happen, and no one was seriously hurt."

"Why would they want to kill people, just for buying stuff?" Ellie's face screwed up in perplexity. "That's just stupid!"

"No one ever accused the Guards of being rational," I said, finding my voice. My eyes shifted to Mags. "Does this happen often?"

She shook her head. "We haven't had a raid in, oh, a couple years. Thank God we weren't there when the last one happened. I don't know what sparked this one."

"The Guards get bored," Kilte said, unnaturally sober. "Or they need a quota. We're still trying to figure out how they find us."

I gave him a little smile. "Thank you," I mouthed.

He nodded, his answering grin a trifle shaky. I wanted to ask him about the knife, but not in front of the girls.

"Meryn!" Ellie gasped, looking at my shirt. "Is that blood? Are you—"

"What?" My eyes followed her gaze, then I laughed, brushing at the dried brown spatter. "No, no, it's just mud from the truck bed. That reddish mud from the south side, I guess. No worries."

"I keep telling Walk we have to wash out the bed on occasion." Annoyance infused Kilte's voice, but his eyes on mine held gratitude—and respect. Slow and casual, his hand slid to his side, pulling his jacket forward to cover a splash of blood on his pants. Ruthlessly I stomped down a sudden, hysterical urge to laugh.

"Let's take this day to the Lord, shall we?" Mags extended a hand across the table at Kilte. The rest of us clasped hands and bowed our heads, and as we prayed, Lisha stopped weeping at last.

~

"I think we might have been too ambitious," Mags observed an hour later as we stood, gazing into the truck bed.

"So we go more often and get less?" Kilte suggested. He'd changed into a fresh pair of work pants.

Bree frowned. "That's risky."

"We kept finding what we need to survive winter." Mags shrugged.

On the mad dash home, the three of us had wedged between the potatoes and turnips, a couple bags of fresh onions, a case of home-canned spinach, two bags of dried kale and other greens, and a single, precious, glorious jar of ground cinnamon. My plastic packing boxes showed some damage; they'd insulated us from the cold metal and the worst of the jouncing. I'd also purchased lots of used bedding and clothes on the cheap for insulation. One gorgeous, cozy synth comforter looked new—it was still in the original packaging—and I thought it might just end up on my bed.

Mags had picked up a few skeins of synth-wool yarn in beautiful colors, and Kilte scored some necessary tools. We found two pairs of used but sturdy shoes for the twins—a desperate need, as Lisha was to the point of limping. Mags traded away their old shoes on the spot in exchange for the cinnamon. The only member of our group who bought nothing was Bree. "I have everything I need," she told me with a quiet smile.

Mags's phone beeped, and she checked the screen. *"The boys and I recovered from that nasty infection,"* she read.

Bree blew out a breath. "Keziah's okay."

Mags nodded. "I'll be sure to tell Lisha."

The girls stayed inside and stirred up the fire while the rest of us set to unloading, taking turns going back and forth, quickly getting all the food inside. As I settled the last twenty-pound bag of potatoes in the tiny kitchen, I wondered where Mags could possibly store it all. Then I hurried out to unload my boxes.

Hefting one out of the truck bed, I heard the screen door slam. "That's doing it the hard way," Kilte called, his eyes crinkling. "Hop in and let's drive around to your place."

Chatting in his usual gregarious fashion, Kilte eased the truck along the frozen ground to the back of my tiny tin house. I opened the door, flicking on the overhead light as Kilte brought in the first stack of boxes. When we finished, I gave him a formal bow. "Kilte, I couldn't have done this without you. What do I owe you?"

He snorted, waved away my thanks. "Not a darn thing, Meryn. You and the twins have been doing my kitchen duty. Consider it an even trade."

"Fair enough." I smiled, then sobered. "How bad did you hurt him?"

He grinned and pursed his lips with mock sympathy. "Awww, don't tell me you care about da poor widdle scumbag."

Shrugging, I let out an embarrassed laugh.

"He was going to trade you for his freedom, his and his buddy's." His eyes narrowed, and his thumb and forefinger rubbed together in a nervous fashion. I wondered if he was aware of it. "Happens all the time. The Guards get to play with some young girl and the guys walk."

My mouth dropped open. "That's what he meant by insurance? They were going to—"

Kilte nodded. "If he survived the raid, he'll be okay. I just wanted to get him off you, not kill him. He might not be able to type for a while." He eyed me, his mouth quirking. "Not that you needed much help. Never seen a woman break a guy's nose before. Nicely done."

"I've had some training," I admitted. "Don't publish it, okay?"

"My lips are sealed." Then he chuckled. "You *are* full of surprises. When Walker gets back, we'll do a postmortem. Look at what worked and what can be improved. We got lucky this time." A moment of silence as I digested that, then he clouted me on the shoulder much the same way he did Walker, only with less force. "C'mon. Let's go help Mom get all the food put down."

I was unsure of what he meant, but we headed back to Mags's.

"Thing about City Trade, you never know *what* you'll find," Kilte said, the frozen mud of the walkway crunching under our feet. "The downside is, you never *know* what you'll find. Last winter we went for food and came back with cases of tomatoes, and Mags had put up tomatoes all summer. We ate a *lot* of spaghetti."

"At least it's food," I said, remembering one winter when Mom and I had gone to the grocery store only to find the shelves bare. Before the rioting started, the RD had trucked in some outdated staples, but it was a near thing. Since that awful season, Mom had stocked up on canned goods when they were on sale, storing them under my bed, in the bathroom—anywhere she could find space in the apartment. The following winter saw more shortages, and some stores were looted and burned, but we didn't run out of food.

A few flurries swirled about us as Kilte and I crossed the porch and let ourselves in the house. To my surprise, all the curtains and blinds were closed. I turned toward the kitchen and let out a gasp. Kilte laughed as he locked the door.

The kitchen floor had disappeared. A section of flooring—the kitchen rug flopping over its edges—had been opened on a hidden hinge and now sat propped against the lower cabinets. Mags and Ellie knelt, handing our purchases through the gap, which was letting a draft of refrigerated air into the house.

"Got it!" Bree's voice, muted. Curious, I edged closer.

Mags looked up and smiled. "Come see our cellar, Meryn!" she whispered.

"How—"

"Didn't know a tiny house could have a basement, didja?" Kilte murmured in his amused fashion.

"We keep our voices quiet because we don't want to risk people finding out about it," Mags explained. "A couple of my close friends know it's here, but if the homeless found out, it could be a problem."

I shuddered, thinking of street violence.

"Hey, it's cold down here," Bree complained softly.

"Sorry, love." Kilte grabbed a sack of potatoes and handed me Bree's jacket. He grinned and jerked his head toward the cellar. "Go on. Check it out."

I approached the hole. Ellie was handing a bag of onions down a steep ladder to Lisha, who passed it to Bree at the bottom. Lisha came up and I moved out of the way so she could slip by me.

"It's easier if you face the steps and brace on the floor," Mags suggested.

I complied. On the way down, I found handles affixed to the sides that made the descent easier. The basement was illuminated, and as I stepped off the ladder, I could see how the cellar had been built.

All THOWs were constructed on trailers with metal crosspieces; the space between was plywood flooring and insulation, and the hatch was cut from that space. Someone had built a wooden box around the space between the THOW and the top of the cellar, which was at least a foot below ground level. Even though Mags's house had a skirt to hide the wheels, I applauded the extra caution: a little noise or a flash of light from the wrong spot could tip off passersby to the cellar's existence.

The round room was constructed of concrete block painted white. Prefab concrete panels covered the ceiling, and shelves lined the walls, most of them stuffed with dozens of jars of home-canned food. LED rail lights, festooned with cobwebs, crisscrossed the ceiling.

Bree was gently setting the bag of onions on a shelf by the far wall, and I crossed the space to hand her the jacket. Kilte came down, toting a bag of potatoes on one shoulder. The cellar was chilly but not freezing, and not a bit musty. The food we stored here would stay edible for a long time.

"Meryn!" Mags called in a whisper. I hurried back to the stairs and caught the bag of onions she lowered. We spent the next few minutes carrying, sorting, and storing.

"This is amazing," I murmured to Bree as we worked.

"It comes in handy," Bree agreed, hanging a braid of garlic from a hook in the ceiling. "Originally this was a bomb shelter."

"It still is," Mags said, coming down the steps. Kilte sprang to relieve her of the flat of glass jars she was balancing in one hand. "We had to do something to keep ourselves safe, especially with all the rumors of DRUSA incursions at the Paradise border. It's handy for severe storms, too. Kilte, the spinach goes over there," and she pointed to an open shelf. "We keep blankets, water, and a camp stove down here, just in case."

"How do you keep it so dry?" I asked.

Mags gestured toward a pipe system in the far corner. "Sump pump," she said, dusting off her hands. "We tied the waste line right into the city sewer so it doesn't give us away. And"—she gestured toward the ceiling—"we have an air vent with a fan that runs to the sewer access. It doesn't always smell nice, but we won't suffocate if we have to light the stove, and this way our air doesn't depend on the house."

"This is all so clever," I said.

"Needs must when the devil drives." Mags nodded. "When we expanded the garden—and our harvest—we had to find more storage. So Walker and Kilte cleaned up the old bomb shelter and built the stairwell frame." She motioned to where Bree had organized the root vegetables. "These two shelves are bunks. And more people could sleep on the floor, although that's not comfortable. I must contrive some cots."

Kilte had gone upstairs, and Bree started after him. As I climbed into the kitchen, I noticed hinges on the side of the frame. I meant to ask Mags about it, but the girls needed help with supper, and it slipped my mind.

As I was slicing bread, Mags touched my arm. "Meryn, I know you will be discreet about the cellar."

"Of course," I said.

"One person unaware of its existence is Tamar," she said, low. "I would like to keep it that way."

"I won't mention it," I promised, but I was curious. Mags seemed to like Tamar, and I suspected she and her daughter would become part of the family soon. *Maybe she knows Walker and Tamar might break up?* Firmly I pushed the thought (and the odd hope that came with it) out of my mind and turned to the dull matters of dinner prep.

# 24. CHAOS

Walker joined us for our meal, his eyes widening as we told him what had happened at City Trade. "Wish I'd been with you," he said, his eyes veering to Kilte.

"Ah, you'd've just slowed us down," the young man cracked.

Walker's eyebrows went up, and I wondered if he was offended.

"Seriously," Kilte rattled on, "it was your idea that saved us. The tree was perfect, and the girls managed it with no problem."

Walker smiled and turned to his mother. "I figured you'd have no trouble. Any word on casualties?"

She shook her head. "Keziah lost the rest of her harvest. They had to abandon everything, of course. She said the Guards arrested Sabine and the man with the birds and Delia."

"Who?" Bree asked.

"The girl singing." Mags took a measured breath. "She's been arrested several times before. Keziah said they were treating her . . . badly."

I winced, remembering Kilte's words. "Does she know if anyone—" I broke off. I couldn't say *died*.

Mags shook her head. "The shooting we heard may have been intended to intimidate. Keziah didn't mention fatalities."

"How'd Keziah get out?" Walker asked, taking a bite of bread.

"She didn't say—everything was in code. We have to be so careful." She paused. "They got some Liberté people, including my contact."

Kilte's face was tight as he turned to me. "Come on. Let's get started on your place."

Fatigue pulled at me, but I didn't argue.

"So how will I pay you for this?" I asked him when the door to my tiny tin house closed behind us, and I mentally winced at my phraseology. *Lord, don't let him ask for something I can't give.* I wondered about the appropriateness of working alone with him, unsupervised. Mores at Shady Dell were very different from what I was used to, and I wasn't sure how I felt about that.

He looked up, doing some rapid mental calculations. "Let's say . . . two months' worth of kitchen duty?"

I folded my arms. "I think two weeks of kitchen duty sounds fair."

He grinned, and I grinned back.

"A month," he said.

"Deal."

We bowed and set to work, cutting the crates apart with Kilte's power saw, measuring the distance from stud to stud and drilling holes for screws. The frigid temperatures forced us to wear jackets and hats, but the tiny stove cast off enough heat to keep our fingers from freezing.

Walker had spent a rare free morning earlier in the week stringing my electricity (much to my astonished delight), so Kilte and I cut holes for the outlets. As each panel went up, we shredded and stuffed pillows or blankets or old jackets into the space and started on another panel.

We'd been at it for about forty-five minutes when Bree stopped in.

"Nice!" she said, looking around.

"We haven't even finished one wall yet!" I laughed.

"No, but it looks great." She turned to Kilte. "How late are you working, love?"

He finished screwing in a panel before turning to answer. "Maybe another hour at the most. I'm pretty tired."

"We all are," I said, and Bree nodded.

"Rough day," was all she said, and she kissed him and settled on my rolled-up pallet to watch us work, handing us screws or insulation as necessary.

The job required two people at minimum, and Bree's help made it easier. Kilte's serious dedication surprised me. Behind his jocular and fun-loving personality, the man displayed an impeccable work ethic. I felt blessed to have him working on my house, and I told him so.

"Well, I figured out that if I didn't do a job right the first time, I'd have to do it over," he said, stepping back from the panel we'd just put up and tucking the drill under his arm. "Mags taught me that. And if Walker and I are going to turn this illegal house thing into a real business, we need good examples to show. Can't have our work falling apart!"

He grinned, and Bree and I laughed. Kilte was turning into a real friend, to my relief.

I fell into bed in the loft that night sore and exhausted. We'd finished the walls, but we needed to insulate the ceiling before I would dare spend a night in my house. He reassured me it wouldn't be difficult. "Same principle," he said, "just upside down on a ladder."

"Bree," I whispered, nudging my friend.

She rolled over to face me, her eyes a question.

"So . . . what's the deal with Tamar? She doesn't seem to like me." I didn't mention my suspicion that the woman was gossiping about me.

Bree snorted softly. "She doesn't like anyone who isn't Walker. Look, don't let her fuss you." She settled back against her pillow. "I think she's just an elevator operator in heavy makeup."

I tried not to laugh. "Seriously? You think she's a climber?" We all knew the girls from school whose sole aim was to marry up-caste.

Bree nodded, her eyes on the sky. "Hagar told me she'd heard Tamar telling someone that the only drawback to Walker was his Indigent status. How awful is that?"

I bit my lip. "Bree . . . are we . . . gossiping?"

Now my friend's green eyes met mine. "No." Short, decisive. "She's the gossip. The whole community knows it. And Walker is my brother—well, technically he's my uncle, but we grew up together. I have a right to know about anyone who has an interest in him." She scrunched lower in the bed, grimacing at the cold, and pulled the comforter to her chin. "I think the minute some green-ringed guy at Kwale's tilts his head at her, she and Pris will be out of here so fast it'll make your head spin." She yawned. "I hate to think of what it will do to Walker. He thinks she walks on water, and he adores Pris."

"Hmm," I said, my thoughts indecipherable.

Bree's eyes closed, and a moment later she drifted off. I thought of Charity and Keturah, and guilt nagged at me. I asked God to watch over them and keep them warm and safe. To heal Charity's feet, and Keturah's heart murmur. Before I got too sleepy, I pulled out my phone and took a few minutes to jot down Zipporah's odd prophecy. I'd prayed, asking God for understanding, but the encounter still puzzled me. I fell asleep mulling the old woman's cryptic sentences, and trying *not* to think about Walker.

~

The next morning over a breakfast of porridge with dried apples and a bit of new cinnamon as a treat, Mags informed us we would have church at home. "The thermometer read fifteen below when I got up this morning and it has dropped since then. It's far too dangerous to drive in this. I'll call our carpool folks."

Walker, who had joined us for breakfast, nodded assent.

"We can still work on your house, Meryn." Kilte swallowed a mouthful of coffee. "I'll run over after breakfast and start up the stove."

"Working on the sabbath, Kilte?" Mags murmured.

He grimaced. "I know, but it's important to get Meryn into her place as soon as possible. You know how hard it is to have this many people in a THOW."

"I do," Mags admitted, "but I think God gives us grace."

"Your call, Meryn." Elbow on the table, Kilte eyed me over his mug.

I hesitated. Much as I wanted my tiny tin house finished, I didn't want to alienate Mags. "Well . . . you guys have a heavy week ahead, and I'm closing at Mrs. That'll put us off a few days. It's a drawback, but I'm okay with waiting if you all can put up with me."

"It's not a problem for me," Bree said. "You keep the bed warm."

Laughter rattled around the table.

"Let's wait, then." I smiled at Kilte.

"Sure thing," he said, eyes crinkling. "Keeps me out of the doghouse. Doesn't seem right to me that we can't work on the Sabbath, but Bree has to."

"Doesn't seem right to me, either," Mags observed, sipping her toast coffee.

"Why does the RD allow it?" Ellie asked.

"Money," Walker put in, and Mags nodded.

"They say God gives a special blessing to those who work on the Sabbath," she said. "It used to apply only to those who worked in essential services—Guards, medAngels, doctors and so forth—but that changed pretty fast despite the CSA Constitution and frowns from the rank and file. Anymore, it just comes down to good old-fashioned greed."

I scraped together the last of my cereal. "The church teaches that if you work on Sunday, you are giving up your Sabbath for God. But the Bible doesn't say that."

"That is hyper . . . hycri . . ." Lisha was trying to get the word out.

"Hypocritical?" Bree offered.

"Yes!" She scooped up a bite of porridge. "I was telling our teacher how hypocritical it was that . . ."

"Ohhh." I winced at a memory. "Don't argue with your teachers."

"But she tells us to ask questions," Lisha protested.

"About normal lessons, yes," Mags said. "But Meryn is right—be careful not to object to RD theology or the Bible."

"You can get marked as an apostate." I picked up my coffee. "And that could get your Mom in trouble."

Lisha's eyes rounded, but Ellie nodded. I noticed neither twin had to ask what the word meant.

"That's why you don't discuss our business with your friends at school," Mags said. "If they find out we have our own Bible study, we grow our own food—"

"We know, Mom." Lisha was sober. "We'll go to jail."

"Just smile and nod," I advised. "It's safer."

"It's stupid," Kilte put in, rising and crossing to the stove to add another scoop of porridge to his bowl.

"Amen," Ellie said.

"This is the stuff that is supposedly guiding our very lives." Lisha's face was a study in amazement. "And we can't ask questions or raise objections?"

Mags nodded. "It isn't fair, but that's how it is." Kilte returned to the table, and she passed him the pitcher of soymilk. He nodded his thanks.

"I can't believe the stupid RD is looking over our shoulder at school, too!" Ellie set her mug down, hard. "I thought we had a democracy! What about how the government is supposed to be responsive and listen to the people? Can't we object to what our carvenor or popresident is doing? Our civics text says—"

"Civics teaches that the popresident is considered God's man on earth," Walker said.

"That's a difficult one." Bree turned to Ellie. "We have a representative government—"

"Ha!" That was Kilte. "After what we just went through at City Trade? A representative government requires a free society that truly has freedom of speech and religion."

"Well, we were breaking the law, I guess," Ellie said. "Technically."

"Should surviving be against the law?" Mags lifted her mug, sipped.

Ellie grimaced. Lisha looked confused. "We don't have a representative government?"

"Try it sometime," Kilte said.

"Not yet," Mags put in hastily. "Not until you're older. Much older."

Ellie frowned, her eyes darting around the room.

"I've thought about it." I said. "Going to a City Council meeting and bringing up a question or an issue. Just to see what happens." I had in mind the housing problem, and how single men and women—especially women—couldn't find an affordable place to live.

Walker was smiling into his porridge.

Bree looked triumphant. "That's what I mean! We should be able to do that without worrying! If not, what is the City Council for?"

"Are you the same Bree McCafferty who drove us home, hell-bent for leather and screaming curses, during an RD raid?" Kilte asked.

"Those were Guards! How do you not get it—that circumstance was different!" Exasperation lit her eyes. "Aren't we supposed to be able to function within the system? Isn't that what they ask us to do?"

"Tell us to do," he muttered into his mug.

"Sometimes they listen," Mags admitted, "but I've heard stories. You must be careful what you bring up and how you present. You have to go prepared. And if you're a woman," she shook her head, "you'll run into a lot of resistance."

"That's exactly the problem." I leaned forward, my eyebrows up. "There's one woman on the council. *One.* For all of Silvermine? How will women be represented if we don't step up and create it for ourselves?"

"The RD says women's husbands represent them." Mags nodded toward Lisha. "That's in the text, too."

"But is that right?" Lisha asked, looking from Mags to me. "What if my husband is a jerk, and he doesn't listen to me?"

"Good question." I tilted my mug in her direction.

"Of course it isn't right," Mags said.

"Why is there a woman at all?" That was Ellie.

"She's a token." Kilte shrugged. "One voice carries little weight, and she always sides with the men."

"And if a woman doesn't have a husband?" I was thinking about Steff and trying not to be angry. "We can vote, sure, but almost all of the names on the ballot are men. How can a man understand the needs of single women? Maybe someone should ask the City Council about *that.*"

Lisha got up and started clearing away the breakfast dishes. Ellie was watching me, her eyes dark and thoughtful.

"Try it and see how that works out for you," Kilte said. "Give us a heads up when you're going—I want your house before someone else gets it."

I rolled my eyes at him, and Bree laughed, poking him in the arm. "You don't get her house, bum. Besides, it's just a Council meeting."

"And from a legal standpoint, you're a runaway," Walker put in.

"Point taken," I acknowledged, sighing. "It will have to be done carefully." I was lost in thought, wheels turning. *Why shouldn't single women have affordable housing? The RD says they listen. How would Mom's life have been different if she hadn't been forced to marry Ray?* Hurt and anger simmered below the surface of my mind. *She would still be alive.*

"Very carefully indeed," Mags said, her eyes clear and distant, as if looking at something I couldn't see.

~

Two days later, my wrist buzzed while I was hanging up garments at Mrs. At break, I went to the stockroom and dug my phone out of my tote.

Ray. One sentence. *You'd better be at the funeral.* My lips tightened, but I didn't reply. I slid to the floor, head resting against the wall, looking at everything and nothing.

Because land was precious and expensive, only the Exalted Caste could afford to have a loved one interred—generally, at American Reformation Memorial Park in Charleston, our nation's capital. You needed an invitation from the RD to merit a plot there. The rest of us were cremated after we breathed our last. The State of Paradise handled all services, with little input from family members; prinisters performed the necessary offices on a barge out in the ocean, several miles off Silvermine's coast. After a short ceremony, the decedent's remains were launched skyward to "touch the face of God." The capsule exploded at altitude and ashes scattered to the wind.

Those who had the means sometimes purchased fireworks to embellish the explosion, marking a colorful end to an often gray life. But Ray didn't have that kind of money, and it didn't matter, anyway. I sighed, tears swelling my eyes, my emotions denying the display on my phone.

I wanted to go to Mom's funeral, of course. But I didn't want to do it with Ray. *He will use the occasion to get me back under his thumb—force me back home. And that's not going to happen.*

Only I didn't have a clue how to prevent it. *Maybe Bree will have some ideas.* I vowed to ask her when she came in later.

~

By the time Mags came in with the girls that evening, I had a large pot of vegetable soup simmering on the back of the stove and was slicing a fresh loaf of bread.

"Oh, Meryn!" Mags beamed, shaking snow from her coat. "Bless you!"

"Is that for us?" Lisha asked, her eyes big.

"Of course!" At their reaction, a flush of pleasure burned my cheeks. "It's about time I started helping around here!"

"You help a lot." Ellie was trying to hide a grin. "I got an A on my math test, thanks to you."

"Ellie, it was all your hard work!" I said as she laughed and came to hug me. "I just nudged you in a new direction."

"We stayed late at school because we're rehearsing for the Christmas pageant." Lisha tossed her backpack on the futon.

"Hang it up please," Mags said. "It's snowy."

Lisha grimaced and grabbed the offending pack, swiping at the futon fabric.

"We're the camel *again*." Ellie rolled her eyes and sat at the table.

"What would you rather be?" I asked, setting bread slices on the grate to toast.

"An angel." Lisha hung her backpack on a peg and slipped by me to get the pitcher of tea out of the fridge. "The one who talks."

"I want to be Mary," Ellie said. "She gets all the press."

"Now *that's* a good reason." Lisha said tartly, thumping the pitcher on the table so the tea splashed. "The play isn't *about* us. It's—"

"Girls, why don't you set the table and keep an eye on the toast," Mags said. "Meryn, can I tear you away from your cooking for a moment?"

"Of course," I said, mystified. I wiped my hands on a towel and followed her to the girls' bedroom.

"I'll do flatware!" Lisha said.

"You did flatware last time," Ellie said. "It's my—"

Mags shut the door on their argument. "Meryn, dear." Her expression was hesitant. "Bree and I have no desire to intrude on your very private grief. Nor do we wish to add to it. However, Bree shared with me your conundrum about your mother's funeral. And I may have hit on a solution . . . if you're open to talking about it?"

My stomach knotted, but I laid a hand on her arm. "Mags, of course. I welcome any ideas you may have."

She pressed her hand over mine. "Thank you, dear." Briskly she turned to the closet, pushing hanging clothes aside until she found a garment bag at the back. Unzipping it, she drew out a dress and hung it on the back of the door. My gasp melded with her sigh.

A cascade of stunning, full-length black lace openwork flowed over a solid black sheath. The underdress's modest, U-shaped neckline accented the lace—handcrafted by artisans using the finest crochet hook—that buttoned to a chin-skimming high collar. The long sleeves were designed intentionally narrow to hug the arms. More jet glass buttons ran from elbow to wrist, and lace extended down the hand to a loop meant to slip over the wearer's index finger, creating an elegant, pointed finish. Wealthy women wore ringlets with such a dress—gold or silver rings attached to fine chains that looped around the wrist, down to the buttons and back to the fingers.

The dress spoke of a different, more elegant time—and a much higher caste than Mags's current Indigent status.

"Mags!" My fingers caressed the bodice. "This isn't . . . silk?"

"It is." Mags's voice warmed with a touch of pride. "It belonged to my mother."

"This is stunning!" I'd never seen a silk garment, much less worn one, and I didn't know anyone who had.

Mags smiled. "I'm so glad you like it. I was thinking you could wear it to your mother's funeral."

I gawped at her, too stunned for a moment to respond. When I found my voice, I said, "Mags—I couldn't."

"Why on earth not?" Mags asked, her eyes widening; then they narrowed critically as she examined the dress. "Well yes, the skirt might be a bit short—mother was small, you know—but with a pair of black tights, the thicker ones, for warmth . . ."

"Mags, what if—God forbid—something were to happen to the dress while I was wearing it? I could never forgive myself!"

Mags tilted her head, her eyes crinkling. "Well, I would forgive you, Meryn dear. Besides," she went on in a more practical tone, "clothes are for wearing. It would delight Mama no end to know this old rag was getting some use."

"Well," I said, shaking my head, "this dress is a miracle. But . . . it doesn't solve my problem."

"No," Mags agreed, raising an index finger and turning back to the closet, "but this might." She took down a large round box from a high shelf. Coaxing off the lid, she lifted out a dark shape—small, covered with lace. A hat. "May I?" she asked, smiling.

At my nod, she pulled the girls' stepstool over with her foot and stepped up. As she set the hat on my head, my hands rose instinctively. "This was Gamma's. It's modeled after an old Spanish mantilla," she said, pushing my hands away and snugging the hat down on one side, "with a few alterations to make it stay put. These were all the rage right after the Reformation when husbands didn't want other men to see the beauty of their wives." She fluffed the hat on one side and drew the veil down, and I was enclosed in a little tent of lace. "There!" She turned me toward the mirror.

I could hardly see my jaw drop. "I'm invisible!"

"Close." Mags grinned. "But notice you can still see. It's the reflectivity of the lace. Chinese product, of course. I was thinking"—and she swept my hair back and twisted it up, tucking it behind my head—"your hair is a giveaway, but if we change it . . ."

I studied the effect. "This is marvelous, Mags! We could do a bun, perhaps. Or—will the hat still fit?"

Mags nodded. "It was designed to hide the hair, as well as the face. Hair is sexual, you know." Her mouth quirked. "We'll have to pin it in place, but it will work." She released my hair, put the stepstool in its corner and settled on the foot of the lower bunk.

"I had one more idea," she said. "You can't do much if the Guards are there with a chip reader. Short of taking out your chip, and then you'd get busted for that."

*Take out my chip?* I was dumbfounded, but Mags was still talking.

"If you go in the guise of a married woman, Ray won't look twice at you."

My hands were reluctant as I removed the hat and placed it back in its box. "Borrow someone's wedding ring?" I joked.

Mags smiled. "Yes. Mine. And you will need a husband."

My smile faded. "That might be more of a challenge, unless you have a spouse stashed somewhere, too."

Mags laughed. "I'm not that resourceful! No, Walker has volunteered to stand in for the future Mr. Flint."

"Walker?" My eyes opened wide, and a swirl of conflicting emotions beset me. *Walker? He doesn't even like me.*

Mags arched an eyebrow. "Is Walker . . . unacceptable?" she asked delicately.

"Well, no—I mean—" I stammered. "Wait. He volunteered?"

"He did." Mags's tone was unequivocal, and she sighed. "Don't let what he said in the bathroom trouble you, Meryn. Walker is just very . . ." She paused, and her voice gentled. ". . . protective."

"And wisely so," I said, but the memory still smarted.

"It would be easier, of course, if you could just wear an MT," Mags said, and we traded a wry look. The funeral barge was the one place women were exempt from that law, the odd reason being that MTs weren't made in black; if I wore one there, I'd stand out like a goldfish in a shark tank.

She rose and patted my arm. "Give it some prayer. Sleep on it."

# 25. GOODBYE

But lying next to Bree on the futon four hours later, my eyes refused to close. Insomnia was becoming an uncomfortable habit, but this night at least I understood why. My stomach knotted every time I thought about possibly seeing Ray, being recognized, being caught. I kept telling myself that if Ray wanted to turn me in, he would have done it already. But I also knew Ray's mental state might change during or after Mom's service. And Guards were always on the funeral barge to prevent any unseemly displays of emotion.

I rolled over, wishing I'd asked Mags for a dose of her potion. I tried to pray, but that felt hypocritical, given how angry I'd been at God since Mom died. I kept slipping into scenarios of the funeral, which all ended with me in handcuffs, being escorted to a Guard station. My eyelids blinked, sagged, closed.

A Guard seized my arms and dragged me toward the back of the funeral barge. Despite fighting with every move in my arsenal, I couldn't break free. I heard Ray's voice behind me. "Take her away! Stupid witch. She doesn't deserve a husband."

"Finally," the Guard said. "You're mine. You can't get away this time." He pushed up his faceplate, and I gasped; it was Steffan. His mouth flattened into a cruel line.

"No. She is not for you." The new voice came from behind us, and I twisted in Steffan's grip. A slender, red-haired mermaid sat on the edge of the barge, her tail dangling in the water. When our eyes met, she rose.

"Mom!" Joy overwhelmed me. I struck Steffan's hands away and ran toward her.

She wore only the coral-bead necklace, her hair modestly covering shoulders and bust, her face glowing with a serenity and purity that took my breath. Holding out her arms, she smiled. "Mer-child!"

"Well, now." Steffan pushed me aside. His eyes on Mom were greedy.

He reached for her, but she shook her head, sobering. "You cannot have everything you covet, Steffan Hagen."

His face contorted with the rage of a petulant child. "Who are you to tell me what I cannot have, woman?" In his mouth, the word became an epithet, and he lunged at her, his hands balled into fists.

She held up a hand. Steff's entire body jerked as if he'd struck an invisible wall, and he stumbled backward and fell. The moment he hit the barge deck, he disappeared. I blinked in surprise; just as quickly, the memory of him vanished.

Mom's gaze shifted to me, her expression so loving, so full of understanding, tears sprang to my eyes. Twining the coral necklace around her fingers, she lifted it from her neck and looped it over my head. Then she touched my cheek. Her warm hand smelled of the delicate rose perfume I remembered from childhood. "Don't be afraid, Meryn. God is always with you. He's not angry, darling—He knows you're hurting. And I will always love you."

She turned toward the water then, her face reflecting the same yearning I'd seen when we were on the beach together—a look that said she'd been too long away from the ocean, her heart's home. "I must go."

"Mama," I whispered, pleading. "Let me come with you."

She shook her head. "You cannot, Meryn. You have yet to walk." Before I could speak, she executed an amazing backflip and dove cleanly into the waves.

"Mom!" I threw myself on my stomach, my head and arms dangling over the edge, hands desperate in the frigid ocean, and watched as she swam deeper into the Stygian gloom, finally fading from sight. My hands delved the water until my fingers turned blue, trying to touch her, trying to touch anything that touched her.

~

Despite my insomnolence, my eyes opened early the next morning. I gazed through the skylight at the stars as they blinked and began their slow retreat from the morning light. A psalm came to mind, and I whispered, "Awake, harp and lyre! I will awaken the dawn." Listening to Bree's even respiration, I thanked God for another day of life. I'd been doing that a lot in recent days. Life seemed fragile, precious.

Abruptly I remembered my dream. "Mom!" I whispered. My hand darted to my cheek, my thoughts lingering on how real it had felt to be with her again, to talk to her. What was it she'd said? It wasn't my time? No. Something I had to do? What? *Lord, please help me remember. It was just a dream, but this feels important. I have to swim? No.*

I shook my head on the pillow. Closing my eyes, I plumbed my memory for every moment of the dream. Ray. Steff as a Guard. I grimaced. Mom . . . as a mermaid. "Walk," Mom had said. *She couldn't walk because of the tail, but I still could. She had to walk?*

*No.* At once, the words surfaced. *"You have yet to walk."* I smiled in triumph. *But what did she mean? Especially since she had a tail in the dream, so she couldn't walk. Her walk is over? And she has become who she was always meant to be?*

I had more questions than answers. But the anxiety that had kept me up the night before was gone.

The sky above smudged a brightening blue. The day was coming, whether or not I wanted it, whether or not I was ready. Careful to not wake Bree, I slipped out of bed, gathered my clothes, and crept downstairs.

~

Two hours later, after a shower and quick breakfast with the family, I stood in the bathroom, surveying the effect.

Except for the hem length, the dress might have been made for me. The black silk sheath skimmed my torso and flared around my calves. Delicate lace snugged up my neck, almost to the chin, and wrapped its way down my arms to the wrists, arrowing across the backs of my hands to loop over the index fingers. The opaque sheath covered my décolleté without hiding my shape, and sheer lace swirled to my ankles. I'd bought a pair of black leggings for warmth, and a new pair of black winter shoes with modest heels. The shoes had consumed most of my paycheck, but Mags had taken one look at my open-toed sandals and insisted on covering my food needs for the next two weeks.

I didn't dare wear jewelry: everything I owned, Ray would recognize from across the barge, so the only item I'd put on that morning was my blue Caste Ring.

The darling hat perched on my head, covering my hair in its conservative, braided bun. The lace I'd pulled up and back—no need to cover my face yet—but I was pleased at how it disguised my hair color. To my surprise, I looked much older.

I'd never been vain about my looks—Mom was the knockout in our family—but this morning I was delighted with my reflection in the mirror. I found myself wishing for a different occasion so I could enjoy wearing such clothes. Then shame struck me from two directions.

A pounding on the door shattered my thoughts.

"Meryn? I'm sorry, but I gotta go!"

"Oh, I'm coming, Ellie!"

I opened the door, intending to slip past, but Ellie stopped me. "Whoa." Her eyes traveled the length of me, lingering jealously on the black glass buttons and delicate lace. Her gaze wandered up to the little hat, and she smiled into my eyes. "You're gorgeous!"

"What?" Lisha poked her head around the doorframe. "Wow! You look like a high-caste lady!" She proffered a formal bow.

Heat bloomed in my face. "Thanks, girls," I said, sounding shy even to myself.

"Mom!" Lisha ran down the hall. "You should see Meryn!"

I could hear Walker with Mags, his voice murmuring low. Taking a deep breath to summon courage, I moved hesitantly into the living room.

For a moment there was silence, broken only by the sound of Walker's car keys hitting the floor. He cleared his throat and bent to retrieve them as Mags came toward me, beaming, arms outstretched. "Ohh, Mama would be so very delighted! How glorious you look!" She circled me, inspecting the fit, gently tugging the hem in the back. "It works well, I think. Don't you? In spite of the height difference."

I fumbled with the wrist buttons, grateful for the distraction. "I was afraid it might be too short through the waist," I said, "but . . ."

Mags shook her head as she buttoned them for me, tightening the lace to my arms. "The design just skims the waist and hips. There. Meryn, it's perfect!" She stood on tiptoe to kiss my cheek.

"I can't thank you enough, Mags." I smiled, nervous, trying not to lick my lipstick. "I'll be careful."

"I know you will, dear," she said.

Finally, I let myself look at Walker. He wore a formal dark blue suit and patterned tie, and held two coats draped over one arm. His freshly washed hair was drawn into a ponytail, but his expression shuttered, cautious. "You look very nice, Meryn," he said, polite.

An unexpected disappointment drew in my breath. "All glory to God," I said, formal in turn. "May we honor Him on this occasion."

"Meryn," Mags said, "We got out the 'house' dress overcoat for you." Walker dropped one coat on the futon and held out the other, and I pushed my arms into the heavy synth-wool sleeves as he pulled it up and settled it on my shoulders. Immediately its warmth wrapped me, and I worried less about freezing out on the barge.

Mags went on, "Bree and I share it, but we thought it would go well with the dress." She fussed, rolling down the cuffs and kneeling to fasten the lower buttons, which made heat rise in my cheeks. "There," she said, satisfied.

I thanked her as I buttoned the rest, and Walker pulled on his black overcoat. It was secondhand; the sleeves were slightly short, and one arm sported a neatly sewn patch, nearly invisible. Wrapping a black scarf around his neck, he turned toward the door.

"Wait," Mags said. "One more thing." She stepped close, pulling the wedding ring from her left ring finger. "I'm hoping this will fit," she said softly, handing it to me. "If not, I'll get out Will's."

My hands shook, and I couldn't get the ring to cooperate. "Oh . . ."

"Allow me," Walker said quietly, taking the ring from me. I held out my hand, and he gently slid the ring onto my left ring finger.

My breath caught, and I cleared my throat, turning away. "It fits just fine, Mags. I was afraid it would be too tight . . ." I dared not look at Walker. *He doesn't trust me. But Mags does. But what if he—no. I can't think about anything else bad today.*

Mags cut off my thought. "Now don't forget to cover your face when you get there," she said, and her eyes registered a sudden blaze of memory, an incandescent pain untarnished by time, and I experienced a brief vision of the older woman standing on a barge, the sea wind whipping this same dress into a lace-trimmed flag as her tears joined spume from the waves, fireworks painting the sky red with grief. "I'll be praying for you both." I shook my head to dispel the scene, my emotions already on overload.

"Shall we?" Walker opened the door for me, and we crossed the porch and descended the stairs to the sidewalk, where salt had carved safe circles in the ice. The cold, pellucid air cleared my thoughts; just a few high clouds filtered the sun, and the breeze was kind.

We walked to the bus stop in silence, my new shoes squeaking on the snow. I didn't know what to say. I felt slow and stupid, as if in an odd dream, standing on a stage without a script, cast in a performance but didn't know the name of the play.

We didn't have long to wait; the bus arrived moments later. "Careful," was all Walker said when we boarded.

"Here you are, goodwife." A white-haired man stumbled to his feet and gestured for me to take his seat in the Worker Caste section.

"Thank you," I said, hiding my surprise and gathering up the overskirt so it wouldn't brush the filthy floor. The seat was still warm.

Walker stationed himself next to me as the bus jerked forward. His gloved hand gripped the bar, his Indigent Caste ring screaming to anyone who bothered to look that he was in the wrong section. Not for the first time, I whispered a prayer of thanks that Guards rarely patrolled the buses. *Should I ask him to move to the back? Just to keep him safe?* Glancing at his implacable expression, I decided to hold my peace. The bus was too noisy to do much talking, anyway. *I should have chosen to work today. Too late, too late.*

We debarked one bus, walked to a different stop, boarded another. I was content to let Walker guide me so I didn't have to think. "You okay?" he asked at one point, and I nodded numbly. My hands cramped with cold; abashed at my thoughtlessness, I fished in my pockets, drew on my gloves. The nanites in my Caste Ring dissolved and reassembled outside the leather, tightening to a comfortable fit.

*This isn't real. We'll get to the barge, and Mom will be there. She just had to go to the hospital for a few days. Yes, that's it. Ray just picked her up, I'm sure. They'll call this whole thing off. Didn't that happen once—some guy showed up at his own funeral? His wife almost had a heart attack. We'll laugh about it later. I'll go home, and Mom will fix tofu, and I'll sleep in my old room. Everything will go back to normal, and . . . we'll laugh. Of course, we will.*

Another stop. Another bus change. No seats this time. Walker's hand on my elbow, guiding me, supporting me, his body sheltering me from curious eyes. The kindness warmed me in a distant way. *Is this one of the functions of a husband? They didn't teach us this in school.*

I looked out the window. Docks. Warehouses. Workers doing normal things. *Normal. Will life ever be normal? What is normal, anyway? Oh, the docks. We must be close. Why did I come? I should've worked. This is silly. What is it supposed to—*

The bus groaned to a stop, and I lurched and gripped the overhead bar. Walker guided me toward the door. Three people got off ahead of us. A man with thinning hair . . . *Ray?* My breath sucked in, nerves knotting my stomach. *No. Hair too light. Not Ray.* I stepped off the bus. Moved forward, uncertain. Smell of the sea, damp and salty. Low clouds scudding in from across the bay, blotting out the sun.

"Mary," Walker said.

*Someone he knows?* The bus doors closed, the bus—

Something jerked my elbow, hard, whipped me around. *Walker? What—*

Before I could ask, he reached up with gentle hands and pulled dark lace across my face. The world shuttered gray.

"Oh," I said.

He smiled a bit, then pulled up the coat's hood to shelter my head from the wind. "You just forgot, Mary. Here. Let's put the scarf around the back of your hood and tuck it, so your neck won't be cold in the wind." He matched words to actions, crossing, tucking, and tying, and buttoned the topmost button. "That will keep your hood up."

"Thank you," I whispered.

He offered me his arm; I put my gloved hand on it, and we walked down the sidewalk to the docks, joining a queue of other quiet, sober, black-clad people, joining ritual, joining ourselves to the community of death and mourning and life, loss and love and pain. A gate. A thin man in black, holding a pad. A larger man, wearing Guard white. *Disrespectful. Guards should have black uniforms for . . .* My insides clenched. I swallowed, hoping I wouldn't vomit.

"Barton, Esselin, Frank, Hopewell?" the man in the black suit asked the couple in front of us.

"We're here for Joseph Barton," a man answered.

The black-suited man scanned their chips and nodded.

*Oh no.* My mind scrambled for prayer but found no purchase, a cat on ice skates.

"Last queue on your right, Mr. and Mrs. Munson, highest castes toward the front." They filed past him, down to the barge. He looked at Walker. "Barton, Esselin, Frank, Hopewell?"

"Hopewell," Walker said. I envied his composure. My lungs had forgotten their function. The Guard's eyes scanned the barge, bored. I forced a breath, trying not to gasp.

A muted cry. An umbrella flew past us, bouncing toward the water. "I told you to leave that closed!" An angry male voice, behind us.

The black-suited man ran after the umbrella and returned it to the group behind us. Then his hand fell on my shoulder, pushing me forward. "Hopewell is first queue on your right, ma'am, highest castes toward the front," he said, and just like that we were past him and the Guard, floating down the gangway and onto the funeral barge, its space partitioned into four sections, railings festooned with streamers of black crepe. Abruptly I could breathe again. Sparks swam in my vision, and I clutched Walker's arm.

A sign to our right read *Hopewell*, but the space overflowed with mourners. *How odd*, I thought, *seeing dozens of women wearing black, not an MT in sight.* "Here," Walker murmured, guiding me to the second space, marked *Frank*. It was only half full, but we lingered toward the back. More people filed past, regarding us with detached curiosity.

"Bad idea," Walker said, low. "Come on." He guided me past the area with a sign reading *Esselin*—my guts performing acrobatics beneath my ribs—to the space for *Barton*, where we mixed with the small crowd.

I darted glances toward the Esselin queue, where I recognized several people from church, including Bart and my friend Ruth Wittier. Something in my heart warmed, a brief candle. Mom loved Ruthie. People still crowded onto the barge, filtering themselves into each queue. The throng pressed us forward as our section filled. Mourners weren't formally separated by caste at funerals, but we stayed toward the back, anyway, and allowed people to move past us. The last thing we needed was a Caste Insult accusation.

A gate clanged, and the tugboat's horn blew twice—loud, startling. Mottled seagulls circled, crying angry objections overhead. The breeze blew much stronger here, tainted with odors of diesel and rotting fish. It threatened to pull off my hat, despite the profusion of bobby pins I'd used to secure it. I tucked lace into my scarf, gripped the edge of my hood. The barge jerked forward. Several women cried out, and I stumbled.

"Easy," Walker said, low, his strong hand steadying me. Ahead of us, a woman sobbed inconsolably. A man standing with her scanned the crowd, his eyes wide and white, and whispered urgent words in her ear.

The barge jerked again, not as hard this time.

"We're moving, Mommy!" A child's voice, happy. *Mommy.* I bit my lip, memories flooding. Walker's hand tightened on my arm.

The dock floated backward—no, I corrected, the barge was moving forward. At a speed seemingly measured in inches, we drifted into the bay, the tugboat pulling and chuffing. The whole scene was eerily silent except for the slap of waves, muted sobs, and gentle conversation between mourners.

"How did you know Joe?" The question came from a blonde woman wearing a dark blue hat and black coat. I recoiled, gripping Walker's arm; I hadn't seen her approach.

Walker bent toward her. "We're with Hopewell, but it was full."

"Ah," she said. "I'm sorry for your loss."

"Thank you," I managed. She nodded and moved away.

People shifted in the Esselin queue, revealing Ray standing toward the front, talking to someone. His eyes wandered in my direction. I turned and strode toward the far railing, my back to the barge.

Walker moved with me as though the shift were a mutual decision.

I grasped the metal bar, its cold burning through my gloves. The wind danced past us, rising in strength as the barge cleared the sheltered harbor. "Thank you," I said, not looking at him.

"No problem," he said. "That balding guy . . ."

"Yes." Abruptly, the image of Ray registered on my brain. "Was he with a woman?" I whispered fiercely.

"I believe so." Walker was quiet, diplomatic.

Fury bisected me like lightning through a dead tree. For the first time in my life, I wanted to hurt, to maim—that flaming, consuming desire overriding training and faith. I whirled away from the railing and marched toward the Esselin queue, an odd, hard smile curling the corner of my mouth.

A split second later I was trapped against Walker, his arms pinning me fiercely in place, my face flattened into his coat, nose pushed to one side at a painful angle.

"I know it's upsetting, Mary," he said in soothing tones. "I know. Family can be hard."

I struggled, but it was like play-fighting with Ray when I was four: pointless. A curse that had never passed my lips burst from me now in a toxic hiss. "Let go of me!"

"Don't be stupid!" His whisper matched mine for urgency. "Do you *want* us to get caught?"

*Us.* That stopped me cold. I finally realized: Walker was in this with me—all the way. Escorting an illegally homeless woman, and without her father's permission. Falsely representing himself as my husband. His punishment would not be mild.

My eyes rose to his, my mouth open. Rage cooled, morphed into shame at my rash display of emotion, for the jeopardy I'd put him in, and for my hideously sinful desire to harm my stepfather. "I'm so sorry,"

I whispered. "I'm a fool." Tears flooded my eyes, and impatiently I tried to brush them away under the veil, but only succeeded in plastering the lace against my face.

"I forgive you." He held my gaze and his mouth gentled. "Mary."

I shook my head, unwilling to accept his quick forgiveness, unable to forgive myself.

"Can I let go?" he asked, still in that gentle tone. His eyebrows lifted, then furrowed in concern. He shook my shoulders slightly. "Hey. It's okay."

The blonde woman with the blue hat moved into my field of vision, studying us. My heart leapt into my mouth. "We're being watched."

Walker pulled me closer so quickly I was startled, and patted my back. I tried to relax. It felt awkward, but I didn't know if that was because he was uncomfortable or because I was.

It seemed an eternity before Walker spoke. "She's gone." We released a breath in unison, and moved back to our position next to the Esselin queue. *God, what have I done, putting Walker in jeopardy like this?* My stomach knotted.

Walker supported me as the tug drew the funeral barge farther from shore. The wind gusted and the seas had become choppy, making my footing on the deck uncertain. I shivered uncontrollably despite Mags's thick dress coat. Walker positioned himself as best he could between me and the wind and wrapped his arms around me.

"Thank you," I said. He nodded.

It seemed I had an awful lot to thank Walker for, this morning.

The trip seemed endless—the odd silence broken only by the cries of birds, the wind, the rocking cold, and the occasional murmur of mourners. I wondered how deep the water was beneath the barge. *Half a mile? More?* The thought unnerved me. We were so far from shore. *Could the barge sink? Of course, it could—it's metal, after all. How long would we live in the cold water?* I looked at the slate waves and shuddered.

Almost imperceptibly, the tug slowed and turned, angling the front of the barge downwind of us. Far out on the ocean, the squat form of a tin-transport ship violated the broad sweep of horizon. I wondered where it was going. I wondered if I could swim to it, if it could bear me away from my guilt and my fear, away from the RD, away to some exotic land. *If the weather were warmer, maybe—*

A prinister stepped up on a platform at the front and led everyone in a short prayer. In the Barton queue, a man frowned, folded his arms, and muttered something to his wife, who gave him a reproving look.

Then the prinister launched into the life of Joseph Barton. A second man, tall and lanky, his black hair whipping in the wind, stood and shared humorous anecdotes; then a shorter man, heavyset and well bundled against the cold, detailed Barton's support of his church. A respected accountant, Barton had become a pillar of his community, and left behind three fine sons and seven doting grandsons, as well as other assorted relatives.

After an exhortation to "all men" to live an honorable life before God in the manner of Joseph Barton, the service concluded. The grief cannon fired, launching his ashes into the sky. We all heard the faint *boom* when the canister exploded. A woman in the Barton section wailed her grief. A Guard at the back of the barge—I hadn't noticed him before—moved through the crowd toward her. I lost sight of him, but a moment later the wailing stopped. I ground my teeth. *Lord, please comfort that woman in her bereavement. In spite of the Guard.*

Prinister Severs stepped up to the platform. My hand tightened on Walker's arm. "Dearly beloved," he said, his tones sonorous and reverential, "We are here today to honor the life of our dear sister, Rose Caroline Esselin, beloved obedient wife of St. John Raymond Esselin, mother of Maureen Anna Esselin."

"He couldn't even get my name right," I muttered to Walker. His gloved hand pressed mine, and a dull headache started between my eyes. *Oh, Mom. This isn't happening. In a moment I'll wake up—this is a bad dream. Just a horrible dream.*

The rest of the service was a blur. Two of Mom's friends from church stood up and said nice things, praising her selflessness and her volunteer work in the bookstore. That warmed a remote part of me, but mostly I felt wooden, disconnected. Our neighbor Hannah spoke of her concern for the widowers. The crowd had shifted again, and I couldn't see Ray. I wondered if he'd brought Constance, or someone new.

Prinister Severs reclaimed the podium. "We will miss our sister Rose. But we take great comfort in knowing she is resting safe in the arms of Jesus. Now Rose's friends St. Bartholomew and Damaris Deborah will sing Rose's favorite hymn." He yielded the space to Bart and DeeDee. Bart opened with some chords from the chorus. I knew what they would sing, and they did.

*Why should I feel discouraged?*
*Why should the shadows come?*

*Why should my heart feel lonely*
*And long for heaven and home?*

Tears formed in my eyes and ran in warm rivulets down my face, melting into the lace around my neck. Soft and careful, I sang the alto line with Dee's soprano.

*When Jesus is my portion*
*A constant Friend is He*
*His eye is on the sparrow*
*And I know He watches me.*

*This is real. Dear Jesus. Mom, why did you have to die? How can I possibly live without you?* A sob rose in me, but I fought it down with fierce anger, bowing my head as Dee and Bart segued into the next verse.

When they came around to the chorus again, I joined in and let my voice soar. I couldn't stop it—my sorrow and grief, so long suppressed out of fear and necessity, the pain of missing Mom, my conflicted feelings over running away after Mom's death, my guilt about leaving Ray and hating Ray and missing Ray, and feeling like I was taking advantage of Bree and her family—all of it coursed out of me in a paroxysm of grief and tears and love and rage. It was foolish and risky. It was cathartic. It was my tribute to Mom.

When the song stopped, I noticed several people in the Barton queue darting looks in our direction. An older woman beamed at me openly, tears streaming down her face. I wanted to feel afraid for her, but I didn't have the space. Walker pulled me to him and covered the back of my head with his hand, careful not to jostle the hat. I didn't know if he was trying to comfort me, hiding me from the fallout from my foolish gaffe, or just playing the part. The truth was, I didn't care. I needed to be held, and I clung to him, desperate, trying to keep my twisting face from releasing the sobs inside, coughing my grief in quiet gasps. His arm tightened around my waist, and I relaxed into his strength, letting him support me, taking in his warmth, the masculine smell of him, the hint of woodsy—

And at that highly inappropriate moment I thought of Tamar, and I remembered who I was and who he was and why he was here. Confused, crushed with a disappointment I didn't understand and didn't have the strength to parse, I loosened my grip. Walker gently let go, and I turned away, my unreleased pain eating acid holes in my soul.

"Farewell, beloved child," Prinister Severs chanted. "Ashes to ashes, dust to dust."

The grief cannon fired, carrying the remains of my beautiful mother into the clouds. We all traced the faint trail of its ascent. After a moment, the capsule exploded. I jerked reflexively; Walker steadied me.

Without warning, bright green streamers appeared in the sky. My eyes widened—how had Ray managed to spring for fireworks? I watched the iridescent trails as they looped, then coalesced into a perfect green rosebud. The bud turned pink, opened, and blossomed into a layered flower in glimmering, variegated shades of rose and merlot. There were *oohs* and *ahhs* from the mourners. A moment later the whole image dissolved, green sparkles raining into the ocean.

I closed my eyes, releasing tears. "Mom," I whispered. *Oh, Mom. Why did you have to die? Why did you leave me?* Of their own volition, my eyes searched the back of the barge, but no feminine figure lingered there, dangling a tail in the water. My teeth crushed my lip; I tore my gaze away. *It was a dream, Meryn. Don't be stupid.*

The other two services were a panoply of words, hymns, scrupulously checked emotions and well-choreographed odes. Each time the grief cannon fired, I jerked again. Walker supported me, his arm around my waist.

No one else had fireworks.

People milled about in each queue, talking in low tones. A few women wept, soundless, wrapped in their black lace and comforted by somber spouses. Someone in the crowd gave a laugh, quickly extinguished. A baby wailed, the sound grating on nerves already raw. The barge's Guard walked toward the sound, and a moment later, the cry was muffled. *Not even babies can cry on this barge,* I thought, but the cynical part of me was distant and tired. A black crepe streamer tore free of the railing beside me and sailed on the wind, far out to sea until it was lost to sight. Idly I wondered how much black crepe papered the ocean floor.

"What are they waiting for?" a man muttered.

As if in answer, the tug gave a double blast on its horn, startling me. People quickly grabbed the closest railing as the engines gurgled to life. The barge jerked, then jerked again. The acrid smell of burning diesel fuel wafted over the crowd, and several people—including me—coughed uncontrollably until the tug turned downwind and we could breathe again. Walker guided me to the outside rail where the air was fresher, and I held on and looked down at the slate-colored waves as they bounced and slapped against the side of the barge. I couldn't stop shivering, but he did not put his arm around me again and I was glad.

I searched the water the whole way back to Port Silvermine, as if looking for something I knew I would never find.

# 26. RECKONING

An odd change in the rhythm of the waves brought me back to the present moment. My eyes lifted from the waves, and I blinked: We were passing the breakwater. The tone of the tug's engines dropped, and the barge slowed, the slosh of water against its hull waning to a quiet hiss. For a long moment I gazed out at the ocean, my whole body a yearning—then my shoulders sagged, and I turned away.

With deliberate slowness, the tug guided us past whirling gyres of plastic trash, dead fish, and frozen seaweed; past derelict fishing trawlers, rusted and half-submerged, frost riming their superstructures; past the ruin of Old Port Silver, its houses up on stilts but nevertheless mute corpses, victims of sea level rise. The broken windows seemed to watch the port like lifeless eyes in a face gone slack. Here and there, boats bobbed at the base of rickety, slime-festooned ladders that led up to each house.

The state had dug out the bay near the city and expanded the port to accommodate the rising seas, but no one had the money to clean up the thousands of miles of flooded shoreline with its houses, condos, dead trees, and shops. The city's attempt to elevate the pricier structures and prolong their use had failed.

A huge series of levees surrounded the still-dry Silvermine Historic District, and pumps ran day and night to keep the seas at bay. But every storm sent waves of seawater over the barricades, and we all lived in dread of the hurricane that would breach the walls and finally destroy that part of our city's history. The most recent Category 8 storm had all but obliterated New York City, in DRUSA; Silvermine's bishopmayor,

Oral Heibeluft, had relished telling us about "the wrath of God on unholy Babylon." We'd heard that New York's mayor vowed to pump out the floodwaters and rebuild the city. Privately, I found that foolish.

"People still live there," Walker murmured. I started; I had forgotten him.

"That's dangerous," I said. "Those houses are infested with mold and swamp rats and Lord only knows what else."

"Yes." Walker stepped forward, his gloved hands on the railing. "But the poor have nowhere else to go. At least here they have shelter and can put fish on the table."

We drifted past the burned-out shell of a house, its missing wall exposing what had once been a kitchen. What hadn't burned had been plundered, appliances cannibalized for parts. All that remained were the outlines of cabinets and a cheap, half-melted plastic crucifix nailed over the kitchen door.

The barge drifted as the tug disconnected and circled, shifting its duties from pulling to pushing.

"I thought the Guards cleared everyone out of there," I said softly, leaning on the railing. Within seconds, the cold ate through my coat sleeves, and I stepped back. From the corner of my eye, I caught a glimmer of light from one house—a flash from a distant star—but when I looked for its source, I saw nothing.

"They did," Walker said. "But the people come back."

"That's disgusting!" A man near us addressed his wife, pointing to the burned-out house, his voice too loud. "They should clean this up!"

"They have tried, dear," his wife said, low, her hand on his arm. "The cost—"

"The cost!" His tone dripped scorn. "What did we elect Bishor Heibeluft for, anyway? He promised to roust all the trash out of there!"

"Perhaps you could call the bishor's office on Monday." She fussed with her gloves. "He's sure to listen to you, darling."

"A fine thing," the man said, pulling his expensive synth-wool overcoat more tightly about him.

The red Governance Caste Ring worn over his glove made me lower my eyes lest he look in my direction. Then I remembered he couldn't see my face, and I looked up again, emboldened and curious. Beneath the veil, my eyebrows rose. *What a small man he is. Small and frightened.*

"Shouldn't have to tell the bishor how to do his job." His head jerked as he caught sight of someone through the crowd. "Prinister Fichert!"

With no courtesy, the man pushed past the people surrounding him. "Prinister, do you see that disgraceful . . ." The noise of his diatribe faded as he moved up the barge, his wife following.

The Guard paid no heed.

The wind blew stronger, foul now with the odors of rotting fish, mildew, burned wood, and human waste. A woman cried out as it swept off her hat. Her husband jogged to retrieve it before it blew overboard, and she smiled, quick and sad, as he handed it back to her.

"It's the dead bide there." A voice at my elbow, as if we were in the midst of a conversation. A little girl—perhaps six or seven—grasped the railing next to me, looking out at Old Port Silver. She was dressed all in black, and a black tam-o'-shanter failed to contain her yellow curls, which blew in random chaos around her face. Her little black mittens gripped the railing.

She looked at me, her odd, pale purple eyes blinking. "They are set free in the sky, and they fly there to live."

"Why do they live there?" I asked, half curious, half playing along. "Can't the dead go anywhere they want?"

She shook her head soberly, curls bobbing. "The good people go to heaven with God. The bad people go there." Pushing her tam higher on her forehead, she nodded toward the ghost town. "The cursed ones. You must never go there," she said, her voice a warning. "The cursed ones will haunt you forever if you go there."

"I thought bad people went to hell." I whispered it. Nervous prickles ran up my spine, and I wondered where the barge Guard was.

"That—" She took a deep breath and pointed toward the house nearest to us, a pale-pink structure covered with irregular strips of black mold. "That's where they go, before they go to hell. They have to wait their turn because hell is so crowded with the homeless and the indigent and the sinful rebellious, the devil has to add more room. So they scare people here before they go. Sometimes—I—my gamma says sometimes they're so evil, they invade your body and take you over and make you do bad things. So you must never go there." She looked up at me, blinking back tears. "My gampa is there now."

"I'm sorry for your loss." I wanted to hug her, but I didn't dare; instead, I put my hand on the railing. "It's sad to lose someone you love."

"I didn't love him." Her eyes riveted on Old Port Silver, her tone turned truculent. "He was evil. The prinister's a *liar*, all that stuff he said. My gampa *deserves* to go there. I hope he *rots* there and doesn't take me over." I exchanged a startled look with Walker, who gave his head an infinitesimal shake. My eyes dropped to the little girl again; her tears were fear, not grief.

"Well, Jesus watches over us all. I don't think you have to worry about your gampa or any other dead person taking you over," I said in what I hoped was a reassuring tone.

She nodded. "'Cause I'll never go there. I know smarter."

"Elizabeth Jochebed, come away from the railing," a woman's soft voice called. The little girl lifted her chin and walked back to her queue without another word. I was glad I hadn't touched her; only the high caste addressed their children by their full names, and at the same moment, the significance of her purple eyes hit me: she was Exalted Caste, a pureborn direct descendant of one of the Founders. *What on earth are those people doing on a funeral barge?* My blood ran cold, and Walker blew out a breath.

The tug didn't dock our barge at its embarkation point as I expected; instead, it nosed us by inches toward the end of a different pier. I chewed my lip. Our queue would get off first, not last . . . increasing my risk of being seen.

The barge kissed the dock, mack-clad workers scrambling to secure the bollard lines. Deckhands extended the auto-gangway and rousters secured it, then opened the pier gate. What seemed like hours later but in reality must have been just a few minutes, a deckhand opened the barge gate and invited us to debark.

Our queue filed toward the pier, some mourners still weeping, trying to hide their emotion in handkerchiefs and scarves. The deckhands stood, silent and respectful, as we passed.

Walker and I started down the gangway, following an elderly woman who moved with a slow shuffle, leaning on a large metal cane. About halfway to the dock, her stiff blue fingers lost their grip, and the cane flipped out of her hand, clanged on the rail and fell into the filthy brown water, lost to sight.

"Oh no!" she said with a gasp, gripping the icy railing and looking over the edge. "No! It's gone!"

My eyes fell on her swollen ankles, mushrooming out of overtight shoes—she wasn't going far without help. Her Caste Ring was blue, so I let go of Walker's arm and stepped forward, touching her sleeve. "Mother, forgive the intrusion, but may I walk with you? I'm terribly cold."

She turned to me in surprise and smiled. "Why yes, child," she said with quiet dignity. "I will be honored to help keep you warm."

"Thank you, mother." I wrapped my arm around her back. Once we cleared the gangway, Walker moved to her other side and offered her his arm, and the three of us proceeded along the pier, other mourners swirling past us.

"A lovely service," the old woman said, puffing a bit. She peered up at me with rheumy blue eyes. "How did you know Joseph?"

"I'm afraid we didn't," I said. "We were with another queue."

"We listened to the service. He was a good man," Walker said.

She smiled up at him. "Oh, yes. He took good care of his family, including his lame old mother."

"He was your son?" I exchanged an astonished look with Walker. Mothers rarely survived their sons.

"My eldest," she said, and we couldn't fail to hear the pride in her voice. "I married his father when Joey was five, but he took to me right away, and I to him. He grew up to be a fine man. A fine man," and she gave her head a sharp nod to emphasize the point.

She was telling us about Joe's successes in school when I heard a familiar voice.

"Glad you came."

*Ray!* I stiffened but didn't turn.

"You knew I would."

*Steffan? How did I not see him on the barge?* Fear fed my chill.

"Sorry she wasn't here."

"I'm telling you, Ray, she's here somewhere! I heard her singing!"

I winced, trying to block out the old woman's chatter so I could focus on what Ray and Steff were saying.

"And here or not . . . utterly disrespectful, not showing her face and expressing the appropriate condolences to you and everyone who loved Mrs. Esselin . . . failed in her Family Duty. Obviously, she's not mature enough . . . You should bring her home. Discipline, Ray—that's what she needs."

I turned my head toward the old woman as the two men came by, so close that Steffan's coat brushed my hip. *Oh Jesus, help me!*

Ray grunted, and my lips tightened. I hoped he was remembering what his so-called "discipline" had done to my mother. I hadn't forgotten mine.

Steff cleared his throat, and his voice dropped, oozing persuasion. "You do understand, Ray, when I marry the girl, that could elevate you, too. As my wife, she'll bounce two full caste levels, right up to the red. A girl's father doesn't often see that kind of a change, but I have some friends on the City Council. They're reasonable men; we could almost certainly get you a management slot. The green ring, of course, and corresponding increase in your salary. That would be an added comfort and extra security for Meryn, if God forbid, anything should happen to me."

I felt Walker's eyes on me.

"Maybe you're right." Ray, thoughtful. "You're a good man, Steffan. And you've been very patient, waiting through her chastisement the way you did."

"I appreciate that more than I can say. I've been good as gold to that girl. But I just found out she even quit her job. How will she survive? I can't imagine these friends of hers will look kindly on her freeloading after a few weeks. And it's already affecting the family name."

Ray coughed, spat. "I had hoped through all of this she would have turned to you for love and support."

Shock forced me to pause. Fortunately, the old woman hadn't noticed, and I forced myself back into a walk. I glanced up in time to see Steffan turn to Ray, earnest. "I can take her in hand, you know. I'm ready, but I can't do it without your support. You have the final say. She's a good person—she just needs the firm guidance of a loving husband."

*Guidance? From you? Do you remember what you were screaming at me a few days ago?* Anger and fear fought through my grief.

Ray's murmur became unintelligible as they moved forward.

"Do you understand what I mean, child?" The old woman looked up at me.

I didn't dare speak. Steff wasn't ten feet ahead. I muffled a cough in my glove.

"Oh child, have you caught a chill?" she asked, solicitous.

"It was freezing on the barge, with that wind," Walker said. I silently blessed him for his quick thinking. "But mother, what about your cane?"

"Well, I have an old one at home," she said. "If I can get to the bus, I should be able to manage."

Wary, as if my gaze might alert them to my presence, I peered through my black lace curtain at Steff and Ray. They'd moved several paces ahead, out of earshot, and I released a breath. And in that moment of relief, I realized no one else was walking with Ray. *I was wrong. He didn't bring her. God!* Shame and guilt pricked me inside my coat.

Walker and I visited with the old woman until we reached the bus queue. People thronged the bus parked at the curb; as soon as it pulled away, another motor coach took its place. The city had long ago learned to accommodate funeral traffic.

As the jostling crowd surged toward the stop, I redoubled my grip on the old woman, keeping an eye on Ray and Steff as they boarded the vehicle. With growing horror, I realized we were too close—we'd end up on the same bus. I tried to hang back, but the press of people made it impossible.

"Here you go, mother," Walker said as we approached the door. We helped her onto the steps, Walker stepping up behind her, but I turned around.

"Get on the bus!" a man behind me said, stamping impatience.

"Wrong one," I muttered, pushing past him and fighting through the multitude until I'd worked my way to the front of the bus and onto the cracked sidewalk, with its patches of ice and random bits of broken plastic and *khat* wrappers. Without the wall of bodies around me, the wind off the bay felt like an icy river, and I pulled Mags's coat tighter around my torso.

"Mary!" Walker yelled. Angry voices behind me; the sound of a brief scuffle, and Walker appeared in my peripheral vision, between me and the broken road. Behind us the bus doors hissed shut, and a moment later the big vehicle thundered past, belching its toxic black clouds.

Walker said nothing. He just matched my pace, step for step, past the dockyards and the mechanical loaders, past rows of dilapidated houses with their warped doors and splintered, boarded-up windows, gaps stuffed with rags against the cold.

After several minutes, he spoke. "I'm sorry. I was so focused on the old woman . . . Ray got on ahead of us?"

I just nodded. We walked on in silence, our shoes crunching over ice and shattered glass, as the residential area gave way to long rows of warehouses, abandoned and sagging, the chain-link fences along the sidewalk rusted and broken, some still supporting decades-old signs touting Silvermine's dockhands: *The Industrious Pride of the RD*, and *Silvermine Port Authority: God's Finest Workers*. That sign was broken, the bottom half of the word *Workers*, missing. Profane graffiti covered the initials *RD*, and I looked away.

"Why are you so afraid of him?" Walker blurted. "I mean, you don't have to tell me if you don't want to . . . Mom said you're worried he'll turn you in, but . . ."

*What?* I stopped walking and turned toward him. "Mags didn't tell you?" I asked, pulling the black curtain from my face.

He shook his head, confused. "Tell me what?"

Was he lying? How could he not know—especially since Tamar obviously did? But no, I saw no guile in his eyes.

"Ray killed my mother," I said simply, as the sullen clouds lowered and the cold wind blew past us, carrying spits of fresh snow and the reek of diesel oil and burning trash.

Walker couldn't fake the shock that drained his cold-reddened face of color. "Dear Jesus." His eyes closed briefly, then searched my face. "I am so sorry, Meryn. No, Mom didn't tell me. Neither did Bree, if she knew."

I nodded. "I told her the day it happened. I was late to work. I—"

And it all poured out of me, every detail, moment by moment, me standing on the port sidewalk in the freezing wind in a borrowed dress and coat. Every element, every nuance of the drama that took my mother and shattered my life paraded across my memory and coalesced into words, and I couldn't stop it any more than I could have stopped singing at Mom's service. It seemed Walker's kind sympathy was drawing the narrative out of me. I continued right up to when Bree invited me to come home with her and Mags, and then the words ran out and I stood, silent and utterly spent, rocking a bit from the force of the wind and wishing I could sit down. Another bus roared past us, and I grimaced, turning away.

Walker's eyes were troubled. "They chose not to press charges."

"Obviously," I said, my voice far harsher and more bitter than I intended. "She was just a woman. She had committed the unforgivable sin: she burned the pork chops. And you know the worst part? The . . . worst . . ." I coughed a humorless, bitter laugh as the full, awful realization struck me, my memory of that awful day clear now, brutally so.

"What?" Walker asked, still in that gentle tone, but I couldn't hear him, didn't see him reach forward to grab me as some raw, vile emotion punched me hard in the stomach, doubling me over, and an animal scream I never knew was hiding inside came shrieking out of my throat, an inchoate, feral, searing cry, ripping my vocal cords, pulling me into a fetal position as my mind scrambled to escape the awful truth I'd been fleeing like some wild thing ever since Mom died.

I know I screamed the word *"NOOOOO!"* several times, over and over, my fist pounding the cold pavement, trying to hurt myself physically enough to distract from a pain so awful it threatened to drive me past the edge of sanity. Then words and reason abandoned me and all I could manage was screaming cries, great racking sobs that barely left me enough space to breathe, tears freezing on my cheeks, breath coughing out in clouded gasps, and it went on and on as time suspended and I was locked in some dark purgatory with nothing but the searing, soul-shredding pain.

Gradually I became aware that I wasn't on the ground; my right wrist was locked in a vise, hand clenching and unclenching, waist supported, my left hand balled into a fist and hitting . . . something. Not cement. My face was buried in . . . wait. *Walker's chest?* I opened my eyes, still gasping, tried to focus. *Oh no!* I had been hitting Walker! A remote part of my brain ordered me to move, step back, apologize, but grief still paralyzed me and all I could do was breathe. Every exhalation came out a moan—"Mommmmm . . . mommmmm . . ."—and at last my heinous sin burst out of me, Walker my prinister, my confessional the sky: "I killed her! God help me! *I killed my mother!*"

"Stop," Walker said, his voice commanding. "Meryn. Stop it."

I barely heard. "I killed her! Walker, I killed her! Oh, dear Jesus, *why?*" The word trailed off into screaming sobs.

"No, Meryn."

"She died"—a gasp—"because of me! Don't you— She died because of *me!*"

"She died because Ray hit her, and she fell and struck her head." Walker's voice was low, measured. "Meryn." He shook me, still holding my arm, my hand spasming open and shut. "Meryn, it wasn't your fault."

*"The button!"*

"No!" His word had the force of a slap. "Meryn, listen to me. *Listen.* Your mother was a wonderful, kind, generous woman. I heard every word those people said about her—they *loved her.* Her death was not your fault. More importantly"—and now I was listening, finally, his words starting to pierce the darkness surrounding my heart—"her death wasn't *her* fault, either. Are you hearing me? It wasn't your fault. And it wasn't her fault. It *wasn't!*"

Through gasps, I tried to reply in a coherent fashion, but all that came out was a thin wail. I looked up at him, my hood falling away, his face distorted through my tears. Releasing my wrist, he drew me in and held me, supporting me as my body shuddered, my hand clenched tight on the lapel of his coat.

We stood like that for several minutes, Walker patient, kind. In my memory I heard echoes of the second verse of my mother's favorite hymn, but instead of Dee's voice, it was Mom singing.

*"Let not your heart be troubled," His tender word I hear,*
*and resting on His goodness, I lose my doubts and fears.*
*Though by the path He leadeth, but one step I may see;*
*His eye is on the sparrow, and I know He watches me.*

And a quiet whisper spoke in my spirit. *Let not your heart be troubled.* That was all, but it was enough to wash peace into the roiling storm in my soul, calming, soothing. As my sobs wound down, I heard Walker's voice again, ineffably gentle and compassionate.

"We all know loss, Meryn," he said, his breath warm in my ear. "We put a brave face on it, but we all know loss. Some of us just meet it sooner than others. And it is soul-killing and excruciating and consuming and there is no escaping it, no bargaining with it or defying it or denying it. Fair does not apply. It hounds our sleep at night, and it is there, waiting to pounce with claws and teeth, when we wake in the morning. It comes with all the strength of hell, showing up when we least expect it and refusing to leave."

Each breath came in a gasp, me holding on to him as if he were a lifeline, willing myself to listen, hear, understand . . . and divert from the raw, gaping wound in my heart . . . *Oh Jesus . . .*

"I think the pain of grief is one of the strongest forces in the universe." His tone was thoughtful. "But it can't compete with what is truly strongest. When you feel like the pain is going to win, remember that. There is something stronger." He patted my back with a gloved hand, willing my attention. "You tracking? You with me?"

I sucked air, nodded against his chest. "God," I croaked in a voice that wasn't mine.

He chuckled, and the rumble of it rattled his chest and resounded in my ear. "I was going to say love, but they're the same. Love's what keeps us going when we don't have the strength to fight anymore. My love for Mom and Bree kept me going when I was ready to give up."

*What?* "Can't imagine you . . . giving up," I said, weak.

He pushed away slightly, tilting my head up to look at him, his face severe with my grief. "No one is unbreakable, Meryn. Any of us can be gotten to. Our place of greatest joy is also our place of greatest vulnerability. The enemy knows that. I think that's why he targeted your mom. Not only to destroy her, but also you and Ray.

"Pain can drive us toward God. But I think more often, it confuses us. It drives us away."

"You think Satan targets—" I broke off, trying to release his coat, but my fingers seemed frozen.

"You've read your Bible." His head jerked, a trifle impatiently. "Do you think Christ was joking when He said the thief comes to steal, kill and destroy? Do you think that was just symbolism?"

*Good. Good. A different topic.* With my free hand, I fished in my pocket for a handkerchief. Walker handed me his, and my other hand finally thawed and I blew my nose in a horribly unfeminine fashion, even though tears still leaked out of my eyes. I tried to focus on his words. "Prinister Severs said too many people blame the devil for their own flaws." I wiped my eyes. "That's why we have heaven. He said while we're here, we're responsible for living right, and that would keep the devil away." The black lace kept falling across my eyes, and Walker gently lifted it away from my face and over the top of my head, then pulled up my hood, tucking the lace behind my hair. I tried to thank him, but I couldn't smile.

"Yeah, Sanctioned Churches." His shrug was annoyed, dismissive, his eyes intense. "But when you start living your life for God—really doing it, not just showing up at church and giving God lip service—you become a target. And God gives us ways to cope."

*Church . . . God . . .* The reality of what I had done came crashing into my grief: I had cried, wailed, and pounded on my friend, a *man,* for pity's sake—in public. Where anyone could see. "Oh, no." My hands covered my flaming cheeks, my eyes. I spoke into the false dark. "I cannot—Walker, how do I begin to apologize? I'm—"

Strong hands grasped my wrists, interrupting me, but he didn't try to force my hands from my face. "Meryn," he whispered. "You have lost the one person in this whole world who was closest to you. The one person who understood you. You are *grieving.* God gave you the space to do that here, unobserved except by me. Isn't that miraculous?"

My breath sucked in—he was right. We should have been seen by now. *Maybe, God . . . maybe.* I nodded, trying not to cry.

"And I don't think less of you. Quite the opposite. Meryn." Now, as he drew my hands away, I didn't try to resist; my eyes opened on his, a deep brown: not intense, not wary or shuttered, but kind. Compassionate. I'd never seen such an expression on a man's face, and I lingered a moment in my astonishment while something tight and frightened inside of me uncoiled. He didn't look away, and I didn't want him to.

He spoke again; oddly, I wanted him to stop, so I could take in what I'd just learned—*he is different, this Walker*—but I said nothing, listening.

"That you allowed yourself to mourn your mother—especially in front of a man you hardly know—well, it shows an emotional honesty and strength of character that's missing in most people."

*Strength of character? Wow. Well, I don't think that's what Prinister Severs would call it.* A tiny corner of my mouth lifted, and I chuckled without mirth, but I didn't stifle an odd blush of hope. I wasn't sure I agreed with him, but he didn't give me time to argue.

"Now." He relaxed his grip but kept his hands in place. "Can you walk?"

# 27. HOME

I nodded, but as I stepped back my knees buckled. Without effort, he caught me.

"Whoa! Maybe not," he said with a hint of a smile. "Try again but hold on, just in case."

I complied. It seemed a sensible precaution. We took a few steps; the physical purging of my grief had left me feeling weak and headachy, and I was grateful for Walker's arm in mine.

"Where did you learn that stuff you told me about the enemy?" I asked, choosing my steps with care.

"I grew up with it. You've noticed we do a lot of Bible study."

I nodded.

"Well, a lot of what we study, and our interpretation of scripture, isn't exactly . . ." He looked away.

"Sanctioned," I said bluntly.

"Well . . . no."

I stopped. Walker's expression had closed, guarded.

"Walker." My voice was a fatigued rasp. "I understand why you are afraid for Mags."

He stiffened. "I am concerned for our whole church family."

It was too soon. I longed to rewind our conversation by two minutes, to return to the kind Walker, the unguarded one . . .

"I know I can't give you any reassurance you will believe," I went on, my voice flat and emotionless, as if everything I could ever feel had leaked out all over the front of his coat. "All I can tell you is that I love Mags and I respect your church and I would never do anything to endanger either."

His expression softened. "I do want to believe you, Meryn."

"Besides," I went on, too tired to smile, "I'm an unprotected woman, on the lam from her father. How could I turn you all in without jeopardizing myself?"

Walker's sudden grin looked almost boyish. "There is that, I guess."

We headed down the sidewalk again, me dodging broken pavement and shattered glass. Another bus stop waited some distance ahead, but every step made me aware of a blister forming on my left heel.

"You're limping," Walker observed.

I grimaced. "New shoes, and we still have at least a half mile to go."

"Yeah, they don't make shoes the way they used to. Not even in New Korea." He didn't smile. "Do you need more support?"

"I'm fine," I said, my voice firm, but we hadn't taken another dozen steps before the pain forced me to stop.

"Not fine," Walker said.

I blew out a breath in exasperation. I hadn't thought to bring athletic shoes because I wasn't expecting to do a lot of walking. *Stupid mistake, Meryn. Never again.*

"I'm going to take off my shoes." I looked about for a safe spot to sit down.

"On this sidewalk? With the cold and all the glass?" Walker's eyebrows rose. "That wouldn't be wise. If you will allow me, milady," and he gave me a high court bow, "I shall carry you to the bus stop."

*Carry me? I'm not his wife!* I rasped a chuckle, mirthless, to cover my surprise. "Walker, I'm hardly a lightweight!"

"Well, neither are the logs Kilte and I have been hauling."

I folded my arms, regarding him with angry resignation. "What if someone sees?"

His lips thinned, our sober expressions silently acknowledging the risk. After a moment, he spoke. "We'll just pray no one does. I haven't seen a vehicle come by since the last bus."

That was true enough; the normally busy port road was oddly deserted, but that could change at any moment. I was running out of excuses. "If I'm too heavy, do you promise to put me down?"

He put a hand over his heart. "I do." A faint smile tugged at his lips.

I let myself glare. "Seeing as how I don't have a choice . . ." *Lord, please protect us!*

In one expert move, he swung me into his arms and started down the sidewalk. At the press of his body against mine, my heart pounded, and I tried not to gasp. "I would ask one favor," he said.

"Of course." My voice sounded high and thin, and I swallowed.

"Don't mention this to Tamar, please. She can be a bit . . . jealous."

His warmth penetrated my coat, easing my shivering. "She has nothing to be jealous about." It came out more tartly than I intended. "This is out of pure necessity."

He smiled at the pavement as he walked, acting for all the world as if he were carrying a loaf of bread. "I doubt she would see it that way."

"I won't say a word."

If I thought holding hands with Walker was uncomfortable, being carried by him took it to a whole new level. This was an intimacy I would expect only from a spouse. With a man I barely knew, it was frightening. I caught the fragrance of soap—or could that be . . . aftershave?—and was beset by a roiling wave of emotions: fear of an intimacy violation, shame, relief from pain, and an odd feeling in the pit of my stomach I couldn't identify. I tried not to shudder, and I wondered if he could feel my heart's rapid tattoo against my ribs. *What if someone sees us? Well, there's no help for it. I have to get to the bus somehow. I'll just insist there's no need to press charges. Except . . . I'm unescorted.* That would be Ray's call, not mine. Walker's every exhale washed warm breath across my face. I studied his profile. Was he enjoying this, or was he uncomfortable, too? Was this an imposition? But no, he seemed quite normal, chatting in an amiable fashion about his work and Kilte's merits as a business partner, and I tried to relax.

The conversation shifted to Pris and the twins, school and work, and I was surprised at how quickly we covered the half mile to the stop. When he set me on my feet, holding my arm until he was sure I was steady, an unexpected disappointment mixed with my relief, and heat rose in my face. I bent down, unnecessarily fiddling with my shoe.

"So you'll be taking her with you in the mornings?" I straightened, hoping he couldn't read my thoughts, and he nodded, an odd expression crossing his face. It was gone before I could pin down an emotion.

"Mom shared your story about Debbie, and Tami was horrified. And the girls love the idea of riding together—they're good friends."

Our timing was perfect: not two minutes later, a bus chuffed to a stop next to us, the wind of its arrival scattering exhaust and snow into my eyes. We climbed aboard, and I noted with relief that the heat was working, and the bus held only one other passenger. I sank into a blue seat, Walker standing next to me like a benign guard, holding the grab bar. I was glad I remembered to keep my skirt off the floor. A few people got on at the next stop. I knew I should watch for someone who might recognize me, but I didn't have the energy to care.

~

As he had guided me to Mom's service, so Walker guided me home. Fatigue made me clumsy, unaware, and I strove to keep my eyes open. Bus change. Arm under mine, supporting me, sheltering me from wind, people, curious faces. Bus stops, starts. Talk. *Laughter?* I felt a distant spurt of rage.

A jerk. Bus, stopping.

"This is us, Meryn." Walker, gentle. Guiding me down the steps. Cold. Wind. The surprise of pain in my feet made me stumble.

"Oh no." It came out a whisper; I was still hoarse. I'd forgotten about my blisters, but Walker caught me before I could fall.

"Ah," he said. "Once more, milady, for king and country."

I croaked a laugh. "No," I whispered, then cleared my throat. My mouth was dry. It hurt to swallow. Snow pelted my face, and the wind ran cold hands up my skirt. "Too close. People. Tamar will . . ."

"Nobody in this neighborhood will care. And you let me worry about Tamar." Walker's tone was gentle, harsh. "Up you go," and he hefted me into his arms again, blocking my face from the wind. Weary, I laid my head on his shoulder. It reminded me of Mom carrying me when I was a little girl.

*Mom.* She didn't meet me, as I'd almost hoped. She'd sprinkled her beautiful sparkles into the ocean where she'd always wanted to be. She was mer-woman, immortal now, swimming with the ocean denizens she loved so much. Did she remember me, wherever she was now? Tears stung my eyes. *Tears, again?* My private ocean, freezing grief to my skin. *Could Mom swim in a teardrop? Of course she could, she—*

*Mer-child, I was there.* Warmth. Mom's voice.

*What?* My eyes fluttered open, reason manifesting in disappointment. *Oh. Mags, not Mom. Asking if Ray was there, I think.*

"Yes. But your idea worked brilliantly."

"What happened to her?"

"She's just exhausted, Mom."

"Cold. So cold," I whispered.

"It's understandable," Walker said. "And she developed blisters. We did a lot of walking . . ."

"Walker, can we put her in your place? She needs to rest, and the tiny house is chockablock. The girls brought over Iscah and Gabe—"

"Yes, of course."

"Let's get her clothes. Bree!" Mags's voice moved away.

"Walker, no, I . . . I'm fine, I . . . just tired."

"What did she say?"

A baritone reply. "She's tired. Of course you are, Meryn. You had a rough morning. No arguments, now. You rest in my place. I'll go watch the game with Kilte."

Walker's footsteps, a lock beep, a door creaking open. Too much effort to look. Arms under me replaced by a bed. Soft.

"I'll get it warmer in here . . ." Someone fiddling with something. A squeak of hinge. Heat bloomed.

A tap at the door.

"Come in, Mom."

Door opened, steps, more steps. Door shut.

I forced my eyes open.

Mags, sitting next to me. "Don't talk, Meryn. Let's get you into your sweats. Bree?"

*Oh, Bree! My angel friend.*

Walker cleared his throat. "I'll just . . . go . . ."

"Walker!" I put all my strength into it, my voice unavoidably harsh.

"Shhh," Mags whispered.

I opened my eyes to see Bree glance from me to Walker, her eyebrows lifting.

He crossed to the bedside. "It's okay, Meryn. You're safe here with Mom and Bree. You rest now."

I grabbed his hand and pressed it to my cheek in mute gratitude. "Thank you," I whispered, closing my eyes. Tears leaked out, squeezing between my cheek, his hand. Tears again. *God . . . my ocean . . .*

"You're welcome, Meryn," he said, covering my cold hands with one of his, warm. "You're most welcome. You eat now, and rest."

"We brought you some clear broth," Mags said as Walker let himself out. "But first we need to get you into your jammies."

I worked hard to produce a smile.

"Atta girl," Bree said in her best bracing tone. "I'll just take this," and without a tug, she removed the plethora of bobby pins in my hair and lifted off the elegant lace hat. Mags supported me as I stood, and she helped get me out of the coat, but it took both of them to disentangle my fingers from the loops, manage the buttons, and pull the dress over my head.

As Bree reached for her tote and Mags folded the dress, my skin prickled with goose bumps. "Cold," I whispered. "So cold." *Is Mom cold? Does she feel now? Has she left all worldly cares behind?*

"Here we go." Bree unfolded the sweatshirt and pulled it over my head, its fleecy warmth wrapping me as my arms found the holes. Mags helped Bree get my legs into the matching pants, pulling them up over my hips before settling me to the bed.

Bree chaffed my cold-reddened toes with her hands, whispering a mild oath over the blisters. After a few minutes my feet warmed, and she pulled cozy synth-wool socks over them.

Settling next to me, Mags handed me a mug of something hot and steaming, and set a clean cloth napkin with two slices of dry toast in my lap. "Try to drink, Meryn," she said, helping my shaking hands support the cup. *Shaking?*

"You're just hungry," Mags said soothingly, and I realized I must have spoken aloud. "It's well after lunchtime, and Walker said you traveled quite a distance in the cold. That was too hard on you, after living on the street. Here now, take a bite of toast."

The broth warmed me, and the toast helped fill an emptiness I hadn't noticed until that moment. I tried not to get crumbs on the bed.

When the mug was empty and the napkin folded, Mags eased me supine, Bree lifting my legs and tucking them under the coverlet. A warm water bottle found its way in next to my feet.

Someone must have pulled the coverlet over me, but I had only a moment to wonder about the appropriateness of sleeping in Walker's bed before oblivion took me.

~

A noise startled me awake. I looked around, disoriented. *Where— Oh.* Walker's place. Mom's funeral.

And Mom—*dear God, no*—Mom was really dead.

A figure loomed over me. Surprised into fear, I gasped.

"What are *you* doing here?" A woman's voice—harsh, familiar. I blinked in the gloom, trying to focus, and sat up.

Tamar. Arms crossed, glaring, fury radiating.

"Until a moment ago, I was sleeping." My voice was still strained, raspy. I didn't try to sound polite. "I don't know where Walker is, if you're wondering. Try Mags's."

"I want to know what *you're* doing in my boyfriend's *bed!*"

"Ask your boyfriend." I rolled over, pulling the covers over my head. A long silence. Angry stompings to the door, the creak of it opening, and a slam that shook the hipster.

I closed my eyes. Even in my half-awake state I was aware that the bedclothes smelled faintly like Walker. Comforting. I smiled. A tendril of guilt intruded, and I shoved it away. *It's okay. Mags's idea, after all, my sleeping here.* The warm darkness beckoned me to sleep, and . . . my wrist tingled. I burrowed under the pillow, but a moment later the tingle came again. Groaning, I sat up.

The text was from Steffan. *We missed you at the funeral. Why didn't you come? Was it me, or Ray? You don't have to be afraid, you know. We could—*

I deleted it. Tossing the phone on the bed, I leaned against the wall.

For the longest time I just sat, wrapped in the coverlet, staring at nothing as daylight dimmed and faded from the window, the sound of the wind outside transporting me back to the barge with its press of people, the sobbing, the muffled *whump* of the grief cannon. *Mom is gone. I failed her. I failed in my Family Duty. Who am I? Who is Meryn Flint? I am nothing.* A breath. It hurt. *Life got a little rough, and she just . . . ran away.*

A quiet thought drifted into my mind. *Giving up, Meryn?*

I didn't have the strength to laugh. *What's to hang on for?* The question hung in my thoughts, haunting the shroud of my grief. My eyes felt sandblasted, and I let my eyelids sag shut. *Mom sent me away . . . so I would be safe. Safe from Ray. Safe from Steffan. And the church. I finally did what she wanted. And for what?* Slowly through the fog, an answer came. *So Rose Flint's daughter survives, and something of Rose lives on.*

My mouth jerked, curled down, and I looked at the ceiling. *Yes. That's what I hang on for. Mom's legacy. I guess it's the least I can do.*

I took a deep breath. "Okay, Mom," I whispered, tears scorching my eyes. "Meryn Flint is the repository of your DNA. Your memories and your humor, your mores and your beliefs, your incredible, limitless love." I sighed, shoulders straightening, not bothering to wipe my face. "I will guard it all as best I can." I almost laughed aloud at the irony, thinking of Severs and his basement room, of Shady Dell's odd mix of friendly and hostile neighbors. "No guarantees."

Sleep was now an utter impossibility, and I stirred myself to click on the bedside table lamp. My eyes roamed Walker's place without purpose, noting that it was as neat as the day Mags had shown it to me. A book on the bedside table caught my attention, and curious, I twisted a bit to read the title. *A Humble Path: The Life and Social Justice of Pope Francis I.*

My eyebrows lifted. "I never would've expected that one," I murmured. Unable to resist, I climbed out of bed and padded on sore feet to the dresser to look at his other books. "*Standard's Bible Commentary*," I croaked aloud. "*The Life of Leonardo da Vinci*. That's a thick one. *The Walk of Forgiveness* by a Josiah Millken, PhD. *Healing the Damage: A Family Plan for Coping with PTSD* by Dr. Ananiah Baker. Wow, that one's old." The paper was yellowed, the spine worn and cracked. I flipped to the copyright page, noting the publication date was prior to the Reformation. That made it illegal . . . which meant Walker trusted me far more than he let on. A slight smile touched my lips. I was looking around for more books when my wrist tingled, and I hurried back to the bed, trying to convince myself I hadn't been prying.

A text from Ray.

*I'm terribly disappointed in you. You're coming home. Better start packing.*

I sighed, settled onto the soft surface, and started typing. *I was there.*

A moment later, *Nice try. I didn't see you!*

*Of course not. I didn't want to be seen.* I wiped wet cheeks on my sleeve.

*You're lying!*

My mouth firmed. *The model of tact, as always,* I wrote. *The fireworks were a nice touch. A rose, no less—Mom would've loved it. And Bart and Dee did a lovely job on her favorite hymn. Too bad Severs couldn't remember my correct name. Did you remind him it's Meryn Athena Flint, not Maureen Anna Esselin?*

A long pause.

*Should be Esselin, anyway. Huh. Guess you were there.*

*Not lying!*

*Your friends missed you.*

I sighed, typed. *I know.*

*Peanut, you don't have to be afraid of me.*

*Are you kidding?* I wrote, discarding tact. *When you threaten to sic the Guards on me? And show up at Mom's funeral with Steffan, of all people? What were you planning to do—force me to marry him on the spot? Convenient, that, with Prinister Severs right there. Good grief, Ray, what do you expect? I have a host of reasons to be afraid of you, not the least of which involves Mom. And have you forgotten how you dragged me to church and turned me over to Severs for discipline? I haven't. It was a whole lot more than just a "little talk," no matter how he wants to paint it. But you don't care about that, do you?*

Silence.

# 28. HOURS

"More hours?" Carole looked up from where she knelt in the stockroom, doing inventory. The morning rush at Mrs had slowed, freeing me from the floor, but I kept an ear out for the door chime.

I realized I was biting my lip and smiled, tried to take a deep breath.

"Actually, I'm glad you asked; I could use you. I don't like to overload a new hire, but Britt had to cut back her hours—she's still out with that broken leg—so I'm in a pinch. Besides, you're good." She stood, pushing her fists into the small of her back and rotating her neck. "I'm impressed with how quickly you've picked up the details. I can give you thirty-two hours a week starting tomorrow, if you're interested."

I gasped, and my stomach relaxed. "I am, Carole—thank you!"

"I don't know for how long," she cautioned. "When Britt comes back, I may have to reduce them again." She tossed a size-six working girl blouse atop the others and gave me a bright smile. "But this gives us a chance to train you on some additional duties, and I can make a case for keeping your hours up."

"Oh, that's incredible, Carole! I look forward to it!" *It might even position me for a raise.* I could live more comfortably in my tiny house with a little extra financial padding.

"Let's get started," Carole said. "It's slow, so let me show you how we do the online ordering and inventory. We'll set you up with the retina login . . ."

Three hours later, my head spun with new information, but I was awash in euphoria.

"Go take lunch," Carole said, taking the scanner out of my hand. She grinned. "You need time to process. I'll finish this."

I smiled, grateful; even though it wasn't yet noon, my stomach had been rumbling for the last half hour. Picking up my tote, I headed for the back door and clocked out. Some mall employees purchased a meal at the food court, but I couldn't afford that, so I always brought something from home. Today it was leftover pea soup and a couple slices of toast. Invariably I got sidelong looks from the higher castes when I unpacked my homemade lunches, but I'd long since gotten over any embarrassment.

The truth was, I wasn't just hungry—fatigue dogged me from the moment I struggled from my covers in the morning until I collapsed on the futon at night. Bree said it was from the emotional storm of the funeral, and I had to agree, but the weariness made my shifts seem longer, even when we were busy. Traversing the access corridor, I pushed through the crash bar to the mall's walkway, took three steps and stopped. Shock froze me to the floor, and the blood drained from my face. *No.*

From the spot where he lounged against a potted ficus, Steff smiled. "Hey, girl," he said, brushing his blond hair out of his eyes.

I took a deep breath, and my muscles unlocked. Watching Steffan with a wary eye, I turned and headed for the escalator.

He moved forward and fell into step beside me. "Meryn."

I clattered down the escalator stairs, weaving past the people standing quite properly in place, Steffan following. A large woman with a shopping bag screeched a protest as he pushed past her and grabbed my arm.

"Mer, I'm here to apologize!" He recoiled at the look on my face, and his hand fell to his side. "I mean it," he said, his face twisting with discomfort. "I'm sorry. Sometimes I'm a real jerk."

"Well, it sounds like you're thinking straight . . . sometimes." Stepping off the escalator, I headed into the food court, searching for a small table.

"Over here." Steff gestured toward a vacant booth—marble, with red plush banquette seating.

"That's the Governance section." Sitting there would get me a quick trip to the Guard station.

"You're with me." He shrugged, his smile too smug.

Trying not to roll my eyes, I turned toward the blue section, searching until I found a small two-seater.

"Okay, whatever." His face crinkled with amusement.

I let my annoyance show. "I don't remember inviting you to join me."

He tried to assume a mien of humility. "Just . . . let's talk for a few minutes, okay? I promise if you ask me to leave, I'll go."

I headed toward the table and nodded. "Good. I'm asking you to leave." Settling on the hard plastic chair, I pulled my lunch from my tote.

Without invitation, Steff sat in the chair facing me, and my patience vanished. Slamming my thermos on the table, I glared at him.

A woman at an adjoining table looked over, frowned.

He sighed. "Just . . . let me get this out, okay?"

*Dial it down, Meryn. You don't want to spend lunch at the Guard Station.* Ignoring the woman, I sat back, crossing my arms. "I don't have all day."

A hint of satisfaction crossed his face. As I opened my thermos and started on my soup, two children ran by, screaming with laughter. Their mothers, clad in blue MTs, claimed the last table in the Worker section.

"Mer, I'm so sorry. I was a complete jerk to you. I've been seeing my prinister."

I took a bite of toast. "Faith is a good thing."

Steff's face clouded, cleared. "He's been helping me with my temper. What happened with us, well . . . it showed me that I have a problem. I'm fixing it."

"I'm glad to hear it." I kept my tone positive. "That will be such a blessing for your wife and kids."

"That's why I'm here," he said, and I winced internally, mad that I'd given him an opening. "You know I dated other girls after things with us didn't work out, but no one compares to you." A woman sitting nearby glanced at us, her eyes demure, and smiled into her stir-fry.

*No, honey, you are not witnessing a proposal.* "I'm sure if you keep at it, you'll find someone." I shrugged, avoiding his gaze.

Steff reached across the table and picked up my other piece of toast, took a bite. My eyes rounded, but he didn't seem to notice. "But I don't want anyone else," he said, chewing. He looked at the toast in his hand, eyebrows lifting. "Hey, this is good. You've really learned how to cook."

My spoon clattered into the bowl, and his eyes met mine. "Steff, I am asking you to leave."

He set down the toast. "And I am asking you to give us another chance." To my surprise, no anger clouded his voice. "Your dad said I should. Just . . . let's try a date. This Friday night. We'll go see a vid, have dinner, get to know each other again. I'm different now, Mer. I want this to work out. I want *us* to work out." His eyes were wide, guileless.

I paused, gauging his sincerity. He took that as encouragement.

"We could go to Kwale's. They make an amazing filet mignon. Tender, juicy—it cuts with a fork. And all the trimmings, you know—baked potato, sour cream with chives, fresh, crispy green salad." His eyebrows lifted, his hands widening. "And they have this incredible chocolate volcano for dessert. Big enough for two to share. It melts in your mouth."

My mouth was watering. I swallowed.

He looked at my soup, and so did I. "I suspect you're getting tired of split pea," he said gently.

Tears pricked my eyes, and I blinked, hoping he wouldn't notice.

"And I don't blame you. A woman, trying to survive alone? Working all the hours God put into the day? It's a noble attempt, Mer. It's just the kind of strength I'd expect from you." His voice softened. "But you don't have to do this. You don't have to face this world alone, vulnerable to any psycho with an ax to grind.

"I understand why you don't want to go home."

Despite myself, I looked up, my eyes meeting his.

He nodded. "I wouldn't either, after what happened. Don't get me wrong; I like Ray." He gestured toward me. "But you're not a girl anymore. The young woman you've become needs security. Safety." He leaned forward, smiled, and I wondered briefly if he knew what had happened to me at St. Mike's. "Let's make our own home, Meryn, you and me. A safe place for us, and our kids. Together."

I looked at the man sitting opposite me, his expression open, frank—kind. Steff, yes, but different. Mature, more controlled. Maybe he really was growing up? My resolve softened. *God, is this real? Is this kind person in front of me the same man who tried to knock my head off a year or so ago? The one who screamed obscenities at my last job? Can I trust—*

At once, the memory of Steff's voice cut off my prayer: "*. . . failed in her Family Duty. Obviously, she's not mature enough . . . You should bring her home. Discipline, Ray—that's what she needs.*"

I exhaled, the fleeting hope slipping away. "I'm really happy you're getting the counseling you need. I'm glad you're healing, and ready for a relationship." I picked up my spoon. "But it won't be with me."

Steff's eyebrows lifted. "Are you sure, Meryn? You may regret this."

I searched for malice or fury on his face, saw none. Just gentle concern. Biting the inside of my cheek, I looked at my soup and counted ten. "I'm sure."

Steff sat back. I held my breath, expecting anger now, but he just sighed. "I understand. Thanks for listening, Mer."

I blinked, but his expression didn't change. Rising, he smiled wistfully and walked away without another word.

I went back to my soup. *God, did I just make a huge mistake? Maybe I should've—*

My eyes fell on the piece of toast lying on the table where Steffan had been sitting—a piece of toast with one bite out of it.

~

"Okay, that's just weird," Bree said.

We sat on the futon, getting ready for bed. I set my phone on its charger while she pulled the privacy curtain closed.

I still struggled with ambivalence. *He was so nice. So controlled. There was none of that black rage—* "So you think I did the right thing?"

She sighed, pulling off her house shoes and setting them beside the bed. "I can't make that judgment for you. But what we know about him, and what you told me about his comments at your mom's service— yeah, I think you did. Sounds like he was buttering up Ray on one side and you on the other. That isn't love; it's manipulation." She pulled off her blouse and handed it to me, and I tossed it in her clothes hamper, biting my lip.

She caught the gesture, and her eyes on me were sharp, even though her tone was gentle. "Do you miss him?"

"A little," I admitted, folding my legs under me. "We had such good times, before—" I broke off. "I keep thinking, maybe he's really grown up."

Her eyebrows lifted into her hairline. "Sweetie, are you that desperate for a husband? When did this happen?"

I sighed, impatient with myself, with something I didn't understand. "Don't you ever think Family Duty means something? That I really do owe something to the memory of my mother, and that by doing all this"—I gestured around—"I'm dishonoring her? I mean, even if we agree to forget Ray, but what about Mom?"

"Let me ask you something." Bree tossed on her pajama top, pulling her long blonde hair through the neck and giving me her full attention. "Do you think your mother forgot about Family Duty when she told you to leave?"

"No," I said, "but—"

"Do you think your mother would've wanted you to marry Steffan?"

The intensity of her gaze pinned me, and I couldn't look away. She and I both knew the answer to that one.

"She didn't tell you to call Steffan. She told you to leave. The reason is pretty obvious, at least to me. And don't think you have to leave Shady Dell because of us." Bree smiled, kind. "You know we've had more than one runaway take shelter here—right here in this house."

"But I don't belong here, Bree!" My whisper was harsh with desperation. "I'm the wrong caste—and I don't belong with Ray or at St. Mike's, I don't belong at Our Lord's Church, I don't belong anywhere!" Tears stung my eyes, the pain of loss and abuse too fresh.

Bree looked at me with a combination of anger and compassion. "Do you think you're the only one who feels like she doesn't belong? I've felt that way my whole life. When I was little, Marian made it clear she thought Gamma was taking on too much by raising me. Don't you get it? Nobody belongs." She leaned toward me, her green eyes thoughtful now, her fingers pulling at the hem of her nightshirt. "We like to think we do. We set ourselves up in families and communities and clubs and castes, and we think that's going to make us feel less lonely. But it doesn't. Because nobody on this earth is going to truly understand you. You'll never belong *anywhere*. The only person you belong to is God. And the only place you will belong is heaven. And until you realize *that*, Meryn, you won't be happy anywhere."

I was too busy formulating a response to really listen to what she had said. "Well, I overheard what's her name . . . Marian . . . saying—"

"And we don't care!" She stopped whispering, her volume ramping up with her glare. "Don't you get it, Mer? All the Marians and the Rays and the Guards—and yes, the whole putrefying RD—will happily let you die in the gutter just so they don't have to deal with what made you run in the first place!"

My eyes darted to the curtain; a warm flush crept up my neck.

"Look, it's your call." She'd dropped back to a whisper, but her face was cold. "I'm going to brush my teeth."

Slipping on her house shoes, Bree descended the ladder, and I sighed, grateful for the white curtain. I knew she was miffed, but I didn't know what else to say. *Should I have kept this to myself, Lord? I thought Bree would understand.* I bit my lip. *How can I expect Bree to understand when I'm not sure I understand, myself?*

My wrist tingled. Without looking, I took the call.

"I'm so glad you answered!" a woman's voice said.

"Ruthie! Oh, it's good to hear from you." Grateful for both the distraction and the source of it, I settled on the bed.

"I am so sorry about your mom," Ruth said in her gentle way. "I've worried about you."

"Thank you, sweetie." I sighed. "I'm holding up."

"She was such a remarkable woman. Always had a smile, a kind word, always thinking of others before herself. A truly godly woman."

Tears stung my eyes. "Yes. I still want to be like her when I grow up."

"You couldn't do better than Rose." She paused. "I'd love to see you, Meryn. Would you like to get together after your shift sometime? We could go to Thorhild's, get some sweet biscuits. My treat."

Her offer touched me. I knew Ruthie didn't have a lot of money, either. "I'd love to; I just don't know when. Life is pretty chaotic right now—I—"

"I totally understand," Ruth said at once. "Why don't you text me when you're ready? And maybe I could check in with you in a few days? I don't mean to impose."

I smiled. "Ruthie, you never impose. That sounds great."

"And I'm always here, Meryn, if you need to talk. Just a tingle away." I could hear the smile in her voice.

"I'll be in touch soon, I promise," I said warmly. "Just need to check my work schedule."

It wasn't a hollow promise, I thought as we disconnected. I missed Ruthie. She was one of the few people who'd welcomed me back to St. Mike's with open arms after the shunning. She never once asked what happened. Never even alluded to my absence. When the other girls whispered and giggled behind their hands, Ruthie linked my arm in hers and walked with me to Bible class, to service. Her quiet witness calmed the gossip and helped restore some normalcy to my relations at church and school.

And it was because of Ruthie that I told Mom I was okay staying at St. Mike's.

~

Mrs had become my refuge, a hub of normalcy as my personal life slipped farther away from anything I could call "normal." I wondered what my client, a young woman looking for a special date outfit, would think if she knew I was building my own house. What Carole would think if she knew I'd narrowly escaped a raid on City Trade and was living with a member of Liberté. Would she turn me in? I didn't want to find out. I created a mental and emotional firewall between my work life and my home life. It seemed . . . hypocritical. Shameful.

"It isn't," Bree told me in a whisper when she came in for the later shift. "Everybody has to do it—otherwise we get accused of bringing our problems to work."

"But isn't that hypocrisy?" I said, low. "Being somebody different at home than you are at work?"

"I look at it like this," she said, folding a synth-wool sweater and putting it in its cubby as I hung up a blouse. "I have my 'work' self and my 'home' self. That doesn't mean I try to be someone I'm not. But when I'm at work, that's what I focus on. I try to leave everything else at the door. Does this make sense?"

"It does," I said, "but I don't see men having to do this."

"Men are held to a different standard," Bree said. "You know that, Meryn."

*I know that. But I'm getting tired of hearing it.* As I turned toward the front, my eye caught movement in the hallway. Someone with blond hair, ducking behind a live-quin.

Despite a stab of fear, this time I didn't hesitate. I bolted to the front of the store and through the doors. "Steffan!"

He was running down the walkway. I easily identified him from the back, but he didn't turn. I clenched my fists, biting my lip hard, and made my way back inside the store.

Bree's eyes widened to round saucers. "It was him? Are you sure?"

"Positive." My hands were shaking. "Bree, I can't have this. What if he follows me home?"

"How did he find you?"

I gave her a look, and she sighed. "Ray. Your bank account's still linked to his. Well, it's obvious Steff isn't going to let you go." Annoyance infused her tone. "Doesn't he have a job, or something?"

I shook my head. "His father, the right honorable, distinguished, eminent John Hagen, gave him a trust fund. Steff's independently wealthy. He should be working for his father, but he told me the two of them couldn't get along in the office together."

"Dear Jesus." Bree's eyes closed. "The former Bishor Hagen, who eliminated homeschooling in Silvermine and created the model for the RD to take it nationwide. His boy has no schedule or responsibility. No accountability."

I nodded. "What am I going to do?" I tried not to let panic show in my voice. "He could jeopardize my job!" *I can't just leave Mrs. I don't want to leave Mrs!*

Her eyes opened, her gaze frank. "Or worse. What if he abducts you and forces you to marry him?"

*What?* My mouth dropped open, but then the absurdity hit me and I laughed, careful to keep it quiet. "No, no. Those are urban legends, Bree."

"It's been done." Her face settled into grim lines. "You know it's happened, Mer."

The door chimed, and Bree handed me her armload and hurried out to greet a customer. I turned to the clothes rack, my mind racing, palms sweaty, despite my assurances to Bree. *Lord, I need to resolve this. Please help me. This is . . . beyond scary. But Shady Dell is my home now.* My jaw firmed. *I can't go back. I won't go back.*

The rest of the week passed without incident, although I spent every free moment at work constantly scanning the walkway. The hypervigilance was tiring. On the other hand, Carole expressed unreserved appreciation of my work. The books were impeccable, and the inventory so well organized she could find anything she needed within seconds. When we had a slow day, I busied myself steaming wrinkles out of new inventory; the crazy days were best because I was distracted from worry, and my shifts flew by. I didn't see Steffan again. I vacillated between hoping he'd given up and worrying that he'd followed me home, despite my careful attention.

Worse still, the insomnia was back, horrific nightmares jerking me from sleep almost every night. Mom sinking into the ocean off the funeral barge, frantically clawing for the surface, me diving as deep as I could but unable to reach her, watching her drown before my eyes. Me, inexplicably forced to crew on a fishing trawler, finding my mermaid mom dead in a net full of fish. And the worst one: walking through a packing plant, finding her dismembered body on a processing line, cans sealed with red curls looping out of the tops. The first three nights after the funeral, I'd woken the entire community with my screaming. Lately, I only woke Bree. Although dark circles rimmed her eyes, she remained sympathetic and understanding. But I was exhausted and heartsick. I prayed, and I knew everyone was praying for me, but nothing seemed to help.

God seemed very far away. I knew it was my fault, but I didn't know what was wrong, and I couldn't seem to bridge the gap.

Tuesday night, Kilte, Walker and I finished half of the ceiling in my tiny tin house. We used two ladders to support a wide board as a work platform; Walker separated the boxes, and I held the panels in place while Kilte attached the screws. Bree sat on my pallet, thumbing her phone, occasionally offering to help or laughing at Kilte's jokes.

After an hour she rose, stretched, smiled. "I'll be right back."

The door closed behind her, and Walker set a layer of panels next to where I stood on the ladder. "This should do you." He smiled, and I caught the subtle, essential combination of odors that was *Walker*—a spirituous blend of wood, hard work and an indefinable maleness—and my memory catapulted me back to his hipster, back to his bed, the fragrance of him comforting, the warmth of him wrapping me, driving away the cold of my bereavement . . . and ruthlessly I shoved the memory aside, even as I realized it was the memory of Walker's arms around me—steadying me on the barge, holding me at every explosion from the grief cannon, carrying me home as if I weighed no more than Pris or Ellie—it was that memory that lulled me to sleep every night after the nightmares roused and shrieked and stalked—

"That's all of them, so I'll leave you to it." He closed the door softly behind him without looking at me, and a flood of disappointment mixed with relief made me sway on the ladder.

Kilte grimaced as he jumped down and set another armload of panels on the board. I blinked, smiled a bit, grateful for the distraction. "What? I can do that, you know."

"Nah, it's not you." He climbed up beside me. I held a panel firm against the plastic studs while he drilled pilot holes, then I rotated my shoulders as he switched out the bit. Fishing in his breast pocket for a screw, he affixed it to the magnetic end of the screwdriver. "Where'd she go?"

"Bathroom."

"There's a loo in the corner."

I suppressed a laugh. "She doesn't like to go where people can hear."

He snorted a chuckle, shook his head. "She lives in a tiny house, for pity's sake."

It always surprised me that he used a manual screwdriver for the first screw, and finished the panel with the electric, and went back and tightened all four screws with the manual again, but I didn't have the courage to ask why. He finished three screws before he spoke again. "She doesn't trust me."

My head jerked in surprise. "What? Why do you think that?"

"She's here, isn't she? I mean, except to go take a whizz." He nodded at the empty pallet and crouched down, rotating his neck.

I lowered to my haunches, too, gripping the ladder. "Well, no. I mean, isn't she here to chaperone me? She knew Walker was leaving."

"Oh, hell no, Meryn. It's me she doesn't trust." He straightened again, rolling the final screw in his fingers. "I didn't know I was marrying the damn Silvermine Guard station when I asked her." He placed it on the screwdriver and drove it into the panel.

For a long moment, I didn't know what to say. Of course, such an escort was normal in our society. I should welcome her company. But to my surprise, I felt annoyance building. Did she really think I would poach her fiancé? Didn't we know each other at all? But even as that awareness hit, I made the decision to keep it to myself. Sometimes friendships are made on what isn't said, Mom used to say.

Picking at a cuticle, I settled, finally, on cliché. "Surely it isn't that bad. I mean, I know she loves you."

Kilte didn't reply immediately. He picked up the final panel and I held it in place as he drilled the holes, dust flying around our heads.

"Yeah, she loves me all right." Now his tone was soft as his smile. Inserting the first screw, he changed the subject. "Heard you've had some trouble at work."

I stifled a sigh. "An old boyfriend. He can't seem to take no for an answer."

"Well." He focused on the screw he was turning, the muscles in his forearms tightening and relaxing, tightening and relaxing as the panel edged into place. "If it gets bad, you let us know. Me and Walk. Okay?" His eyes flicked to mine.

*If it gets bad? It's already bad. What can you do? Beat him up? Stab him? Then you'll get in trouble. No, I have to fix this myself.* What I said was, "Thanks, Kilte. I appreciate it."

~

I worked double shifts the next day, opening and closing. My eyes felt like sandpaper, and fatigue stole along my bones like a feral cat in a dark alley. I'd never been so happy to hear a boss tell me to go home. Trying to smile at Carole through my exhaustion, I headed to the back and clocked out.

As I stepped on the escalator, something grabbed me from behind. Desperate, I twisted, my muscles too tired, too slow; something sharp pricked my butt. The world went hazy, and I folded; something kept me from falling. Oblivion dragged at me, but adrenaline coursed through my veins, an unlikely ally. *Stay awake! Stay awake, Meryn!*

"Is she all right, sir?"

My mouth was a desert, my tongue swollen. I forced my eyes open against an odd brightness. Head back, knees up; I was being carried.

"She's fine."

*Steffan! Bree was right—I'm being kidnapped!* I tried to scream, but it came out a groan. *Jesus, help me! Help me!*

"Let me call for the medAngels, sir." Solicitous.

I recognized the voice: it belonged to Guardian Quisten. He patrolled the mall during the evening shift. The brightness came from the mall's overheads.

"She'll be okay. I just have to get her home."

"Help me." It came out a whisper. Desperate, I tried to focus on Quisten, but my vision blurred, and my tongue refused to cooperate. "Kid . . . napping . . . me . . ."

"She wants a nap." Steffan chuckled.

Quisten shook his head, turned to Steff. "She's Worker Caste? That's very generous of you, sir. You take her on home. She's had one too many."

Fury mixed with fear. "Don't . . . drink. Help . . . me!"

Steffan turned toward the doors. "Thank you, Guardian."

Desperate, I grabbed Quisten's jacket. He jerked, startled, then disengaged himself and patted my arm. "Go sleep it off, Miss Flint. Let your boyfriend take care of you." Seizing his sleeve, I opened my mouth, trying to form words, and his voice turned disapproving. "A lovely young lady such as yourself should not indulge in this unbecoming display of public drunkenness. The shame you have brought on your family!"

Fear mixed with failure rose like bile in my throat, choking me.

A chuckle. Steffan moved forward, tearing the Guard's sleeve from my grip. No longer able to resist the drug, I sank into blackness.

# 29. PREY

Pain roused me, and I groaned, disoriented. *Am I late for work? Why am I—*

"Glad you're back." Steffan's voice.

Memory cascaded back, and with it, panic. Something hard under my back. *Where am I?* Ignoring the fierce pounding in my head, I forced my eyes open. Light stabbed my brain, and I winced. "Wha' ya do to me?" My mouth felt dessicated, my tongue three sizes too big.

"I had to get you someplace where we could talk," Steff said.

I tried to lift a hand to shield my eyes, but pain lanced up my wrist, and the cold bite of metal. *What? I'm handcuffed?* A strong arm slid beneath my shoulders, lifting me to a sitting position. My tongue worked its way around my mouth, stimulating saliva, and I blinked several times in succession. Finally, my eyes focused.

I was sitting on a desk in a small room—an office? The musty odor and a dark bank of windows to my right suggested an old warehouse. Steffan stood next to me, his solicitous expression that of a man whose friend took a small tumble. In front of me was . . . Prinister Severs?

*Oh, no.* My heart dropped into my stomach. *No.*

A moment later my eyes found Ray, who stood by the door as if guarding it, his face sober, impassive. Betrayal washed over me in an icy wave, clearing the last of the cobwebs from my head. *Of course. They've been working together this whole time. Ray just can't resist the lure of that green ring.*

"We have nothing to talk about." To my relief, my voice sounded steadier.

"On the contrary." Prinister Severs's voice boomed in the small space, increasing the pounding in my head. "It is time for you to behave like a responsible young woman, instead of a dissolute whore. You have disrespected your father and disgraced your family. Obviously you did not take to heart the little chat we had at church." He peered at me, hard. I wondered if he was confused as to why his nanotherapy hadn't worked. "The only reason I am condescending to this travesty of a marriage is because your father begged me to restore the family honor."

"I tried to give you time, Peanut." Ray stepped forward. "But this can't go on. You know that."

"What can't go on?" I shifted my weight off the desk. My legs buckled, and I grabbed the edge with both hands just as Steffan seized my arm.

"Whoa," he said. "Give yourself a minute."

I wrenched away and stumbled a step or two, desperate to put distance between us. "Me living my life? How does that offend you? You certainly—"

Severs cleared his throat, interrupting me, his brow furrowed. "You are a fallen woman. Your reputation—and that of your poor family—is forever sullied because of your selfish behavior. The fact that this young man is willing to marry you in spite of it is a testimony to his generous and self-sacrificing character. Do not debase yourself further by refusing him."

"So that's what this is about." I took a cautious step forward; to my delight, my legs supported me. But the headache stomped through my brain, relentless. "You're here to force me into a marriage I don't want." I turned to Ray, unleashing my glare. "How could you?"

His eyebrows drew together. "You gave me no choice. And I'm out of patience."

"Patience!" I began with some heat. "You—"

Severs cut in. "Technically, I should not sanction this marriage. You have been too long away from the bosom of the church." He sighed heavily, his jowls falling into sorrowful lines. "But Ray is a good and faithful servant—"

I stifled a laugh.

"—so I am here as a favor to him, provided you return to St. Michael's after your consummation, and attend such classes as are assigned to you."

*Classes? In that charming little room in the basement?* My mouth tightened, but Severs was still speaking. "You have abdicated your Family Duty, Miss Esselin. You have much to atone for."

I had only one card left to play, and I knew it could cost Ray everything. My heart pounded in my ears, but I stood erect, my gaze on Severs, and nodded at my stepfather. "Did he bother to tell you that he was entertaining another lady friend before my mother's body had even made it to the morgue?" Ray blanched, but I went on. "That she was staying in our *apartment*? That's why I couldn't go home! And you have the audacity to talk about *my* unfaithfulness and reckless behavior?"

Ray jumped forward, gesturing wildly. "I didn't—I—" He turned to me. "Why didn't you tell me you—"

Severs raised a placating hand. "God understands the needs of a man. Whatever your dear father had to do to assuage his devastating grief after the loss of his beloved wife, I'm sure God will look upon with grace and forgiveness."

*What?* Shock glued me to the floor. Ray let out a sigh, avoiding my eyes.

The prinister's expression hardened. "But *you* are another matter altogether."

I couldn't breathe. "I . . . see." Finally, I did. *In the eyes of the Sanctioned Church, it doesn't matter what the man does—only what the woman does. Mom was partly right; the church is about control, but controlling men is only done to further the ultimate goal of controlling women. Why didn't I get this sooner?* Tears pricked my eyes as the true import sank in. *Oh, God! There's no way out for me.*

Severs was regarding me with the mask of smug superiority I had come to know so well, and bile rose in my throat at everything he represented. I couldn't look at him another minute. I headed for the door.

"Hey!" Steffan said, as Ray moved to intercept me.

He spread his arms, and I had to stop to avoid running into him. "Just . . . listen to Steffan, will you?"

"Listen to what? He can say nothing that will change my mind." I moved to step around him. "And neither can you."

"She's right." Steffan appeared next to me and took my arm. His other hand held a knife to my chest.

My eyes widened. *He can't be serious!*

He looked down at me, his voice an impassive threat. "I'm talked out. We're getting married. Right now."

I laughed; I couldn't help it. "Proposal at knifepoint? With the bride in handcuffs?"

"You refuse to listen to reason." Steffan's eyes were manic, irrational. "This is your fault! This is what you have brought me to."

Ray turned away from my imploring gaze. Severs's expression hadn't altered at the appearance of the knife. *Not a word, prinister? Was the knife your idea?*

Turning to Steffan, I couldn't keep the contempt out of my voice. "You're blaming me for *your* decision to use violence? That's rich, Steff." My eyes darted to Severs. "And you are a spineless hypocrite, allowing any kind of violence against a woman to justify your control. My mother is *dead because of you!*"

Ray flinched, but my vitriol missed its target; Severs stood, unmoved. Tears crowded my throat, forcing me to a whisper. "And you destroyed the only father I ever knew."

Ray's eyes lifted to mine. His mouth twisted, and he turned away.

"Come on. We're getting married." Steffan tugged my arm, and I pulled back. A split second later, the knife point jabbed my throat. I couldn't suppress a gasp, and my eyes locked with his. I saw no mercy, no affection—just a ruthless calculation that made my blood run cold. "If you think I'm joking, I recommend you think again," Steff said, his voice soft. "I will not be denied, Meryn. Do you understand?"

"I do." I couldn't muster a smile at the irony. No words would get me out of this. I was in big trouble.

"Prinister, if you will." Steffan kept the knife to my neck as Severs launched into the wedding ceremony.

The whole thing was surreal. I stood in my work clothes (all dirty down one side; Steffan must have dragged me at some point), my hands cuffed together, in front of Severs, who was immaculate in his vestments. I felt stiff, constricted, like when I was six years old and still trying to wear my favorite dress even though it was far too small. Ray took his place next to me as if my future husband holding me at knifepoint in an abandoned warehouse was the most normal thing in the world.

Despair flooded me, and a sob forced its way through my lips. In my memory, I saw my childhood friend, Debbie Delaney, who'd been raped on the school bus those many years ago. I wondered if she felt this same sense of panicked hopelessness, the same weight of inevitability.

Maybe this was just. Maybe it was right—God's recompense for my bad behavior. *Maybe this whole time I really have missed God's will.* I'd let my grief over Mom blind me to the truth.

I'd always known men and women were regarded differently by the church and society. I saw it everywhere, in example after example, year after year—how men were promoted, excused, and cozened, while their wives were disregarded, their pain or problems nodded off with a laugh or an insult or a backhand across the face. And I'd accepted it all because everyone else did, even as my discomfort and my questions increased.

But I'd never expected it to destroy my future so completely. I'd always held out hope that somehow, my life would be different. I was smart—resourceful. *Shouldn't that matter? I guess not.* I gave a mirthless snort, and Steff eyed me.

*What made me think I was so special that I could elude the strictures that afflicted every other woman? This is our burden. That's what Mom always said. This is what God has given me—marriage. Children. Mom accepted it, and so must I.* But my stomach twisted, nausea rising. *Am I rebelling against God?*

Deep in my spirit, a still, small voice spoke. *No. Steffan is not My will for you.*

I didn't know if it was God, or my own defiance.

"Steffan Caulfield Hagen, do you take this woman to be your wedded wife, to have and to hold, to guide and direct, to rebuke and correct in the way of life everlasting, to love and to cherish as the mother of your children, as long as you both shall live?"

"I do," Steff said, his voice full of pride.

*No, no, no, God, how is this happening?*

Severs turned to me. "And do you, Maureen Anna Esselin, take Steffan Hagen to be your lawfully wedded husband, to love and to honor? Do you agree to become one with him, to obey him without question, to to put him and your children before yourself, to submit to him as unto the Lord, as long as you both shall live?"

I hesitated, and the knife nicked my neck. "Say it," Steffan hissed. A trickle of warm blood oozed down my skin and dissolved into my collar.

*I can do this. God, help me do this. Just say it, Meryn.* "I do."

And then something—a warm, comforting presence—pushed its way between me and the other men in the room. Was it an angel? I don't know. But it separated me from them—their intentions, their desires, their authority—as effectively as if someone had dropped a wall between us. And Someone spoke. *No, Meryn. No more.*

The lights went out.

Before I could think, my elbow drove deep into Steffan's gut. As his breath expelled in a rush, my clenched hands shot out and came around with a full-strength chop aimed at his Adam's apple. The emergency lighting clicked on, illuminating everything seemingly in slow motion:

the knife twirling upward in lazy arcs—my strike must have knocked it out of Steffan's hand—while his body curled forward, his arms tightening around his stomach, his lowering chin deflecting my blow. That miscalculation on my part probably saved his life.

Somehow, I caught the knife as it came down, despite the handcuffs; whirling, I shook off Ray's clumsy attempt to grab my arm.

Severs stepped forward . . . to meet the knife, pointed at his face.

Ray gripped his bruised hand. His jaw dropped. "Meryn!"

Severs's eyes widened, then narrowed. "How dare you threaten violence against a man of God, you Jezebel whore!"

I didn't waste breath on a reply. Backing away from Severs, I turned toward the door, but Ray blocked my path. Adrenaline and fury pulsed through my veins. "Out of my way!"

"Now, Meryn," he said, spreading his hands.

Steff stood, coughing, using the desk for support. "Are you really going to stab your father?"

Heat suffused my face. "I am *leaving!* What do you not understand about that?"

Steff approached, rubbing his jaw. I lifted the knife as I backed away. "That's close enough."

"Think about this, Miss Esselin." Severs stepped toward me, lifting a hand placatingly, but the benevolence was absent from his expression, replaced by the same hard judgmentalism I'd seen at the trial.

"I've thought about nothing else since Mom died! What option have you left me?" Tears sprang to my eyes.

"We just want what's best for you." The prinister's tone belied his words.

I bumped against something: the wall. Steffan stood in front of me, Prinister Severs to my left, and Ray blocked my path to the door. I had nowhere to go. Cold from the concrete block ate through my thin work clothes and penetrated my back.

His steps slow, measured, Steffan eased toward me.

I lifted the knife. "Stop." My voice went up an octave. *"Stop!"*

He didn't. Instead, he spread his hands. "What are you going to do, Meryn? You gonna kill me?"

Oh, how desperately I wanted to call his bluff. A big part of me wanted to plunge the knife straight through his vile, hating heart and end the whole horrible charade. I could eliminate Steff and disable Ray; I had the skill. But if I did that in front of Severs, it would guarantee me a trip to the nearest Guard station. To escape, I would have to kill all three of them.

And I couldn't do it—it was a bridge I couldn't cross. My eyes traveled from the knife to his face, and my fury ebbed to a slow simmer.

Tears flooded my eyes, ran down my face.

Steffan's mouth curled into a grin, mirthless and cruel. "Yeah, that's what I thought." He reached forward to take the knife, and at that moment everything clicked together in my mind. *I can't kill Steff. I can't marry him. That leaves just one option.*

I raised the knife and held it to my throat.

# 30. CHOICE

Severs's face contorted into a mask of rage. "Stop this ridiculous self-ishness at once!"

Steffan's eyes widened, but a moment later the office echoed with his laughter. "Oh, please. A last dramatic bid for attention!"

"I am leaving this room a single woman." Tears caught in my throat, but I pushed on, my voice cracking. "Even if I leave in a body bag. But I will never marry you, Steffan Hagen." My voice dropped to a harsh tenor caw, my mouth twisting with contempt. "I will die, first."

The silence lingered, unbroken. Wind fluttered along the eaves, whispered through chipped windows. Somewhere out in the warehouse, water dripped in three-quarter time. I wondered, oddly, if it was raining. *I wanted to see the sun again. Just once more. Look out at the ocean—Mama, can you see me? Mama, are you waiting? Will you welcome me home? Or is Prinister Severs right, and I will live in an eternity of torment for what I'm about to do?*

The prinister sighed, then spoke, entreating, as one would to an errant puppy. "Come now, child. Everything is going to be all right. Marriage is a joyful union—you have no reason to fear. Just trust us. We know what is best."

"Trust you?" My eyes shifted to him. "Every one of you has betrayed me! *Every one!* The people I trusted most!"

"Betrayed you?" Steffan's bafflement seemed genuine. "How is wanting to marry you a betrayal?"

Severs turned to Ray, his voice a warning. "Control her, Raymond! It is your duty as her father."

My eyes followed his, hope crowding into my despair. "Ray," I whispered through swollen lips. *Maybe Ray will realize . . . maybe . . .*

Ray said nothing. His eyes dropped to the floor, and bitter disappointment soured my mouth.

Steff stepped back, his eyebrows lifting. "You're ready to die? Okay." He shrugged, crossed his arms, casual. "Go ahead."

I looked to the door, still blocked by my stepfather. *Even if I can get there before Steff gets to me, I'll never make it out of this room.* My eyes shifted to Steff, who was grinning. *And this is how it will be for the rest of our time together. Him mocking my pain. Manipulating me. He doesn't love me. He doesn't know how to love.* Severs stood, hands clasped, his face impassive.

*Not one of them cares.*

"I can't—" *live.* I couldn't stop the tears, and something inside crumbled into shards of frigid ice, devoid of life. The knife was shaking against my throat. *God, forgive me! There's no other way.*

I heard a faint thought—*There is always another way*—but I couldn't trust that I wasn't hearing myself, my vain hopes for escape, for life. My thumb found the carotid artery, pulsing strong against my skin, and I adjusted the angle. *One sharp cut, swift and deep, should do it.* My elbow lifted, ready to—

"Stop."

Surprise froze me.

Ray stepped forward, hand lifting. "Rose, stop."

*What?* I blinked. The pressure of the blade on my skin lessened.

"Don't leave me." It came out a whisper. His eyes dark and ancient with pain, Ray paused, as if afraid to take another step. "Not again."

Severs turned to Ray, lifting a hand in admonishment. "Raymond—"

Steff's snarl cut across the prinister's words. "The hell I will! She's mine, Ray! You told me so! Besides." He eyed me, supercilious, calculating. "She's bluffing; look at her shake. She's a coward."

"Mr. Hagen, perhaps you should reconsider." Severs's tone and manner were conciliatory. "Obviously she is damaged goods. We don't even know if she is still a virgin. And look at her cry—shedding tears in front of us! I thought the church could heal her"—he shook his head, ponderous and mournful—"but she's far too damaged to be salvageable if she's willing to harm herself. Think of what she might do to your children."

Steffan's mask of fury didn't alter. "She's mine. I'll control her."

Ray's gaze traveled from the shaking knife to my face. He shook his head. Something in his eyes softened, and he cleared his throat. "Come on, Meryn. I'll take you home."

"Now, Raymond," Severs began, "first discuss your bargain with—"

"What home?" I spat the words, contemptuous. *Really? You expect me to trust you?*

Weary, beaten, Ray spread his hands. "Wherever you feel safe. I'll take you there."

"This is bullshit!" Steffan ground it out, but my eyes were on my stepfather.

Severs cleared his throat. "Raymond, I see what you're trying to do. But this doesn't speak well of your discipline. Let me correct her. Just a few minutes in my office can—"

"Correct her? Like you chastised Rose?"

*What?* My mouth opened in a gasp, but Ray's eyes on the prinister were a frozen lake, unyielding and remote. "I obeyed your instructions, and you still think my discipline is too lax? What's happened to your heart, Noah? Did they destroy it, like they tried to destroy mine? Do you think I don't remember that you went in to the same prinister I did— Mordman—for that coveted 'individual instruction in godly manhood'?"

My stomach dropped. Severs paled, his eyes darting to my face, but I couldn't see anyone but Ray through my tears. My flawed, alcoholic stepfather. Who hated church, but went anyway to keep his job and support his family. *Oh Jesus, they didn't*—Nausea rocked me, and a whimper escaped my throat. It all made too much sense. *And Mom; what did they*—

Ray stepped toward the prinister, his face taking on the angry, uncompromising lines I knew so well. "How can you stand there and watch all this, and say nothing? Were you really going to let my daughter cut her own throat? Does her life mean so little to you?"

Severs' mouth set in a firm line, and his eyes narrowed. "You made an agreement! You let her walk out of this room, and any future elevation is *forfeit*. In fact, I can have your job for this. Do you hear me?"

Ray gave an oddly lighthearted laugh as he removed a key from his pocket. He reached forward, his eyes on my face, his expression encouraging me to trust.

At Ray's silence, the prinister's voice rose. "You'll wear that blue ring for the rest of your natural life, Raymond! I might even get you busted down to Indigent!"

My stomach clenched at the threat, but Ray didn't so much as blink. I took a cautious breath, my eyes on his, and slowly lowered the knife. He avoided it as he unlocked the handcuffs. A tendril of relief curled through my mind, but I shoved it aside, ruthless. *Don't. Don't.*

"You're right." Ray's face was bleak. "You can easily take my job. You can knock me out of my caste." Dropping the cuffs on the floor, he took my free hand, his gentle, tentative. "But you cannot have my daughter. And you cannot have my soul. That belongs to God alone."

Something inside of me thawed, warmed. The shaking slowed, but I didn't let go of the knife.

"We'll see about that." But Severs's words were thin—powdered milk made with too much water. A moment later his eyes shifted to me and hardened. "And you. You are in gross violation of the Women's Code. I expect to see you home and attending services with your father on Sunday."

My eyebrows lifted. I tried to speak, failed, and cleared my throat.

"Meryn—" Ray began, but I cut him off.

"Then I expect you'll be disappointed. As for St. Mike's—" My voice turned to iron. "I'd rather have a front-row seat in hell."

Ray tugged my arm, hard, and I let him pull me toward the door. I glanced at Steff, expecting rage or condemnation, but except for narrowed eyes, his face was impassive.

"Miss Esselin."

We paused. My eyes met the prinister's. And for the first time in my life, I didn't look down.

His pasty face reddened. "No one can stop that now. Not even God."

It wasn't worth my satisfaction to laugh as Ray led me through the door and into the night.

~

"You know I can take you wherever you want," Ray said, but he slowed the car to the curb a stone's throw from the Jordan Avenue bus station, its lights throwing harsh shadows along the street.

"I appreciate that, but this is fine." I removed his handkerchief from my neck. The bleeding had finally slowed. Adrenaline still fired my responses, but fatigue was creeping from dark pockets in my body and I knew I didn't have much time before I was exhausted and vulnerable.

He put the car in park, opened his mouth, closed it. His hands trembled on the steering wheel.

I fought sympathy and failed. Took a deep breath, looking out at the night. "Thank you."

A sparrow landed on the chain link fence next to us. It cocked its head and chirped.

"I, uh, wanted to—" He stopped. "Well. I didn't do you any favors."

"You did." I shook my head, twisting the bloody, tearstained hand-kerchief in my hands, and now I looked at him. "I'm alive because of you. You and God. I—" My throat closed. *Mom is dead. But I'm alive.* I didn't know what to think; my stomach knotted.

I tried to hand him the handkerchief, but Ray shook his head, his eyes on the city lights beyond. "Keep it." His laugh was harsh. "It's the least I can give you. No, you're alive because of you, Peanut. You're braver than—well." He turned to me, wearing the defeated expression I'd seen in the warehouse. "If you need anything—and I, uh, I mean that—you know how to reach me." He paused, his eyes dropping. "I didn't know you tried to come home."

The sparrow flew away.

"Yeah, well." I fumbled for something to say. "Walking up and say-ing hi didn't seem like the thing to do."

"No." His laugh was mirthless. A long pause. "Look, Peanut—"

I cut him off. "Don't. Just don't." The rest of the words jammed in my throat, a derailed train. I managed to force out, "Take care of yourself." No longer able to control the tears, I fled the car.

~

"He *what?*" Bree's voice was a screech.

"Meryn, your neck!" Lisha gasped, her eyes wide and frightened.

The girls said nothing during my recital, Ellie wrapping one arm around her sister as they ate breakfast, the kitchen light driving back the early morning dark.

As I wound down, Mags set a bowl of oatmeal in front of me and sighed, her brow furrowed. "I'm so sorry, Meryn. You could have come here last night, you know." Her expression said, *You should have.*

"I didn't want to risk it." My voice was still high. I didn't tell them I didn't come straight back to Shady Dell after Ray dropped me off; instead, I'd gone looking for Charity and Keturah. I didn't understand, myself, why I'd sought them out first—but the alley where they'd healed me from Severs's poison had been swept clear of people and structures, as if they'd never existed. I'd stood on the pristine concrete and wept. I had no clue where they'd gone, so I went home to Shady Dell.

I hadn't slept much after I locked myself in my tiny tin house; it was cold, even close to the stove, and the incident kept replaying in my mind, underscoring how very close I had come to joining Mom.

Now, taking a swallow of tea, I shook my head. "I still don't know how much Steffan knows. He may know exactly where I live."

Lisha gasped. "He could come here?"

"I'd like to see him try." Ellie's voice was a growl.

"It is unlikely," Mags said soothingly, "but if he does, we will certainly deal with that when it happens." She pinned me with a gentle look that cut through the anxious and angry responses of the twins. "Are you working today?"

I shook my head. "I called in sick. I can't risk—I can't—"

"We'll manage." Bree settled next to me, hugging my shoulders.

"But my job—"

Mags moved to the cupboard, selected a tincture, and handed it to me. "Three drops in your tea. Your eyes are burned holes in your head, child. Take the loft. I'll be right here on the futon, knitting, all day."

Her kind commitment to my safety warmed me, and my shoulders sagged relief.

Ellie nodded. "You look terrible. You should see yourself."

"I'd rather not." I tried to laugh; without argument I measured the medicine into my tea and stirred.

"Carole understands that sometimes people get sick," Bree said, a trifle testy. "Especially after the week you've put in, you—"

"I can't be sick for the rest of my life!" Fear clutched my guts, and I pushed my bowl away.

"You should tell Carole what's happening." Mags poured soymilk on her cereal.

"But I'm not supposed to take my problems—"

"I agree." Bree patted my back and moved to her seat. "This no longer affects only you, Mer. It could compromise the store."

Hope flared, died as quickly. "What could she really do?" I asked, and took a deep swallow of tea, trying to calm myself. I eyed the girls nervously. *I shouldn't have brought this up in front of them. Lisha—*

"An official complaint from a store manager requires the mall Guards to address the problem." Bree sifted a spoonful of sugar into her tea. "Unlike management at On the Mark, Carole takes this sort of thing seriously. And because this happened at the mall, you have the legal right to access mall surveillance video and build a court case."

"A court case won't do me much good if the person I'm suing is my husband," I said, my face bleak.

Mags stirred her oatmeal. "You're right. They'll throw the case out."

I buried my face in my hands, fighting tears. "This is hopeless. I should just go home. Move back in with Ray."

"Don't you do that!" Bree grabbed my wrist, her green eyes intense. "This isn't hopeless. You escaped Steff last night, you know. We'll find a solution. Besides, you know as well as I do the moment you go home, Ray will marry you off to someone else, anyway."

Ellie gasped. "You mean, you can't choose your own husband? Your stepfather can—" Her eyes veered to Mags, who turned to her with a reassuring expression.

"Don't worry, sweetie, I will never force you to marry someone. You will make that choice yourself."

"But why can't Meryn?" Lisha asked. Tears brimmed her eyes; oddly, that made me feel better.

"Our society has created unreasonable expectations for women." Mags's hand closed into a fist around her napkin. "We'll figure something out, Meryn. We didn't come this far to give up."

"Hear, hear." Bree's face was fierce.

Ellie looked out the window. "Bus!" she yelled. "Bus, Lisha!"

Both girls scrambled from the table, running for backpacks and coats, Lisha wiping away tears. As I struggled to finish my cold oatmeal, listening to Mags's kind nattering, Bree went out to where Kilte and Walker stood in the cold morning predawn. Kilte greeted her, his voice cheerful, and Pris emerged from the gloom to hug Walker.

I was glad the guys hadn't come in. The door closed behind the twins and I watched them run to the truck before I turned to Mags. "I have to leave."

Her brow wrinkled. "But Bree said—"

"I don't mean work. I have to leave Shady Dell. This whole situation with Steffan is jeopardizing you, this house"—I fought tears, and my voice dropped to a whisper—"*the girls . . .*" and then my throat closed, and I couldn't go on.

Mags reached across the table, her hand warm on my arm. "Meryn, listen to me. Yes, there is jeopardy. Yes, this situation presents a danger. But danger waits for every woman who insists on living her own life." She pulled a clean handkerchief from her apron pocket and handed it to me, her face kind, worried.

I tried to smile, pressed it to my eyes. The world seemed safer in the dark.

"If you decide you truly want to go home, I won't stop you. But don't go just because you're afraid of what Steffan might do to us. The Steffans of this world will always find an excuse for violence."

Uncertain, I dropped my hands and met her eyes. "But—"

"And if you cave now, you will live at the mercy of every man's whim for the rest of your life. Is that what you want? Is that the future you envisioned for yourself?" Her head tilted. "More to the point: do you think that's what God wants for you?"

That hit like a fist to my stomach. "I don't know," I whispered, hating the whine in my voice. "Doesn't God call us to obedience, as women? Doesn't the Bible?"

Mags nodded, her eyes thoughtful. Opening her phone, she pulled up a screen and turned it toward me. "Do you remember this scene in Luke? When Martha told Jesus to make Mary help her in the kitchen?"

I experienced a moment of mental whiplash. *What?* I read the passage, perplexed. "Um, yeah, of course. Mary was in the other room, listening to Jesus talk instead of helping her sister. It's the basis of the Women's Code—our dual duty to worship and to serve."

Mags tapped a finger on the table. "But what was Mary doing? We tend to couch it in terms of her worshiping, but wasn't she actually sitting under the teachings of Christ?"

I nodded. *So? Where is this going?*

"Why do you think Christ let Mary stay? Wasn't she being disobedient, sitting there with the men? Wasn't she supposed to submit, like Martha?"

I blinked. I'd never considered that; it wasn't taught. "Well, I suppose she was doing something important in His eyes." *Besides, that was Mary and that was in the Bible and it was a different time—*

"Something more important than Mary's obedience," Mags went on, setting the phone on the table where I could read it. "Something so important to Mary's worth as a person, that Jesus Christ Himself let her stay in a roomful of men and learn from Him. Direct—no husband, no prinister, no filter." She smiled slightly. "At that time, Jewish women were not permitted to study the Torah as men were. The fact that Christ not only allowed Mary to sit under his teaching but encouraged her to do so—well, that was revolutionary. Downright heretical!" She sipped her tea. "He could have been arrested."

My eyes widened at that. "Wait a minute. It was against the law for Mary to listen to Jesus? The Lord broke the law?"

Mags nodded. "And if Christ loved Mary enough to overturn centuries of Jewish tradition and Mosaic law, don't you think He loves you that much, too? Don't you think God values *your* life"—she gently shook my arm—"just as much as He values Ray's or Steffan's or anyone else's? Do you really think God would ask you to marry a violent man just to placate your father, or placate the Sanctioned Church? Meryn!" Her lips parted in a delighted laugh. "Do you really think Jesus would tell you to go back in the kitchen?"

My mouth dropped open, and I stared at the older woman with dawning wonder. *He values my life . . . as much as He values Ray's? Or any man's?* The scene played across my mind: Mary's eyes on her teacher, ready to obey, waiting for the single word that would tell her to leave, to become only what the law said she could be, and no more. And on its heels, a stunning revelation: the moment Mary knew her life, and the lives of all women, had changed forever. "He loves me that much?" I whispered, my voice breaking. "So much, He was willing to break the law . . . for me?"

Something shifted inside me. A hard, impenetrable shell—one I'd never known was there, one that had long confined my soul—abruptly shattered into a million pieces, leaving me broken, exposed . . . *free.* I gasped with the shock and wonder of it. As my vision transformed, things that were once so dark now came easily into view. "But that means—" I broke off, my mind reeling. *That means He loves every woman that much—so much that He destroyed thousands of years of tradition in one revolutionary moment in Martha's living room. And if He loves all women that much, that means our entire society . . . is based on a lie.* The revelation rocked me to my core, and I gasped a sob. "Oh, my God! My God!" The tears started and wouldn't stop.

"Yes." Mags's face was radiant with my joy. "He loves us—*every woman*—that much."

A warmth invaded my heart, healing and softening places that had been hardened and cold for far too long. Burying my face in my hands, I yielded to sobs as all the doubts I'd quietly harbored—doubts that God loved me as much as He loved Steffan, doubts that God could still love me if I wasn't obedient to Ray, doubts I didn't even realize had kept my heart chilled and alienated from God—they all melted away like snow beneath a blowtorch. Mags held me close and let me cry.

At some point I garbled out something about asking God's forgiveness for being so stupid, and Mags chuckled. "Revelation comes in its own timing, my dear. There is no sin in that."

Wiping my eyes, I sat up and hugged her fiercely. "Oh Mags, how can I thank you. You have given me such a tremendous gift!"

"It's nothing I can take credit for, Meryn." Mags dashed tears from her own cheeks, her smile watery. "The Holy Spirit whispers. We have but to listen."

I remembered the mysterious force that had separated me from Steffan in the warehouse, and I laughed, overcome with a joy I'd never known. Mags sipped her tea, and I sat, contented, looking around at the tiny house and everything outside, somehow seeing it all differently: my friends and neighbors, the world, and my place in it. *I belong. Finally . . . I belong.* I understood now why Mags had joined Liberté, and why she worked so tirelessly to help every woman at Shady Dell. *Because the only One Who has a right to tell a woman anything about herself . . . is God.*

My thoughts flew to Mom, and I wondered if she had ever felt this sense of belonging, of belovedness—and immediately on the heels of that, a profound doubt. "But why can't—" I broke off, lost in my musings. *Why can't all women know this? Why doesn't God—*

Reality intruded. My thoughts shifted, my smile slipping away. "Mags, all this doesn't change the fact that Steffan kidnapped me."

"No," she said softly. "It doesn't."

Fear and doubt permeated hope and revelation, like ink tainting water. My laugh came out an odd croak. "Then how can I possibly go to work tomorrow? How can I—"

"You can, the way I can," she said, "the only way we all can. Through prayer. Through trust in God. It's the only way to find peace in this dangerous place. Steffan may not leave you alone. But Bree and I will not take away the only refuge you have. And we cannot let fear do that, either." She smiled, tentative, opened her hands. "Shall we pray?"

Trembling, I nodded and clasped her hands in mine.

# 31. DOПE

The rest of the week was quiet and uneventful, but I vibrated on a knife edge. Every time I left the store, my eyes searched for a tall, blond-haired man. Every time I boarded the sub, I scanned for someone following. I knew Steffan wasn't going to give up. More than once I caught sidelong glances from one man or another, and I immediately studied the floor. I took to changing my route home, walking from one sub station to the next through the frigid wind, trying to throw a potential tracker off my route. I kept wondering if Steff was working alone, or if he had someone helping him. If he did, I could be followed home and I'd never know it. My meal breaks shrank; I was too nervous to eat at the food court, but I couldn't eat in the store; it was against policy. My body thinned, but I couldn't seem to relax. Bree watched me, her eyes worried, but she couldn't help, either.

Mags, Bree, and I set aside a time of Bible study and prayer every night, petitioning God for protection, for a resolution. Sometimes the girls joined us. It was the only thing that kept me sane.

Tamar walked in one night during our prayer and waited patiently until Mags said, "Amen." When our eyes opened, the blonde woman shook her head and turned into the kitchen, rummaging through the pantry. "Why you don't just marry him is beyond me." She tossed that off, tucking two cans into her tote. "I mean, good God, he's a *Hagen*."

I resented the intrusion. *How is this Tamar's business?*

"She doesn't love him." Bree's eyes were razors.

"A red ring is all the love a girl needs," Tamar retorted as she slipped out of the house.

Mags sighed. "Someday she'll understand. It's hard to maintain perspective on money when you're living brown."

Bree snorted.

I did file a report with Carole, who was sympathetic. "Do you have a photo?" she asked. "That way I know who to watch for. And we'll attach it to the complaint." I swiped through my phone photos and found one from when Steff and I were dating.

When we submitted the report, the Guard on duty studied the shot. "He's a well-favored young man. I haven't seen him, but this is good to have. With this information, we can program the door to notify us if he enters." He looked up and smiled. "Seems like he's pretty gone on you. And Governance Caste? Cute little Worker Bee like you—you should marry him."

Exasperation and rage warred for space in my head. "Reward the man's violence?" I said, trying to keep my tone even. "No, thank you. And I want to request video from the evening he abducted me. I can show you exactly where—"

"Miss Flint," the Guard interrupted, impatient, "you're a woman. I cannot release Silvermine Guardian Angels' property to you without authorization. You will have to obtain a request from your father or your husband."

My mouth dropped open. "Steffan Hagen kidnapped me—*me*, not my father—and you can't—"

The man's voice was rote. "We don't know he kidnapped you—"

Carole broke in, smiling. "We appreciate your assistance, Guardian Killingham, in keeping our workplace safe." She turned away from the desk and I took the hint.

~

On the way home from work, I caught a flash of flaxen hair through the sub's connecting doors before the man vanished in the crowd. I bolted off at the next stop, running up the stairs and past late afternoon commuters walking home through the blustery weather. Ducking into a narrow alley, I tried not to cry, willed my heart to slow.

*Lord, this is insane! I can't live like this. But I can't stop it either. What can I do? What on earth can I do?*

My back against the rough brick wall, I watched people walk by, chatting on phones or with each other, the women dressed in coats with their tan or blue MTs reaching to their ankles, the single women standing out in their jeans or patterned, full-length skirts. No one noticed me. A blond-haired man walked by, and my heart jumped, but it wasn't Steffan. I lingered in the alley for a long time, my hunger growing, as the sky overhead spun slow into night and the freshening wind tossed trash across the concrete.

"Help a poor sister?"

Startled into a gasp, I turned toward the voice.

A young woman sat on the cold pavement just across the alley, propped against the wall, wearing an expensive but soiled jacket and a green Caste Ring, her bare feet wrapped in plastic burlap onion bags.

My eyebrows lifted. *My God. How long has she been—*

"Of course," I whispered, and fumbled at my tote, digging for scrip.

"You're running from *him*, aren't you?"

I froze, and my eyes met hers. "I—he was my boyfriend."

She nodded, pushing a curl of dark hair beneath a tattered cap. "I'm running, too. He said he'd kill me if I wouldn't date him, and he threatened my family, my little sister—" Her lips twisting, she cast her eyes down the alley. "He's still chasing me. Never stopped. We all run," she went on, her voice hoarse from fatigue or the thick smog. "We run, or we die." She shrugged, her chin lifting. "I'm not ready to die."

I gave her the fiver, crouching so I could see her. "You live here?" I whispered. "In this alley, alone?" My mind overlaid the dim corridor with a collection of blue tarps, Charity smiling as she tended the fire . . .

She tucked the scrip away, her expression plaintive. "We all do." She gestured toward the alley, the street. "It isn't safe to stay in one place. The girls come and go, depending on if they get a warm bed or a warm meal. Where else can we live? Every place has its demons. Every place has its price. Every place." She put a hand on my arm, earnest, intent. "Don't you let him get you, sister. Don't you let him win."

Tears gathered in my eyes. She nodded as if satisfied and glanced down the alley, and her kind expression faded. "No!" She scrambled to her feet, clutching a worn tote to her side.

I rose, my eyes following hers, but saw nothing but a few battered dumpsters and the gathering darkness. "What? I don't—"

"You don't see him? He's right there." She gestured, backing toward the street. "No, John, you aren't taking me again!" Her voice ratcheted up to a scream. *"Nooo!"*

Passersby glanced in, curious, amused, but no one even broke stride.

"Sister! No one's there," I said, low, trying to break through her hallucination without drawing more attention.

"You!" She pointed at me, her face morphing from fear to betrayal to rage in the time it took to draw breath. "You brought him! You're with him! *Damn you!*" Before I could reply, she'd whirled, lurched into the crowd, and vanished down the street.

I had to stay in the alley until the tears stopped, the people passing without noticing, each one focused on their own demons, their own price. My eyes kept searching the metastasizing dark, wondering if he really was there, if it was my own vision that was faulty. The curtain of night had fully fallen when I made my way back to the sub station, checking behind me every few steps and wondering if I'd know when the caution turned to fear and the fear to paranoia and the paranoia to madness, and wondering if the boundary between them was even visible, or if it was as thin as a crack in the new sidewalk beneath my feet.

~

"I just wish it were over." I whispered it.

Bree and I lay in bed, wrapped in darkness. A faint snoring mixed with the hiss of the woodstove below. Above us, a full moon played hide-and-seek with the clouds. Guilt dogged me—the guilt of the faithless, of so quickly finding myself in the valley of doubt after leaving the shining mountaintop.

"It will be," she whispered back. "This can't go on. Steff will get bored." She shifted a bit. "We'll just have to keep you hidden till then."

*That could be . . . a long time.* "I texted him, you know."

The bedcovers rustled as she turned to me, her astonishment clear in the moonlight. "What, you texted Steff?"

Not looking at her, I nodded. "Tonight. I asked him to stop."

A long pause. "What did he say?"

My stomach tightened at the memory, and I closed my eyes. *No. No more tears.* "He said, 'I'll stop when you're dead, you Jezebel slut.'"

"He said *that?*" Bree flopped back against her pillow. "Well, that's a nice proposal."

I chuckled, humorless. "I guess that means he's . . . going to kill me." It took effort getting the words out, even though they'd been ricocheting through my brain since I read the text. *Jesus . . .*

"No, he isn't," Bree said. "You humiliated him. Men can't stand that, so he's trying to get back at you. Tomorrow when you go in, attach his text as an amendment to Carole's report."

"As if they'll do anything. I just wish he would find a rich girl and move to Zion State, or something." I lay quiet for a moment, absorbing that truth. And then something came out of my mouth that was so appalling, I could hardly believe I'd said it. A whisper—profound sin barely aspirated. "Or walk in front of a bus." As soon as it was out, I gasped. "Bree, I didn't mean that! I didn't!"

Silence. *She's angry. Of course she is. I can't believe I said—*

"Bree," I whispered. Rolling over, I raised up; her eyes were closed, her breathing deep and regular.

Stifling a mirthless laugh, I flopped back on my pillow. The moon hid behind a cloud, and I sighed. Even though my friends were kind and supportive, this was my burden, something no one else could share or mitigate. *Maybe not even God.* I watched the sky for a long time and tried to pray, tried not to feel so profoundly alone as the stars winked off, one by one.

~

The next morning, stormy gray clouds dominated the sky. Getting to work meant a fight through freezing wind, smog, and hostile, hurrying crowds. I arrived five minutes late, but Carole said nothing, just greeted me with her usual kind smile. To my relief, she took Steffan's threat seriously and escorted me to the Guard station on the first floor.

The Guard shrugged. "These boys, they get carried away. I'm sure he didn't mean it." Quisten eyed me. "You really want to file it? This kid is Governance Caste; you could get him in trouble. And once it's filed, you can't delete it."

*"Kid"? He's nearly twenty-nine.* "He should've thought of that before he sent it." My mouth bunched. "I'm sure."

He sighed impatiently. "Miss Flint, you want to ruin this boy's life over something that isn't a problem?"

"Isn't a—" Heat stung my face. "He's threatening *my life!* How can—"

"Miss Flint's one of my most valuable employees," Carole interrupted, smooth and professional. "It's important that she's free to focus on—"

"Valuable?" The Guard's laugh echoed through the mall. "She isn't valuable until she's whelped. Three puppies, minimum." He rummaged for something behind the desk, muttered, "Well, at least she's sober today."

My mouth dropped open, and I drew in a breath to deliver a stinging reply—just as Carole stepped in front of me.

"Guardian Quisten, we appreciate your diligence in keeping our workplace safe," Carole said, smiling. She turned away from the desk. This time she had to pull my sleeve, hard, to get me to follow her back to Mrs.

As we ascended the escalator, I tried to tamp down my fury. "This is unbelievable. He isn't even taking this seriously, Carole!"

"I understand your frustration," she said, her voice soothing. "I know it's no consolation, but I've been through the same thing. Usually, the boy gives up once he knows there's no hope for him. Mine did."

My lips compressed in a thin line. *Steff hasn't been a 'boy' for ten years. And what happens if he doesn't give up?*

On Thursday evening, Kilte, Walker and I finished the interior of my tiny tin house. The light tan packing boxes made the walls almost as attractive as if I had painted, and they reflected light effectively.

"Can you feel the difference?" Kilte grinned.

"I can!" I was awed. "It's amazing!" A fire crackled in the stove, insulation keeping the heat in. I vowed I'd sleep in my own house that night.

"Insulation does the trick," Walker said. "I think you're good to move in now."

"What do I owe you for the electrical work?" I asked. Walker had strung the power in my house, and the main line running from Mags's.

"Your silence," he said with a lopsided grin. "Handy usually installs the electrical at Shady Dell. He'd be plenty mad if he thought I was muscling in on his market. But I need the practice. Just tell him you had a contractor do it. It's the truth. You don't have to name names."

"Will do," I agreed, aware I knew nothing of Shady Dell's informal political structure. It was easier to comply than question.

Kilte's expression darkened. "Handy considers himself the king of Shady Dell. Moved in here eons ago, even before Will and Mags. With his business doing so well, he could live someplace nicer, but he likes the power. Especially over women."

Walker caught my expression. "Don't let it worry you. Just try to stay away from him."

"Gladly." Then, deciding I wasn't going to let Handy ruin my joy over my house, I smiled. "I'm so grateful to both of you for your work."

"Well, I'm grateful I don't have to do the dishes tonight." Kilte chuckled as he moved toward the door. "Fair trade, Meryn. Enjoy your house in good health and long life!"

"And lock your door," Walker said, pushing a handful of braids over his shoulder. "Shady Dell is usually okay, but sometimes the homeless come over and try random doors. Some of them are a bit odd."

Fear warred with sympathy. "I will!"

# 32. ERRAND

After work the next evening, I went to Mags's. I still hadn't moved all my stuff to my tiny house, but I'd promised to help Lisha and Ellie with their homework. Despite that welcome distraction, worry lurked in the back of my mind like a chirping smoke alarm, impossible to ignore.

We were deep in Ellie's fractions when Bree burst through the front door and slammed it against the frigid wind. "Whew!" She hung her coat on its peg and smiled, breathing on her cold-reddened hands. "Gamma, is there anything hot on the stove? The temperature is plummeting like a stone out there!"

Mags looked up from her knitting. "Sure, the kettle's still hot. I just fixed myself some tea."

I tried not to resent Bree's cheerfulness. Swallowing, I turned to Ellie's next problem. Bree patted my shoulder on her way to the stove, and I bit my lip.

"Meryn, would you do me a favor?"

I looked up. "Of course, Mags."

Her expression reflected annoyance. "I forgot to bring in firing this afternoon. Would you run over to Walker's and ask him for a few logs? We won't make it through the night with what's in the wood box."

"Of course." I rose and pulled on my coat. "Give problem four a try, Ellie. You saw how we did the last one."

The girl nodded. "I think I can do it this time."

The night was clear but profoundly cold, and the snow squeaked as I made my way down the steps. The salt Mags had sprinkled that afternoon hadn't yet thawed the ice. Crunching along the path to Walker's place, I paid close attention to my footing in the moonlight.

"Sure, tell Mom I'll bring it myself." Walker stood at his open door wearing just his work clothes, as if not feeling the cold at all. "Kilte and I haven't had dinner, so we'll be along in a few."

"I will." I smiled, trying not to be annoyed at leaving Ellie for what turned out to be nothing. On the way back to Mags's, I took a firm hold of my temper. *Not her fault. Or Walker's. It isn't like—*

"Nice digs."

I froze in place, my nightmare crystallized in front of me. Steffan leaned against the back of the house next to Mags's, hands in his coat pockets. Darkness shadowed his face, but the voice was unmistakable.

"Did you really think I'd give up? You must think I'm stupid."

My heart pounded in my chest, stealing my breath. "No, I don't think that."

"I'm giving you one more chance to do the right thing, Meryn. One more shot." He dug in his pocket and something crinkled. Stepping into moonlight, he held up a sheet of paper. "You know what this is?"

I couldn't find my voice. Swallowing hard, I shook my head.

"It's a Writ of *Emptio Iumentis*. Ray signed it this morning."

My heart plummeted into my stomach and kept falling.

In essence, an *Emptio* Writ meant Ray was giving up his parental rights and transferring them to Steffan. I would become Steff's legal ward, which would make me his common-law wife. Because such a marriage was unsanctioned by the church, society would regard me with the same scorn they would a Sweet Pea.

My shaking now had nothing to do with the cold. *Oh, Ray. You didn't. You didn't.*

"I didn't have to push very hard to persuade him." Steffan refolded the paper and tucked it in his pocket. "I think your little trick with the knife was the last straw, girl. So." He gestured toward the U. "Let's go."

"No." I was relieved that it came out clear and firm, but not angry, not frightened. "I haven't changed my mind."

Steff folded his arms. "Submit, Martha!"

That phrase didn't elicit the obedience it once would have. "Aren't you breaking the law right now?" I countered. "Cross-caste fraternization?"

"The law is on my side." His eyes narrowed. "You know, I didn't object when my friends made fun of me for dating a Worker Bee. I told them how beautiful you are, how mature for your age. I showered your father with gifts. I gave you everything!" His mouth turned down. "And this is how you repay me. You force me to make you a slut."

Sending up silent prayers, I clasped my gloved hands. "You can't force love, Steffan. And you can't buy it. Not from me."

He shrugged and his gaze swept Tin Town, his grin malicious. "So you'd rather live in this filthy, rat-infested warren, instead of a habitat? Never knew you enjoyed slumming." He sauntered forward, his expensive boots kicking frozen clods of snow out of his way. "Just look at all these pretty little houses. And I'll bet not one of them is legal. Right?"

*Oh no.* I backed away, keeping my distance.

"This'll give the Angels their quota for the year. I've been watching for a few days now, trying to figure out just which cockroach you're staying with. Easy—the old woman. You really should look behind you once in a while."

Fury rose, displacing fear. This time I didn't resist it. *How dare he call Mags that!* I chuckled. "Oh, Steffan. You were pitifully obvious."

*"Enough!"* His hands yanked out of his pockets, and in one hand he held a gun. "You're coming with me! Now!"

In that instant, everything changed.

*Assault with a firearm.* I'd been trained in how to deal with it, but I also knew the Guards were unlikely to believe what I told them. Stepping back, I assessed the space around me. A lot would depend on how the interaction went down. I could disarm him, but I knew there was no way I could persuade him to leave. *It's time to end this.*

The voice of my *sensei* echoed in my memory: *You must not kill.* My jaw tightened. Steffan had already demonstrated his inability to take no for an answer. Dropping into controlled breathing, I stepped back with my right leg, balancing—

"You must be Steffan."

The gentle voice curdled my guts with fear. "No!" I shrieked. Steffan whipped around, pointing his weapon at the silver-haired woman standing just feet behind him. "Mags, he's armed! Don't—"

He cut me off. "So you're the soft-headed idiot Meryn suckered. You hashers are a stain on Silvermine! All of you need to go!"

Mags laughed softly.

"Ah, the arrogance of the rich." The snow chirped underfoot as Kilte stopped next to me. His stance was casual, his arms relaxed, but I wasn't fooled. "Always telling us poor folks what we have to do to make you happy. Bow, kneel, scrape, you hashers!"

Adrenaline pounded through my veins; I maintained my focused breathing. *In. Out.* A wall rose in front of me, around me—a wall of discipline, created by my breath.

A crunch; Walker's bulk filled the space to my right.

Steff turned toward us with a laugh, lining up the handgun on Kilte. "Well, well. I knew a brave defender would show up. Are you doing her? Careful, man, she'll give you some disease. The whore's probably slept with every guy on the street." His eyes flicked from me to Kilte. "Well, I'm doing you a favor. Give her to me, and I'll leave you in peace."

"Whore?" Kilte didn't acknowledge the gun. His gloves made cracking sounds as his hands balled into fists.

Rage for myself, for my friends, boiled beyond the wall of breath, but I clung to peace. *No fear. No anger. Accept what is. Allow it to unfold.*

"Kilte." The word came slow, careful; Walker crossed his arms. Even though I knew his strength, the size of his bicep astonished me. "Yeah, Steffan, you'll leave us in peace." His tone was amiable. "And you'll leave without Meryn."

A light came on—the back porch of the THOW behind Steffan, illuminating the scene. Another light, two houses down. More footsteps approached: people from Tin Town.

"I have a Writ!" Steff's face contorted, his words coming fast. "I take her now, or I come back with the Guardian Angels. I have a feeling they'll find more than just a runaway in this hasher nest."

Mags met my eyes. "Meryn, do you want to go with this man?"

"No." I said it loud so everyone could hear. "Never."

"What you want doesn't matter." A corner of Steffan's mouth lifted. "You belong to me."

I shook my head. "No, Steff. The only One I belong to is God." My voice rose, truth surging through my veins like an elixir. "I have the right to choose—who I love, who I marry, and how I live. *I choose.*" My hand splayed on my chest. "Not you, not Ray. Me—Meryn Flint. You can't change that. Not even with a gun."

His laugh was derisive. "You've gotten some radical ideals, living with these traitors to our faith. After we consummate, I think I'll turn you over to Prinister Severs. He'll drive that heresy straight out of your head."

I didn't doubt his threat. *Meryn, if he takes you tonight, he will kill you or imprison you. You won't get another chance. He'll make sure of it.*

The sound of footfalls. Mags no longer stood by herself; a crowd surrounded her, more people arriving as I watched. Steffan's eyes darted from side to side, his scowl deepening, and I cursed mentally. *I want this to end. Lord, this has to end!*

A gasp; Marian pushed through the crowd, her hands fluttering. "Oh, Mr. Hagen! Right honorable, distinguished, eminent, exalted sir, you honor us with your presence!"

*Please, Marian. Steffan will never be Exalted Caste.* I couldn't believe she'd used the honorific.

Steffan didn't turn, didn't even acknowledge she'd spoken—a horrible insult. Casually, he reached out and shoved the older woman to the ground. Someone gave an anguished cry; I think it was Bernice.

Instead of rising, Marian scrabbled to her knees, her face white with pain, her hands pressed together in supplication. "Forgive us, good sir! We don't—" Then Bernice had Marian by the shoulders, murmuring in her ear as she helped the woman to her feet.

"We don't much like strangers." Taylor stepped in front of Marian. "I don't care what your caste is, in this community you don't go insulting our young ladies, or knocking old ladies down."

I blinked in surprise.

"You've overstayed your welcome." Junia. "Meryn is family here."

"An insult is a terrible way to say hello, but a pretty terrific goodbye." Behind me, Hagar's voice turned to iron. "Take the hint, jerk."

*What's . . . happening? All these people are defending me?* Euphoria rose quietly behind the wall of breath but, like the rage, found no purchase.

Mags stepped back, the people around her forming a phalanx that opened like a tunnel, creating a path for Steffan.

"Time to go," Kilte said tonelessly.

"How dare you hashers tell me what to do?" Steffan's face contorted. "I'll kill every last one of you! The Angels won't care." He laughed. "Hell, they'll probably give me a medal.

"In fact, I could just shoot someone." Stefan put a hand over his eyes. Smiling, he swung the pistol in a blind arc. People gasped, ducking and backing away. All but Mags, who didn't move.

The moment the weapon was aimed away from me, I tensed to spring, but as if he felt my intent, he dropped his hand. "Ah, ah, ah." He wagged a finger in reproach.

"I don't care who you are." Hagar's voice was a snarl. "If you so much as nick my neighbors with your little popgun, you'll pay for their blood."

I wanted to cheer. From around me, murmurs of agreement, dissent, and a scraping of snow as Junia turned. "Now Hagar, we—"

Steffan took advantage of the distraction. "You're coming with me!" He lunged, his hand poised to grab, the gun aimed at my head.

*No. No more!* Adrenaline fired, and my body dropped into defense posture, pulling my head out of firing range, my deflection of his grab textbook perfect. A split-second later I processed the counterstrike. As if in a dream, the gun separated itself from Steffan's hand, his scream blending with a loud *snap* as his trigger finger broke. The weapon evaded my grab, rotating off the back of my hand and dropping to the snow. Steffan hit the ground, the entire contents of his lungs emptying with a grunt that echoed off the walls of Tin Town.

The next second hovered, paused, stretched into eternity.

*This ends. Tonight. Now.*

I stood, my right foot planted, weight shifting. The edge of my left foot lifted with balletic grace. I'd rehearsed the move hundreds of times, the sequence clear in my mind: a simple kick, straight to the throat.

A kick that would kill.

I heard nothing but my breath, the inhale in preparation. The shift as my right leg took my weight, my arm lifting in slight counterbalance—

Hands gripped my shoulders, interrupting.

"Nicely done." Kind, benevolent.

Walker.

My breath exhaled in a rush. The pause splintered; my foot dropped; time resumed its march.

Still pulsing with fury, I rounded on him; his deflection of my strike turned into a gentle squeeze, and his eyes bored into mine, conveying respect, understanding, caution, and a deeper message I couldn't read. He released me, his gaze flicking to Steffan, who lay doubled over on the ground, retching from the blow and cradling his injured hand.

"Guess you must've slipped on the snow." Walker's voice, devoid of emotion.

Somewhere behind us, a man laughed.

Steffan's eyes, wide with fear, met mine—then narrowed. He pushed to his knees, trying to rise.

"Stay put." With casual exasperation, Kilte stepped forward and kicked Steffan's good arm out from under him. Shrieking, Steffan collapsed. Kilte bent, pocketed the gun, and crossed his arms. "You don't deserve to stand on the same ground with her." Kilte's expression of utter implacability was one I'd never seen—and one I never wanted to see directed at me. I knew if my defense hadn't worked, Kilte would have stepped into the breach. *Who would have stopped him? Walker? Would Kilte have stopped himself?*

My gaze dropped to my former boyfriend, and an odd surge of compassion surprised me. "Steffan, enough already. You cannot have me." My brow wrinkled. "I don't know why you want to be with someone who doesn't love you, anyway. So don't make excuses for me anymore. Just date somebody else." I extended my hand.

"Well, I never!" Marian huffed. "Why a respectable young woman wouldn't accept—" She broke off as Bernice pulled her away, through the crowd.

Snarling profanities, Steffan slapped my hand away. He climbed to his feet, pointed and tried to speak, but coughed; wincing, he clutched his broken hand. "Your father gave you to me. This isn't over!"

Exhaling, I forced back anger, forced myself not to look at Kilte.

Steffan turned to my neighbors, a sweep of his good arm encompassing them all. "This isn't over—for any of you! I'll be back! I'll burn this trash heap to the ground and piss on the ashes! It isn't over!"

"Oh, I think it is," Mags said quietly, her smile odd. "You see, you're known here, now." Several people in the crowd nodded, and I heard someone taking pictures.

Kilte didn't smile. "Time to go."

Steff opened his mouth, but when Kilte stepped forward, Steffan swung at him with his good hand. The punch connected, and I winced, remembering the power behind that fist; then Kilte straightened, and I heard him laugh. "You hit like a red-ringed pussy. You wanna try that again?"

Steffan's eyes narrowed in fury. His hand flashed beneath his coat, bringing out the knife he'd used on me in the warehouse, and he leaped forward, aiming at Kilte's face. Kilte ducked easily, then slammed a hand into Steffan's broken fingers.

Steff's scream rent the sky. Before he could recover, Kilte grabbed the bigger man and easily wrenched him into an about-face. The knife fell to the snow. A hard kick in the butt forced Steffan to run several steps to maintain his balance. The people behind me flowed forward, creating a wall, escorting Steffan up the U and out of Shady Dell.

And I stood, mouth open, watching them go, warmed by a response I didn't expect. After experiencing betrayal after betrayal—losing my faith in Ray, St. Mike's, and the Guardian Angels—and thinking I had no one to trust, my Shady Dell family had stepped into the gap. I could say that now: *my family.* With nothing to gain and everything to lose, they had placed themselves between me and the man who wanted to take my life.

And kept me from making a mistake that would have changed my life irrevocably.

Tears sprang to my eyes. *God! How did You—* It was too much to fathom. Wiping my face, I turned to the men standing at my side. "I, uh—there's no way I can thank you." It came out rough, uneven.

"No need." Walker's smile was very kind. Behind him, Tamar tossed her head and turned to follow the crowd.

Kilte chuckled. "You did the heavy lifting."

"And man." My uncertain smile at Kilte conveyed awe and respect. "Remind me never to piss you off."

He laughed, ignoring my profanity, and that restored my equilibrium. "Ah, you can't. You're too good."

Walker touched my arm and gestured up the path. "Let's head over to Mom's. We'll have supper on the table when they get back." He looked at Kilte, and his expression shifted somehow—a caution, a remembering. "Don't be long." An odd edge to his voice perplexed me.

"Nah, it's not a night to stay out." Kilte grinned at his friend, and some unspoken awareness flew back and forth between them, infinitely fast; then the blond man gave me a nod. "Sleep well tonight in your tiny tin house, Meryn Flint—you've earned it. We're just a shout away." Stepping back, he turned and strode toward the street, following the murmuring crowd.

~

Late that night, after the dinner dishes were washed, the guys had headed home, and the twins had gone to bed, I crunched over the snow to my tiny tin house. The moon was full, bathing the walkway in its muted light as I closed the door and locked it behind me.

For several long minutes, I just stood, contented, regarding my home: my pallet on the floor, my uniforms hanging in their closet, a cheery fire crackling in the stove. Then I lifted my eyes. "Thank You," I said. "You brought me to this community. You've given me a new family, and a safe place to live. Even after all my—" I broke off, fighting tears, and hung my coat on its nail by the door. *My unfaithfulness,* but I couldn't bring myself to say it. "You are so patient with me, God, sometimes I can't even believe it. How do I begin to thank You?"

Crossing to my pallet, I lifted Mom's coral-bead necklace from around my neck and set it on my bedside table next to the mermaid pin.

She smiled at me, coy, and I remembered my dream, her loving regard, her hand warm on my cheek. *"God is always with you. He's not angry, darling—He knows you're hurting. And I will always love you."*

"Please tell Mom I'm—" I whispered, and then tears closed my throat and made further speech impossible. *Tell her I'm okay, God. I miss her so very much, and I still grieve every day. But tell her I love her, and I've found my new home.*

~

"Meryn Flint?" The voice through the voder was impersonal.

Startled, I turned from where I was restocking a rack at Mrs, my stomach tightening. "Yes?"

The Guard handed me an envelope. "I'm serving you with an official warning. Your report of Steffan Hagen's kidnapping and harassment has been determined to be false, and he has filed a complaint."

"What?" My cheeks went chill. Carole came out from behind the counter, crossing to where we stood. The Guard ignored her.

I tore open the envelope, scanning the page with its official seal. "How can you possibly—"

"I must advise you that any further action you attempt against this young man will be considered Caste Harassment, and you will be arrested and charged."

Fear yielded to a wash of fury. *Caste Harassment? For trying to keep myself safe?*

Carole lifted a hand. "Just a moment, Guardian—"

"Do not involve yourself in this, Miss Stilwell, or you too will be held culpable. Your employer status has no bearing on this case."

Carole's mouth dropped open. A second later it snapped into a thin line, and she folded her arms.

The faceplate turned to me. "A copy of this notice has been sent to your father. You've been warned, Miss Flint." He exited the store. As his footsteps faded away, my eyes met Carole's.

She shook her head. "That's it," she whispered. "If Steffan filed a Caste Harassment warning, there's nothing you can do."

# 33. FALLOUT

"There's always something we can do." The steel in Bree's voice matched her expression as we walked up the U toward home, our feet crunching the snow.

"You know he's going to come back here," I said, chewing slow on my next sentence. "Steffan can't stand humiliation."

She stopped walking and turned to face me, the wind scattering her blonde curls across the front of her jacket, her face sober. "Well, I don't know anybody here who's going to lose a bit of sleep over it. Steffan isn't the first snooty jerk to try to leverage his caste to bother people here, and he won't be the last. If he comes back, that just shows how foolish he is. You're family now, and this community doesn't take that lightly." Her lips twisted into an odd grin. "Some people just completely underestimate us."

I smiled, a trifle grimly, thinking of Kilte. "More the fools, they."

"And don't you forget that."

We walked on, but thoughts churned in my head. "You know, Bree, the problem isn't just Steffan. It's our entire society. Men are held up as being superior to women—like they're more intelligent, or more acceptable to God, or these strong protectors of women—but obviously that's a complete lie."

She shook her head. "Come on, Mer. Not all men are—"

"Wait." I stopped to face her. "Just hear me out. Our entire society is engineered to benefit men and suppress women, and I don't see men opposing it. Even great guys like Walker and Kilte, who know how to treat women right. We've been talking about this whole thing since before I moved in here—how the RD uses all its time and resources reinforcing its control, especially of women. Don't you see how wrong it is? Don't you think it needs to change?"

She sobered, eyeing me as if she wasn't sure if I was serious. "Of course, but what do you want to do? Overthrow the government?"

I sighed, my eyes following the brisk wind as it chased dead leaves and trash up the U. "Yeah, why not. I think I'll just fly to Charleston tomorrow and tell them everything has to change. That should do the trick, right?"

Bree regarded me for a long moment, and when my mouth quirked, she broke into a laugh. I laughed with her, but it didn't feel funny. "C'mon," she said. "Let's go get some tea and see if the boys are home. It's Walker's turn at supper. He's a really good cook." Throwing an arm around my waist, she nudged me back into a walk, and I shortened my steps to match hers.

I chewed my lip, not wanting to drop the subject. *God, she doesn't get it. How can she not get it? Her gamma's a part of Liberté, for pity's sake. Well, maybe I'm just nuts. What can one unmarried runaway woman do, anyway? I'd just get thrown in jail, and that would be the end of it.* Thinking of Zipporah's prophecy, I frowned. *What did she say, exactly? 'The paths through the waters'? I'll have to look at it again.*

As I followed Bree up the narrow walk to Mags's, a sparrow alighted on the tree in front of the house. Bree went inside, but I paused to look up at the tiny bird. She chirped, cocking her head this way and that, her voice launching into a silvery tune that gradually brought calm and order to my troubled thoughts. The song continued as I crossed the porch into the cozy house and closed the door, smiling.

Then she flew away.

# PROFOUND THANKS

I have so many people to thank—so many people without whom this book would not exist. And if I've forgotten anyone, please forgive me—it's been a long journey.

God, Who gave me the idea in a dream and then gave me the crazy notion to turn it into a story. You are the love of my life, my strength and my song, my joy and the reason I live. Thank You.

My friend Norma told me, "There's a book inside every person," and she was right; she encouraged me to stick with it and gave me great cover feedback, as well as providing me a strong shoulder to lean on when my doubts became overwhelming. That you're holding this book right now is due in large part to her. Many thanks to Rick, who encouraged me to follow my dream before I even knew it was possible. Can you see this book from your spot on Cloud Nine, Rick? You saw the passion in me before I did—and had the courage to tell me.

Peggie wanted to read it on the strength of the cover design alone (I love it when that happens!) and kept bugging me until I finished it. Cindy supported, encouraged, and prayed without ceasing. And Jennifer listened to my constant money/logistics/faith challenges with a compassionate and patient ear and kept me on her prayer list. My friend Kenny taught me to trust God without flinching, to climb through fear, and rappel (mostly) without screaming—emotional and spiritual lessons that have served me well in this journey. John gave me valuable tips about structure with unflinching honesty.

Much thanks to Cortney Donelson, whose early read provided terrific feedback and an "attagirl" right when I needed one. Ginny Smith got me a little farther along the publishing journey and gave me hope that it was possible.

Without my phenomenal editors, Annie Mydla and Catherine Jones Payne, this book would not be what it is. Thank you both for taking the long view when I was way too close, giving me the courage to take a machete to overgrowth and dead wood, and answering my constant stream of publishing questions with unwavering patience.

And without you, Mom, this book would not exist—for myriad reasons. You never lost the distinction between church and state, and taught me why it was important.

As always, you were right.

# ✝iny ✝inDEX

| | |
|---|---|
| Abortion | Illegal. Penalty is execution. |
| Adah | Lives in the Widow House at Shady Dell. |
| American Reformation | What the CSA calls the Second American Civil War |
| Bart | St. Bartholomew, the worship leader at St. Michael's church. |
| Bishor | Bishop-Mayor. Title for the head of a city or town in the CSA. The bishor of Silvermine is Oral Heibeluft. |
| Britt | A saleswoman at Mrs. |
| Burris, Connie | Meryn's friend from school; member of Liberté. |
| Calumet, Joy | One of Meryn's classmates. |
| Carvenor | Term for a state's Cardinal-Governor in the Christian States of America. |
| Castes | A system of social stratification that separates people by birth and/or financial status. From lowest to highest, castes are Indigent (aka, Hasher, pejorative), Worker (aka, Worker Bees, pejorative), Management, Governance, and Exalted. Worker and Management Castes are medium level, while Governance and Exalted Castes are high, and require the most deference from the lower castes. |

An entire system of linguistics has developed within and around the caste system. To use an inappropriate form of address to someone of a higher caste is an offense that can result in arrest. "Mid-Caste Casual" is the idiom most often used by the people in Meryn's orbit.

| | |
|---|---|
| Chip | A combination ID, banking and tracking system created by the Reformation Directorate. Permanently embedded in a person's wrist between birth and age five, the chip substitutes for an ID, driver's license, credit card and health insurance card. It vibrates when the user is receiving a phone call or other communication. |
| Chisholm, Chastity | DNN broadcast personality. Host of a morning show, Chatting with Chastity. Her (unflattering) nickname is Chatty. She is well married to a Governance Caste spouse and wears pink or red MTs and bonnets. |
| Cirque, Bilhah | A resident of Tin Town. |
| City Trade | Silvermine's largest flea market. Illegal, it's run by Liberté and rotates its location regularly to avoid attention. |
| Coffee Drop | A coffee-flavored candy that's concentrated caffeine. Very expensive and generally only used by the upper castes. |
| Cornwall, Asher | A young man who lives with his parents in Shady Dell. |
| CSA | Christian States of America. A conservative collection of states that seceded from the United States of America after Civil War II to form a Christian theocracy. |
| DNN | Divine News Network: propaganda arm for the Reformation Directorate. |
| DeeDee (Dee) | A soprano who sings with Meryn on the praise team at St. Michael's. Dee is witness to Meryn's argument with Bart, the worship leader. |

| | |
|---|---|
| Delaney, Debbie | Childhood friend of Meryn's, gang-raped on a school bus when both girls were twelve. |
| Diploma, LT | Girls receive their Diploma, Limited Training (or Diploma "Light") when they graduate after two years of high school. A girl who wants a four-year diploma must pay for the last two years herself. Boys are provided a full four years of high school. Occasionally, a smart girl will find someone who can sponsor her last two years of high school; but more often, wealthy benefactors will spend the money on a boy's college education, instead. |
| Dixon, Clare | Pastor of Our Lord's Church, a non-sanctioned church attended by Mags and her family. |
| Dixon, Hamilton | (Hamil) Clare's son |
| Dixon, St. Peter | Clare's husband |
| DRUSA | Democratic Republic of the United States. The states that rejected the Christian theocratic government formed by the CSA after Civil War II. The nation is considered pagan by the CSA. |
| Eberhard, Tyler | Owns a THOW at Shady Dell. Judith is his wife. |
| Emily | Owns a THOW known as the Widow House II because several widows live with her, including Orpah and Naomi. |
| Espinosa, Hagar | Resident of Shady Dell. Single mom who owns a THOW. Three children: Jeb, Zeke and Hadassah. |
| Esselin, Rose Flint | Meryn's mother |
| Esselin, Raymond | Meryn's stepfather |
| Flint, Meryn | Young woman who moves in with her friend Bree and her gamma, Mags, at Shady Dell. Works at Mrs@18, an upscale clothing store at the Silvermine Mall. |
| Gambit's Grocery | An affordable grocery store with limited stock. |
| Gamma | Grandmother |
| Gampa | Grandfather |

Gamma/Gampa Abuelos

What Meryn calls her father's parents, whom she never knew.

Gamma/Gampa Flint

Rose Esselin's parents. Died in a hovercar wreck when Meryn was three.

GM
A Genetically Modified person. Only the wealthy can afford to have a baby modified in ova. Parents choose features such as build, eye and hair color, while genetic anomalies like illness markers and disease are screened and edited out. Babies not manipulated are NMO: Non-Modified Organisms.

God's Abundance
An upscale grocery store in Silvermine.

Guardian Angels
Known by the upper castes as Angels; the lower castes call them the Guards. The police force for the Reformation Directorate (RD).

Gunderson, Jerusha Meryn's classmate. Twin sister Jobette.

Gunderson, Jobette Meryn's classmate. Twin sister Jerusha.

Handy
Clarence Peters, aka Handy. Lives in Shady Dell. Owns The Handyman's Shop.

Hagen, Steffan
Meryn's former boyfriend. Governance Caste and independently wealthy.

Harris, Kilte
Bree's fiancé. Lives in Shady Dell. Co-owns a landscaping business with Walker.

Heibeluft, Oral
Silvermine's Bishor (bishopmayor)

Hipster
Another term for a tiny tin house—when they were first built, the little houses were "hipped on" to a THOW.

Historic District
An older section of Silvermine, subject to flooding when the seas rose. Protected by levees and pumps.

Honey Pot
An illegal bar on Sweet Street.

| | |
|---|---|
| Honorifics | The Indigent Caste are addressed as the "right," as in, "The right Magdalena McCafferty." Not often used between peers. Worker Caste are addressed as the "honorable." The salutation for the Management Caste is the "distinguished," while the Governance Caste are greeted as the "eminent." Exalted Caste are known as the "exalted." If one wishes to be scrupulously appropriate, one might combine honorifics, e.g., "The right honorable distinguished eminent Steffan Hagen." But it is only proper to use honorifics of the correct caste and below. To address a Governance Caste woman as "exalted" is a Caste Insult to the higher caste and may be punishable by imprisonment. Similarly, to eliminate the proper honorific by addressing her using a lower-caste honorific is also a Caste Insult. |
| Hovercar | An anti-gravity auto conveyance made in China. Expensive; only the Governance or Exalted Castes in Silvermine can afford one. |
| Huldah | Resident of Shady Dell. |
| Humboldt | Popresident of the CSA. |
| Jiang Robot | An AI-driven mechanized robot built in China, generally used for domestic work and other unpleasant jobs. The domestic models are finished with care and look almost human, while the industrial models are basic metal skeletons. |
| Jojo | Nickname for Joseph Sweet (see "Sweet, Joseph"). |
| Junia | An unofficial leader of Shady Dell. Usually presides over the town meetings. |
| Keren | One of Marian's roommates in the Widow House. |
| Kilmargh's Grocery | A small grocery store on Sweet Street that offers mostly canned goods, sundries and pantry supplies. |
| Kwale's | A very upscale restaurant in Silvermine. Tamar works there. |
| Lane, Candace | Resident of Tin Town. |

| | |
|---|---|
| Liberté | A group actively working to overthrow the RD. The group is splintered into cells so no one person can compromise the entire group if someone's arrested. Each cell focuses on a specific area: Some cells help provide food to people in need, while other cells help with healthcare or medicine, and others focus on political issues. |
| Live-quins | Mobile mannequins: Jiang Robots with synthetic skin and battery packs. They look human, although they are manufactured with the lowest-level neural processor available. Used at Mrs (and other stores) to display clothes. |
| Magicia | Meryn's childhood doll. |
| Marian | An older woman who owns a THOW at Shady Dell. It's known as the Widow House because several single women live there with Marian, including Keren, Lydia, Mary, Adah and Asenath. |
| Married Topper | Also known as an MT. A polyester overgarment married women wear outside the home to discourage the attention of men. MTs are color-coded by caste: Indigent Caste wear tan or brown; Worker Caste women wear shades of blue; Management Caste, green; Governance Caste, pink or red; and Exalted Caste, purple or lavender. |
| Mary-Sarah | Meryn's manager at On the Mark, her first job. |
| McCafferty, Bree | Meryn's closest friend. Engaged to Kilte Harris. |
| McCafferty, David | Mags and Will's son; Bree's father. Murdered in a mass shooting when Bree was still a baby. |
| McCafferty, Ellie | (Elijah) Young girl adopted from an orphanage by Mags. Has a twin sister, Lisha (Elisha). |
| McCafferty, Lisbet | (Elizabeth) David's wife and Bree's mother. Died of cancer shortly after David was killed. |
| McCafferty, Lisha | (Elisha) Young girl adopted from an orphanage by Mags. Has a twin sister, Ellie (Elijah). |
| McCafferty, Mags | (Magdalena) Bree's grandmother (gamma), who owns a THOW in Shady Dell. One of Shady Dell's |

unofficial leaders.

| | |
|---|---|
| McCafferty, Will | Mags's husband. Deceased. |
| MedAngels | Medical first responders. |
| Merica | Resident of Shady Dell who works as a Sweet Pea. Merica is her professional name. |
| Miners Stadium | Home of the Silvermine Miners football and baseball franchises, Miners Stadium can hold 80,000 people. It is also used for concerts and large events. |
| Mother | A term of respect for any woman with gray hair. |
| Mr. Josephus | Invited Meryn to be his companion at a fancy hotel. Real name: John Sweet. |
| Mrs@18 | A clothing store for young unmarried women. Meryn and Bree are employed there. The parent company also owns Mr. Right and Mom@20. |
| MT | See "Married Topper." |
| Musgrave Moose | A children's program. |
| NMO | A Non-Modified Organism: a baby conceived with no genetic modifications in ova. Babies who are altered are known as GM: Genetically Modified. |
| Old Port Silver | The portside section of town flooded by sea level rise. The city attempted to salvage the area by putting homes and businesses up on stilts and pilings, but the attempt was unsuccessful, and the city ultimately built a levee on higher ground, abandoning the area and evacuating the residents. Although the houses are not safe for habitation, many poor people still live in them illegally. |
| Owle, Iscah/Gabriel | Brother and sister who live at Shady Dell. |
| Paradise | A state in the CSA where Silvermine is located. |
| Patterson, Liz | A resident of Shady Dell. Husband owns a THOW. Has a nephew, Nicodemus (Nico). |

| | |
|---|---|
| Popresident | Pope-President. Title of the head of the CSA. The current popresident is Humboldt. |
| Praise Team | At St. Michael's Church. St. Bartholomew (worship leader), DeeDee (soprano), John (tenor) |
| Prinister Severs | The spiritual head of St. Michael's Church. As a prinister—a combination priest/minister—Severs also holds a government position. Without his approval, church members cannot graduate from school, hold jobs or marry. Under CSA law, prinisters also have the legal right to discipline and punish parishioners. |
| Pris (Priscilla) | Daughter of Tamar. |
| RD | Short for Reformation Directorate. |
| RD motto | Guided by the Hand of God. |
| Raven, Mr. | Taught "God's Design for the Family" class at St. Mike's. |
| Reformation Directorate | Also known as the RD. Post-Reformation government of the Christian States of America, a Christian theocracy created at the end of the Second American Civil War (Civil War II). |
| Rivercrest | Very upscale neighborhood in Silvermine known as a "habitat" because it is sealed beneath a dome. Tamar cleans houses there. |
| Sanctioned Church | Any church that is legally approved to operate as a religious institution under CSA law. Sanctioned Churches receive their sermons and other teaching directly from the RD. Unsanctioned churches are illegal. If discovered they are raided and shut down. Parishioners are imprisoned or executed. |
| Silvermine | A coastal city in the state of Paradise, CSA. |
| Silvermine River | A river that runs through the City of Silvermine. |
| Silvermine Bay | The City of Silvermine was built on its shores. |
| Shady Dell | A community of tiny houses on wheels (THOWs) in an old part of Silvermine. |

Shady Dell Residents

A short list includes Tamar Brisom, Pete and
Tabitha Cavendish, Thad, Celeste (older woman),
Bernice Karough, Lydia, Absolom Stephens, Faith
and Zeke (Zechariah) Stewart and their kids,
Taylor Wilford, Sarah, Katia Willis and her father,
John Paul Willis, Candace Lane, Celeste, Tyler and
Constance Eberhard, Merica, Huldah, Miriam and
John Morton, Junia, Handy, Joanna (Handy's niece)

| | |
|---|---|
| Squires, Andrew | Carvenor of the state of Paradise, where Silvermine is located. |
| Stilwell, Carole | Manager at Mrs@18. Bree and Meryn's boss. |
| Sweet, James | Jim Sweet. Oldest of the Sweet Brothers, he is the head of a well-known organized crime family. Owns a hover limo with the license plate *Sweet B*. |
| Sweet, John | Jim Sweet's middle brother. Deals drugs. Owns a hover limo with the license plate *Sweet T*. |
| Sweet, Joseph | AKA Jojo. Youngest brother; works as a pimp. Owns a hover limo with the license place *Sweet P*. |

Sweet, Josephus and Salome

The Sweet Brothers' parents, deceased.

| | |
|---|---|
| Sweet Pea | Euphemism for a prostitute. |
| Sweet Street | Colloquial term for Main Street. Part of Shady Dell's neighborhood. Known as "Sweet Street" because it is run and controlled by the Sweet brothers, and known for its debauchery and crime. |
| Sub | Subway |
| Tamar | A resident of Tin Town who is dating Walker. Has a daughter, Priscilla (Pris). |
| Thinwall | An expensive type of drywall. |
| Thorhild's | An inexpensive restaurant in Silvermine. |
| THOW | Tiny house on wheels. |

| | |
|---|---|
| Tin Town | Illegal housing constructed behind Shady Dell. As the population of the THOW community grew, more room was needed. Most of the tiny houses in Tin Town are made of tin and wood, and are known as "hipsters," or Tiny Tin Houses. |
| Virtuous Veggie | A grocery store. |
| Walker | His full name is Fawzia deGraff Walker because that's the name that was pinned to his baby blanket when he was found on the orphanage doorstep, but he goes by Walker. A resident of Tin Town, he co-owns a landscaping business with Kilte Harris. Walker spent several years of his childhood in an orphanage before he was adopted by Mags. |
| War of Northern Aggression | |
| | The American Civil War, fought 1861~1865. |
| Weeks, Kyle | An architect of the American Reformation, the secession process that created the CSA. |
| Wilton, Jael | Meryn's friend. Attends St. Michael's church (St. Mike's). |
| Wittier, Ruth | Meryn's friend. Married to Ananiah; attends St. Mike's. Supported Meryn after the shunning. |
| Zipporah | An old prophetess who speaks to people she meets at City Trade. |

*Follow the author on Facebook at lmaristatterauthor,*
*and on TikTok at lmaristatter.*

*Find out more about the next book in the Tiny Tin House series*
*at niffycatpress.com*

Made in the USA
Monee, IL
07 September 2022

13514878R00204